DECEPTIVE CADENCE

KATHRYN GUARE

THE VIRTUOSIC SPY ● BOOK 1

Kathryn Guare

DECEPTIVE CADENCE

KILTUMPER
CLOSE
PRESS

Published by

KILTUMPER
CLOSE
PRESS

PO Box 1175
Montpelier, VT 05601

Cover Design by Andrew Brown
Print Design by Chenile Keogh

Dedication

For my parents
Claire and Paul Guare
My familial basso continuo
Always with me, holding me up

February 2004

Jammu/Kashmir, Indian Subcontinent

She's come for me.

He woke with the words on his lips, his eyes searching the dim room, looking for someone to tell. It seemed important to tell someone.

Turning his head, he felt the fibers of a rough, homespun blanket catching at his unshaven jaw while a residue of acrid smoke scraped at the back of his throat. He gagged, struggling weakly as pain seared the interior of his chest. Sounds of tense, frenetic activity surrounded him followed by unfamiliar voices, hollow and distorted.

"He's nearly out again. He's in a lot of pain, and both lungs are bad. My guess is pleurisy along with pneumonia and—well, check out these pills I found in his pocket."

"Oh, Christ. That makes it interesting. What about getting him away from this stove? He'll die of smoke inhalation."

"No time. He's not inhaling anything right now. This guy is going down if we don't trach him right now."

"Using what, for instance?"

"Shit, Craig, I don't know. Give me your knife. Go look for something—drinking straw, fucking garden hose, whatever."

As he sank further into the shadows, he remembered where he was: a small, Kashmiri village called . . . what? Bunagam. It was called Bunagam. A Samaritan-souled resident had heaved him into an ox cart to bring him here and then summoned two American doctors from the next village.

He sensed their determination but resisted it, drifting further away, a weary guest trying to slip off unnoticed. The pain was already gone, and when the knife punctured the cartilage of his neck with a sharp, resolute slice, he barely felt it.

They didn't understand, and he couldn't tell them. He didn't want their help. His mother was there. She'd waited for him, and it was time to go. He could see her now, standing near his elbow and then by the foot of the bed. Then she was moving away. He stared after her, and like a lost child running toward reunion, reached out, struggled to follow—and was too late. They had dragged him back.

He surfaced to renewed agony and a stupefied sense of loss. Again, he heard the fuzzy murmur of voices.

"Did the phone number work?"

"Yeah. I talked to three different people. They obviously know who he is but wouldn't tell me. They've already got a medevac on the way. I think you're right, Nick. He must be some kind of agent."

"That would explain the gun."

His gun.

The muscles of his arms locked in spasm, and he opened his eyes. Two concerned faces stared at him, and the larger of the two crouched closer, his shaggy blond beard coming into sharper focus.

"You've been pretty sick, haven't you? You've got pneumonia on top of everything else, but you're going to be all right. We found a card in your wallet—a guy named Frank Murdoch? They're sending a medevac up to get you."

Frank won't be happy. The thought floated through his mind like an inscrutable riddle before he remembered who Frank was, and an instant later, he remembered everything else.

No, Frank wouldn't be happy that the card was in his pocket long after it should have been memorized and destroyed, but that aggravation would pale by comparison if he ever discovered how far astray his amateur operative had drifted. According to Frank's definition, the mission had failed, but he didn't give a damn what Frank thought.

He was still moving among ghosts, hovering at the edge of a boundary he longed to step across. But she kept pushing him back, gentle but insistent, and he couldn't find it without her. His mother had always known and walked in such places, like a goddess crossing over worlds. She would go on without him. She knew the way.

1

Seven Months Earlier

Dingle Peninsula, Ireland

When he heard the faint, friendly trill, Conor didn't know what the hell it was; he didn't recognize it. He'd only had the mobile phone for two weeks—the last man in the country to buy one, it seemed—and nobody had called, so it hadn't rung.

On the second ring, he turned an inquisitive face to his friend and farm manager, Phillip Ryan. They were on the ground at the edge of the pasture, their legs hanging over the drainage ditch they had been digging at all morning. It was nearly noon and the August afternoon had grown warm but not too warm for the flask of tea they had just polished off before lighting up their cigarettes.

Phillip jerked his head at Conor's jacket with a smirk of friendly derision. "It's the mobile, you bleedin' eejit."

"Is that what it sounds like? I thought it was a cricket." Frowning, Conor dove for the jacket and slapped at its pockets to locate the phone. It chirped out a fourth ring before he could answer it. "Is that you, Ma? What's the matter, are you all right?"

He spoke in Irish, or Gaeilge, as it was called in the ever-shrinking corners of Ireland that still kept it in daily use. It was the language his mother preferred, and it had to be his mother calling, because she was the only one who knew the number. He'd purchased the phone for the peace of mind and freedom of movement it brought him. Since her diagnosis, he had become nervous about how often she was left home by herself.

"Fine, fine. Sorry to frighten you, love." Brigid McBride's voice was calm and light. "It's only there's a gentleman from London come to see you, and he's so dressed to the nines I hadn't the heart to send him down to that muddy ditch."

A vague anxiety carved a deeper wrinkle in his brow. In his experience, unexpected visitors often carried unwelcome news. "From London? Who is he? What's he want?"

"Well, he wants to see you, doesn't he? I didn't quiz the man, Conor."

He smiled at his mother's tone of mild reproach. "All right, then. Tell him I'm coming."

He snapped the phone shut and tossed it onto his jacket with a dispirited oath.

"Everything OK?" Phillip asked.

"I doubt it. There's a man in a suit come to see me. From London."

His friend whistled in mock sympathy. "Can't be good. Still, it could be worse. At least it's not the Garda."

"Ah, shut up, ya fecker."

He tossed the end of his cigarette into the ditch with a resigned sigh and started for the house, following a path worn thin from regular traffic, both human and animal. On his left, a long rock wall divided the field into parcels, and on his right, the pasture rolled into the distance, bisected by the main road before continuing on to the rocky shoreline. The weather was fine, but he could see clouds coming together over the ocean. Rain was on the way within the next hour, he estimated.

Trotting down the stairs onto the backyard's flagstone terrace, he saw his mother standing in the open doorway. She looked tiny and frail, dwarfed by the massive farmhouse that framed her. He had stopped asking her every day if she felt all right. He knew she lied, and it made them both uncomfortable. Instead, he had learned to read the lines on her face as a more honest answer to his unspoken question. Looking at her as he came through the back door into the kitchen, he felt the heaviness in his heart lighten a bit. It was a good day.

Wordlessly, Conor raised a questioning eyebrow at her. His mother shook her head and spread her arms, impatiently nudging him forward. He stepped through into the large living and dining room, still brightly lit from the sun that poured through the casement windows opposite the fireplace. A tall, silver-haired man stood at one window, a teacup cradled in his hand as he looked out at the green pastures and the distant ocean. He appeared to be lost in thought. Conor made his presence known with a discreet shuffle of feet before speaking.

"How are you, sir? I'm Conor McBride. I'm sorry to have kept you waiting."

Without a hint of being startled, the figure gracefully turned to face him, a smile of welcome on his face. For a fleeting moment, Conor had an impression of role reversal, as if he were the one paying a visit.

"Conor. It's very good of you to see me." The man's voice had a deep, rich timbre. The accent was quintessential public school English, and his attire—beautifully tailored suit; tasteful, striped tie; and gleaming cap-toed shoes—indicated a fastidious sense of style. "I'm taking you from your work I'm afraid."

"You are indeed." Conor smiled. "Don't think I'm not grateful. Will you take another cup of tea?"

The offer was graciously declined. Conor invited him to take a seat next to the fireplace and sat down in the one across from it. He waited for the visitor to introduce himself. The visitor seemed in no hurry to do so.

"I had the opportunity of hearing you play last evening in

Tralee," he said, crossing his legs and looking as if they were already old friends. The unexpected opening startled Conor.

"I hope you enjoyed it?"

"I enjoyed it immeasurably." The large hazel eyes widened for emphasis. "I have rarely heard Locatelli's capriccios played so confidently or so well. It was an extraordinary display of virtuosity."

"Thank you."

"I must admit I was quite astonished. Do you play often with that ensemble?"

"No. No, they're just over from Dublin for a few nights. I'd played with them before, and the manager rang last month to ask me to be in the program." Conor twitched a self-deprecating grin. "Most nights you're more likely to find me fiddling for the crowd down at the pub here."

"Certainly a far cry from the National Symphony Orchestra, isn't it?" The elegant stranger inclined his head in sympathetic appraisal. "What a waste. I didn't fully comprehend it until I heard you last night. Not your fault, of course, but what a criminal, bloody waste."

Offered in a silky undertone, the observation struck with precision, like a concealed switchblade sliding between his ribs. It left Conor speechless. The voice across from him continued in a low murmur. "How bitter that must have been to lose your seat in the first violins, not to mention your growing career as a soloist. To trade hard-won success and recognition for this ... pastoral obscurity on the edge of the sea, all because someone had to do penance for your brother's crimes."

Conor's face had already lost its polite smile and most of its color. At this last remark, he came up out of the chair, rigid with anger. "I half expected something like this," he said coldly. "Who the hell are you?"

The mysterious visitor seemed content with the reaction

he'd provoked. He too rose, produced a card from an inside pocket of his suit, and presented it. "I beg your pardon," he said, smiling an apology. "Small talk is not my strength. My name is Frank Emmons Murdoch. I am an agent with the British Secret Intelligence Service, more commonly known as MI6."

Made of thick stock, with letters embossed in a tasteful font, the card was an appropriate match for its owner and equally inscrutable. No address or phone number. No contact details whatsoever. Conor examined it with a frown.

"MI6. Are you a spy, then?"

"Certainly not. I'd hardly be doling out business cards if I were, would I?"

"It's not much of a business card. Don't you have a badge or a warrant card, or something?"

The question prompted an indulgent smile. "And how would you authenticate it if I produced one? Have you ever seen an MI6 warrant card?"

"No, I suppose not."

Conor continued glaring down at the card. The anxiety he'd felt earlier settled into an undefined dread. He turned his attention back to the extraordinary specimen in front of him. His speech, demeanor, and appearance were like those of a character pulled from an Edwardian drama. Conor had his own clichéd assumptions about the British upper class, but even he found it hard to believe their ranks could produce such a comprehensive stereotype. Was the man a genuine anachronism or was it an act?

"So?" he prompted, irritably. "I expect you've not come all the way from London to chat about my short-lived musical career. Let's have it."

Frank sighed, his mouth twisting sardonically. "It's your brother, as I believe you've surmised. Thomas has made rather a bad mess for himself, I'm afraid, and he's going to need your help. The matter is urgent, and your assistance will be required almost immediately. For an extended stretch of time, I'm afraid." Frank took the card from Conor's hand and began writing on the back of it. "You'll need to be in London one week from today. The afternoon flight from Kerry to Stanstead is already booked, and so is your room at the Lanesborough Hotel. Quite nice, you'll like it. Meet me in the hotel bar at six o'clock."

"Hang on a minute," Conor sputtered in slow-witted confusion. "What do you know about Thomas? Where is he, and what kind of mess—"

"All excellent questions, but I haven't the time to go into them just now."

Frank handed the card back. He reached for his briefcase, appearing to consider his errand complete.

"That's it? You're off your nut." Conor stared at Frank incredulously. "I can't just go flying off to—"

"Yes, quite." Frank gave a perfunctory nod. "A good many arrangements to make, no doubt. I'd best leave you to it. Until next Thursday, then."

His mother had, of course, been listening from the hallway. She stepped forward to see the visitor to the door while Conor stood, nailed in place, in the middle of the living room. He saw Frank's patronizing smile falter as he turned to her, his lips straightening to a sober line of deference.

Anyone with a shred of intelligence needed only a glance at the fathomless gaze of Brigid McBride to recognize it as something unusual. It radiated a powerful, undefined force that seemed too big for such a small frame. Some looked and felt a twinge of uneasy fear and others a sense of wonder. Conor saw that Frank fell into the latter category. So far, it was the sole point in his favor.

"A pleasure to meet you, Mrs. McBride." The velvety voice sounded quite different without its flippant jocularity. "A pleasure to meet you both."

The glance he threw over his shoulder as he followed her out of the room was grave with respect and, Conor thought, sympathy.

2

Following Frank's departure, he argued with his mother as they had not done in years—in fact, not since the last time they had discussed his brother. He didn't know how to measure the "extended stretch of time" Frank had indicated, but a glimmer of inherited prescience told him it would be longer than he could bear. There were any number of reasons he couldn't afford to be gone for very long; only one of them really mattered. In fear and frustration, Conor paced the living room, storming at her.

"Why must I do this, Ma? Thomas is a criminal and a fuck-up, and God only knows what he's up to that has MI6 over here looking for my help. Let him lie in the hole he's dug for himself. He's caused us enough trouble."

"You don't mean that, Conor," his mother said. "He's your brother."

"And don't I wish he wasn't. He nearly ruined us, in case you don't remember, and it's been almost six years of my life and every penny I could earn to undo that damage."

"I never believed it." She turned away and walked toward the kitchen. "I don't believe it now. He wouldn't have done it on purpose. There must have been some reason he—"

"He's a thief, Ma! He stole grant money meant for poorer farmers and disappeared with it. He blackened our name. He nearly sent me to jail and the two of us into bankruptcy. Now he's shoveled up some new pile of shite that I'm supposed to dive into? Well, forgive me if I don't leap at the chance. I don't mean to spend the rest of my life following my brother into trouble. Isn't it enough, already, what he's taken? Can you think of anything I've left to give up, now?"

His mother hesitated in midstride as if struck, her thin shoulders slumping in defeat and sorrow. He would have given almost anything to have those last words back again, rattling irritably around in his head, maybe, but hurting only himself. After all, he was more to blame than anyone was, after Thomas. He'd signed his name to everything. If he'd paid a bit more attention ...

His anger dissolved in a sigh of regret. The argument was over. It had been an academic exercise, anyway. They both knew he was going, and they both knew why. Despite the undeniable evidence, his brother's crime was a continued source of grief and confusion for both of them, inconsistent with the person they thought he was. Conor wondered what kind of tale Frank had in store for him in London—another half-baked financial scheme or something worse? It seemed unlikely that the UK's secret intelligence service would be stirring itself for a simple case of grant fraud.

In the end, he had to leave it all in Phillip's hands—the farm, the house, his mother's life—and when Conor presented the situation a few days later, he saw his own dubious misgivings reflected back at him.

"It's a lot to ask of you, Pip," he said, watching Phillip's face uneasily. "Tell me now if you don't think you can do it."

"Will you ever leave off with that, for Christ's sake?" Phillip's cheeks reddened. "It isn't that. Your ma has been good to me; it's no bother. I was just thinking that it all sounds a bit ... well, crazy. Who is this fecker, after all? You think he knows where your brother is or how to find him?"

"Who the hell knows?" Conor sighed. "Everything that's to

do with my brother turns out to be crazy, it seems. I don't know if I'll find him or not, but I feel like I have to try."

As he wrote out instructions and prepared, they all pretended it was for just a few days, but on the day he left, his mother dropped the charade. He could tell the pain was bad that morning, and the cool damp of the farmhouse didn't help. He placed a lounge chair on the flagstone terrace behind the house so the late summer sunshine could warm her a bit while he took a quick hike into the upper pasture with his violin.

"Don't go so far that I can't hear. I'll want to remember how it sounded."

Her soft voice was almost carried away by the morning breeze rolling up from the ocean, but he caught it just in time. Pausing on the sloping hill, he turned to look back, a sudden ache in his throat preventing any reply for several seconds.

"I'll stay close." His husky reassurance was too faint for her to hear, but he gave her a nod and a wave of acknowledgment.

He climbed a little farther to a corner alcove created by one of the many intersections in the pasture's network of stone walls. The spot was one of his favorites. Quiet and intimate, the little corner was sheltered enough to keep the sound from disappearing but airy enough to let it wander among the wall's cracks and boulders in their endless variety of shapes and sizes.

Conor carefully lifted the rare and valuable Pressenda from its case for their final session together. After some internal debate, he had decided to entrust it to a climate-controlled vault at the local bank rather than leaving it to absorb the variable Irish weather without his regular attentions.

It was impossible to explain the relationship he had with this violin. He'd spent years learning to understand it, adapting to its quirks and changing moods and allowing it to lead him to whatever magic it wanted to project on any given day. It was a conversation that never grew old—one that engaged all his senses. His jawline could register the occasional, temperamental buzz before his ear had discerned it, and from the range of breathed aromas in the wood—thick and loamy in the damp, sharp and spicy in the heat—he could predict the adjustments needed to coax out the sound he wanted.

Lifting it to his shoulder, Conor brought the bow down across its strings in a light, affectionate greeting. A bright answering chord rose from the instrument, pressing up through the morning air. He started with vibrato exercises to loosen his hand and then settled in to the rhythm of his standard technical practice. The scale for the day was the four-octave G major, and the technique was legato. The musical articulation calling for the seamless transition between notes was one he could easily lose himself in, endlessly experimenting with posture, arm movement, and wrist angles while losing all track of time in the process.

Today he was more mindful of the clock and of his mother, who was waiting to hear something more interesting than the G major scale. He limited the practice to ten minutes and spent the rest of the hour running through a number of airs and traditional songs that he knew she would like. He finished by switching genres to play Rachmaninov's *Vocalise*, an appropriate piece for that day's concentration on legato.

The *Vocalise* was a complex composition concealed within a simple melody. It meandered in a stream-of-consciousness flow, and with a continuous motion, Conor's bow pulled out phrases that looped and followed each other so closely that it was impossible to tell where one left off and the next began. It was a gorgeous but elusive narrative that escaped entirely in its final seconds, leaving a single note hanging in the air until it thinned and faded.

Leaning against the wall, Conor cradled the Pressenda in the crook of his arm and stared out at the ocean without seeing it, unable to make himself move. At last, he pulled the case forward, gently lowered the violin into its velvet-lined cocoon, and closed the lid.

Back on the terrace, his mother appeared to be sleeping, but her eyes opened immediately when he approached and touched her arm. A silent understanding passed between them before he spoke.

"Just off now. I left the mobile with Phillip. I'll ring you when I get to the hotel."

She passed her fingers lightly over his face, pushing away the dark hair that fell across his forehead. "I'm thinking you need a haircut." Her shadowed eyes grew bright with tears. "Isn't it silly? Such a foolish thing to be saying to my fine, grown son when he's come to say good-bye to me."

Conor lowered his face, afraid he would not be able to look at her again before leaving. With a fierce tightening of his jaw, he raised his head and forced out an answering smile. "I'll get it done in London. I'll come home looking so grand, you won't know me."

His mother sat up and took his face in her hands, and he felt their familiar, tingling heat. Holding him in a firm grip, she stared into his eyes, whispering a fragment of prayer. Her hands traveled down under his chin and rested protectively against his neck and chest. She closed her eyes, her brow creased in concentration. There was a flavor of ceremony in her movements, and he had witnessed it often enough to know what was happening.

"What do you see?" he whispered.

"Pain."

The calmness of her voice contrasted with the disquieting pronouncement. "Pain that a mother should be allowed to stop, but I won't be. I'm afraid it will be a long journey for you, my little love, but he needs you. Without you, he'll be lost. He'll be too afraid. He mustn't be lost, Conor. You must tell Thomas to come to me."

He eased her back into the chair and kissed her cheek. "Don't worry, Ma. He won't be lost. I'll find him and tell him you're waiting here for him."

He winced at the sudden strength of her grip on his wrist. His mother's dark eyes, so like his own, swallowed him with their intensity. "You'll know what to do," she whispered. "Tell him I'm waiting."

He arrived at the hotel in London in the late afternoon with just enough time to drop his bag on the bed before venturing downstairs again. He walked into the Library Bar and wished he had taken an extra minute to make himself more presentable. The dark, paneled room was sprinkled with smartly dressed examples of the moneyed class languidly getting started on the cocktail hour. His tatty wool sweater and crumpled pants provided a contrast that the host in the doorway did not appear to appreciate.

"May I help you, sir?" he asked, nostrils flaring. Conor wondered if he might be getting a whiff of something off the sweater.

"Thanks. I'm just meeting someone here." His Irish accent produced an immediate effect. He wryly watched the man's demeanor become even more glacial, but before their relationship could further deteriorate, Conor saw Frank waving to him from the end of the bar. He slipped past the frigid little character with an apologetic shrug.

As he might have expected, Frank was immaculately dressed and wrinkle-free. He was smiling with pleasure at the sight of him. "Ah, Conor," he said, offering a firm handshake. "Welcome to London and to the Lanesborough. All settled in? Room all right?"

"It's very grand. A bit rich for a government budget, isn't it?"

"Not as rich as you might think. We've had a room here for years. Long story. You might get chivvied along, though, if someone more important turns up, so enjoy it while you can."

"I might get chivvied along anyway," Conor said, observing the glances along the bar aimed in his direction.

"Nonsense. What can we get you to drink?" Almost imperceptibly, Frank raised an index finger from the lustrous surface of the bar, and a bartender instantly responded.

Conor hesitated. He was panting for a pint of stout but thought it was what everyone within earshot was expecting the "Paddy" to order. He hitched his chin at the frothy cocktail sitting at Frank's elbow. "One of those will be fine," he said shortly.

The icy drink soon appeared. At least it was cold. He lifted the glass and took a sip, squinting against a withering tartness.

"It's called a whiskey sour." Frank's tone was professorial.

Conor set the glass on the bar with a grimace. "I'm aware of that. I didn't know anyone over the age of eighteen drank them. That's the last time I did, and they're as foul as I remember."

Frank laughed. "Would you rather have a Guinness?"

"I would."

With the earthy, dark elixir soothing his taste buds, he began to feel a bit more at ease in his surroundings and a bit more kindly toward his host. Frank lit a cigarette and offered one to Conor, sliding the box and lighter across the bar.

"Here is your first lesson. Given the choice, it is advisable to do what is expected of you, because it is easiest and—most of the time—it is safest."

Conor lit a cigarette and passed the lighter back. "Should I be getting out my notebook, now?"

"Not yet. Plenty of time for that."

"Is there?"

Leaning back on the stool, Conor aimed a doubtful squint through the smoke. "I'd have to disagree with you there. I need to know how long this is going to take. I don't have a lot of time to be dawdling around London in flash hotels. I've got things to attend to back home that won't wait."

"Yes, of course," Frank said. "There's another year to go paying back the farm assistance funds Thomas chiseled out of the European Union and a few more payments to the solicitor who kept you out of bankruptcy, and out of prison. We know about all that."

"Yeah, well there are a few other things that I've—"

"Your mother's cancer. We know about that, too."

Conor's face became very still. He took a long pull at his drink and withdrew from the conversation, letting his eyes travel vacantly around the room.

Frank's unctuous manner dissolved. He put a finger to his temple and cleared his throat. "I'm sorry, Conor. I didn't mean to—"

"No." Conor cut him short. "Listen to me. You want to show off how much you know about me and how you've studied every bit of me going back to the first solid food I ever ate. Fair play to you. It's about what I expected, and it doesn't particularly bother me. I'd be grateful, though, if you didn't spit out the details of my life as if they were just so much trivia."

He spoke without raising his voice, but its clipped intensity brought a flush to the agent's face. Frank ground his cigarette into an ashtray and folded his hands together, staring at them as the silence grew between them.

"It doesn't come naturally, you know," he said, finally. "A breezy disdain for the concerns of decent people takes years of practice. One needs time to ... harden the callous. I apologize. It was unforgivable."

Conor's posture relaxed. He didn't trust him, but he found it difficult not to like the rare old dazzler with his glossy hair and spit-shined shoes. He allowed himself a small grin. "It's not unforgivable, just bloody rude. Order another round, and I may lose the urge to fight about it."

The next round appeared. It soon grew apparent that Frank

had resolved to avoid "shop talk" on this first evening, which left them with limited avenues for interaction. The subject of classical music proved easiest to pursue—an area in which their incongruous personalities found common ground.

At the end of an hour, Conor was no better informed about his brother's situation than when he'd arrived, but when Frank rose to leave, he indicated he would be more forthcoming when they met for dinner the following night.

"We'll go to my club in Portman Square. I'll pick you up at seven, and for God's sake, wear a jacket and tie."

"I didn't bring a jacket and tie."

"What on earth did you bring, apart from your decaying sweater?" Frank's lip curled, surveying the offending garment.

Conor grinned. "I've got a fairly respectable pair of khakis."

With a sense of déjà vu, he watched as Frank removed a card from his jacket, wrote something on the back of it, and handed it to him. "Go to the first address on Jermyn Street at eleven o'clock tomorrow. Quinn will deal with the evening attire. When you're done there, go to Bethany at the Grosvenor Gardens address. Her assignment is to outfit you for traveling. I'll ring them both in the morning, so they'll be expecting you."

"Outfit me for traveling where?" Conor asked.

"Tomorrow." Frank brushed a manicured hand over Conor's arm. "We'll have a good dinner and a bottle of wine, and I promise we will tackle all the details. Now I'm late. Don't forget—seven o'clock. I trust Quinn implicitly. You'll look suitably stylish, I'm sure."

"Stylish," Conor repeated, watching the silver-headed figure glide through the room and out the door. Turning back to the bar, he wiggled his empty glass at the bartender and was pleased to see him respond to his signal just as quickly as to Frank's.

He watched the nitrogen bubbles churning in his glass, and when the cloudy brown mixture had settled into a uniform darkness, he raised it to his lips with a salute to the room and its stylish patrons.

"*Slainté.* Here's to your health ... and mine as well, God help me."

3

The pretty blond server was back again. She lifted the bottle of mineral water from the table and topped off Conor's glass, offering a coy sidelong glance as she poured.

"Is everything all right, sir? Can we tempt you with anything else this evening?"

He offered a meaningful smile. "Ah, well, you can always tempt me."

"We're absolutely fine for the moment." Frank's assurance had a waspish edge. "You've been extremely efficient with the water service—yes, thank you for noticing my glass as well—it's quite commendable. But I believe we are equal to the task now."

With a parting smile for Conor and a haughty look at Frank, the woman replaced the bottle on the table and drifted to the other side of the dining room.

"It's the suit you know," Frank said, eyes glittering. Conor gave a grunt of laughter. "Don't laugh, it's true. You cut quite a dashing figure when you care to try. A pity the entire kit has to be returned tomorrow. I knew Quinn wouldn't disappoint, but I am surprised he trusted you with cufflinks."

"Contrary to what you seem to believe, it's not the first time I've worn a suit. I even have two fairly sharp tuxedos in a closet at home."

"Oh yes, I know," Frank said with gleeful mischief. "Now, can you tell me the last time you wore one of them in London?"

Conor rolled his eyes. "I suppose I could remember if I tried, but no doubt you've got the facts on the tip of your tongue. There's something of the stalker about you, Frank. It's a bit creepy. Go on and tell me."

"The Savoy, eight years ago. It was a gala charity event for the University College hospitals. You were the soloist for the Tchaikovsky concerto."

"Oh. Right." Conor grew thoughtful. He absent-mindedly pushed stray breadcrumbs around the table, grinding them into the cloth under his finger, and looked out onto the street.

They were seated in a secluded corner of the second-floor dining room next to a window overlooking Portman Square. Suffused with soft lighting and a subdued ivory-and-beige color scheme, the restaurant's atmosphere seemed especially snug compared with the scene outside. An unseasonably cold rain obscured the small park below them. Waves of gusting wind shook leaves from the trees, and raindrops beat against the windows with rolling, staccato pops. Frank leaned forward to pour more wine, watching Conor's profile with curiosity.

"It's not a pleasant memory?"

"No, it is." He shifted his gaze away from the window and smiled. "That was a good night. My ... friend, Margaret Fallon, came over with me, just for the *craic*. That means a bit of fun," he explained.

Frank nodded. "I'm familiar with the term."

"You're also familiar with the details about Maggie, I'm sure."

"Of course." Frank's response was immediate, but his tone was neutral. "Something a bit more than a 'friend,' wasn't she? You had plans to marry, I believe."

"Oh, I had a lot of plans a long time ago." Conor waved his hand, a conscious parody of Frank's habitual gesture. "Anyway, like I said, that was a good night. I nicked two bottles of champagne from the after-party. We drank them in the hotel room with a couple of cheeseburgers. Yeah, it was good ... "

He trailed off, remembering that night in London—the gorgeous Art Deco theatre with its shimmering, multicolored curtain, the energy of the orchestra, and the current of connection he'd felt running from himself to the other musicians, to the audience members, and to Maggie Fallon.

She was a black-haired, emerald-eyed beauty inhabiting a self-contained universe of pleasure and fun that he'd been happy to believe was real and could last. She wasn't made to deal with trouble—at least not the sort of trouble he ended up bringing. He couldn't blame her, really. At least she'd sent a letter. He wondered where she was now.

While still lost in thought, another memory of that evening came to mind. He emerged from his reverie with a slight smirk.

"You're wrong, Frank. That's not the last time I put on my tails in London. The Lord Mayor came backstage after the concert and asked if I'd come play at his house the next night. He was throwing a little party."

Watching Frank's twitch of surprise gave him a devilish satisfaction.

"A private recital?"

"Yep. That one must have slipped by your lads in the office. Makes you wonder what else they might have missed, doesn't it?"

"Champagne, cheeseburgers, and a command performance for the Lord Mayor." Frank shook his head. "You're a rather unorthodox virtuoso, my boy."

"Sure, I heard that often enough." Conor's eyes narrowed. "And a lot of other things that weren't meant as flattery. One critic said I played Vivaldi's *Four Seasons* like it was a pub session."

"How could that not be construed an improvement?" Frank drawled. "I should have thought such a style refreshing."

"Some did but some thought it proved you can't make a classical musician from an Irish fiddler. Anyway, I haven't rattled anyone's delicate sensibilities for a long while now."

"Thanks to your brother."

"Thanks to my brother and my own lazy stupidity," Conor corrected. "I owned half the farm, but I never took any responsibility for it. Thomas wrote to Dublin, saying, 'We'll do this,' and I wrote back, saying, 'Right, good man.' I'm sure you've seen the forms. My signature is all over them. Nothing was forged. Maybe if I'd ever bothered to read the feckin' things, I'd have asked some questions. More likely I wouldn't have, though. It was easier not to know."

In the pause that followed, he drained his wine glass in one long gulp and pulled a packet of cigarettes from his pocket.

"So, what's he at now, Frank? Is he stealing something from someone again?"

"Don't smoke those horrible things." Frank pushed his box of Dunhills at him. "When one is courting lung disease, one should at least do it with style."

They both lit up, and Frank blew a stream of smoke at the ceiling.

"What's he at now. Well, perhaps we should start further back to properly set the scene. It began ... " Frank hesitated. "Well, I can't say 'innocently.' Let us say it began unremarkably. It's not an especially clever or original idea to loot the European Union. It's not even that difficult. These multilaterals are so choked with internal intrigue that they spend most of their investigative resources on themselves. Thomas was not a figure of distinction to anyone at this stage. He was just one of a crowd of thieves and con artists all eager to fleece the EU of the farming subsidies it scatters about like bread on the waters."

"'Fleece' is an apt term in this case, isn't it?" Conor remarked. He smiled bitterly.

"Yes, it is," Frank agreed. "Awfully good at counting sheep, your brother. Let me see now, he inflated the number of his herd by approximately—"

"By exactly one hundred percent. We don't keep sheep at

all. It's a dairy farm. And he jumped up those numbers as well."
He didn't need Frank to fill him in on this part of the story. He
was already well acquainted with the circumstances leading to
the arrival of two officers of the Garda at his Dublin flat on a
Sunday afternoon in 1998—just over five years ago this week, he
realized. One woman and one man, both polite and apologetic.
Ordinarily, there would be no need to take him into custody, they
explained, but since his brother had "done a runner," they had to
assume he might try it too. After all, his signature was on all the
paperwork, wasn't it?

It had been a simple story to explain in the general sense. He
was being arrested for conspiring with his brother to defraud
the European Union of farm subsidy funding by falsification of
records and documents related to the operations of their farm.
Thomas had disappeared from the farm, from Dingle—from
Ireland altogether, it appeared. He'd been gone for days.

The Gardai took turns laying it out in straightforward
language, and if they didn't believe his blank incomprehension,
they were diplomatic enough to hide it.

"So far, you're not telling me anything I don't already know,"
Conor objected.

"I realize that, of course," Frank said patiently. "I am merely
trying to highlight the irony that this particular incidence of
fraud—which ended your engagement and your career in music
and which made you essentially a serf on your own land—was
a subject of concern to very few beyond yourself. They made a
token attempt to find your brother, but neither the authorities in
Brussels nor Ireland were much interested. They had you to foot
the bill, and they had other fish to fry—committee members
taking bribes, that sort of thing. How much did it end up costing
you?"

"With the fines and legal fees, over a quarter million," Conor
said.

Frank whistled, and after a brief pause, he continued. "At any rate, about eight months ago, Thomas became rather more interesting when someone at the EU—no doubt one of those tiresome auditor chaps who enjoy such minutiae—had another look at the documentation and noticed the grant payment had been wired to a bank account in Belfast. Rather suspicious, that, thinks the auditor chap, since neither Thomas nor his farm were anywhere near Belfast. The information got passed on to the Irish authorities, who confirmed the bank as one with historical connections to the IRA."

Cursing internally, Conor poured the rest of the bottle of mineral water into his glass and drank it. He wiped his mouth, ran a hand through his hair, and lit another cigarette. After drawing deeply on it, he rested it against the ashtray and began flicking his thumbnail against the filter tip. The nervous gesture did not pass unnoticed.

"Perhaps you'd care to have a brandy or a whiskey?" Frank asked.

"Yeah, whatever."

His eyes wandered to the votive candle next to the ashtray and fixed on it. Inside its glass chimney, the flame burned straight and motionless, as if frozen. He no longer heard the quiet hum of conversation around him or the rain slapping against the windows. When the whiskey appeared at his elbow, he barely noticed it.

He'd been reluctant about coming here for this story, and now more than ever, he didn't want to hear it. He continued staring into the candlelight, his mind searching for an avenue of escape and telling himself it wasn't too late. He could demand that Frank stop, or he could leave London, pretending not to have understood any of it. He might persuade himself that it was the right decision and that there was nothing he could have done.

Conor finally noticed the older man's silence and looked up.

Apparently, there was no need to think of ways for stopping him. The story had reached its natural tipping point, and Frank's eyes had shifted, their sympathy displaced by professional appraisal. For the first time, he felt the full impact of an intelligence officer's cold-blooded stare.

"It's time to decide, Conor," Frank said evenly. "You can finish your drink now and bid me a fond farewell. I won't try to stop you. If you choose to stay, however, I will take that decision to mean commitment. You'll be making it without understanding what will be asked of you. It is neither comfortable nor fair, but there it is: commitment nonetheless. I warn you now that I shall take it very seriously."

They watched each other warily, until at last Conor shifted in his chair. "Go on with the rest of it," he said.

"Are you quite certain?"

"Of course I'm not 'quite certain,'" he snapped, shattering the spell of Frank's scrutiny. "The only thing I'm certain of is that it's not up to me. I have no decision to make. So, let's you and I stop pretending that I do and get on with it. Tell me the rest. It's what you brought me here for, isn't it? Tell me what's going on and then what the fuck you expect me to do."

Frank removed a document from his inside pocket, unfolded it, and placed it before Conor with a fountain pen on top. "The Official Secrets Act. You need to sign it before we continue. Take a few minutes to read it over, if you like."

Conor impatiently skimmed through the document. "How does this apply to me? I'm not a Crown servant or government contractor."

"You are about to become one."

"The hell I am."

"You are being tiresome," Frank said irritably. "Sign or do not sign, whatever you choose, but if you do not sign, our business together is—"

"Oh, shut up, Frank, for Christ's sake." He signed his name and shoved the paperwork across the table. "You're pretty tiresome yourself."

The document disappeared into Frank's jacket. Settling back with a satisfied sigh, he warmed his brandy glass between his hands and smiled.

"Good. Very good. By all means, let us continue. MI5, the UK's domestic service, is engaged in a number of complicated activities involving the IRA, and as you've perhaps read in the papers, some of them have gone rather poorly. No one welcomed a new case that didn't fit their existing profiles, so the file floated up and down the hierarchy for a few weeks before someone had the bright idea of tossing it to me. Because of my ... unique ... connections with the Irish network—I serve as the MI6 liaison to MI5 in IRA-related matters—they thought I might be useful to them. I think they'd also grown weary of having me at their meetings dissecting their various cock-ups. They wanted to get me busy with something that didn't involve them directly."

"What's so unique about your connections to Ireland?" Conor asked.

Frank playfully swirled a mouthful of brandy around in his cheek before responding. "I spent the first thirty years of my life there—born in Kildare, grew up in Monaghan. I'm as Irish as you are, Conor. Have I surprised you?"

"Go on outta that, Frank." Conor threw back the whiskey and reached for the decanter that had been left on the table. "You're spreading it a bit thick now. You don't seriously expect me to believe that?"

"I confess that I expected you would. It pains to hear you have so little trust in my word. I flattered myself we had established some rapport."

"Rapport is not the same thing as trust."

Frank acknowledged the retort with a nod and watched him

pour a generous measure of whiskey into his glass. "Don't you think you've had enough?" he asked.

Conor raised an eyebrow at him. "On the contrary, I don't think I've had half enough, and if you were really Irish, you'd know the difference. Don't stop now, though. This is good. Tell me all about your Monaghan boyhood and how it made you the perfect recruit for MI6. Because the British love telling their secrets to the Irish, don't they? We can hardly shut them up."

"All right. Never mind." Frank shook his head in bemusement. "It's irrelevant whether you believe me or not, and it's a different story altogether. We don't have time for it now."

"Oh, sure. You need a bit more time to come up with a proper stem-winder? Christ, spare me that. You're about as Irish as the Prince of Wales."

"Fine. Suppose we return to our principal theme?"

"Fine."

Frank took a deep breath before continuing. "We made the usual round of inquiries around Belfast. No one had ever heard of Thomas McBride from Dingle, and no one knew of any large amounts of cash filtering into IRA coffers from fraudulent EU grants. Eventually, though, information surfaced about a skunk-works operation within a cast-off element of the IRA. It seems some financial wizard has set up a system to support money-laundering projects developed with hundreds of thousands of euro cadged out of the EU. One of the operation's clients is rumored to be a Mumbai group fronting the cost of weaponry for a paramilitary group in the Jammu-Kashmir region of South Asia. They need to disguise the money as well as its purpose. In return for a hefty commission, this quasi-IRA group provides its services, and they have placed a man on the ground in India to manage the client and the flow of money."

"You're saying this man ... " Conor paused to stifle his shrill incredulity and started again more quietly. "You're saying this man is Thomas?"

"Yes."

"Ridiculous. He's not capable of it. He's not that bright, Frank. Apparently he's a con artist—no argument there, although even that was hard to believe—but I can tell you for certain he's no technical or financial wizard."

"We're not talking about anything so awfully complicated," Frank said. "The system is already in place for him. All he needs is a bank account, a laptop, and a satellite connection for electronic transfers. Beyond that, we have established proof of his connection to two known representatives of an IRA splinter group originating in Armagh."

Hunched forward with his elbows on the table, Conor tried to explain the disparity of Frank's description with the man he knew. "It doesn't sound like Thomas at all. I can't believe this is something he would—"

"He's there," Frank said with finality. "We have a contractor in India who confirmed your brother's presence in Mumbai, and MI6 sent an agent over to investigate."

Frank leaned forward across the table, his eyes locked on Conor's. "Now, listen to me," he said, his tone low and vehement. "Believe or don't believe whatever you like about me. It means fuck-all to me what you think. But if you are going to be any use to me, or your brother, you will believe this: Thomas has allied himself with a group of IRA cast-offs. He is a primary figure in an international money laundering operation. He is in regular contact with a group of terrorists based in Kashmir, and he is in shite up to his eyeballs. I understand it is painful to hear. I realize it is difficult to absorb. I also know it is quite possible you represent the only chance he has to come out of this alive, so it is imperative that you begin hearing and absorbing it as quickly as possible."

He noticed Frank's elegant upper-class accent had changed. Just for a moment, it had taken on a hint of the lilt and cadence of Northern Ireland. Conor felt his resistance collapsing and closed his eyes. "Yes, all right. I believe you," he whispered. His throat tightened. "What are you going to do?"

"I am going to send you to India to get him and bring him back to us."

He opened his eyes and stared at Frank in confusion. "You just said you already sent a man over there to do that. What happened to him?"

"That agent was not the ideal resource for the assignment." Frank scowled. "We need to have your brother's cooperation, and with the right approach, he might be persuaded to offer it."

"Why do you need his cooperation? Why can't you just arrest him and be done with it?"

Frank offered a thin smile of patient pity. "We believe this to be a global money laundering operation. There might be any number of field operatives running projects within it to prop up terrorist networks. We just happened to get lucky in identifying one of them. We don't want the field operatives; we want the person running them. We want the wizard. Your job will be to reach Thomas and talk him into helping us with that. If he does, we'll be able to help him."

A shiver passed through Conor even as a trickle of perspiration rolled down the side of his face. His hands were ice cold, and his head was pounding. Maybe he had drunk too much. Pinching his fingers against the bridge of his nose, he could think of only one last question to ask. "Why me? For God's sake, Thomas hasn't cared enough to contact me even once in more than five years—not even a postcard to say he's alive. Why would I have any more influence than your last agent?"

"Why you? Indeed. I wonder that it took so long for you to ask," Frank said. "After the initial failure with our own agent, I enlisted a local asset through contacts within the Indian Army. It was a blind assignment to seek out a 'person of interest' through a casual encounter, engage in a recorded conversation, and then send the tape back through Indian intelligence channels. Within two weeks, I had a transcript on my desk detailing the conversation from a two-hour drinking session with your brother at a local Mumbai watering hole. The transcript provided nothing in terms of actionable intelligence, but it persuaded me that you could be precisely what we need for the operation. It took some time convincing others within the service, but I ultimately prevailed."

"Again, why?" Conor asked with a weary sigh. "What was in the transcript?"

"You," Frank said softly. "You were in the transcript, all through it. They went on for a few hours, most of it inconsequential rubbish, but it always eventually and inexorably led back to the only thing Thomas wanted to talk about, which was you—the brilliant, talented little brother who can do anything, especially with a fiddle in his hands. He may not call or write, Conor, but he thinks about you. Clearly, he thinks about you quite a lot."

Although not embarrassed by it, out of some sense of decorum, Conor put a hand over his eyes to hide the sudden swell of emotion. He didn't see Frank slip from his chair, so the gentle pressure of a hand on his shoulder a moment later startled him. He rubbed his fingers against his eyes and looked up with an apologetic shrug, not trusting his voice.

"It's enough for tonight, I think," Frank said. "Let's find you a cab. You could do with a good sleep."

4

The following morning, Conor woke—as he always did—at exactly four thirty. He was still tired, but the internal clock regulating the rhythm of his days made no allowance for a break in routine. He had always been an early riser, even during the years in Dublin. Once a farmer, always a farmer, he thought wryly.

As he shifted onto his back, a hint of warning tickled along his spine. He sat up, wiping the residue of sleep from his eyes, and strained to see in the darkness. The hotel room—a suite, in fact—was appointed in classically English style: tasteful, elegant, and conventional to the last detail. There were large Georgian windows with brocade curtains, and a sitting area in front of the bed with a sofa and chairs arranged around a small fireplace. There was also an unnerving stillness in the room, like a heavy, watchful presence.

Conor stifled the sound of his breathing and sat listening, trying to interpret the silence. Before he could get a fix on it, the tension released, and the room seemed natural again in its early morning quiet. Still suspicious, he vaulted from the bed and went to the door. Yanking it open, he stepped out and looked up and down the hallway. Empty.

He closed the door and leaned back against it, drawing a long breath. He was wide-awake now.

It might not mean anything. He was skittish. It had been an

eventful trip so far, and with the company he'd been keeping, it was hardly surprising that his imagination would find something sinister about a quiet room. On the other hand, the feeling was similar to other instances of heightened awareness he sometimes experienced—a faint echo of his mother's stronger gifts. They usually meant something.

Whether premonition or paranoia, the feeling was gone. His tensed shoulders relaxed and gently flexed again to propel him from the door. He glanced at the bed, dismissed the idea of returning to it, and looked at the illuminated clock on the bedside table. It was four thirty-three. Frank had promised to return at nine o'clock to reveal the next steps in his implausible engagement as a Crown Servant, and until then, Conor preferred not to think about it.

He needed distraction, something to compensate for the absence of his morning drill. He went to the window, pushed aside the curtains, and looked out at the misty, half-lit city. It had stopped raining, but the pavement was still wet, darkly reflecting the streetlights with an oily gleam. The scene was not inviting, but he decided to go for a walk anyway. It was something to do.

On the ground floor, he stepped off the elevator into a deserted lobby. Even the ubiquitous doorman was absent as he exited the hotel onto Hyde Park Corner, but as he crossed the street and automatically glanced behind him, a movement beneath the hotel's portico caught his eye. A figure had moved abruptly back into the shadows.

Once again his skin prickled, and the intuition was not as easy to shake a second time. Someone was watching him.

Without breaking stride, he continued across the street, disguising the kinetic emotion that wanted to drive him forward at a more reckless rate. It wasn't fear; it was anger, and he embraced it with a cathartic intensity.

He had given years of his life as penance for signing his name in ignorance, but it still wasn't enough. It wasn't enough to have been his brother's hapless pawn in a financial scheme that destroyed his career and future. Now, he was also expected to be the cat's paw in some contorted intelligence game that was likely to get them both killed.

To make the irony even more exquisite, when Frank had presented the papers, Conor had signed them without blinking, as if five years had taught him nothing. Well, he'd signed up for the match, and someone appeared to be wasting no time in getting it underway.

"Let them come, then," he said, resisting the urge to look behind him again. "Whoever the hell they are, let them come. Maybe we can get it over with fast."

He reached the large archway of Apsley Gate and passed under it into the park. It was more active than he would have expected for such an early hour. A small collection of runners and dog-walkers moved along the paths, and a group of Tai Chi practitioners was already gathered near the water's edge of the Serpentine. After pacing off a quick hundred yards, he risked a furtive glance over his shoulder and detected one figure stepping along with a more purposeful gait.

When he arrived at the Lido, he was alone again. The park's sunbathing and recreational area was deserted, its facilities locked, shuttered, and swept clean. The Lido's restaurant offered a temporary screen from observation, and he passed around its far corner before pausing to consider his options.

Ahead of him, the path—with a wide, empty lot next to it—straightened out again, carrying on toward a bridge that spanned the Serpentine. A little to his left, an enormous weeping willow stood near the rear of the building. Its branches spilled down to the ground in a green curtain of lance-shaped leaves. Conor moved closer to study it, and then, parting the tangle of drooping branches, he stepped through to crouch behind the trunk. As the rustling leaves settled back into stillness, a broad-shouldered form appeared around the corner of the restaurant.

Conor pressed against the trunk and squinted through the branches. The man carried a briefcase and was dressed in a dark blue suit and gray raincoat, looking like a businessman on his way to work. He had a head full of brown, curling hair, and as he passed the tree, Conor caught a brief glimpse of a square-jawed face. The man walked a few paces down the path and then stopped and rotated slowly, scanning the empty space around him, looking bored and irritated. He pulled a mobile phone from the pocket of his raincoat and impatiently stabbed at the keypad.

"Yeah, it's Shelton. I've lost him."

The voice was gruff, carrying the strong, matter-of-fact tone of an East London accent.

"Well, I had to stay well back, didn't I?" he snapped. "It's a bloody big, open park. I had him in sight about two hundred yards ahead and then he went into dead ground and disappeared. Might have gone on to the bridge or he might have cut through the car park back to the street."

The burly figure turned. His eyes swept across the willow tree without pausing and looked back along the path in the direction he'd come.

"Bollocks," he snorted. "I told you I stayed well back. He couldn't have noticed me. I think he's either—ahh, what the fuck?"

"What the fuck, indeed." Conor grunted as he flew forward, tackling the man in his muscular midsection.

The two of them tumbled to the ground with Conor on top, but before he could establish a grip on his pursuer, he found himself flattened against the ground, with a knee planted on his back and his face slammed against the gravel path. From the corner of one eye, he saw a hand stretch out to retrieve the phone lying next to his head.

"Jessie? Yeah, never mind, love. I've got him. You were right, though. Silly bastard was hiding from me. Send a car down to the

Lido, will you? I've had me exercise for today."

The weight shifted on Conor's back, and a hand grabbed him by the hair, lifting his bloodied face from the ground. A leather wallet covered in clear plastic was thrust in front of his eyes.

"Metropolitan Police, Special Branch," the voice growled above him. "You want to watch yourself there, Paddy. You're a long fuckin' way from Tipperary now, aren't you?"

When the hand abruptly released him, Conor allowed his forehead to settle wearily back onto the bits of stone and dirt. He'd always hated that song.

"Well, I see we needn't waste much effort training you up for antisurveillance. You appear to have a natural aptitude for it." Frank studied Conor's bruised face with a faint smile. "That will free up some time to counsel you on the inadvisability of attacking your followers. Depending on the nature of the surveillance, you will almost certainly wind up either arrested or dead."

"Why did you have me followed anyway?" Conor slipped his tongue out across his swollen upper lip and winced in pain and annoyance. It hurt like hell every time, but he couldn't seem to stop doing it.

"To see where you would go, naturally. Stop talking and put the ice back on before it starts bleeding again."

They were back in the hotel suite, where Special Branch Officer Lawrence Shelton had deposited Conor without ceremony or sympathy before disappearing again. He had returned a short while later, bringing Frank and a bucket of ice along with him. The two of them now sat comfortably arranged around the fireplace drinking coffee. They watched him—Frank with amused pity and Shelton with a sneer of contempt—as he gingerly dabbed at his lip with a towel wrapped around the ice cubes.

"To see if you'd bolt for home or someplace else," the officer added in a flat voice. "To see if you were going to be as useless as your good-for-nothing brother."

"Now, Lawrence," Frank chided. "I'm sure it rankles to have your surveillance exploded by a mere amateur, but accept it as a learning experience. There's no cause for incivility."

"He baited me," Shelton retorted and would have continued, but Frank's icy stare stopped him in midsentence.

"Yes, I think it's rather obvious that he did. But tell me, how is that less humiliating?"

Shelton's face tightened, but he subsided into silence, and Frank turned his attention back to Conor. "Perhaps you could relieve our concerns. You were up and about awfully early this morning. Where were you going?"

Conor exhaled a sigh and tossed the towel into the ice bucket. "I'm always up and about that early. You're forgetting what I do for a living. I woke at half-four, like always, and thought I'd go for a walk. Is that not allowed now? Do I need a pass to leave the premises?"

"Of course not. We just weren't aware of your plans." Frank shot a sidelong glance at his colleague. "Obviously, you caught us a bit off guard."

"Obviously." Unexpectedly, he found himself amused by the eccentric pair. "Why don't you give me your home number, Frank? I'll be sure to ring with the news next time I go off to the jacks. And to be honest, I hadn't even considered 'bolting,' which is a shame, really, since it would have been fairly easy to get away."

He couldn't resist the dig at the Special Branch officer, whose hostility seemed excessive since he'd already taken his revenge. Shelton did not acknowledge the remark but slapped his cup and saucer onto the table and got to his feet.

"I've got work to do if I'm to take him to Gosport today," he grumbled. "What time do you want him there?"

"It doesn't matter," Frank said. "There's nothing planned for today. Try to get a few hours' sleep first, Lawrence. It will improve your mood."

Without responding, Shelton lifted his raincoat from the back of a chair and moved to the door with a step that seemed unusually light in comparison with his bulk. Before leaving, he swung back toward Conor with a baleful glance. "Be out front at two thirty, packed and ready to travel. Don't make me wait."

Conor expected the door to close with a punctuating crash, but instead it slid shut without a sound, which somehow felt more menacing.

"Looks like I've made a friend," he said, hoping the remark sounded more rakish than he felt.

Frank laughed. "Don't take it personally. Lawrence is the quintessential misanthrope. He despises everyone."

"And you're expecting me to get in a car with him and ride to Gosport?"

Frank tapped the tips of his fingers together and gazed at him without expression. "It would be more accurate to say I require it of you. This is part of the bargain you agreed to, and you bloody well need to understand it from the beginning. You are nothing so melodramatic as a prisoner, but you are not entirely free. There are plans in place for this operation that involve others besides you. At some point, lives may depend on your capacity to take direction when it is given. We cannot continue having this conversation."

Conor placed his head back against the plush upholstery of the chair. He opened his mouth and this time consciously sought the tender spot where his lip was swollen and split. When he found it, he pressed against it until his eyes smarted and he tasted a warm trickle of blood running over his tongue. "What's in Gosport?" he asked, staring up at the ceiling.

"Everything you need to know."

He briefly lowered his gaze to glare at Frank but let the cryptic remark pass without challenge. "How long will I be there?"

"Ten weeks."

He allowed the news to sink in, his fingers tightening on the arm of the chair. "After that, I go to India?"

"Correct," Frank said, and then continued in a softer tone. "I know that personal circumstances make this difficult for you, Conor, and I regret it. Of course, you'll want to let your mother know you'll be away, and ... out of contact, for some time. We can't allow you to share specifics, however. It's for the best—for her safety as well as yours."

Lifting his head from the chair, Conor nodded and retrieved the towel from the ice bucket. He would make the call, naturally, but the information would be redundant.

I'm afraid it will be a long journey for you, my little love.

She'd known it already on the day he left, and even after all he'd learned in the past two days, he expected that on some level, she still knew more than he did.

W hen Shelton appeared at two thirty, Conor was encouraged to see the officer had apparently taken Frank's advice. It would be a stretch to say his attitude was friendly, but he looked rested and refreshed and less inclined to violence.

With more than two hours of driving before them, he thought it was worth another try with the Special Branch officer.

"Can you tell me at all what I'll be doing in Gosport, Lawr ... er, Officer—"

"Shelton. Just call me Shelton."

"Right. Shelton. And you can call me—"

"Whatever the fuck I please," Shelton snapped. "Look, it's not a little trip to get to know each other, is it? We're not going to be chatting all the way down to the seaside. I'll sit here and drive, and you sit there and shut up, right?"

"Yeah, right. Whatever." He turned to watch the outskirts of London passing by, adding in an audible murmur, "Wanker."

He heard a low grunt of amusement, and after a moment, Shelton spoke again in a more temperate tone. "They're having you down there for training at Fort Monckton. It's where MI6 sends its recruits to prepare for field operations."

"Does Frank do any training?" Conor asked.

"No."

"He's just a recruiter?"

"No."

"Well, what's he do, then?"

Shelton's eyes continued to focus on the road in front of them. His large, square face remained neutral. "Frank's got his finger in a bit of everything."

"Meaning what?" Conor asked.

"Meaning exactly what I just said, smartass," Shelton snarled. He pulled into the passing lane, and the police car shot down the motorway. Flipping on the flashing lights, he scowled a warning at him. "Chat's over, Paddy. Shut it now, right?"

"Right." He sighed, and settled back into his seat for the long ride to Fort Monckton.

They had to cross a golf course to get to it. It was a small detail, but it accentuated Conor's sense that he had stepped onto the stage set of some absurdist theatre piece. Sitting at the tip of a peninsula overlooking Portsmouth Harbor—mere yards away from the scene where pensioners duffed their way around the sand traps—Britain's most secretive installation was taking in recruits and training them up to be players in the deadliest game of all.

They rolled to a stop in the courtyard, and as he stepped from the car, a tall, angular woman with graying blond hair greeted him. She introduced herself with a brisk, utilitarian manner that belied her exotic name—Valencia Mathers—but offered nothing to identify her position within the Fort's hierarchy. From her smooth blend of deference and authority, he thought she could be anything from the housekeeper to the senior agent in charge.

She escorted him to his room, which proved a stark contrast to the plush coziness of his suite at the Lanesborough. It was spacious enough but almost devoid of decoration or character. Its austere atmosphere seemed perfectly designed for the nameless recruit whose purpose was to become expert at being nondescript.

Only one item disturbed the anonymous uniformity. It lay at the foot of the bed, its antique leather shining with incongruous brilliance in the colorless room. At Valencia Mathers's slight nod of permission, he released the clasps of the violin case and lifted up the instrument inside. Sweeping his fingers over the cinnamon-hued varnish, he peered through the f-holes at the label inside.

"My God—a del Gesù?" Conor pulled his head back in surprise.

"Correct," she replied crisply. "Bartolomeo Giuseppe Guarneri, made in Cremona, 1726. Mr. Murdoch secured it on loan from a private collector. He thought you might enjoy playing it during your stay at Fort Monckton."

He studied her with a curious frown. "How long have you had it here?"

"Mr. Murdoch had it delivered by special courier a week ago."

"Did he, now?"

He turned his attention back to the violin with a private smile. Frank had evidently held a high degree of confidence for the success of his recruitment mission. It was a magnificent instrument, but he wasn't tempted. The Pressenda demanded his loyalty. He placed the del Gesù back in the case, snapped it shut, and passed it to his aloof hostess with a look of apology. "I'm sorry for the trouble that was taken, and I appreciate the gesture, but please tell Mr. Murdoch it's one I can't accept. I won't be playing the del Gesù or anything else until I'm finished with all this."

Valencia Mathers mastered her surprise and accepted the case with a curt nod. "As you wish."

She directed him to an informational binder on the desk to obtain an orientation to the grounds and services and informed him that dinner was served at eight each evening. "I expect someone will be in contact shortly to arrange your schedule. I do hope you will find your experience at the Fort useful, Mr. McBride. Good day."

He tested the door after she left, dispelling a vague paranoia that she might have locked him in, before making a cursory inspection of his quarters. He paged through the informational binder disconsolately and flipped it back onto the desk with a sigh.

Nothing so melodramatic as a prisoner, Frank had assured him. Why, then, did he feel so much like one?

5

A t the end of his third week of indoctrination, close to midnight on a Friday evening, Conor rapped on the frosted glass door of his lead instructor, Hamilton Bestor. "Sorry I'm late," he apologized, sticking his head into the office to assess the mood before committing to anything further.

Bestor was a middle-aged, translucently pale oddity, with a shining helmet of hair combed into furrows suggestive of black licorice. The two of them met twice a week to assess progress, and their relationship to date had been uneven, primarily due to Conor's glib attitude about the entire enterprise.

He was finding the experience far from dull—some of the exercises were downright entertaining—but the sheen of adolescent escapade overlaying all of it inspired a dismissive contempt. It was hard to take any of it seriously or imagine putting any of the tactics he was learning to practical use.

He'd been trained on surveillance, countersurveillance, and antisurveillance. He'd received direction on the establishment of "dead letter boxes" for exchanging clandestine information and had been turned loose on the unsuspecting populace of Gosport with hidden camera technology. He'd even been given a class in secret writing. He went through the motions, obeying the rules and performing as required, but the remote superficiality of his engagement was a constant irritant for Bestor.

"Right, come in." The agent motioned him inside and indicated a folding chair next to his desk, against the wall.

Conor pulled it forward before sitting on it. Bestor's office was in the subterranean nether regions of the fort's main building, and its walls sweated with a malodorous moisture that made his skin crawl.

"I'm told you made a good fist of it with tonight's exercise," Bestor remarked. "Fill me in. How did you manage it?"

He held out a hand for the file, and Conor dutifully slid it across the desk. The evening's activity had been an exercise in the gathering of personal information from strangers. He had just finished writing up the notes.

"The assignment wasn't entirely unfamiliar," he said, mildly. "I've had some prior experience chatting up women in pubs. I told her I was the hiring manager for the Cunard Cruise Line."

"Full curriculum vitae. Impressive." Bestor traced a long, tube-like finger down the page. "How did you get a copy of her passport?"

"That was her idea. She popped back up the street to her office and made the photocopy while I waited."

"Excellent. Let's have a look." Bestor swiveled toward his computer, and Conor stiffened.

"What are you doing?"

Bestor pulled the file forward for easier viewing and replied while still focused on the computer screen. "Putting her into the database, obviously. Let's see what she's been getting up to, if anything."

Conor stood and plucked the file from the desk. "Nobody said that was part of the exercise. She was out with her friends for a bit of fun, and I just spent two hours telling lies to her. I got an entire life story out of her, and you've run your eyes over it; that should be enough. Why should she be filed in your database just because she had the bad luck to run into a student taking one of his spy exams?"

Bestor swung back to face him with a flat, disinterested gaze but then lurched forward and snatched the file from his hands.

"Who are you to tell me what's enough, you poncey little shit?" he snarled. "You think it isn't fair you had to talk rubbish to a pretty girl? This is how it's done. We gather intelligence, we analyze it, and we act on it. You need to get your head round that, and stop smirking your way through this training as though it were a *Boy's Own* adventure story. The men and women dedicating their lives to this service deserve your respect, not your snide condescension."

"I have plenty of respect for the men and women in this service," Conor said. "I just have no desire to join them. This isn't a career choice for me."

"A point you've clarified more than once," Bestor growled, "to the perverse distress of your trainers, who appear to consider it a bloody shame."

"Why is that?"

"Never mind." Bestor let the file drop onto his desk. His anger dissipated with a sigh. "At any rate, the field techniques section is finished. We realize, of course, that many of them are archaic. The main objective was to instill a sense of discipline and a respect for cautious, methodical process. Whatever you might have thought of them, you performed well."

He paused, staring pointedly down at the desk, and Conor realized he was expected to acknowledge the compliment. He dipped his head apologetically.

"Thanks. Listen, I'm sorry. I don't mean to make anyone's job harder. I'll work on my attitude. What comes next?"

"Intensive language lessons, weapons and martial arts training, and computer labs," Bestor responded promptly. "Tomorrow you'll be briefed on the methods of international money laundering. Britain boasts the preeminent expert on the subject, and he's coming down from London to spend the day with you."

"What's his name?"

"Lawrence Shelton."

"Ah. Brilliant."

Shelton appeared bright and early the following morning as promised and proved every bit as surly in his new role as faculty member. Despite his attempts to stupefy him with the arcane details of tax shelters and fraudulent invoicing, Conor found the basic concepts of money laundering easy enough to understand.

"It's pretty clear Thomas is taking in the money from the source," Shelton said, jabbing a stubby thumb at the puzzling hieroglyph he'd circled in the center of a whiteboard.

They were conducting the session in one of the Fort's smaller seminar rooms, and Conor had patiently watched him draw a bewildering series of figures and arrows to illustrate the methods by which funds could elude the finance mechanisms meant to track them.

"Somebody has a shitload of cash they want to use to arm this pack of lunatics up in the mountains. Well, nobody deals in cash anymore. They can't just throw it into sacks and head off for their meeting in Bahrain, Vladivostok, or wherever the hell. They need to put it somewhere, and Thomas is taking care of it. He's managing to get it deposited without tripping any alarms. How's that, then? Couple of possibilities. Either he's got a high-level partner in a bank somewhere that's binning the transaction reports, or he's cutting out the banks as the entry point altogether. Personally, I'm plumping for the latter theory."

Shelton pulled up a chair and leaned forward across the table. Conor saw a gleam of sharp intelligence in his muddy brown eyes and found he could afford a greater measure of respect for a man who brought such a keen sense of curiosity and analysis to a subject that seemed impossibly dry.

"They don't need a bank, you see. As far as they're concerned, he is the bank."

Conor exhaled a small sigh of exasperation. "Thomas has become a banker, now. Is that what you're telling me?"

"Not in the regular sense. I think some schemer a good bit smarter than your brother took all that money that got filched out of the EU and incorporated a shell company to look like it had some legitimate business taking in all that money."

"A shell company. What the hell is that?"

Shelton's face darkened in its familiar scowl. "Jesus Christ, McBride, it's not an act, is it? You really are a cretin. Do you ever read a newspaper? Have you ever been to the movies, even? Every mafia film ever made has this shit in it."

Conor's expression of blank ignorance did not flicker. Shelton took a deep breath and made a conspicuous attempt to gather his patience. He got to his feet again and paced a few times in front of the whiteboard before resuming the lesson.

"Here's how it works. For the money to come out looking clean, it's got to get itself into a bank account and slosh around with a lot of money from a legitimate business. That means Thomas has either latched onto an existing business and started mixing the dirty deposits in with the clean ones, or he's working with a sort of purpose-built company—a shell company that produces nothing, sells nothing, and basically does nothing but sit there as a front for deposits into a bank account. Once the money is in there, Thomas can whip out the laptop and start transferring it around to other accounts."

Another slap at the whiteboard.

"Now, for your average criminal, the money comes out smelling fresh and new and goes back into the legitimate economy to buy holiday homes and diamond necklaces. But our boys are using it to buy boxes of M-16s and rocket launchers, aren't they? Thomas just bounces the money around a bit and eventually wires it into the account of Fecky-the-arms-dealer, who's no doubt got his own shell company all set up and ready."

Shelton plopped once again into his seat.

"So. Right."

The room fell quiet as Conor absorbed the implications of such an operation. It was pointless to mention the sophisticated skills required were incompatible with what he remembered of his brother's capabilities. At this point, he had to admit his opinions about those capabilities might be naïve or at least out of date. In a fairly short time, he'd gained some surprising skills of his own.

Shelton shifted in his chair and abruptly broke the silence.

"I suppose you've got questions, no doubt most of them brainless. Go on, then."

He shot the officer a jaded look. "Who's supplying the money in the first place?"

"We don't know, and for the purpose of our current mission, we don't much care."

"You don't care?" Conor's eyes widened. "How do you expect you're going to stop all this if—"

"No, no, no! Jesus!" Shelton pounded a fist against the table. "You're not focusing on the mission. Once again, as I said at the beginning, as I've been saying all bloody day: the mission is not to shut down international terrorism. It's to shut down this left-behind IRA crowd and stop them from making a living as money managers for international terrorism."

"Well, then, shut it down, why don't you?" Conor shouted. "You've just told me you know how the whole plan works, and you know my brother is running it. You call me brainless. What more do you need, for Jesus' sake? Go find him. Get the names of the people who taught him how to do it, and then throw the lot of them in jail. What are you laughing at, you pompous fucker?"

The final insult made Shelton laugh harder. When he had collected himself and wiped his eyes, he looked at Conor in derisive pity. "It's what we hired you for, you silly prat. Go and find him yourself."

Shelton's tutorial marked a turning point in Conor's career at Fort Monckton. As Hamilton Bestor had inferred, he had been merely tolerating the experience, behaving not unlike a sullen but acquiescent teenager forced to endure a family holiday, but once the architecture of his brother's new vocation was spelled out in all its insidious, finely calibrated detail, something changed.

That night, tossing restlessly in bed, he experienced an unwelcome epiphany. As implausible—ludicrous even—as the scenario might appear, these "Crown servants" were intent on turning him into a passably competent intelligence operative. They were about to send him overseas and actually expected him to wrestle his brother away from a horde of terrorists and the high-rolling fanatics who loved them.

Given the enormity of his situation, he realized his detached manner was childishly counterproductive, and more important, a self-indulgence he couldn't afford.

"Christ, they're going to go through with this. I need to stop feckin' about and get to work."

The Glock semiautomatic pistol was in a pouch inside his backpack, stripped down to its component parts. There wasn't much light in the alley, but he couldn't wait any longer to assemble it.

Ahead of him, he saw strings of lights hanging in a festive, haphazard pattern that connected the stalls of the village's night market, but their bright glow only made the surrounding darkness more complete. He heard fragments of animated conversations in English and Hindi as well as other South Asian dialects he couldn't identify. They were growing louder, which meant he had very little time to get ready.

Quickly moving along the wall, he felt for the small alcove he knew lay somewhere along its length. He found it after a few steps and released a quick breath of relief. Scrambling into a kneeling position inside the confined space, he swung the backpack from his shoulders.

He made a mental note of its location along the wall and conducted a cursory exploration of its dimensions. Pulling the backpack forward, he removed the pouch and shook its contents into his hands. He closed his eyes as his fingers traced over the components and nimbly locked each into place. With the Glock assembled, he tucked it into his waistband and pulled his shirt down over it. Then he stepped back into the alley.

Less than a minute later, Conor was in the center of the market, his eyes sweeping back and forth over the crowd in anticipation of two encounters: one with the agent he'd been instructed to meet there and the other with an individual who had been hired to kill him.

He didn't know what either of them looked like. Was the assassin a merchant at the market or a customer? Old or young? What was the strategy, and what kind of weapon would be used? What about the agent—was it a man or woman? Was he supposed to make contact first or wait for a signal? The brief had been too vague to be of much use. He was operating on instinct and adrenalin.

Sweat beaded above his brow and coursed down between his shoulder blades. A thick, sticky humidity hung in the atmosphere, and he wondered why he hadn't noticed it earlier.

He continued to scan the faces and figures as they proceeded through the aisles between the stalls and observed those in his immediate vicinity: a well-dressed, heavyset man whose wife trailed along behind him; three children with ice cream dripping over their hands; a young mother with a baby swaddled against her breast; and a small group of Maryknoll nuns. The voices around him were more distinct now, and as he warily marked the passing throng, he allowed part of his mind to follow some of the conversations, translating snatches of Hindi as they floated forward.

"Finest Kashmiri wool, three hundred knots per square inch ... "

"Sweet, made from cardamom and pistachio ... "

"Gauri's mother-in-law will not let her ... "

"Conor, over here ... "

"Chai, chai, chai ... "

"Two days until salwar is finished ... "

His head snapped around in the direction of the voice that had spoken his name, and his hand went to the gun at his waist. In the same instant, he realized it was a mistake. Such a reaction could give him away. To his left, a tall, rugged man with a deeply tanned face was signaling him with a surreptitious movement of his head, but just behind him, the young Indian mother who had passed him earlier was observing the exchange. She could not have identified him until that moment.

Her hand disappeared into the bundle she held gathered against her chest. He still had time to get off a shot, but instead he turned and launched himself back at the alcove, diving for cover. It was too late. The shot hit him before he landed, and an explosion of pain immediately followed.

"Shit, shit, shit!" He sprawled in the doorway with a hand pressed to his side, emphasizing each exclamation with a vicious kick at the wall.

The lights snapped on, and the images of the village night market faded from the screens around him. He was once again surrounded by the sterile, fluorescent glare of the Fort's simulation facility. With a small hum, the air conditioning powered on, and his mouth twisted in annoyance as a door at the end of the corridor opened, revealing the compact, muscular figure of his weapons training instructor, Joanna Patch.

She strolled forward and squatted down next to him. From the hint of laughter in her light brown eyes, he could tell she was in a playful mood. Ordinarily, he would have jumped at the opportunity to widen this crack in her professional demeanor, but now it increased his irritation.

"It's no good trying to put a foot through the wall, you know," she said lightly. "It doesn't change the fact that you are now lying in a dark alley in Gwalior with a bullet in your side."

"Yeah, I don't need the detailed narrative, thanks." Conor shifted painfully against the wall. "The physical evidence of your handiwork is realistic enough. What the hell was that, anyway? Sure, I'd be dead right now if you'd clipped me in the head with it."

"It's a small ball made of concentrated felt traveling at sixty-five miles per hour when it hits you." Joanna gave him a serene smile. "And if I'd wanted to hit you in the head with it, I would have done."

"You might give me a vest or something for these exercises." He rubbed a drop of sweat from his nose, still feeling peevish.

"Ah, but you won't have such luxuries in the field, now, will you?"

"Yeah, and haven't you been telling me I won't have a gun in the field, either?"

"I said we wouldn't be issuing you a gun," Joanna corrected him. "But you never know when someone might pitch one at you and tell you to start firing, so we think it's wise to teach you how to use it. Now, let's have a look. Ooh, yes. Nasty, that. Not much fun getting shot up, is it? Best avoided at all costs."

Conor pushed her hand away and yanked his shirt down over the spreading bruise on his side. He sat up a little straighter.

"Was she carrying a baby in that bundle of rags or not?

"Is that why you didn't fire?" Joanna asked. "Because

everything else was going splendidly. You assembled the Glock in record time. I don't think I've seen anyone do it faster, working in the dark. We've already established that you've a quick draw and a deadly aim. You had plenty of time for a preemptive shot, and yet you didn't take it. Is that why? You thought you might shoot an innocent baby whilst saving your own life?"

She waited for an explanation, but when he didn't offer one, she sighed and rose to her feet. The mischievous attitude fell away as she gazed down at him with an expression of cool disappointment. "It was just a bundle of rags. No baby. So you sacrificed yourself for nothing, you see. You should have taken the shot. You need to grow a bit more comfortable with moral ambiguity, Conor. Being able to act on the lesser of two evils might save your life someday."

She left him then and headed back to the control room, but at the sound of the Glock being once more stripped into pieces, she stopped and turned to face him. With deliberate care, and without taking his eyes from her face, he sent each piece sliding across the floor to rest at her feet.

"With all due respect, Joanna, your little aphorisms are a nightmare to me, because the day I grow comfortable weighing a child's death against my own survival is the day I will no longer know who the hell I am."

"The service doesn't give a damn whether you know who you are, only whether you can act the part." Her face assumed the flat, expressionless gaze of the model bureaucrat. "This simulation is completed, Mr. McBride. Thank you for your attention and participation. You may go now."

The control room door slid shut. He heard the muffled conversation of technicians as they powered down the facility. He continued sitting there for several minutes, looking pensively at the locked door. Finally, he levered himself off the floor and walked out into the fresh air.

6

Skimming through the briefing book spread out on his knees, Conor silently reviewed the details of his alias, absorbing it with the help of some internal commentary.

Briefing Profile for Con Rafferty.

Brilliant. I've spent half me life telling people not to call me Con.

Okay, then. Anyway ... Con Rafferty. Unmarried, thirty-two years old. Born in Dundalk, parents dead, two brothers in Dublin, one sister in Minneapolis. Bachelor in Business Studies, Trinity College Dublin, graduate degree ... right, blah, blah.

Present employment with eco-tourism company, Benefi ... Benef ... Christ, I can't even say it, and I'm supposed to work there. Beneficent Tours. There we go. Next item.

Position of Director, New Product Development. Assignment to India, investigating the feasibility of trekking tours in Kashmir ... past assignments ... countries visited, passport number ... medical history, inoculations, dangerously allergic to peanuts ...

Allergic to peanuts?

Conor looked up from the briefing book.

"Why am I allergic to peanuts?"

"Aren't you?" Frank asked.

"No."

"It's probably a typo. Different aspects of the profiles get recycled, and details occasionally get missed by the proofreaders."

"Is that so?" Conor closed the book. "I'm lucky you got my blood type right."

Considering the hazardous nature of the trip he was to begin, he felt in remarkably good spirits. He was back for one last night in the sumptuous surroundings of the suite at the Lanesborough. After spending ten weeks in the chilly, ascetic quarters of Fort Monckton, he had a greater appreciation for its comfortably snug environment. He was also gratified that some kind of productive action was finally on the horizon.

In contrast with his cheerful mood, Frank was in an uncharacteristically sober frame of mind. He ignored the good-natured dig and indicated the second book near Conor's elbow.

"The second dossier contains all the information we know about your brother's activities. Much of it is already familiar to you, but if there is any new information, you should read through it tonight and commit it to memory, because I will be taking back both dossiers in the morning."

"You can take that one now." Conor pushed the file across the coffee table. "I took a look before you got here. There's nothing in there Shelton hasn't already told me."

"Excellent." Frank slipped the documents into his briefcase and looked at him with a skeptical frown. "Have you any concerns? I realize it is a pitifully small amount of information with which to work."

"I'm fine with it." Conor smiled. "You, however, seem a bit jumpy, which makes a nice change for me. What's the story?"

"Not at all," Frank said briskly. His gaze slid away to the floor, and with an abrupt movement, he rose and reached for his coat.

The dodge was transparent and clumsy, handled without any of Frank's typical feline grace, and Conor had been trained to notice such things. He regarded the aristocratic face with heightened concentration.

"'Not at all,' huh? Not too convincing—you're a bit off your game there, boss. Having second thoughts about me, are you?

Wishing you'd gone with a more orthodox plan?"

"No, no, not at all."

"Yeah, 'not at all.' You said that already." Conor scowled. "What the hell's the matter with you? Here's your newly minted agent cheerfully preparing to head out for crown and country, and there's you looking like the eve of the apocalypse. Not much of a send-off, and it's giving me a peculiar feeling."

Frank stood looking down at his fingers as they drummed against the back of the chair. Conor groaned in exasperation.

"Will you ever just give over, for Jesus' sake? Why am I always needing to winch it out of you? It's a little late to be saying it, but if you think I can't do this—"

"That is not what I was thinking. Not. At. All." Frank tapped the chair for emphasis and appeared to reach a decision. He sat down once more and faced Conor. "There is a complication with this operation that I did not anticipate. I am irritated with myself for not anticipating it, and more important, I am troubled by the possibility it will make your task more difficult and more dangerous than it already is."

"More difficult. More dangerous. Grand."

It was an uncomfortable piece of news, but notwithstanding the sincerity of Frank's concern, he received it with ironic amusement. More dangerous compared to what, after all? Nothing in his life experience could serve as a yardstick for whatever he was about to begin, so what capacity did he have for measuring the degrees of difference?

"You'll have seen in your brief," Frank continued, "that upon arrival in Mumbai, you are to rendezvous with the agent who will serve as your controlling officer in country."

"Curtis Sedgwick, thirty-six, American, blond hair, thin, medium height," Conor recited. "I'm to hang about outside the arrivals hall and let him find me."

"Correct."

"I was surprised. Didn't realize you hired Americans."

"I was surprised as well," Frank muttered. "Unpleasantly so. I'm familiar with Curtis Sedgwick, or more accurately, with his reputation. He is not an official member of the service. He works as a 'NOC'—a nonofficial cover agent—in the South Asian sector, with mixed results, I might add."

"So, not one of your favorites," Conor said drily. "What sort of repu—"

"His performance is spotty, his habits are detestably foul, and his lifestyle exposes him to unacceptable levels of risk. When he is not on assignment—but for all we know, even when he is on assignment—he carries on a number of sordid commercial enterprises, some of which are criminal. He is exactly the sort of questionable asset that inevitably ends with the service writhing in embarrassment."

Conor felt his stoicism giving way to a twinge of alarm. "Criminal in what sense of the word?"

"In the most literal sense of the word," Frank snarled. "Among other things, he is a small-time drug dealer, and if reports are accurate, an addict."

"An addict?"

"To be more precise, a heroin addict."

"A heroin addict! Are you having me on, Frank?" For a long moment, he stared in speechless disbelief. Then, with a surge of incredulous rage, he exploded. "A fucking heroin addict? What kind of bullshit is this? I've signed papers that promise to string me up if I even think about straying from the straight and narrow. I even had to read a handbook on deportment, for fuck's sake, and now you're telling me that my supervisor, my guide, my all-important in-country controlling officer, is some drug-dealing junkie?"

"I learned only this afternoon that he had been engaged for the operation," Frank said.

"And what are you going to do about it, then? Oh, no you

don't," Conor hissed, seeing a familiar guardedness beginning to form in Frank's eyes. "Don't you give me some secret agent bollocks and tell me you can't do anything, because I'm not having it. You'd better pull your socks up and do something or else find some other miserable bastard for this nonsense. There's a limit to what I'm prepared to swallow, and we've bloody well reached it."

"I understand," Frank said. "Your reaction is predictable and justified, which I expect is why I hesitated in sharing the information with you. The fact is, much as it distresses me, I cannot have him removed from this assignment. He has a unique qualification that makes it quite impossible."

"A unique qualification! Jesus and Mary, can you tell me at all what that might be? What sort of intelligence work does a heroin habit qualify you for these days?"

"I can explain that to you in a minute, but I first wanted to—"

"Explain it now!" Conor shouted. "I'm not listening to anything else you've got to say until—"

"He knows your brother."

It took several seconds for the statement to catch up with his brain. When it did, he felt as though a pair of clammy hands had suddenly gripped the back of his neck.

"He knows my brother? He knows Thomas?" He swallowed hard. "What are you saying to me?"

Frank raised his hands to forestall another eruption and quickly continued. "Not as a customer. I'm not saying that. There's absolutely no evidence of anything of that kind, but they have crossed paths a number of times. Let's not forget the main point here, Conor. Thomas did not go to India on holiday to visit the temples. He and Curtis Sedgwick travel in similar circles. They know the same people, and, as I've learned this afternoon, Sedgwick was the original source in Mumbai who confirmed that Thomas was there, and he was the officer MI6 hired to manage the agent we sent over. Although that endeavor was ineffective and counterproductive, there are legitimate grounds for viewing him as the most promising conduit to your brother."

"Unbelievable." Conor shot a hostile glance at Frank as he paced around the suite. "It's all been calculated, assessed and decided, has it? Quite the pack of clever puppet masters you are, and the rest of us just waiting on your pleasure, wondering what string you'll yank on next."

"Listen to me," Frank said with a resigned sigh. "He lies beyond my authority, but my authority where you are concerned is a different matter. If your concerns are overwhelming, I will release you. You would remain bound by the Official Secrets Act, of course, but your obligation to this mission would be removed. It is all I can offer."

Silently now, Conor continued to pace, struggling to retain the intensity of his self-righteous rage. It was pure and honest and represented what might be his last opportunity for rebellion, not just against the last ten weeks, but also against the last five years he'd spent paying the consequences for choices made by others.

Try as he might, he couldn't make it last. The rage evaporated as he finally admitted it was neither pure nor honest. He had been offered a choice. He'd thrown down the challenge to a tug of war and the rope had gone slack in his hands. He dropped back into his chair and regarded the silver-headed figure with a mixture of admiration and resentment.

"You are so very good at this game, aren't you, Frank? Do you still get that ticklish thrill every time you win, or does it wear off after a while?"

Frank accepted the victory and the backhanded compliment with a bow of his head, but his answering smile was forced, and brief. "It does wear off, son. More quickly than you can imagine."

7

He tried to stay relaxed as he joined his fellow travelers in a switchback crawl through the airport security line the next morning, the passport for his alias dampening in his hand. After passing through without incident twenty minutes later, Conor found Frank waiting for him on the other side.

"You might have taken me round by the back door as well," he complained mildly. "Seems like I'm not getting many perks out of this gig. Economy class ticket, too. Nothing but the best for the rookies."

"We needed the extra money for your laptop." Frank gave him an arch smile. "Let's go have a drink."

"At nine o'clock in the morning?"

"My dear boy, this is Heathrow. It is never any particular time of day here."

It wasn't the first time Conor had nursed a beer before noon, and as they sat surrounded by the general tumult of a population in transit, he appreciated the symbolic truth of Frank's statement. The duty-free zone was a municipality unto itself where the natural progression of day into night existed only in theory. Immersed in the bright, unblinking atmosphere of perpetual commerce, its temporary citizens were left to decide for themselves which time zone best suited their needs. Their self-selected position in the twenty-four hour rotation was most notably evidenced by their menu selections, and Conor was intrigued that the demand for eggs and toast seemed evenly matched against that of sushi and white wine.

"I brought you a bon voyage gift." Frank reached into his briefcase and handed over a brown bag with a smaller plastic one inside it. "A mixture of Chinese herbs. Mix them with hot water, and they serve as a wonderful sleep aid. Perfect for long plane rides."

Conor took a drag at his cigarette and squinted through the smoke at what looked to be a small bag of dirt. "Jayz, what a great gift. I'm touched. Really. I'll be sure to bring you back something nice as well. What do you fancy? Some powdered elephant tusk, maybe? Sprinkle it on your oatmeal?"

Frank lightly braced his hands against the counter and laughed—not a phony, pedantic warble but a spontaneous, honest-to-God guffaw. It was a good sound. It made Conor laugh too, and he found himself wishing he had more time to spend with this cagey cipher who had thoroughly upended the natural order of his life. Maybe if they could get good and drunk together, some of the secrets might start to spill. Maybe he'd get a glimpse of the interior man. Maybe they'd even get to be friends.

Not enough time for it today, though. His gate number would appear on the screen in another ten minutes. He flexed his foot up and down on the rung of the bar stool and stared up at the screen, conflicted between wanting the wait to be over and wanting the clock to stop. He glanced again at his watch.

"Nervous?" Frank asked, looking not at Conor but at the surrounding scene, as though watching a passably interesting piece of theatre. In contrast, and as usual, he was the very image of relaxed enjoyment, sipping from his drink with leisurely pleasure.

Another droll remark leapt to the tip of his tongue, but before he got it out, Conor changed his mind. He took a swallow of Guinness and nodded. "I am, yeah. Any last words of wisdom for me? To be honest, I feel like I could use a few."

"None that would be of any practical use, I'm afraid," Frank said. "But since my first gift was found lacking, let's see if this suits better." He took a small felt pouch from his pocket and slid it along the bar.

"Looks a little more promising." Conor picked up the pouch and spilled the contents into the palm of his hand. His eyes widened as he recognized what he was holding—a circle of black silk cord with St. Brigid's Cross hanging from it.

"*Nach álainn é!*" In his surprise, he uttered the exclamation in Irish and smiled in bemusement. "Sorry. What I meant to say was it's lovely."

"*Tuigim go maith,*" Frank replied, gently. "I understand you perfectly."

Conor gave a short laugh, shaking his head. "That's right, I'd forgotten—the fella from Kildare. You're a man of many parts, Frank. I can't make you out at all. Quite the character." His face grew thoughtful and remote. "My mother's name is Brigid," he added in a low voice.

"I remember," said Frank. "An impressive woman."

"She was fairly impressed with you as well. The two of you have a lot in common, actually, the more I think about it. How does that line go? 'A riddle wrapped in a mystery.'"

His voice trailed off as he absently rubbed the silver cross between his fingers, feeling himself drift to an interior place of silence. He allowed the sensation to deepen, letting the ambient sounds of luggage trolleys and clattering silverware drop away into a distant background.

For as long as he could remember, he had been able to achieve this sort of meditative state quickly and with little effort—a capacity fused into his DNA, apparently—but he did not indulge in it very often. It put him into communion with a phenomenon that was too strong for him—a sensation of pulsing, unbounded consciousness.

His mother called it *chuisle Dé*, the "heartbeat of God." It seemed an apt description for the feeling of being exposed to something relentlessly infinite and exceptionally alive. The experience unnerved him so he tended to avoid it, but he respected the connection it created between the two of them. It was the only thing that ever brought him close to understanding the enigma of Brigid McBride.

He pulled himself back after a few minutes, and the long breath he drew stuttered with overwhelming sorrow. He looked over at Frank, who was watching him with worried concentration.

"She's not expecting to see me again. She didn't say it in so many words, but she got the point across, and I think she's probably right. She usually is about these things."

"That attitude won't do, Conor," Frank said, his frown deepening. "You can only be effective if you go into this with a belief that you will come out of it again."

"No, that's not what I meant." He saw Frank had misinterpreted the remark. He forced down his grief and cleared his throat. "I don't want to sound overconfident, because I'm far from it. I'm scared as hell in fact, but I do believe I'll get back, mostly because she seems to think I will. It's just ... well, it's just not likely to be soon enough—for her."

"Ah. I see." Frank nodded. "I'm sorry. I wish this could have somehow been made easier for you."

"Thank you." Conor glanced again at the screen above them and saw the gate number for his flight was now posted. "Time to get the show on the road, I suppose." He drained his glass and rose. "Thanks for the parting glass, Frank. And thank you, for this." He slipped the necklace over his head and tucked the cross beneath his shirt. "It means a lot. More than you probably realized."

"I'm glad of that. You are most welcome," Frank said.

"Not that your little packet of dirt isn't special too," Conor added with a grin.

In making their farewells, Frank had a final talisman to bestow, one of his ubiquitous cards, this time with a phone number and password on the back. The implication was clear, and from the briefing dossier he'd reviewed, Conor knew it was a breach of protocol.

As soon as the wheels left the ground on his flight to Mumbai, he was officially serving under the direct supervision of Agent Curtis Sedgwick. No other intelligence officer had any business providing him with instructions, much less the number to a private, secured phone.

He took the card without expression, a slight nod of acknowledgment the only indication that he understood. The two men shook hands and parted. He intended to study the information, commit it to memory once he was settled on board, and destroy the card. He didn't realize as he tucked it into a fold of his wallet that he would never give it another thought.

Once settled into his economy-class seat in the rear of the plane, Conor indulged in some jaded speculation about the mission ahead of him. He didn't expect it to go according to plan.

The briefing books in their elegant detail gave the illusion of having anticipated every conceivable contingency. There were no dead ends in any of the "decision trees" the backroom planners had constructed. Every question had an answer, every problem a solution.

Bollocks.

He had weathered enough life experiences to know the most finely tuned plan could evaporate in an instant. He considered it unlikely that this one would stay intact for very long.

Low expectations notwithstanding, the first stage of the mission was the least complicated: sit on a plane and wait to be collected outside the arrivals hall. He assumed it was likely to proceed as designed, but in reality, the operation was officially underway less than an hour when it jumped the track. More than the speed, he was startled by the ease with which a random circumstance could make hash out of ten weeks of indoctrination. In this case, the random circumstance took the form of the occupant of seat 51B.

The first surprise was that seat 51B had an occupant at all. He was in 51A, next to the window, in one of the few rows with only two seats. His instructions for the flight had been unequivocal. He was to remain quiet and anonymous, avoiding unnecessary conversation and making every effort to appear as invisible as possible. He presumed this meant someone had ensured that the aisle seat would remain empty. Surely an intelligence expert of any quality—particularly a British one—would not expect an Irishman to sit next to someone for nine hours without talking.

No such precaution had been taken, however. Conor therefore felt only partly culpable for the events that began when he turned his head from the in-flight magazine and met the serene, brown-eyed gaze of an older Indian woman. She had materialized soundlessly in the seat next to him and now sat watching him placidly, unmoved by his flinch of surprise. Only her eyebrows twitched with amusement.

"I'm sorry," he said. "I didn't know you were there."

The woman touched her forehead with the tip of a long, thin finger. "You are deep thinking," she said, toggling her head from side to side. "I am watching you many, many minutes. Not reading. But so deep thinking."

Conor smiled. "I guess you're right. There wasn't much in it worth reading."

He tucked the magazine into the seat pocket and glanced forward at the plane's open door. Passengers continued to board at a sluggish pace. He tried looking out the window for a few minutes but finally gave up and turned his attention back to his seat companion.

Her weathered face was thin and lined, but a thick, gray braid of hair draped over her shoulder gave her a girlish appearance. It was difficult to judge her age; she might have been anywhere between fifty-five and seventy. The voluminous folds of her crimson and gold sari suggested a more substantial frame, but the embroidered length of cloth was not sufficient disguise. She was remarkably small and frail, and despite a gleam in her eyes, she appeared to be in rather poor health. Her breathing sounded labored, whistling in and out with a high-pitched wheeze. And she was still looking at him.

She was going to be impossible to ignore. With an internal shrug, Conor surrendered to the inevitable, but before he could speak, she leaned forward with a smile.

"What is your good name, please?" The South Asian intonation added a musical quality to her words.

"My good name is Con." He made a conscious attempt not to grimace. "Con Rafferty. And you?"

"I am Kavita Kotwal."

"*Shrimati* Kavita." He automatically applied the honorific as he had been taught, which made her beam with surprised pleasure. "*Aapse milkar khushi hui.* I'm very pleased to meet you."

"Yes, very pleased. Also." She inclined her head in a graceful gesture of greeting. "You are speaking very good Hindi."

"I'm sure I don't do it justice, but I've enjoyed learning some of it. It's a beautiful language."

"*Haan.* Yes," she agreed. "In Mumbai, the people are also speaking Marathi and Gujarati. Those you speak also?"

"I'm afraid not," Conor replied. "Hindi was about all I could handle. That and a bit of Urdu."

"*Accha.*" She nodded in satisfaction. "Hindi is better. Urdu is best. These are the languages of my home region. Uttaranchal.

You must visit. This is first time in India? You are making the tour?"

"I ... ehm, yes, first time," he said evasively, and turned again to assess the boarding process. "I'm looking forward to it."

"Not making the tour, I think," she murmured, as if to herself. "Not holiday time."

"Sorry?"

"Too much deep inside." She tapped her head again with a meaningful look. "Eyes too much far-off. Not a holiday face."

He closed his eyes for the length of one long sigh, wondering if this might be a final test concocted by his employers. It was an early and unwelcome demand on his prevarication skills, and he felt it particularly unfair that out of four hundred passengers, the psychic Indian grandmother was seated next to him.

"I'll try to work on it," he said lightly and then redirected the conversation. "What about you? Have you been on holiday in London?"

"Yes, for wedding. My grandnephew. Wedding is ... " She paused to take a deeper breath. "Wedding is like good holiday, yes? Many people, all party-party, and beautiful city. We have been—" She broke off, winded, and leaned back in her seat, breathing heavily for several seconds before speaking again. "Sorry, sorry. This is some small chest troubles I am having few weeks now."

Conor regarded her with a nervous frown. "Are you traveling alone?"

"No, no, no." Her hand waved vaguely at the seats in front of them. "Daughter is there, son-in-law. Three granddaughters also there."

"Ah, right." He felt somewhat relieved. "Good."

"Yes, yes. This is good. Many family is there." She appeared to understand his concern and gave his arm a reassuring pat, but then she leaned in closer and offered a mischievous wink. "But no husband. He is not for holiday and party. Husband is home."

"I see." He laughed. "Is that good as well?"

"Yes, good! This is very good!" She sat back and began to laugh—a slow, irresistible chuckle that gave way to a fit of coughing. She covered her mouth with the shawl that had been lying in her lap and looked at him with a helpless wave of her hand, her eyes still shining with laughter even as she struggled to catch her breath.

Conor brought out the water he had picked up before boarding. He was still fumbling to support her and help her drink from the two-liter bottle when reinforcements began arriving. With another quick twist of her hand, Kavita confirmed the first arrivals as her family members and made introductions between gasps.

"Daughter, Parvati. Son-in-law, Sukhet. Granddaughters. Surabhi. Deepa. Bhuvi."

Another eight or nine Indian passengers—later identified as additional wedding guests—pressed up behind the family and filled the aisle across the plane. They strained forward, calling out questions in Hindi. This excited the curiosity of other passengers, who began turning in their seats and peering toward the rear of the plane.

The commotion drew a response from the flight attendants as well, who quickly swarmed up both aisles, asking everyone to take their seats. In whatever direction he looked, all eyes were fixed on him and the small woman beside him. With wry amusement, he realized he had become one of the two most conspicuous passengers on the plane.

Off to a rattling start, he thought. So much for anonymous invisibility.

8

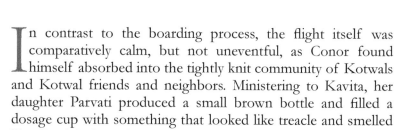

In contrast to the boarding process, the flight itself was comparatively calm, but not uneventful, as Conor found himself absorbed into the tightly knit community of Kotwals and Kotwal friends and neighbors. Ministering to Kavita, her daughter Parvati produced a small brown bottle and filled a dosage cup with something that looked like treacle and smelled like diesel fuel. Kavita tossed it back as though it were a shot of the finest whisky. The cough subsided, and she was soon asleep, breathing in a soft, regular wheeze.

To the acute but helpless exasperation of the flight attendants, a steady stream of visitors filled the aisle when she woke a few hours later. Many bent to touch the feet of Kavita-*ji*, and to Conor, they offered homemade snacks, staring at him with frank, lively interest as he tentatively bit into them. The three granddaughters, teenagers with straight, dark hair and arms bedecked with gold bangles, peeked at him from beneath long lashes and converged in shy giggles whenever he glanced at them. The men gave hearty handshakes and asked a lot of questions. He stuck to the personal history of his alias, relieved that he had taken the time to master its details.

In the last hour of the flight, as the plane descended, Kavita grew feverish, and when they landed, she was too weak to stand. He appealed to one of the flight attendants, a young redhead who had been the most tolerant of all the crew. "Is there a wheelchair that might be brought in for her?"

"Oh, it would take ages to get one. We didn't call it in ahead, did we? And even then it might not be a proper aisle chair, just the standard sort that would never fit down here."

They both regarded Kavita and her surrounding entourage with a puzzled frown.

"Poor little dear. She's quite done in, isn't she?" the flight attendant said. "And none of these blokes look fit for the job. Can you carry her out yourself? I can bring your bags to the jet way, if you like."

Conor nodded. "Yeah, okay. Thanks."

Carrying Kavita was effortless—she weighed no more than a small, thin child—but when they cleared customs and entered the pandemonium of the arrivals hall, he grew impatient with the absurdity of the situation. There still wasn't a wheelchair in sight, his bags were in the hands of some obliging cousin up ahead, and he was caught in the unstoppable tide of Kavita's surrounding entourage. He tried to express a concern to Sukhet, her son-in-law, a short man with a balding, oval-shaped head and large round eyes, but his voice was lost in a cacophony of traffic and shouting as they emerged into a warm and hazy Mumbai night.

Arriving well after midnight, he'd assumed it would be quiet outside the airport and relatively easy for Curtis Sedgwick to find him. He was wrong. The scene outside the arrivals hall was anything but quiet.

The sidewalk beyond the security railing teemed with people standing massed against the barrier, all craning for a better view of the single exit out of the airport. Some stood silently, holding signs with the names of people they'd come to claim. Others gave animated shouts, hailing tourists who wandered through the door and gazed about in confusion. A continuous stream of auto-rickshaws packed the road beyond the sidewalk, and a sputtering roar filled the air as they competed for space with the taxis and vans in their midst.

Conor searched for a thin, blond man of medium height who was presumably somewhere in the crowd searching for him. Then he looked down at Kavita to see her gently fingering the silver pendant that had slipped from beneath his shirt. She gazed up at him with a wise, affectionate expression that stirred an uncomfortable emotion in his chest. Abruptly, he shifted his gaze away and hurried to rejoin the group, which had assembled in front of a black mini coach.

He carried Kavita to a wide bench seat at the rear of the coach and grappled with the seat belts for several minutes, trying to find some way of securing her. Finally, he straightened and addressed Parvati, his voice conveying greater patience than he felt.

"This isn't going to work. There isn't any way to buckle her in while she's lying down. Once you start moving, I'm afraid she'll—"

As if on cue, the mini coach lurched forward. They both leaped to keep Kavita from tumbling onto the floor as the vehicle swung from the curb. Quickly recovering his footing, Conor spun in alarm. "Holy shit, what's he doing? Wait, stop the bus!"

When his shouts produced no effect, he turned his agitation on Parvati. It took several minutes of disjointed commentary, with a number of other passengers chiming in, before he understood the nature of his benign captivity.

From her mobile phone, Parvati had already telephoned Kavita's doctor, who had urged them to get her to the Kotwal's flat in Mahim, a neighborhood of Mumbai, as soon as possible. On top of that, although he was offered forceful reassurances, his fellow travelers could not pinpoint the exact location of his bags. It would take some time to discover where they had been stowed, and if they had to pull over and search ...

"Okay, okay. *Thik hai*, I get it." Conor sighed in acquiescence. "We're going to Mahim."

"*Accha.*"

This most versatile Indian word—used to signal agreement, understanding, skepticism, surprise, or general goodwill—echoed throughout the coach in a chorus.

After driving through surprisingly crowded streets, the coach pulled into the covered parking area of a nondescript apartment building in Mahim. A scene of fresh confusion erupted as a small welcome party of household staff climbed aboard to lend assistance, presenting an improvised stretcher. With a burst of irritation, Conor flatly refused to surrender Kavita to the rickety pallet. He astonished even himself with the colorful Hindi-English directives he employed to clear the aisle so he could carry her out and up to the flat.

Bending to lift her, he was surprised to see Kavita regarding him with a devilish glint in her eyes.

"Hindi is improving rapidly, Con," she whispered, breathlessly. "Welcome to India, land of surprises."

He couldn't resist smiling as he tucked her shawl around her shoulders.

"Is that the official motto?"

"No," Kavita responded with a wheezy laugh. "Not really."

"Well, write someone a letter, Kavita-ji," he said, gathering her up into his arms. "Sure it sounds like a winner to me."

After laying Kavita down in her bedroom, Conor was led to the head of the dining table as the "most welcome, most honored guest," and the family members began feeding him. Moments later, he was further rewarded by the nearly miraculous reappearance of his luggage.

Stupefied by food, weariness, and bemusement at the slapstick nature of his predicament, he fingered the mobile phone in his pocket, unsure of his next move. He knew Curtis Sedgwick had a similar, MI6-issued phone. He had the number for it but had been instructed to dial it only in instances of extreme emergency.

The current situation seemed to qualify, but he continued to stall, postponing the humiliation of trying to explain the mess he'd landed in within minutes of arriving in the country.

He also found it interesting that his controlling officer had not phoned him. It could mean Sedgwick did not yet find the circumstances worthy of extreme measures. In his jetlagged mind, the ongoing silence between them felt like a game of chicken. If he phoned first, would he be reprimanded? Called out as a hopeless amateur?

"Who are you kidding?" a voice whispered in his head. "You are an amateur, but that's not your feckin' fault."

Careful to avoid drawing attention, Conor slipped from the table and stepped onto the balcony of the flat. He dialed the memorized number, and the call went directly to an automated voicemail greeting. He hung up immediately. Voicemail messages were forbidden under all circumstances. Even if they weren't, what the hell would he say? That an Indian wedding party had kidnapped him at the airport?

He lifted his head to gaze around the wide balcony and absently slapped the phone against his thigh. For the first time his senses began to register the exotic, heady atmosphere of Mumbai. The flat was on the third floor, but this exterior space was not constructed for viewing. A cement wall, too high to see over, surrounded it on all sides, so his impression of the city below was formed by the smells and sounds wafting up from the street.

There was plenty to hear in the air around and below him, but the odors most insistently demanded his attention. There were layers upon layers of them, all present at once but individually distinct. They shifted in strength and character with the ocean breeze that blew soft, irregular gusts across his face. First came the sharp tang of engine fuel mingled with an even more acrid burning smell, as though something unnatural had been set alight to blanket the city with a smoldering stench. A shift in the air's direction brought a fresher aroma of salt and brine floating in from the sea. It gave way to the hot smell of spices frying in oil, which in turn incongruously merged with the subtle reek of garbage.

Underlying all these was a consistent undercurrent resembling a scent he had known most of his life. Familiar enough to farmers, but no longer to the inhabitants of developed world cities with robust sanitation systems, it was the dark, organic odor of waste, both human and animal. Back home, it signified a freshly fertilized pasture; here it was the defining smell of a densely packed and largely impoverished humanity. It was repellent in theory, and yet the sensory experience of it was fascinating.

"*Arrey*, here he is!"

He turned at the exclamation and saw Parvati approaching across the balcony.

"I was afraid we were losing you," she explained, waving a hand at him with theatrical exasperation. "Maybe you were sneaking away to find the greeter friend at Mumbai airport. But see, no need for airport now; the friend has found you."

Conor looked past Parvati in the darkness and saw a figure in the doorway silhouetted against the light from the flat—thin, medium height, blond hair.

"The elusive Mr. Rafferty," Curtis Sedgwick announced in a flat, Midwestern American accent. He held up a hand to display the faint green glow of a mobile phone screen.

"You rang?"

9

"So, Curtis ..."

"Sedgwick. Just call me Sedgwick."

"God help me, another one," Conor muttered, remembering his contentious exchanges with Lawrence Shelton. "So, Sedgwick. If you knew it was me calling, why didn't you ring me back?"

He was following the agent through the covered parking area, and although the man was half a head shorter than he was, Conor was struggling to match his stride. The events of the past fourteen hours were beginning to wear on him. He stopped as they reached the street and tried to distribute the weight of his bags more evenly. Sedgwick stopped as well with an impatient sigh.

"I didn't call because I was just a hundred yards down the street." He jabbed a thumb over his shoulder. "I figured it would be quicker to come get you."

"Why didn't you come sooner?" Conor asked.

"Because I didn't know what the hell you were up to, that's why," Sedgwick shot back with an amused scowl.

"And how did you know where I was?"

"Look, dude. Do you mind if we continue the introductory pleasantries in the car?"

Sedgwick flipped a set of keys from his pocket and pointed the entry remote down the street. A white SUV chirped in response, and he started walking toward it.

"You weren't the only thing on my agenda tonight. I'm about three hours behind schedule."

"Yeah, sure. Sorry." Conor hoisted his bags and followed.

He remained silent as they pulled onto the road, yielding the conversational lead to Sedgwick, who at first seemed disinclined to take it. The agent whistled under his breath as he manipulated the standard shift with playful aggression, sending the vehicle speeding up the street. Several times during the ride, Conor felt his core tighten and brace for a crash that looked impossible to avoid, but each time, a sliver of space would appear, and as the SUV shot forward to fill it, he would hear an emphatic whisper of triumph from the driver's seat.

"Boom. Boom."

He took the measure of the man sitting next to him through a series of furtive glances. Sedgwick looked to be in his mid thirties, and although his fine, ash-blond hair reached almost to his shoulders, he was otherwise fairly conventional and clean-cut in appearance. He had a sharp, angular face with thin, dark eyebrows and slate-gray eyes. He was dressed in jeans and a khaki shirt with the sleeves rolled up to his elbows and wore a scuffed pair of motorcycle boots. Most notably, he seemed to be in excellent physical shape. He wasn't a bad-looking guy. He certainly didn't look like a heroin addict.

As if reading his thoughts, Sedgwick took his eyes briefly from the road and glanced toward him. A sardonic grin deepened the vertical lines engraved on either side of his thin face.

"Sizing me up? How am I looking?"

Embarrassed at being pinned so easily, Conor looked away. "About how I expected," he lied.

"Hmm, I'm sure," Sedgwick drawled. His brow furrowed in irritation. "Why so quiet, chum? I thought you had a list of questions for me, although it seems like you have more explaining to do than me."

"I suppose I do," Conor agreed. An enormous, eye-watering yawn prevented further comment.

"I'll cut you a break and start first," Sedgwick said. "But don't fall asleep. It's not my fault you've got to report for yourself this soon."

He shifted into a lower gear and pointed the car at the longest stretch of empty road Conor had seen so far.

"Here's my end of it. I get to the airport a half hour before the plane lands. I see everyone from the flight walk out the door, and I miss you completely. Of course, I'm looking for a black-haired Irish guy wandering around by himself and am too preoccupied to notice the Good Samaritan carrying out a woman obscured by a posse. So kudos, if that was the plan—maybe everything they're saying about you in Gosport is true."

"It wasn't part of the plan." Conor looked curiously at Sedgwick's profile. "What is it they're saying about me in Gosport?"

Sedgwick dismissed the question with a quick shake of his head. "We'll save that for later. Anyway, now I'm standing around at the airport, and I've got no black-haired Irish guy. I'm wondering if he missed the plane, if the MI-whatever boys back in England changed their minds, or if maybe the MI-whatever boys are just fucking with me, which wouldn't be news. Then, I hear these two rickshaw drivers jawing away next to me and realize they are trying to figure out what the story is with that tall, dark-haired *gora* that carried Kavita Kotwal out of the airport. I whipped out the photo I had, and they confirmed it was you."

He paused and looked over at Conor. "A *gora* is what Indians call a white guy."

Conor nodded. "Right. I know."

The agent held his gaze for several uncomfortable seconds before switching his eyes back to the road. "Good for you," he murmured. "Straight A student."

They rode on without speaking for several blocks before

Conor broke the silence. "So you knew I left with Kavita Kotwal, but how did you know where she lives?"

Sedgwick gave an incredulous snort. "Come on, everyone knows where Kavita Kotwal lives." Seeing Conor's obvious confusion, Sedgwick's eyes narrowed. With a quick twist of the wheel, he pulled the SUV over to the side of the road, cut the engine, and swiveled around to challenge him squarely. "What are you up to, McBride? Are you seriously trying to tell me you don't know who Kavita Kotwal is?"

"Rafferty," he corrected.

"Rafferty, McBride—nobody gives a shit. Answer the question."

"Well." Conor took a deep breath. "I guess I know her now—a little—but I didn't know her at all until she sat next to me on the plane."

"She sat next to you on the plane, purely by coincidence, and that was the first you'd ever heard of her? Is that what you're telling me?" Sedgwick leaned forward to get a better angle at his face. "Is it? Is that what you're telling me?"

"That's what I'm telling you, yes," Conor said, irritably. "For God's sake, it's my first time in India, and I've been here a total of four hours. I haven't had much chance to make friends. What am I missing? She's somebody famous, is she?"

"Yeah, yeah, somebody famous." Sedgwick ran a hand through his hair and shook his head with a sigh. "What are the odds? Fucking unbelievable." He reached into his shirt pocket to pull out a packet of cigarettes and offered one to Conor. "Your turn now. I think we could use a smoke for this one."

"Too bloody right."

Conor lit up, and after a deep, fortifying drag, launched into the confession of how he had managed to botch the first and easiest stage of his assignment. Considering how many hours it had consumed, the story was depressingly quick to recount.

When he finished, flicking a chagrined glance at his companion, Sedgwick responded with a merciless shout of laughter and reached for the ignition switch.

"I'm beginning to like you more than I thought I would, McBride—oh, sorry. Rafferty."

Conor wasn't sure he could say the same, but swallowed his annoyance and returned to the question he'd asked earlier. "Who is she, then? You say everybody knows her and where she lives. She's some kind of celebrity, or what?"

Sedgwick gave the SUV a burst of acceleration as they rejoined the flow of traffic and continued driving south, with the inky, dark water of Mahim Bay occasionally appearing on their right. "She's famous for a few reasons. The newspapers call her the Mother Theresa of Mumbai, and at this end of the city, she's known as the Devi of Dharavi. That's one of the biggest slums in Mumbai, maybe as many as a million people living in it. You probably drove by it on your way from the airport. It's right next to her neighborhood."

Conor shook his head. "I didn't notice. I was ... a bit distracted."

"No doubt." Sedgwick smirked. "Well, Kavita spends a lot of time there. She's pretty much dedicated her life to working with the slum dwellers of Dharavi, and let me tell you, she's a real fuckin' force to be reckoned with. When the UNICEF team showed up at Dharavi with the polio vaccine, they couldn't get anywhere until they started working with her."

Although surprised, he didn't find it very hard to picture the tiny woman he'd carried in his arms commanding a group of UN health workers. There was something decidedly intense and purposeful about her. "How did she get to be so powerful?" he asked.

"Because of the other reason she's famous—her husband. They're not exactly separated, but they don't see much of each other. Separate interests, to say the least. She sticks to Mahim, and he's got the top floor of a high-rise on Marine Drive. His name is Pawan Kotwal, or as he's more commonly known, Pawan-*bhai*. I don't suppose you've heard of him either? No, I guess not." Sedgwick began to laugh—an unpleasant snicker that he made no attempt to control.

Scowling in distaste, Conor refused to indulge it with inquiry. Curtis Sedgwick's physical appearance might have been a surprise, but in other respects, he was shaping up to fit the profile he'd been expecting.

"Sorry." Sedgwick put a fist to his mouth in an exaggerated effort to smother his laughter. "I'm just thinking about the report I'll be filing with London. Not only did their new boy wonder miss his first contact in country, he managed to offer his services to the wife of one of the biggest mafia dons in Mumbai."

"A mafia don!" Conor began spluttering a skeptical protest but then stopped.

He allowed the tense muscles of his back to go limp while Sedgwick continued chortling next to him. Argument was pointless. It was true. Of course it was. He had traveled halfway around the world and arrived at a place that was feeling more like a new dimension of reality rather than any mere country, a place where the mouthwatering aroma of curry fought for air space alongside the pervasive smell of human excrement, and where a tiny old woman with a braided ponytail could fool you into thinking she was no more than she appeared.

It was a place that made briefing books look like the ramblings of some dotty English aunt.

A land of surprises.

When they arrived at the Jyoti Apartments on Malabar Hill, it was after four o'clock in the morning. The neighborhood was quiet, and Mumbai itself was at last moving into a brief respite between shifts. It was the transitional period common to all metropolitan centers of great size. The bass-note vibrations of the night had faded, and the hive-like buzz of early morning had not yet begun. They were moving through that small slice of time when the city descends—like a massive, restless organism— into fitful sleep.

The Jyoti was a fifteen-story "serviced apartments" complex constructed in a long, curving crescent, fronted by an expanse of land scattered with patches of sun-withered grass. Sedgwick explained the site had been selected because it afforded greater privacy and independence than a traditional hotel setting.

"And, frankly, it was cheaper," he added, as the elevator reached the fifteenth floor. "It's a pretty decrepit old building that's scheduled for demolition, so it's also half empty. Not the luxury package, sorry to say. Should be a nice view, though. In another year or two, people will be paying a fortune for it."

The accommodation was indeed extremely modest. It was a large, cement-floored space with a closet-sized kitchenette, a slightly bigger bathroom, and an array of shopworn furniture. The whitewashed ceiling and walls bore evidence of water damage and mold, but the flat had one outstanding feature that more than compensated for its grim characteristics. The wall along its western side was made entirely of glass. It stretched from floor to ceiling with a folding door at one end leading out to a narrow balcony, and it looked out over the Arabian Sea. While Conor stood staring out at it, Sedgwick inspected the quarters and supplied a running commentary.

"They come in to clean and replace linens on some kind of schedule, but I don't have a clue what it is, and even if they'd tell you, it would end up being something different. Looks like they delivered all the food I ordered—fruit, eggs, bread, marmalade, digestive biscuits."

Sedgwick swiveled his head from the refrigerator, his face uncertain. "I didn't know what Irish people eat. I just assumed it was the same as the English. Do you like marmalade and shit like that?"

Still at the windows experimenting with the folding doors, Conor nodded vaguely. "I pretty much eat whatever is put in front of me."

"Dangerous habit in India." Sedgwick slammed the refrigerator shut.

Having satisfied himself that everything was as it should be, he gave Conor the key along with the name and location of a restaurant where they would meet at nine o'clock that night.

"I know you've probably got that 'early to bed, early to rise' farmer thing going on," he remarked sarcastically, "but most of the people you'll need to get friendly with only come out at night, so you'll have to get used to a different rhythm here."

Conor gave a thin smile. "I'm sure I'll adjust."

"Good." Sedgwick's eyes swept over him in a final, skeptical stare, and then he left.

Conor thought about unpacking, but then he thought again. Kicking off his boots, he stretched out on top of the bed. He had time enough to wonder whether the mattress might actually be filled with cement before crashing into deep, insensible sleep.

10

It was clearly a restaurant—there was no disputing that—the question was whether it was the right restaurant. There wasn't a name to be seen anywhere on its exterior, and the immediate surroundings provided no helpful data to determine his location. No visible street sign and no numbers.

He'd already been inside once, and after investigating the restaurant's dimly lit rooms, had confirmed that Sedgwick was not in any of them. Conor stood in the crowded street looking helplessly at the building, while the man at his elbow offered an animated defense of his navigational skills.

"This is the place. I am telling you absolutely, sir. For eleven years, I am guide in Mumbai. I know all these places. You are asking me to take you to Chole House restaurant. This is Chole House. It is not a nice restaurant, but it is the one you asked for."

"Well, I hope you're right, Bishan Singh," Conor said. "Because if it isn't, I might as well get the next plane home. I'll never live it down."

The thought that he might have arrived at the wrong place for the second time in twenty-four hours was unbearable, especially since in all other respects he had managed his first full day on the subcontinent with admirable self-sufficiency.

He had cooked his breakfast on the kitchenette's pump-action kerosene stove without blowing himself up; he had mastered a new method of washing, using the multiple spigots and buckets supplied in the bathroom; and when he had ventured out to explore the city, he had succeeded in choosing an intelligent, trustworthy guide from among the dozen clamoring to offer their services.

He hadn't intended to hire a guide, but it had quickly become apparent that it was easier to pick one rather than combat the unflagging advances of all the others. He'd selected Bishan Singh—a large, solidly built Sikh with a crimson turban—on the basis of his brilliantly white starched shirt and the fact that he had his own car.

He had a deferential but cheerful, self-assured demeanor, and once Conor had made it clear that he was not interested in procuring drugs, women, or young boys, the two of them had passed an agreeable afternoon together visiting the main tourist attractions.

Bishan was an amiable companion, and Conor believed him to be reliable, but the dilemma of the Chole House was putting a strain on their budding friendship. His uncertainty caused his guide's face to stiffen with a dignified, stony expression of injured pride.

"It isn't that I don't believe you," Conor said. "I'm just wondering if ... well, if maybe there is more than one. Is this the only Chole House restaurant in Mumbai?"

"In all Mumbai?" Bishan's thick eyebrows shot up toward his turban. "It could be or might not be, but you said also Ganesh Bazar. This is the only Chole House in Ganesh Bazar."

"Okay. Fair point."

He glanced around the square, searching for additional clues, and when his eyes returned to Bishan, he looked past his shoulder and saw Sedgwick ambling toward them, wearing an unmistakable smirk.

"Ah, sure you're the real cute hoor, aren't ye," Conor crooned, watching the agent's approach. "Just wanting to make me sweat."

Sedgwick dodged between two auto-rickshaws and came to

stand between the two of them. "Sorry I'm late," he announced, watching Conor's face.

"Yeah, no worries," Conor replied. "We just got here as well."

Sedgwick laughed and made a cursory study of the tall, muscular Sikh. "Make a new friend?"

"I did, actually. This is Bishan Singh. Bishan Singh, this is my ... this is Sedgwick."

Unsmiling, Bishan gave a small, curt bow and then turned a questioning gaze back to Conor. He gave a quick nod.

"Right. We're just finishing up here."

"I'll meet you inside." Sedgwick turned and headed for the entrance of the restaurant. "Come to the room in the back," he called over his shoulder. "And don't pay him too much. He'll lose respect for you."

Conor took a wad of rupee notes from his pocket, and after a quick calculation, handed Bishan what he thought was fair.

The guide looked at him with grave concern. "Sir, I do not like this place. And this man, how do you know him? He has a cunning face. He does not look like your friend. I am not happy leaving you with him. I will wait here until you return."

"No, it's fine." Conor grinned. "He's a bit of a prick, but he's not going to hurt me. I'll be fine. Thanks for your concern, though. If I ever do need protection, you'll be my first call."

Bishan nodded soberly. He fingered the bundle of rupee notes in his hands, and with a small shake of his head, handed half of them back. "It is because I do respect you," he said, gripping Conor's shoulder in a gesture of farewell.

Picking his way through the restaurant to the room at the back, Conor could appreciate Bishan's reluctance—the place had an unsavory atmosphere. The series of dingy, half-lit rooms that opened one on to another were small and cramped, and the close, humid air was made even more oppressive by the stale odor of spent cooking oil that drifted overhead in a greasy vapor.

He found Sedgwick in a booth in the very rear of the last

room and slid into the seat across from him. A man, perhaps in his early twenties, sat next to Sedgwick against the wall. He was painfully thin—a long, thin frame topped by a long, equally thin face—with a swath of black hair that hung limp across his forehead. His protruding brown eyes gave him the look of a trapped animal whose initial terror has subsided to taut watchfulness. Sedgwick did not introduce him.

He ordered beer for the three of them, along with plates of *chiwda*. When the dry snacks and large, sweating bottles had been placed on the table, he poured the beer into his glass and raised it to offer a facetious toast.

"Knowing how things work over at the Fort, I'm sure nobody bothered to congratulate you on completing the training, so let me be the first."

"Thanks. I did get a handshake, but that was about it." Conor shot a pointed glance at the unidentified companion, and Sedgwick dismissed the implied question with a shrug.

"Don't worry about him. He doesn't speak English. We'll get to him later. Anyway, maybe they didn't let you in on it, but they were certainly celebrating your graduation," Sedgwick said. "Not many opportunities for that since 9/11, but they're practically peeing themselves over you, dude."

"Are they?" Conor took a sip of beer and tilted his head with polite interest, refusing the bait. He would hear the story eventually. It was clearly one Sedgwick wanted to tell. The silence didn't last long.

"Quite a surprise for them too, since at first they didn't even want you there. Before you showed up, opinion was divided between those who thought you'd be a spindly, weak-chinned musician with oh-so-delicate hands and the ones who were sure you'd be a knuckle-dragging cretin with the barnyard still stuck on your boots. The common link was that both groups thought you were going to be a useless waste of time for them."

Conor had to chuckle at that; the characterization rang true. It was a clever depiction of the class-conscious divide that existed among the Fort Monckton officers, and it helped explain the startled expressions he'd so often encountered during his first few weeks of training.

"Being Irish didn't help either, I imagine. That would have been another point of shared annoyance."

"Yeah. I've never understood that," Sedgwick said. "Shit, everyone else likes the Irish."

"Long story." Conor poured more beer into his glass. "Are you suggesting I turned out better than they expected?"

"So they say." Sedgwick's face became rigid. "Nice for them, I guess. Gives them fresh hope. Recruits often don't perform as well as their officers anticipate. Then again, the recruits don't often anticipate what the officers will ask them to perform. Hard to know who's at fault, since the game requires everyone to be lying to everyone else, most of the time."

Conor regarded the hardened face with a cool gaze and remained silent. He wondered if the agent was blowing off steam or was trying to draw him into more complicated territory.

With a mirthless huff of laughter, Sedgwick sat up and reached across the table for the bottle. The movement exposed the inside of his right forearm and revealed an extensive network of scars. He saw Conor's involuntary glance, and with a tight smile, rolled his arm over and planted it on the table between them.

"Yeah, I figured they'd tell you about that." His tone was nonchalant, but his faded gray eyes flashed in anger. "Go on, take a closer look, why don't you? I don't mind. Maybe you'd like to send a report home. Tell them whether they look fresh or not. What do you think, Rafferty? Think I'm going to screw them over again?"

After a long pause, Conor gave an impassive shrug. "You tell me. To be honest, as long as you don't screw me over, I don't much give a damn."

An unusual change passed over Sedgwick's face, an almost elastic rearrangement of features that—for just an instant—made him look boyishly quizzical. Before Conor could even be sure he had seen it, it was gone. Sedgwick rubbed a hand over the lower half of his face and narrowed his eyes. "You are a cool customer, aren't you? They said that about you, too. A 'talent for repose,' they called it. That, and a gift for languages, a nearly photographic memory, superior balance and athletic ability, and you can apparently shoot the balls off a fly at a hundred yards. You're an intelligence director's wet dream. It's a tricky line of work, though, sonny boy. You'd better go slow in deciding how good you want to get at it."

"I'm not interested in getting good at it," Conor replied. "I'm interested in getting it over with and getting out."

Sedgwick nodded. "Sure. Point taken, but I'm sure you'll understand that after being bombarded with tales of your prowess, I'm eager to see some evidence of it."

He reached down and lifted up a small black bag that had been sitting on the seat next to him. The mysterious young man who had been hunched over his glass of beer moved even farther against the wall. Sedgwick tossed the bag onto the table, its contents jangling as it landed.

He didn't need to open the bag to know what it was and what Sedgwick wanted. Conor felt a rush of intense irritation. The wisecracks and cheap theatrics were wearing thin. He was beginning to wonder if managing a spiteful recovering heroin addict might be a greater strain on his patience than dealing with an active one.

"Here? In the middle of the restaurant?" he hissed. "Is there something about the word 'covert' you don't understand? We might as well slap signs on our backs. And what about yer man, there?" he added, jerking a thumb at the huddled figure. "What's he going to think?"

"Like I told you, he doesn't speak any English."

"Sure, he doesn't need to," Conor argued. "He'll bloody well know a gun when he sees one, won't he?"

"Just get on with it." Sedgwick nudged the bag forward. "Trust me, in a place like this, no one will take much notice."

"Oh, for Christ's sake." With a frown of annoyance, Conor pulled the bag forward and unzipped it. "A Walther," he said, poking a finger among the parts in the bag. "Why not a Colt 1911? Give me a real challenge."

"I only wish I could turn out the lights," Sedgwick said in a soft undertone. "Shall I time you?"

"I assume that's the point, isn't it? And if it's a show you want, let's have the full treatment. *Arrey* ... " Conor rapped a knuckle on the table in front of the young man and pointed to the scarf around his neck. "Let me have that for a minute."

He wrapped the scarf twice around his head, covering his eyes, and knotted it in the back. Then, he carefully tipped the parts of the stripped down Walther semiautomatic out of the bag and onto the table. He assembled it quickly by touch, and when he had hammered the loaded magazine into place and placed the gun on the table, he removed the scarf and threw it back across to the young man, who fumbled with it clumsily.

"Nine seconds. I'm impressed," Sedgwick purred with a mocking grin.

An instant later, the blond agent's face was pressed against the table, and a small trickle of blood was seeping over his lip where the point of impact had forced it against his teeth. With lightning speed, Conor had seized his hair and snapped his head down, and then, still holding him, he had snatched up the gun and come around to the other side of the booth. He slammed in against him, pressing him up against the nameless companion, who in turn was pinned against the wall.

"And how about this?" he asked with icy calm, thrusting the barrel of the gun against his controlling officer's ear. "Pretty good trick, too, right? How many points do I score for this one, boss?"

"Perfect ten," Sedgwick said, his voice muffled by the table.

"Then, if you're satisfied, maybe we can knock off the caustic commentary and horseshit games from now on, right? I haven't known you more than a day, and you're already on my last nerve."

Sedgwick made a strangled, inaudible comment, and his shoulders began shaking with silent laughter. Conor gave him another irritated shove, and the young man against the wall yelped in alarm.

"Who the hell is this guy, anyway?" He released his hold on the back of Sedgwick's neck and dropped the gun back onto the table. The agent sat up slowly, putting his fingers to his lip.

"Don't shoot him. I brought him here to meet you, after all. His name is Raj. He works for your brother."

Conor swiveled around the table, taking his seat again, and looked at the long, thin face with greater interest. Raj watched him nervously and shifted away from the wall. Conor opened his mouth, mentally formulating the words to the question in Hindi, but then remembered himself and stopped, even before he saw Sedgwick's hand flash across the table in a gesture of warning. He was supposed to be a tour operator investigating new trekking tours. He wasn't supposed to know anyone named Thomas McBride.

"Does he know where my brother is?" He addressed the question in English instead to Sedgwick, who shook his head.

"Nobody does. I think your brother got spooked. Frank told you about the agent MI6 sent over last year to flush him out?"

Conor nodded.

"The guy was supposed to find him—with my help—and

offer him an immunity deal in exchange for cooperation. London is after the ringleader—the 'wizard.' Well, their agent managed to find me at the airport, but in every other respect, he was a train wreck. Half the time he was drunk, and the rest of the time he was careening around town interviewing the club owners and bartenders and making no secret about who he was looking for. He blew his own cover and nearly blew mine as well. And they called me a security risk."

Grimacing in disgust, Sedgwick drained his glass and signaled for another round. "Thomas and I used to cross paths occasionally, but he went to ground once that fathead showed up, and I haven't seen him in Mumbai since the beginning of July. I'm not sure Raj here has ever even met him."

"If he's never met him, how can he be—"

"I'll tell you how he can, if you'll shut up and let me finish," Sedgwick said affably. He took a deep breath and arched his back in a long stretch. When he sat forward again, his face had smoothed into a more sober expression. "The money your brother has been laundering belongs to Ahmed Khalil. He's a businessman and a gangster—big in the Bollywood racket and the mobile communications business, but he's got a sideline trade in drugs and prostitution that brings in more cash than anything else he's got going on. The way it used to work is that Thomas would go around to all the collection points in Mumbai and pick up the cash. Nobody knows what he does with it, but eventually it shows up as a deposit in a series of Swiss accounts that he and Khalil control. Then, when Khalil's crazy friends up north need some firepower, Thomas goes to the meetings with the arms dealer and sets up the payment transfers. That's how it used to work."

The waiter appeared with three fresh bottles and placed them on the table, removing the empties. For the sake of appearances, Conor filled his glass again but didn't drink any more. It was hard enough to absorb yet another confirmation that Thomas had become enmeshed in a world as alien as the far side of Mars. He didn't need the fog of alcohol amplifying his distress.

"How does it work now?" He maintained an appearance of unemotional interest, but Sedgwick appeared to sense his discomfort and regarded him with an almost sympathetic smile.

"A few months ago, he introduced a few new layers of security between him and the daily grind, and one of those layers, however skinny, is Raj. He's making the cash pickups now and delivers them to a drop point. Somehow it gets moved on to Thomas, and he does whatever it is he's been doing with it."

"But Raj doesn't know what happens after he makes the drop?" Conor asked. He looked over at the younger man, who perked up slightly at the sound of his name. He now looked simply sleepy rather than nervous.

"Nope."

"Brilliant." He sighed. "So what are we doing here? You brought him to meet me. Who does he think I am?"

"His new body man," Sedgwick said, with matter-of-fact promptness. "Mine too, as a matter of fact. You get to take the gun home with you tonight. And that little acrobatic move you pulled on me was helpful. Scared the piss out of him. You've got him thinking you're a real badass."

Conor stared at him. "I'm not following you."

"Look, McBride—"

"Will you ever please stop using—"

"Oh, fine, whatever." Sedgwick tossed his head. "Listen, I'm sorry if you spent a lot of time memorizing it, but this tour guide cover they assigned you is crap, and as soon as Frank Murdoch heard they were putting you with me, he must have known it was dead. He just didn't have the guts to tell you how it was going to be."

"He gave me a pretty good idea. He offered to let me back out of the whole thing."

"But, you didn't. So, here you are in Mumbai, and this half-assed alias that has you going off on environmental treks is not going to wash. If you want to get anywhere with this mission, if you want to find your brother, then you've got to work from inside the Khalil organization, and I'm your ticket to get there because I'm already inside it. I'm assigning your cover. You'll have to take what I give you and like it."

"So you say," Conor muttered. He didn't like any of it. As much as he had tried to strip away any sense of naiveté regarding the character of the business he had committed himself to, he still found himself seriously shaken by the plan being suggested.

The most obvious argument against getting mixed up in Sedgwick's insider activities was that he would put himself beyond protection or support from his employers if something went wrong. He had been briefed on conditions that would set their "plausible deniability" process in motion, and although playing bodyguard for the bagman of a drug and prostitution ring wasn't specifically mentioned, he was pretty sure it was somewhere on the list.

Of more immediate concern was not the question of what might happen if it went badly but how to cope if he were good at it. Infiltrating an Indian mafia organization required a far deeper level of reinvention than passing himself off as an earnest environmental tour guide, but he knew he had the required skills to pull it off, and it made him uncomfortable.

Already, he felt as though the past ten weeks had turned him into someone that he didn't seem to know anymore. Who would he be when this performance was done? Assuming a criminal alias and living inside it had consequences, and he thought the acerbic, scarred man across the table could tell him more about that than he cared to know.

He slouched against the back of the booth, considering his options. He didn't have many, but he eyed Sedgwick with cautious calculation and exercised one of them.

"You know, the ink on those briefing books was barely dry when I read them two days ago. If they're obsolete already, I'd appreciate having that confirmed by Frank."

"Forget about Frank." Sedgwick swatted the suggestion away without even changing expression. "Frank is off the grid. He appears out of the mist when he's called and sinks back into it when they're done with him. You're not likely to ever see him again." He gave a wolfish smile. "You're in my wheelhouse now, McBride. They threw you to me, and they knew exactly what they were doing. I write the music; you play the tune. The sooner you get used to it, the easier it will be. Welcome to my world."

The cheerful menace and clichéd constructions were too corny to sound threatening, and Conor didn't feel provoked. The more time he spent in his company, the easier it was to see the loneliness and self-doubt lurking beneath the agent's veneer of irascibility. He swallowed the anxiety that had convulsed the muscles in his throat and gave Sedgwick a weary smile of acceptance. "Okay, then. Go on and tell me who I'm supposed to be in your world."

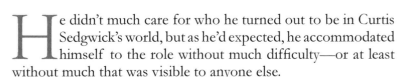

11

He didn't much care for who he turned out to be in Curtis Sedgwick's world, but as he'd expected, he accommodated himself to the role without much difficulty—or at least without much that was visible to anyone else.

His responsibilities, as they were outlined that first night, were not complicated. He would function as an armed guard, and on the evenings when collections were scheduled, he would accompany Raj on his rounds to ensure the smooth transport of funds to a designated drop point. On certain other evenings, he would be safeguarding the supply side of Khalil's drug operation, tagging along with Sedgwick to take delivery of fresh product arriving from the Kabul and Peshawar regions and conveying it to the numerous retail distribution points scattered around Mumbai.

The first step in cementing his latest identity was to settle on what others would call him. A single, easily pronounceable word was all that was required, Sedgwick had insisted, and he found it unnecessarily complicated to create something new. With a perverse instinct to irritate, he selected the half of the official alias that Conor despised most and introduced him to the skittish, skeletal Raj simply as Con.

During the week that followed, he understood that he would soon be introduced to an assortment of leading characters in Ahmed Khalil's underworld army but not before Sedgwick had taken ample opportunity to school him in the details of his new persona.

"Let's get this clear. Your job is not to blend in," he instructed during one of the frequent educational sessions he had convened following the Chole House initiation.

They were on Chowpatty Beach, steering around the lovers and families who had come out to stroll in the evening air and watch the sunset. Conor's attention was divided between the lesson and the large plate of bhel puri he was devouring as they walked. He'd become addicted to the famous Mumbai salad of puffed rice dressed with combinations of potato, fruit, dry noodles, and piquant spices. It was offered in countless varieties at the street stalls lining the beach, and he was making a point of trying them all.

"Not to blend in," he repeated dutifully, wiping a smear of tamarind chutney from his chin. Sedgwick shot him an impatient glance before continuing.

"Your job is to provide contrast, primarily just by being white. That's why Khalil hired me—he wants a few *goras* on the payroll to show around. He thinks it makes him look more international. You also need to have an attitude that contrasts with his regulars. They're a band of *goondas*—thieves, pimps, black marketeers, and smugglers. They're colorful and uninhibited—big personalities. You, on the other hand, will be colorless and self-contained. This is your chance to show off that splendid 'talent for repose' your teachers were so proud of. You need to convey the threat of violence while looking tranquil at the same time. Think of yourself as a monk—a dark, brooding, ass-kicking monk with a sketchy paramilitary past that you don't discuss. That's what I've led them to expect."

"Uh-huh, monkish. Okay."

"In other words," Sedgwick stopped and turned to face Conor, lip curled. "A little less like the sloppy, bumbling tourist you're successfully imitating right now. Christ, how many of those have you eaten today?"

"That was the third." Conor grinned. "Anyway, we haven't started yet—the monkish bit, I mean. Don't worry. I'll be ready."

"That was just a point of reference. Don't overdo the monkish thing."

"Relax." Conor sighed. He threw the empty plate on top of an overflowing trashcan. "I guess it would be more fun for you if I were a complete, bleedin' eejit, but I actually do get the point. You want tall, dark, and silent with a whiff of sophisticated malevolence—enough to command respect without looking psychotic. I've seen that guy in a dozen different films. I can play the part, and I promise not to embarrass either of us while I'm doing it. Feel better?"

The steely gray eyes squinting at him plainly communicated a lack of conviction, but a few nights later, Conor was secretly pleased to watch those same eyes gape in surprised appreciation when he arrived at their specified rendezvous point—the lobby of the Intercontinental Hotel—in character and ready for his debut.

The adjustments he'd made to his appearance were subtle but added up to more than the sum of their parts. With an application of styling gel, he'd combed his hair straight back from his forehead, and it molded to his head like a shining, black skullcap, giving his face a severe, chiseled appearance. The look also gave greater exposure to the thick lines of his eyebrows and accentuated his dark, carefully expressionless eyes. To offer an extra dimension of shadow to his face, he had allowed his beard to grow to a precisely groomed stubble.

Aiding the concealment of the handgun snapped into a shoulder holster, he wore a black cotton blazer over a charcoal gray T-shirt that fit snugly against the muscles of his chest and waist. He'd completed the ensemble with a pair of jeans, black boots, and the silver pendant around his neck.

He'd debated leaving off the unusually shaped cross but was

reluctant to remove it. He finally justified it by considering that its resemblance to the ancient Sanskrit swastika symbol might prove useful, or at least lucky, and transferred it to a shorter string of black leather, furthering the similarity to amulet necklaces commonly worn throughout the country.

Sedgwick lifted the lapel of the blazer to confirm the presence of the shoulder holster, and then, crossing his arms, studied Conor with unfeigned interest. For once, he appeared genuinely impressed.

"It's superb," he remarked. "Better than I would have ever imagined. Amazing, really. You haven't done that much, but you're almost unrecognizable, and you look pretty comfortable with it. How do you feel?"

Unrecognizable, Conor thought. He didn't care to dwell on the process he had engaged in to become mentally and physically acclimated to the role, or how easily it had slipped over him once he was ready for it.

"I feel fine," he said, laconically. Even his voice sounded different to him, its light, lyrical cadence flattened to a subdued monotone. "Are we ready to go?"

Sedgwick looked startled. "I figured you'd want to eat first. Wouldn't dream of having you miss a meal."

Conor shook his head. "Not hungry."

"Not hungry?" Sedgwick laughed. "Well, that clinches it. Conor McBride has left the building. It's too early, though. Let's go to the bar. I'm not as nervous as I was before seeing you, but I could still use a drink."

Conor allowed the barest twitch of a smile to pull at one corner of his mouth. "Me too."

"That was your best effort yet," Sedgwick said when the last of the meetings had concluded and their collection of lively guests had departed. "You handled Abdul Hassan perfectly. Very clever to show him that touch of deference. He's been with the organization longer than anyone, and he's frustrated that he hasn't moved up the ranks. "Problem is," he added, stifling a yawn, "He's dumber than a box of rocks. There's not much he can be trusted to do right."

"I did get that impression."

Conor was stretched out along the length of the booth with his back against the wall. They were both exhausted. He hadn't realized how much tension they'd been shouldering between them until it had dissolved with the departure of Abdul Hassan, who had been the last inebriate to push himself up from the table and totter unsteadily into the night.

At each of the meetings, Conor had spoken very little. He ate nothing, declined to smoke, drank only coconut water, and in his demeanor balanced an attitude of remote equanimity against an undercurrent of intensity. Within the first ten minutes of each gathering, Khalil's *goondas* had absorbed the primary message: "Con" the bodyguard was the real thing, and he was not going to be one of their new drinking buddies.

The line between wary respect and mistrust was a thin one, requiring continuous adjustments in tone and body language to ensure the desired results. It was tedious and nerve-wracking, like a series of interviews for a job he had to pretend to want. But when it was over, he had earned the durable respect of his sardonic controlling officer.

He was relieved to have it over with and relieved that he would not have to put on the performance for Khalil himself, who had decamped to Dubai for the foreseeable future to pursue certain business opportunities. He was also relieved to be able to relax into some semblance of himself again, if only temporarily. He folded his hands against his stomach and closed his eyes, but almost immediately, they snapped open again.

"Jesus, I'm starving. My stomach thinks me throat's been cut, I'm that hungry."

"Glad to hear it." Sedgwick exhaled a weary laugh. "You ate everything in sight for the first week, and then hardly so much as a peanut the last four days. I was beginning to think anorexia was one of your new character traits. Do you want to order something?"

"Not here." Conor's face convulsed with disgust. "I'd like to get the hell out of this place and not see it again for a donkey's year or two. I just need to gather the strength to get up out of this booth."

"This was the hardest part, you know," Sedgwick said. "Getting in smoothly and making everyone comfortable with it. The rest will be easy compared with this."

"Ah, Curtis." Conor sighed, dropping his boots to the floor. "No offense, but that's the biggest load of shite you've dished out yet."

The most disquieting aspect of his budding career as a bodyguard was how quickly it transitioned from perilous endeavor to commonplace routine. The weeks following his initiation into the Khalil gang were not enjoyable, but he had to acknowledge they were not as dangerous as he'd anticipated.

The delivery of drugs operated on a precise timetable, so, much like any other man with a job, he had a schedule to keep and duties to perform, and they had a greater degree of rhythmic predictability than he ever expected.

Several nights a week, he accompanied Sedgwick to grotty, waterfront warehouses known locally as godowns, and these outings were not without suspense. The deliverymen came in two varieties: jumpy teenaged boys and sweating middle-aged men. They were usually tense and ill humored, and, according to his controlling officer, congenitally larcenous. As a deterrent to temptation and to keep them aware of their tenuous position, Sedgwick frequently created some point of conflict around the size of the delivery, the date for the next shipment, or any number of other things to create an excuse for intimidation.

Conor's role in this bit of stagecraft was devoid of nuance. He was to terrify the men by any means necessary while Sedgwick reminded them of their low rank in the hierarchy. In some instances, the desired pitch of fear was achieved without much effort. Standing in the shadows, he sometimes got results simply by stepping forward with a dark, unsettling stare. More often than not, though, Sedgwick wanted more tangible threats of violence, which typically meant the petrified courier found himself pinned either to the floor or the wall with a gun pressed to his temple.

There was also a timetable and rotation for collections from the nightclubs and dance bars, and by contrast these happened in a much more workman-like manner. He shadowed Raj from one end of the city to the other, but the only security action required so far had been to shield the bagman from a rampaging drunk who had mistaken him for someone else.

The delivery of the money collected was equally monotonous. The house Thomas supposedly used as a central drop point was in a residential section of Goregaon East. The ceremony was always the same. They were buzzed in to a small hallway where they sat on low chairs and waited. After about ten minutes, an elderly man in a long white kurta would appear with a tray of biscuits, chai, and an envelope containing their payment. Without a word, he placed the tray on a side table, took the duffel bag Raj placed on the floor next to it, and disappeared back through the door at the end of the hall.

Over a period of weeks, Conor made a surveillance of the property on his own, furtively peeking into windows and analyzing it from every angle. The efforts yielded no results. He never saw anyone enter or leave the building, and except for the nights they were scheduled to be there, he never saw a light inside.

After several weeks, he was discouraged and restless and yearned to separate himself from the entire loathsome enterprise. The sheer banality of the Khalil operation heightened his aversion to it. The corruption and exploitation, carried on with the dispassionate efficiency of a conventional corporate endeavor, was an obscenity he couldn't rationalize. It was hard to stomach the shame he felt for the part he played in keeping it running.

Apart from personal angst, another factor added to his edginess: a nagging sense that they were on the wrong track. Maybe Thomas wasn't in Mumbai at all. Maybe they should look somewhere else. Conor didn't bother to hide his misgivings from Sedgwick, but his boss provided little reassurance beyond an exhortation to stay the course.

"We'll get wind of him sooner or later," he remarked at one point. "He'll make a mistake, or we'll get lucky. That's how it works, and it takes longer than you want it to. You thought you were going to blow into town and wrap it all up in a couple of weeks? Think again. You're only getting started, and if you're finding the routine a little humdrum, enjoy it while you can. The sort of excitement that pops up in this business is not going to be the kind you'll find entertaining."

As usual, he was correct.

12

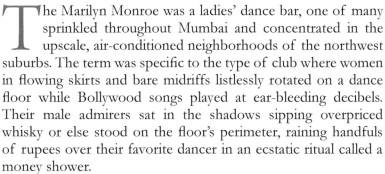

The Marilyn Monroe was a ladies' dance bar, one of many sprinkled throughout Mumbai and concentrated in the upscale, air-conditioned neighborhoods of the northwest suburbs. The term was specific to the type of club where women in flowing skirts and bare midriffs listlessly rotated on a dance floor while Bollywood songs played at ear-bleeding decibels. Their male admirers sat in the shadows sipping overpriced whisky or else stood on the floor's perimeter, raining handfuls of rupees over their favorite dancer in an ecstatic ritual called a money shower.

To Conor, the sight of jiggling, middle-aged men sprinkling banknotes over women young enough to be their daughters was pathetic, but it did offer a marginally healthy contrast to what reigned in the garbage-heaped lanes of Kamathipura.

The largest red-light district in Asia was not known for nightclubs and dancers but for brothels. It was particularly known for the infamous Falklands Road area called "the Cages," where stacks of concrete cubicles hacked out of crumbled buildings were filled with sex workers of all ages.

The Monroe sat in the middle of the district, at the end of a lane just north of Falklands Road. It was accessed from the street through a nondescript door that led up a flight of stairs to a soundproofed corridor. The door at the end opened into a room containing a bar and dance floor surrounded by mirrored walls lined with low, white leather couches.

Conor was sitting on one of the couches, impassively watching the dancers while Raj took care of business with the floor managers behind the bar. On the table next to his elbow sat a piping hot tiffin canister and a bottle of lime soda, along with a sticky packet of *jalebi*—a deep-fried sweet dripping with sugar syrup. The *jalebi* was essentially a bribe. No other incentive proved as effective in persuading Radha to eat her dinner. Since he frequently surrendered a hefty bundle of rupees to the bar's owner, Rohit Mehta, simply for the privilege of giving the young dancer a hot meal, he always made sure the sweet was visible to her from the dance floor.

At thirteen, Radha was not the youngest girl he'd ever witnessed plying her trade during the small hours of the night. Her plight was not the most desperate, but for some reason he had been drawn to her, and within a short time, they had befriended each other.

From halting conversations with Raj, Conor had pieced together her story. She was not an orphan but something worse—a child sold into Rohit Mehta's particular brand of slavery by her own parents. Ever true to his reputation as a man to seize the main chance, Mehta snapped up the child at a bargain rate and put her into the lineup as his "unplucked flower."

She was good for business, and because of her youth—and a drug habit that Mehta supported in a grotesque parody of fatherly indulgence—she was an easily controlled commodity. Conor was determined to help her. Her fragile vulnerability and the beguiling innocence she maintained despite her circumstances affected him in a way he found difficult to explain. So far, the only practical assistance he'd managed to offer was a healthy meal and his friendship.

She was at the other end of the dance floor, a tiny frame enveloped in veils with a long, braided ponytail pulled forward over one shoulder. He checked his watch, confirming that he'd timed his arrival to coincide with her break, and a moment later, the sound system shifted to one of its infrequent acoustical numbers. Radha floated from the stage over to Conor's table.

"It is long time since I am seeing you, Con-ji." She turned her kohl-rimmed eyes on him with reproachful sadness and continued twirling in slow, languid circles. She insisted on speaking to him in English, which despite her lack of formal education was quite good.

"I was here just last week," he said. "You don't remember?"

"I remember that it seems long ago," she sighed, with a melodramatic toss of her head. Conor raised an amused eyebrow.

"So, we're being a bit *filmi* tonight, are we? Rehearsing for your Bollywood debut? Stop spinning around like that. You're making me dizzy."

Radha came to a stop and giggled. She stood undulating in place in front of him, her hands placed on her small, thin hips in a childish imitation of seduction.

"Yeah, and stop doing that as well," he said sourly. "Makes me want to throw a blanket around you. Come here now. Have your dinner."

She slid onto the couch and tried distracting him with a flirtatious pout, which Conor greeted with bland indifference as he pointedly moved the package of *jalebi* away from her groping hand. He began opening the tiffin canisters but then jerked in surprise as an unfamiliar buzz tingled against his chest. The government-issued mobile phone in his shirt pocket was ringing for the first time.

He punched at the keypad and listened, uncertain what sort of greeting was expected. After several seconds of silence, Sedgwick's nasal twang crackled in his ear.

"McBride? Are you there?"

"Yeah, I'm here."

"Well, why didn't you—oh, fuck, never mind. Where are you?"

"Kamathipura. The Monroe. Where are you?" Conor asked.

"Good. That's not far. Tell Raj he's on his own and get your ass over to the Shalimar Hotel. We'll meet you in the lobby in ten minutes."

"Who's 'we'?"

He swore as Sedgwick hung up without answering that question either, and turned back to Radha. "Sorry, I've gotta go. *Biriyani* before *jalebi*, right? Promise?" He ruffled her hair.

He went to the bar to give the news to Raj, who was visibly relieved. Despite Conor's numerous attempts at reassurance, he'd continued to display an attitude of barely contained terror in his presence.

"Make sure Radha eats," Conor instructed without conviction as he headed for the door. It was unlikely the timid young man would be any match for her spirited obstinacy.

Arriving in the lobby of the Shalimar, he found his boss accompanied by Abdul Hassan and two of his *taporis*, who were common street thugs from the lower ranks of the Khalil operation. Conor made no comment until the two of them were alone in the SUV, following Hassan's car on the road north out of the city.

"What's going on?"

"Disciplinary action." Sedgwick's voice held its customary hints of irony, but Conor noted lines of strain furrowing the skin around his eyes.

"Hassan got a tip. One of his suppliers has been stealing from the organization and holding back hashish to sell on his own. Needless to say, it's got them perturbed."

"What's it to do with us?" Conor asked.

"Hey, all in for the team, right?" Sedgwick glanced at him and looked quickly away. "He asked us to come along. I couldn't think of a reason to say we wouldn't."

"What are they going to do?"

"I don't know. It's Hassan's deal. I guess we'll see what he has in mind when we get there."

Conor took a steadying breath. "Not the answer I wanted to hear."

"Sorry, dude. It's all I got for you."

The smallest trace of a breeze trickled in through a six-inch opening in the battered metal door of the godown. Not enough to be refreshing. He nudged the door further ajar, trying to coax in a stronger gust to ease the stifling atmosphere inside. He also hoped the expanded view might offer distraction from the activity going on behind him.

The warehouse was an old, abandoned wreck. It sat close to the water a few miles south of a seventeenth-century fort in Sewri, one of the northern, east coast suburbs of Mumbai.

A movement along the shore caught at the corner of his eye, and he moved into the doorway, peering through the darkness for a closer look. At first, he thought it was an animal snuffling through the refuse being nudged up the beach by lapping waves, but then he realized it was two small boys, no doubt engaged in a bit of nocturnal garbage picking.

He wished he could still feel astonished that two tiny children would be out alone in this desolate spot at such an hour, but the capacity for that sort of bewilderment was long gone. He thought of Radha and other variations of the tableau: children in places they ought not to be, doing things they should never have to. He hoped the boys weren't looking for food amidst the rubbish but thought it likely that they were; and he even more fervently hoped they would stay on their current course, which was taking them farther away from the warehouse. He didn't need that particular headache added to his skyrocketing stress level.

As they'd discovered soon enough on arriving at the deserted godown, what Hassan had in mind for his disciplinary action was in keeping with his limited intelligence and imagination. When the hapless thief appeared, there was an initial false heartiness that put him at his ease, followed by a progression of subtly cutting remarks until all pretense was gone, and the man's uncertain smile melted into stark fear. Only then, when his apprehensive terror was at its peak, only then did the torture begin.

Conor leaned against the doorway and lit another cigarette. He had thankfully drawn the long straw when Hassan began barking orders. As the appointed lookout, he was as far away from the center of activity as he could get, but it didn't feel far enough.

The beating had been going on for more than twenty minutes now. He had not once turned to look at it, but he could not as easily ignore its sounds: the sickening, wet crunch of the blows as they landed; the screams that subsided into sobs and whimpering groans; and the heavy, labored breathing of Hassan's men as they finally began to tire from their efforts.

It stopped eventually, and there was a brief, exhausted silence. After some inaudible discussion, he heard footsteps approaching and turned to meet the haggard eyes of Sedgwick. He straightened and tossed the cigarette aside with a curt nod.

"All clear at this end. Can we get the fuck out of here, please?"

"Not yet," Sedgwick said hoarsely. "Abdul Hassan has ... an order to give you."

"What's that supposed to mean? You're the man who gives the orders, I thought."

Sedgwick attempted a smile but failed to bring it off with his usual conviction. "The organizational dynamics are complicated. I've already talked him down as much as I can."

"Talked him down from what, for God's sake? What's he want me to do?"

The question was met with several seconds of tense silence

before Sedgwick responded. "You're the only one carrying a gun."

Conor stared, stunned into speechlessness.

"Are you crazy?" he finally hissed, lips barely moving. "Are you out of your fucking mind? Do you think I'm going to kill a man just because that fat lunatic—"

"Calm down. You don't have to kill him, just kneecap him."

"Just kneecap him?" Conor struggled to control his voice. "No. I bloody well won't. He can have the gun and do it himself. Or maybe I'll shoot him instead. It's bad enough we've just been standing around for the past half-hour while—"

"Get a grip, goddamn it," Sedgwick said. "We're both under a microscope here, and this is already taking too long. It's a test of loyalty and courage. If you refuse, we're both blown, and once we've been blown, the next thing we'll be is dead. Your call, but he's waiting."

Conor had only a few seconds to make a decision. Once he'd reached it, a cold, unnatural calm settled over him. He felt the muscles of his face arranging into an inexpressive mask. Before forcing his eyes to assume their flat gaze, he drilled Sedgwick with a look of contempt. "Tell me, boss. What kind of courage does it take to shoot a man with his arms tied behind his back and his face so filled with blood that he won't even see me?"

He stepped around Sedgwick and strode across the building, his boots striking the cement floor with clipped, echoing cracks. With one smooth motion, he opened his jacket and ripped the Walther from the holster, chambering the first round as he walked. Ahead of him, he watched the fat, sweating face of Abdul Hassan freeze in fear and then relax again as he moved past him. He stopped in front of the ruined figure that lay slumped on a stack of pallets; pointed the gun at one thin, brown knee; and pulled the trigger.

A burst of blood and tissue exploded from the shot and

spattered onto his jeans. With the man's screams filling his ears, he slammed the gun back into its holster and turned away. Conor strode back toward Sedgwick, who shrugged an apology as he passed on the way to the door.

"There's more than one kind of courage, Conor," he said softly.

"Fuck you," he replied and kept walking.

13

She looked like a little bandit, a diminutive bank robber, with an enormous white triangle of cloth covering her face. The point of it swung back and forth with each movement of her head, reaching down almost to her stomach. Her wide brown eyes, peeking out above the cloth, had been watching her mother solemnly, but suddenly she noticed she was being observed.

She tilted her head back, and a mass of waving brown hair fell away from her face as she peered up and saw him. She stared with the fearlessness of a six-year-old, and without hesitation, she raised both arms above her head and waved them energetically. Conor smiled and put his hands to his chest, pretending to swoon against the marble railing that surrounded the circular opening to the floor below. Instantly, her eyes crinkled with delight. She laughed aloud and called out to him.

"*Bhaiyya!*"

What was left of his heart was lost again.

There had been many such scenes since his arrival in India, instances of unreserved affection and generosity that took his breath away. His wrists had grown crowded with woven bracelets and wooden beads pressed on him by men and women, rich and poor, young and old. From every kind and color of person, he had received tokens of benevolence, but the little girl's cry of greeting was particularly sweet to his ears. It sounded good to hear someone call him "brother".

He'd been lingering in the Jain mandir since early morning, first wandering around on the temple's lower floor, keeping a respectful distance as the devotees chanted mantras. He watched them anoint their deities with sandalwood, their mouths ritually shrouded with the cloth muhapatti to protect the sacred texts from the moisture of their breath.

Later, he retreated to the greater solitude of the second story, alternating his gaze between the colorful temple dome above, depicting the zodiac and other celestial scenes, and the main floor of the sanctuary below. In a dreamlike stillness, he looked down at the meditative movements of the worshippers and offered his own silent prayers of penance, hoping they might resonate with whatever enlightened presence was on hand to receive them.

It was not his first visit to the temple. Bishan Singh had introduced it to him on one of their many excursions around the city. It was within walking distance of the Jyoti Apartments, and he was repeatedly drawn to it as a haven of peace and tranquility, far removed from the frenetic din of the city and the jangling clamor of his thoughts.

He had hesitated before entering it this morning. Following the drive back from Sewri—an excruciating ride during which he had rebuffed Sedgwick with a stony, unapproachable silence—he'd spent the remainder of the night in a sleepless stupor, roaming through the streets and winding lanes of the Malabar Hill neighborhood before coming to a stop in front of the temple as dawn was breaking.

After the night he had just spent, the brutality he had witnessed and the violence he had committed, Conor wondered if even his presence on the temple's threshold might be a polluting influence, an outrageous insult to the Jain religion's prescriptive path of peace and nonviolence. He had almost convinced himself that it was when a single phrase of prayer came to mind.

The sacrifices of God are a broken spirit. A broken and a contrite heart, Oh God, thou wilt not despise.

It was a line from one of the psalms his mother often recited, a prayer of penance and of praise for an all-powerful, endless mercy. His knees buckled with the sensation of homesick loneliness that flooded over him. He wondered how she was and how much further the cancer might have progressed, and he ached for the comforting rhythms of her quiet voice.

He wouldn't have called her now, even if Frank had not forbidden it. It was too painful to consider how his evasions and awkward silences would affect her, but as he stood on the steps of the temple, he could almost hear what she would tell him. Seek refuge. Accept mercy. Grant the forgiveness you ask for yourself.

He couldn't talk to her directly, but he could still feel a transcendent circuitry connecting them in a way that was as mysterious as it was powerful. Without understanding it, he knew it would always be there. In obedience and relief, he climbed the temple steps and entered into its sanctuary.

He felt a greater sense of composure now than when he'd first arrived and watched as the little girl and her mother completed their puja ritual. He gave an answering wave to her salute of farewell as they headed for the street and moved out of sight.

"How was I somehow knowing that I would find you here, my friend?"

Conor turned at the sound of the rich, baritone voice and smiled. "Becoming a creature of habit, I guess. How are you, Bishan Singh?"

"I am well. You are not well." The burly Sikh positioned his tongue against his teeth to produce a sound somewhere between a chirp and a smack. "This whatever-it-is nighttime work is not good for you, *yaar*. You have eyes that are sinking into your head, and you are becoming thin. What have you taken for food today?"

"Now that you mention it, I haven't taken a bloody thing." Conor straightened up, realized he was hungry, and looked hopefully at his friend. "Did you have something in mind?"

"Yes, come, come. We will eat in the garden. I have ordered already some Punjabi foods from the *dhaba*, just there."

Bishan's hand signaled an indefinable location for a restaurant that might have been anywhere within the city limits of Mumbai, but it was good enough for Conor. The mere mention of "Punjabi foods" had already started him salivating.

"Sounds good to me. Lead on, Bishan."

The Ferozeshah Mehta Gardens of Mumbai, more commonly known as the Hanging Gardens, was a gentle transition from the serene atmosphere of the Jain temple. A terraced garden that sloped up Malabar Hill and provided picturesque vistas of the city and the Arabian Sea, it was a popular but still relatively peaceful gathering spot for Mumbaikers.

After eating, they rested on the grass under the hot sun. Before long, the strain of the previous hours produced their inevitable effects, and Conor found it impossible to keep his eyes open.

Without remembering how he got there, he woke some time later, flat on his stomach with his face pillowed against his arms. He rolled onto his back and saw Bishan, his arm resting on one knee, holding a large square of cardboard over Conor's face to shield it from the sun.

"How long have you been holding that?" Conor asked.

"Hmm." Bishan consulted his watch. "Some forty-five minutes now."

Conor groaned and sat up. "Shit. Sorry, *yaar*. Why didn't you wake me? You're making me look like some pampered dick of a tourist."

"A pampered dick of a tourist, I would have roused." Bishan said with unassailable logic. "A friend who is tired and ill, I would not."

"I'm not ill. Tired, I'll grant you, but not ill."

"There are many different kinds of illness, Con-ji," his friend said, quietly.

"Just like there's more than one kind of courage?" Conor muttered.

"*Kyaa*? What is this?"

"Nothing. It doesn't matter." Conor rubbed his hands over his face. "Sorry. I understand what you're saying."

"I will work now for a few hours." Bishan stood up and stretched, his powerful, thick chest straining against the buttons of his shirt. "Come home with me this evening. Meera will brew a tea for you. She has many Ayurvedic skills. My daughter Aashirya will play soothing music. We will make you well."

Conor could not answer immediately. The simple expression of friendship, coming at a moment when he both needed and felt unworthy of it, moved him to strangled speechlessness.

There was something else he needed to do that evening, though—something he needed more than friendship.

"Thank you. I'd like that," he said, when he could trust his voice. "But there's also another place I need to go tonight."

Bishan gave another loud smacking chirp, its note of exasperation transparently clear.

"No, it isn't the usual thing," Conor reassured him. "There's something else ... "

He trailed off, helplessly. He wasn't sure himself why after all this time he needed to see Kavita Kotwal. He only knew it was important.

After dinner with Bishan's family, they left for Mahim. Since Kavita was married to Pawan-bhai—whose gang was in direct competition with Khalil's—Sedgwick had forbidden Conor to have any further contact with her. Although she was in no way involved in her husband's activities, any relations with his family would be tantamount to consorting with the enemy.

It was an argument that had lost a good deal of its power to influence at that point. When Bishan dropped him off in front of Kavita's building, Conor felt a sad sense of nostalgia for the whimsical innocence of his first visit and began to understand why he was there.

As he climbed the stairs to the third floor, he could hear his pulse pounding in his ears. It was not very late—a little after nine o'clock—but the apartment building seemed strangely quiet. There was the smell of something baking on one floor, something with cardamom and ginger, and on the next, someone was burning incense. The air was full of scents and seemed crowded with things he couldn't see, but the only sounds he heard were his steps against the stone floor and the drumbeat of blood inside his head.

On the third floor landing, he looked down the hall at the Kotwal flat and saw that the door was open. The interior was lit with a soft, golden glow. He came in to the small vestibule just inside the door, and before continuing, he removed his boots and placed them with the sandals lining the wall.

She was alone, sitting in a straight-backed chair facing the household shrine. He had arrived at the end of her evening *aarti*, the worship service offering light to the gods. Camphor wicks—soaked in ghee and burning in front of the deity—provided the room's sole source of light. Her hands fingered a string of Hindu prayer beads that lay in her lap, and her lips soundlessly moved to form the words of a mantra. Her face, with the candlelight flickering around it, was radiant.

He watched her for almost a full minute until she opened her eyes and turned to him with a quiet, unsurprised smile.

"There you are," Kavita murmured, as if he had been there all along.

He crossed the room to her. Kneeling, he brushed his fingers over her feet and touched his chest. He spoke to her in Hindi. "*Namaste*. It's good to see you looking so well, *ji*."

"How nicely you greet me," she said, with a mischievous tilt of her head. "I am also glad to see you, Con."

"It's ... my good name is actually Conor."

"Yes. This also is a fine name. Conor." Kavita's smile grew even brighter for a moment, but then her face softened. "As Con, or as Conor, you are most gladly, most tenderly welcome, but you are so much changed. What have you been doing that has made your good face this tired and sad?"

"Things I'd be ashamed to tell you, even if I could," he whispered, struggling to control an emotion building inside him. "Dil gira kahin per. My heart has fallen somewhere, Kavita-ji. I can't ... I don't know what to do."

She took his hands into her lap, and holding them, wrapped the beads around his fingers. "Not fallen. Only heavy. Your heart has not gone missing, *beta*. It is just too, too heavy with love. Love that needs a river to sail on, to let it float and breathe and take it where it is meant to go."

She continued speaking softly to him, but as soon as she'd spoken the word beta—the word son—the struggle had ended. He lowered his head onto her hands and wept.

14

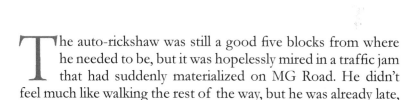

The auto-rickshaw was still a good five blocks from where he needed to be, but it was hopelessly mired in a traffic jam that had suddenly materialized on MG Road. He didn't feel much like walking the rest of the way, but he was already late, and ahead in the distance, he could see a familiar figure pacing in front of the spot he should have reached twenty minutes earlier.

Conor pressed a handful of rupees into the driver's palm with a few words of thanks and headed for the sidewalk without a backward glance. He couldn't spare any energy for haggling— whatever he had left might be needed for an argument with his controlling officer.

The call on the mobile earlier that day—the second he had ever received—had been an unwelcome surprise, first because it was three days early. Sedgwick had left the city more than a week ago, ostensibly headed to Dubai for meetings with Ahmed Khalil and his business associates. Conor didn't know if that story was true or not, but he didn't care. He had been enjoying the respite, both from Sedgwick and at least one part of his undesirable duties, and he'd expected it to last until the end of the week.

His second objection to the call was that it began with a demand for a meeting with no defined purpose. It was all too reminiscent of the last time his boss had phoned him, and that episode had not ended well. His first reaction was refusal, which, not surprisingly, was an unacceptable response from Sedgwick's point of view. Conor finally agreed to meet him in front of the Bombay Gymkhana at eight that evening, but to exercise some level of control, before leaving the flat, he had placed the Walther handgun inside a biscuit tin in his kitchen cupboard.

The packed crowd of pedestrians was moving only slightly faster than the auto-rickshaw, and when he arrived at the entrance to the city's premier sporting club, Sedgwick was almost vibrating with impatience.

"Where have you been? You're a half hour late."

"Lost track of time." Conor met Sedgwick's accusatory glare with a diffident shrug. "I seem to recall waiting around for you more than once. How was Dubai? Business booming?"

The pivot was intentional but too weak to divert the closer scrutiny he'd hoped to avoid. He didn't want to admit he'd fallen asleep on his balcony and would still be there if a boisterous gecko had not landed on his neck. He'd assembled the elements of his bodyguard persona in something of a rush, and as Sedgwick's trained, critical eye swept over him, Conor hoped he didn't look as disheveled as he felt.

"Dubai was just fine. You're looking pretty peaked there, Finnegan. Something bothering you?"

Conor rolled his eyes. He had insisted that the agent stop addressing him by his real surname, so Sedgwick's new habit was to make use of assorted nicknames drawn from his knowledge of Irish drinking songs, which was surprisingly extensive. He'd accepted the eccentricity without further protest. It was mildly entertaining to see how many his boss could come up with, and it had been helpful in easing the discomfort between them after the incident at Sewri.

"Nothing more than the usual," he said candidly. "Just feeling a bit fuzzy at the edges."

Sedgwick snorted. "You should pay more attention to what you put in your mouth. The stuff I've seen you eat, I'm surprised you haven't come down with amoebic dysentery before now."

"You just haven't my sense of culinary adventure," Conor said with a fleeting smile. "Anyway, it's not my stomach."

"No?" The suspicion in Sedgwick's voice became more pronounced. "Then what have you been up to today that's got you feeling fuzzy?"

With an inward sigh, Conor prepared for another of the verbal sparring matches they'd been having for weeks. The truth was that he had been "up to" the same thing almost every day for nearly two months. By night, he was a demoralized amalgamation of an Irish farmer imitating an intelligence agent who was pretending to be a soldier of fortune. By day, he was finding a temporary escape and some small measure of redemption in an unlikely place—the sprawling slum-metropolis of Dharavi.

He'd sought out Kavita Kotwal without understanding why, but from the moment he reached her doorway, Conor had known he was where he needed to be. She had begun helping him the very next morning simply by giving him the opportunity of doing something useful. She had directed him to the small network of health clinics sprinkled throughout the zopadpatti, as Mumbai's slums were called, and he had been volunteering almost daily ever since, going wherever she sent him or following where she led.

The work provided a productive outlet for his restlessness and offered more satisfaction than he felt about anything else at this point. The assignment of tracking his brother and coaxing him to give up his secrets was bogged down in an unproductive strategy that made less sense the longer it continued, and the strange passivity of the controlling officer who was responsible for moving it along had begun to rouse an unfocused suspicion.

Having a daytime occupation that generated some positive karma to balance against the things he did at night was a welcome diversion, but his association with Kavita was yet another clandestine activity he had to manage. He met Sedgwick's eyes with a steady, bland gaze.

"I didn't do much today, really. Read a book. Hung about with Bishan for a while."

"What did you read?"

"The *Bhagavad Gita*. As you recommended."

"So I did." Sedgwick gave him a cagey smile. "You know it's funny, because I ran into Bishan down at the Gateway earlier. He didn't mention he'd seen you today."

"Probably because I hadn't yet. I just came from having a beer with him at the Leopold. Funny, he didn't mention seeing you."

Sedgwick gave in with a roll of his eyes, and Conor smiled. With lies and half-truths, they had dueled each other to a draw once again.

"Where are we going, anyway?"

"We're already there." Sedgwick indicated the club's entrance with a jerk of his chin. "See? I told you not to worry. It's the most respectable place in the whole city. Nobody's going to get shellacked or shot up in the Bombay Gymkhana. The reservation in the dining hall is for nine, so we've got about thirty minutes if you want to hit the bar."

"You mean you're wanting to eat here?" Conor looked at the building with reluctance.

Sedgwick raised an eyebrow. "That's generally what they do in the dining hall. You got a problem with it?"

"No, not a problem, exactly, it's just that I ... ehm, I'm not really ... " As a familiar tickle shot up through his chest, Conor turned aside and cupped his hands over several hard, barking coughs. Sedgwick flinched in surprise.

"Jesus, still? Sounds worse than it did a week ago. I would have thought you'd be over it by now."

"I would have thought so too," he said when he could talk again.

The cough had not particularly concerned him, at first. His

susceptibility to respiratory ailments was above average, dating from a childhood bout with pneumonia and no doubt bolstered by a tenacious cigarette habit. For a while, the present bug had been no more remarkable than any other, but it seemed to be trending in the wrong direction, and that, along with a number of other symptoms—fatigue, weight loss, and a sporadically recurrent fever—had finally captured his attention.

The idea of venturing into Mumbai's healthcare system held little appeal—he had to assume it would be as chaotic as every other facet of Indian life—so he'd been counting on the symptoms to dissipate on their own. On good days, it seemed they might; but on other days, he was unaccountably exhausted, and the cough felt like it was ripping shards of glass from his lungs.

"You've gotten skinnier, too," Sedgwick observed. "Lost that famous appetite of yours?"

"More or less," Conor admitted. "I can't say I've much of one right now, at least, so I'd hate wasting your money on a posh dinner at this place."

"Makes no difference to me. I'm not paying for it. The people we're meeting are picking up the tab."

Conor's cheeks puffed in a deflated groan. "I knew it. What kind of people? Who are they?"

"Very tame people. Very sophisticated. Very safe." Sedgwick's tone was reassuring, but a remote annoyance flickered over his face.

"Are you going to tell me who they are?"

"Yeah, sure, of course." With a hand on Conor's back, Sedgwick propelled him toward the Gymkhana's entrance. "I'll tell you about it at the bar."

The Bombay Gymkhana was one of the oldest private sporting clubs in India. Originally established as a British-only retreat in the 1870s, it now functioned as an equal opportunity status symbol for the upper echelons of Mumbai society.

The main clubhouse was a long, multi-gabled building with an architectural style that resembled a Swiss chalet, and its veranda looked out over an expanse of open ground, which was in a peak state of grooming for the cricket season.

Gym's Inn, the club's bar, and the main dining hall mirrored the chalet theme in décor, with an abundance of exposed beams and polished wood. The bar enjoyed a mythic reputation for dispensing the largest volume of alcohol in all of South Mumbai, but Conor was doing nothing to help advance that reputation. Settling tiredly onto a stool, he asked for plain hot tea with lemon. The request raised the ire of their bartender. With tight-lipped disapproval, he slapped down a cup with a single teabag and a thermos of boiling water. Conor slid a generous pile of rupees over to him with an apologetic smile, which had an instantly taming effect. Sedgwick shook his head in exasperation.

"Haven't learned much, have you? You're still one helluva soft touch. You don't even make it challenging for them."

Ignoring the dig, Conor reached for the thermos, but the bartender, now in a jovial mood, beat him to it. Uncapping it with a flourish, he poured hot water into the cup as though filling a martini glass. He disappeared and returned with lemon slices, three more teabags, and a complimentary plate of vegetable pakoras. Arranging the offerings in front of Conor, he made a slight bow before retreating once more. Conor looked at Sedgwick with deadpan innocence.

"No snacks on the house for you, then? And you the great man of experience?"

Sedgwick conceded the point with a wave of surrender. "Okay, you win that round. Enjoy the spoils."

"I wish I could." Conor looked wistfully at the fried vegetables and pushed the plate across the bar. "You have them."

"Don't mind if I do." Sedgwick extinguished his cigarette

and indicated the box sitting next to the ashtray. "Have a smoke instead, if you want."

Conor hesitated and exhaled an oath as he tore his eyes away from the cigarettes. "I'm trying to quit. Between those feckin' things and the air quality in this city, it's no wonder I can't breathe."

"Good luck with that," Sedgwick mumbled cheerfully around a mouthful of pakora. "I've tried it myself more than once and haven't managed it yet. Getting off heroin was a piece of cake by comparison."

Conor gazed down into his teacup, and Sedgwick continued before the silence between them could become awkward. "Damn. You can't eat, you're not drinking, and you won't smoke. You're getting to be kind of a bore, Clancy."

Conor sniffed in mingled amusement and weariness. "Well, you've only to say the word and your man Clancy will be happy to remove his monotonous presence. I wasn't the one looking for this mix and mingle, after all. It was your idea."

"Not exactly," Sedgwick muttered.

"No? What's that mean?"

"Oh, never mind. Let's just get to it. It's almost nine o'clock."

With edgy irritation, Sedgwick pushed the empty plate away from him. He pulled another cigarette from the box, lit it, and tossed the lighter back onto the bar. Leaning back on one elbow, he gave the inside of his whisky glass a speculative stare. "Do you speak any Russian?" he asked abruptly.

Oh, Janey, what now? Conor thought. He put his cup down and looked longingly at the cigarettes again. "I don't, no."

"Not even the basics? Hi, how are you? How about this weather?"

"Not even a syllable."

Sedgwick nodded, and a gleam of something lit his eyes before he snapped them away to signal the bartender for the check. Conor thought it looked like relief.

"Doesn't matter. It'll just be a little dull for you. They don't like speaking English." Sedgwick patted the pockets of his trousers and searched the inside of his jacket with an air of nonchalance. Conor didn't like what he was seeing in the agent's long, thin face. Despite an effort to appear unconcerned, he was clearly nervous and had been avoiding eye contact for the past several minutes.

"We're having dinner with Russians, then, is that it?" he asked.

"Crimeans, actually," Sedgwick said. "But I don't speak Crimean Tatar, so we'll have to get along in Russian. They're associates of Khalil's, from a 'sister organization.' There's a joint project coming up in a few months, and they're over for a few days. I haven't even met them myself. Khalil wanted them to start getting to know some of the key people on the Mumbai side, especially the foreigners. They're not all that keen on working with Indians, so he wants to show off his *goras*. All you have to do is sit there and look impressively Caucasian."

"I will in me arse." Conor spat out the refusal with a snarl. He felt his blood pressure rising as the agent's intentions became clear and thought he damn well ought to look nervous about trying to make him collaborate on one more diversionary operation. "This is exactly why I didn't want to come here tonight. There's just one project I care about, Sedgwick, and it's nothing to do with any bleedin' Crimeans. I'm already sick to death of the shite you've had me neck-deep in since I came, and it never seems to get anywhere, so you can be dead certain that I'm not about to start foostering about on some ... "

The force of his dissent prompted another round of coughing, preempting the rest of his objection. Sedgwick continued to avoid looking at him. He had located his wallet and began digging for the grimy bills inside it.

"Look, you've got nothing to worry about; I'm not trying to get you involved in anything. It's one dinner, and you're just a stage prop. Seriously. It will all be over in two hours."

"One dinner and done?" Conor asked. "I'll never have to see them again?"

"That's right."

"And can we agree that you'll not be trying to drag me into any more of these sideshows?"

"Agreed."

He pressed the advantage even further. "And that we'll stop arsing around and form a real plan for how to find my brother so I can get the hell out of here?"

"Yes, all right." Sedgwick nodded, throwing the rupees onto the bar. "I agree we haven't made much progress. I know you're frustrated. We'll work on something."

"Do I have your word on it?"

Sedgwick didn't respond immediately. He bit his lower lip and looked down at his hands with a peculiar smile. "If you think the word of an addict is worth anything, then you've got it. Is that good enough?"

Conor hesitated as well. Again, he felt a vague suspicion that he was missing clues, but he still couldn't put his finger on the source of his mistrust. "I guess it will have to be, God help me." He winced as another cough rattled painfully against his ribs. "I may not survive the night, so you could be off the hook soon enough."

"I'm beginning to wonder if you'll even make it through dinner." Sedgwick gave him a worried scowl. "You should get that checked. Sounds like it needs something stronger than tea."

"Well, as it happens, I have something stronger, but I don't like to use it much."

Conor picked up the knapsack sitting on the floor by his feet. From a zippered front pocket, he removed the small brown bottle that he had first seen in a British Airways plane bound for India.

Kavita had been worried about him also. He had so far

resisted her appeals for an examination at the hands of her personal physician, but he'd compromised by reluctantly accepting a bottle of her homemade physic. Although it was remarkably effective, he had used it only a few times. The taste was something altogether shocking, and he didn't know what the hell was in it.

He could detect the presence of ginger, anise, hot chilies, and mustard oil, but these ingredients did not account for the rush of relaxed euphoria he experienced after taking a dose of it. Clearly, there was a pharmacological wildcard in the mix, and since he had no idea what it was, he restricted the medicine to an intervention of last resort.

He put the bottle down on the bar, and Sedgwick immediately picked it up with a look of intense interest. "Where did you get this?"

"Ehm ... "

The question was natural enough, but he wasn't prepared for it. Conor hid his momentary confusion with a gulp of tea. "Bishan's wife, Meera," he said. "She's always pouring her Ayurvedic recipes into me. This one works pretty well."

"Uh-huh." Sedgwick removed the cap. As he leaned over the bottle to take a sniff, a portion of his silky hair fell over one eye, and a slow, reflective smile crept over his face. With a soft laugh, he nodded.

With a sinking feeling, Conor watched him reach across the bar to pick up a shot glass. He didn't know how, but it was clear from the recognition in his cool, gray eyes that Sedgwick knew all about the little brown bottle and its contents ... and knew who had provided it.

He filled the shot glass with the brown, viscous liquid, and their eyes met as he passed it over with a gently sardonic salute. "She probably told you take it like this, right? Meera, I mean?"

Conor played the hand the only way he could—with feigned

innocence. "She did tell me that, yeah."

He accepted the shot glass and tipped its contents down his throat, his mouth puckering at the revolting taste. The heat from the chilies made his eyes water as the medicine burned its way down his gullet, but almost immediately he began to feel its beneficial effects. The tickle at the bottom of his windpipe retreated, and he seemed able to breathe a little easier.

"Better?" Sedgwick asked. Conor nodded.

"I'd feel even better if the ingredients were listed on the bottle."

"That would be telling though, wouldn't it?" Sedgwick said, with a wink. "There's always a secret ingredient. Anything else on your mind? Before we go do this?"

"Nope." He tucked the bottle back into the knapsack. "How about you? Anything you want to add? About your Crimeans?"

"Nope. Except that I'm as anxious to have it over with as you are."

15

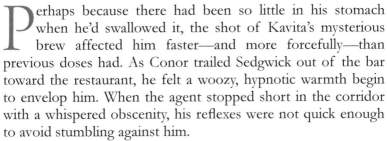

Perhaps because there had been so little in his stomach when he'd swallowed it, the shot of Kavita's mysterious brew affected him faster—and more forcefully—than previous doses had. As Conor trailed Sedgwick out of the bar toward the restaurant, he felt a woozy, hypnotic warmth begin to envelop him. When the agent stopped short in the corridor with a whispered obscenity, his reflexes were not quick enough to avoid stumbling against him.

"*Arrey, gabh mo leiscal, yaar.*"

The apology, offered in a jumble of Hindi and Irish, caused Sedgwick to turn back to him in startled confusion. "What did you say?"

Conor blinked. "Jaysus, I'm not sure. What did it sound like?"

"It sounds like you're drunk."

"Secret ingredient," Conor suggested with an uncharacteristic snicker. "What's the matter? Aren't those your lads up ahead, there?"

Sedgwick released his breath in a long, slow hiss of resignation and nodded. "They're not what I expected. Are you going to be all right?"

"Yeah, yeah." Conor gave himself a slight shake and stood up straighter. "Anyway, I'm the dark, quiet sidekick, right? I'll be a bit darker and quieter for a while. It will wear off before long. I hope."

"I hope it doesn't." Sedgwick started again toward the two

men who were standing near the doorway of the restaurant. "It might be easier for everyone if it didn't."

At first, it seemed Sedgwick might get his wish. They approached the strangers, and during the introductions, Conor wallowed in sleepy affability while trying hard to maintain his role as one of Khalil's mysterious, deceptively tranquil *goras.*

He was cautiously silent as they exchanged greetings, shook hands, and made their way in to the dining room. After taking a seat at a large round table that could have accommodated twice as many people, he began discreetly applying himself to the task of clearing his head.

About fifteen minutes later, the cobwebs began to disperse, helped along by several glasses of water and a few pappadams slathered with hot, mixed pickle. With clarity of thought returning, he began a more discriminating assessment of their dinner companions.

The men had introduced themselves as Grigory Lipvin and Anatoly Kovalevsky. Lipvin, the older of the two, was seated across from Conor next to Sedgwick. He was tall, appeared to be in his early sixties, and had a solid, athletic-looking frame. A shaved fringe of gray hair served as a notional border for the gleaming dome of his bald head, and he had small, dark eyes that looked out from behind a pair of wire-rimmed glasses.

His associate sat on Conor's left. Anatoly Kovalevsky was a short, slender, and dark-haired young man, no more than twenty-five if he was even that old. He had extremely fair skin; red cheeks; large, round eyes; and a conservative hairstyle featuring a straight, severe part down the side. He was the exact portrait of a young overachiever, right down to the conventional navy blue suit, identical in cut and style to the one worn by his elder counterpart.

Kovalevsky had also not spoken after the initial introductions, and as the silence on their side of the table continued, Conor became more aware of the discussion across from them. Lipvin and Sedgwick sat with their elbows on the table, their heads bent toward each other. Although he could not understand their words, he could read the body language, and from the occasional, furtive glance Lipvin darted across the table, he felt confident in his interpretation. They were discussing him.

His stomach lurched, and his brain—emerging from its stupor—struggled to keep up with the incoming stream of data. A dry-mouthed anxiety supplied a visceral substitute for the rational analysis that still eluded him.

Something was wrong.

His muscles twitched in an involuntary shudder, which the young Kovalevsky took as an invitation to converse.

"So, Mr... . er, Con. You have been working in India for some time now?"

Conor turned a smooth, inscrutable gaze toward the voice on his left. "I've been here a while," he said, evenly. "And you, Mr. Kovalevsky? Is it your first time visiting India?"

"*Da.* Yes, this is the first time, but there are no opportunities for sightseeing." Kovalevsky's brow wrinkled sorrowfully. He gave a deep sigh of disappointment. "All business. It is great shame to come so far and not see more of such amazing country."

"That is a shame." Conor's eyes remained riveted on Kovalevsky's face. Since the young man had started speaking, a spark of understanding had begun to grow and smolder, like a flame licking stubbornly against damp wood, and now it flowered into a steady glow. It was the voice, the accent, the face, and the clothes. The entire package was false.

He was wide awake now and beginning to wish he wasn't. If it was accurate, the insight crystallizing in his mind had ramifications so unexpected and disturbing that they threatened to overwhelm him. With effort, he drew on the training intended to guide him in such situations. He forced his thoughts to yield to a methodical process, and with the shadow of a smile, responded to Kovalevsky.

"The Crimean peninsula is quite beautiful as well. At least I thought it was when I saw it."

And there it was. He'd been prepared to watch for something subtle, but no special powers of discernment were needed to register Kovalevsky's immediate discomfort. The slight widening of his eyes and the reflexive glance toward Lipvin communicated his nervousness as eloquently as a verbal admission. He tried to cover the slip with a hum of delight.

"Yes, of course, very beautiful. How marvelous that you have seen it. When were you there?"

"Years ago," Conor replied. "Sevastopol. Is that anywhere near you?"

"Not far." Kovalevsky waved a hand, vaguely. "I am from a small place not far from there."

"On the coast?"

"Hmm, yes. The coast."

"Must be lovely. Right on the coast of ... " Conor paused with a small frown of uncertainty and looked at his table companion in embarrassment. "What sea? Funny, I can't think of it. Is it the Caspian?"

The young man smiled in an attempt to cover his frozen indecision. "It is, um ... "

"Right." Conor nodded. "The Caspian Sea. I thought so."

"Yes. Caspian."

Kovalevsky released his breath in a slightly explosive exhalation, but his relief was short-lived. Conor fixed him with a long stare of contempt.

"Or is it?" he asked, softly.

A dark red flush spread over the young man's face and rose up to the precisely defined line of his scalp. Conor watched it without expression and turned away. The experiment was complete, the results analyzed, and the conclusion indisputable.

Kovalevsky and Lipvin were no more Crimean than he was,

and they'd taken very few precautions to hide the fact. With a dawning sense of incredulous shock, Conor also knew he was the only one their pitiful performance was designed to fool.

They're not what I expected.

The meaning of Sedgwick's remark and the source of his annoyance were now clear. He had been given a cover story only to find his associates had arrogantly neglected their side of the ruse. They had not adequately altered their appearance or demeanor to conform to the roles they were supposed to be playing. They could not have effected a more inept impersonation if they'd tried. They could not have looked more like the pompous Americans Conor was almost certain they actually were.

Turning again to the ongoing drone of conversation across the table, he concentrated on the face of his controlling officer, which looked tense and unhappy, and tightened his jaw against a combination of emotions too numerous to name.

One set of puppet masters was quite enough for him, but apparently not for Sedgwick. Apparently, he preferred to have some skin in more than one game, like a compulsive gambler. Or an addict. The exposure of his deceit was agonizing on many levels, but most harrowing was the realization that he couldn't even be sure how big the lie was, how far back in time it extended, or who had started it.

With that thought, the bedlam inside his head converged in rage and despair, but even in that extremity, his "talent for repose" did not desert him. With quiet, careful movements, he folded his napkin, slid his chair back from the table, and rose to his feet.

"Mr. Lipvin." He nodded to him and then looked at Sedgwick. Their eyes locked for several seconds, and the agent's brow contracted, as though in pain. He whispered something soundless and slumped against his chair.

"Thanks for your hospitality," Conor continued. "And fair

play to you on the success of your Pimsleur language lessons, but I'm afraid I've no appetite this evening—for dinner or any of this."

He retrieved his knapsack, and when he straightened, he swept his eyes over all of them, dismissively, and indicated the young man next to him with a tilt of his head. "If you'd really intended to keep the game going, you should have left this little fart of a fellow back in the States. Neither of us has ever been on the Crimean peninsula, but one of us at least knows it's in the Black Sea."

16

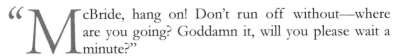

"McBride, hang on! Don't run off without—where are you going? Goddamn it, will you please wait a minute?"

On his way out of the building, Conor had veered from the long corridor, crossed the club's wide veranda to the grounds beyond, and walked quickly across the manicured cricket pitch. He stopped now and spun to meet the shadowy figure advancing on him out of the darkness.

"Is that an order, boss?" he demanded. "In what capacity, please? It's dark out here, so I can't see. Which official badge are you flashing at me, now, MI6 or CIA?"

"I don't have any capacity with the CIA." Sedgwick came to a stop in front of him.

"Sure, and if bullshit were music, you'd be a brass band. Don't even waste your breath trying to sell me—"

"I'm not selling anything. I'm telling you the truth. They're not CIA and neither am I." Sedgwick's chin jutted defensively. "The CIA cut me loose eight years ago. Security risk to myself and my colleagues."

"What the fuck are you, then?" Conor's voice shook with fury. "And what the fuck are they? Whatever you're playing at, I'm guessing MI6 is out of the loop. Am I right?"

Sedgwick's lips compressed into a thin line. He nodded.

"Right," Conor said, bitterly. "As far as I can tell, that puts you and me on opposite teams."

"Not exactly," Sedgwick said with a grim smile.

With a growl of disgust, Conor shouldered his knapsack and turned away, heading across the field into the night. Sedgwick jogged forward to catch up and walked along beside him.

"What are you doing?"

"What's it to you?"

Sedgwick angled his head to the sky with a light groan. "I think you know why I need the information."

"Yeah, well, I think you know why I don't feel the need to give it to you. I've had enough of this game, thanks very much. I'm not playing anymore."

Sedgwick took hold of his arm, pulling him to a stop. "I'm sorry it happened this way. Things aren't what you've been led to believe, sometimes because people didn't know any better and sometimes because they did. I understand that's upsetting. It sucks to be lied to, and if it had gone differently tonight ... anyway, my fault. They don't trust me either. Not surprising. I warned them not to underestimate you, but I should have known they would."

"But, listen." He gripped Conor's arm more tightly. "Even though you don't understand any of it, there's a lot of dangerous and complicated shit going on, a lot of moving parts. It's not a game. We're not dicking around, making up stories for our own entertainment. You need to appreciate that."

Conor shook the hand off his arm. He shifted his weight, squared around to Sedgwick, and delivered a hard punch to his jaw. He watched as the agent tripped backward and sat down hard on the ground, his breath knocked out with a whoosh of astonishment. He loomed over him, fists still clenched, as Sedgwick struggled to breathe.

"I know it isn't a game, you miserable son of a bitch. I'm not that fat in the forehead, but if nobody will tell me what it is, then what am I supposed to call it? Has anyone spoken one word of truth to me since this mad shambles began? Is my brother even in this bloody country? Do you even know who he is? And do you have any idea what it has cost me to come over here for this? Do you have any fucking idea what it's cost?"

He whirled away and began pacing, fists pressed to the sides of his head. His chest heaved with the struggle to control his rage while Sedgwick regained his breath in ragged whoops.

The agent rose to his knees and then got slowly to his feet. He silently watched Conor's struggle before speaking again. "I do know Thomas. I've known him a long time. And he is in India. I've been working with him for years."

Conor's fists unclenched. Recognizing the impotence of his wrath, his hands dropped down to hang at his sides. He stared at the ground in defeat. "You've known him for years, and you know where he is now. You've known from the beginning."

"Yes," Sedgwick said, after a brief pause.

"And you're not going to tell me what this is really about or how to find him," Conor added, tonelessly.

"I wish I could. In fact I wanted to, but now I can't."

"He's never been near that drop house in Goregaon East, has he? All this bullshit I've been caught up in for the past two months—"

"A feint, a distraction," Sedgwick conceded. "I infiltrated the Khalil group years ago to collect intelligence. It was easy enough to bring you into it. It's not the main event, and Thomas isn't involved with them."

"Not the main event." Conor choked a harsh laugh. "Just a minor attraction. And you get it coming and going, don't you? Khalil pays you to help run his crime ring, MI6 pays you to babysit me, and your fake Crimean buddies pay you to keep me chasing my tail."

"That's not quite the way I'd put it," Sedgwick replied, "but the general gist is correct. We didn't want you here. After we sent back the first MI6 agent pickled in gin, we didn't expect London to send another one over so soon, and we certainly didn't expect them to send an amateur. The conventional wisdom on this end was that after I'd trotted you around the hellholes of Mumbai for a couple of weeks, you'd give it up and cry to go home."

Sedgwick looked away and shook his head. "I had a feeling you wouldn't though, and once I saw you shoot that guy's knee apart, I knew you weren't going away. I told them, but like I said, they tend not to believe me. They wanted to get a look at you. That's why they called the meeting tonight." The smile twisted into an expression of jaded contempt. "Their heads are so far up their own asses, they haven't even realized yet how badly they've screwed up with you. The older guy—Lipvin—he's thinking it's all good. He figures you're freaked and headed for the airport and that if MI6 gets a story about me dealing in something fishy—well, it won't be anything they haven't heard before."

"What about you?" Conor asked, eyes still on the ground. "What do you figure I'll do?"

Sedgwick put his hands into his pockets and came up to stand next to him again. Looking out across the darkened field, he gave a wistful sigh. "I figure you won't, but that's not to say I don't wish you would."

"What will you do, then? Kill me?"

"Oh, for Christ's sake." Sedgwick pulled out his packet of cigarettes, shaking his head. "That's above my pay grade, but I have to warn you, they're going to come to their senses soon and realize they can't afford to have you hanging around asking more questions. So, if you give us too much time to get organized, we'll think of something to get you out of the way for a while—get you arrested, kidnapped, something. If you just leave now and keep your mouth shut, it would be safer for everyone, your brother included."

Conor lifted his eyes from the ground and joined Sedgwick in gazing out into a darkness that had grown blacker during the time they'd been standing there.

"Tell me where he is," he said calmly, but without hope.

"I can't do that," Sedgwick began and raised a hand to forestall Conor's protest. "I can't tell you how to find him, but it doesn't matter much, because I'm pretty sure he's about to come find you."

Conor's half-articulated objection died on his lips. He turned to stare at the averted face next to him. "You're saying he knows I'm here?"

"Yeah. He doesn't know what you've been doing, but he knows you're here." Sedgwick paused to light a cigarette. The lighter illuminated his sharp, angular features and highlighted small flecks of gold in his gray eyes. "He promised to stay out of sight as long as we kept things under control, but he told me he knew we would fuck up eventually and that all bets were off once we did."

The agent gave him a hard, steady look. "I wasn't kidding, Conor. This thing has been baking for years, and it's ready to come out of the oven. If you don't leave, my 'fake Crimean buddies' won't take chances. They're going to want you snatched up and put on a shelf somewhere, and Thomas knows it. He'll try to get to you first."

A silence fell between the two of them. Conor closed his eyes, trying to assimilate everything he had heard and turn it into something coherent. He heard Sedgwick's lighter igniting as he finished one cigarette and lit another. He opened his eyes and turned to him again.

"The only way he'll know you've fucked up is if he finds out what happened here tonight."

With an enigmatic squint, Sedgwick dragged on his cigarette and swiveled his head to release a stream of smoke into the night air.

Conor swore in frustration and leaned in closer, his eyes on the agent's face. "Why are you doing this? Why tell me all this after lying for so long? To help me? Am I supposed to believe that?"

"Call it payment on a debt."

"I don't know what that means. Tell me how I can believe what you're telling me. Why won't you tell me the rest of it? How can I trust anything you say?"

"You can't." Sedgwick expelled the retort in a hoarse growl. Grinding the cigarette beneath his boot, he pushed a handful of blond hair from his forehead and looked at him with a tired smile. "You shouldn't. Everybody else knows enough not to. I tried to tell you that earlier tonight. The problem is, you don't have an alternative."

"Is it an intelligence operation? Are you Thomas's controlling officer?" Conor demanded.

The agent laughed softly. "It's probably more accurate to say he's mine, depending on how you look at it."

"I don't—"

"I know you don't understand, and you're not going to, even if you decide to stick around and let him find you. He'll keep you as ignorant as I have; he'll just be doing it for different reasons. I can't convince you to go home without him, but maybe he can. Maybe we should have let him try that in the beginning. Hindsight is twenty-twenty."

They fell silent again. Conor thought there was little left to say and little left for him to do. His soldiering days in Khalil's army were over. The artifice constructed to keep him occupied for two months—an elaborate, self-contained set piece that had flawlessly directed him farther from the truth—had been disassembled and packed away over the course of an hour.

It left a void he didn't know how to fill. He was adrift and becalmed, with no immediate strategy to implement and no controlling officer to coordinate his actions. As he wrestled against the paralysis of indecision, he looked absently at his watch and remembered the other activity that had been on his agenda for the evening. Suddenly, he saw an opening—not the way out but at least a way forward. He turned with such a sudden, vigorous movement that Sedgwick took a startled step backward.

"I'm supposed to be meeting Raj in Kamathipura in two hours."

"Oh, right." Sedgwick nodded. "I'll send someone. We presented you as a free agent from the beginning. I'll tell him and the others you've moved on to something else."

"I don't want you to send someone or say anything yet. I'll go for one more night. There's something I need to do."

Sedgwick's eyes widened but then narrowed in shrewd understanding. "Radha. This is your next move? Really? Rescuing a prostitute from the squalor and indignity of the red-light district? That's wandering pretty far off the track, I'd say."

"She's not a prostitute," Conor said. "Not yet, anyway, and this might be the last chance I get to keep her from becoming one."

"Very noble but it's a bad idea." Sedgwick's face hardened into disapproval. "You're buying trouble when you can't afford what you've already got. You steal her away from Mehta, and you're bringing down a world of shit that is going to—"

"I'm not going to steal her."

Sedgwick's bark of laughter echoed over the empty field. With hands on his hips, he took a short, circular walk before returning to confront Conor, his habitual, cutting sarcasm firmly back in place. "You really are—literally—planning to buy trouble, aren't you? It's going to be a bigger price than you expect, dude. She's had an expensive habit for a while now, and he's been supporting it because it suited him, but he's going to add it to the bill. You'll be paying for her and every molecule of smack that's gone up her nose in the last six months, and that's not to mention how many ways you'll be paying after you've got her."

"Why don't you let me worry about that," Conor said curtly. "All I'm asking is to keep this little psycho-drama running for one more night. Seems a small enough request, considering the circumstances."

"Yeah, sure, okay." Sedgwick threw up his arms in a pantomime of surrender. "Go to it, but I think you're crazy. It's like pissing on a forest fire. Do you know how many Radhas there are in the world? In Mumbai? Do you know how many there are, right on that same lane in Kamathipura?"

Conor looked at the face in front of him, its fine features contorted in the perpetual effort of concealing its owner's insecurity and self-disgust. Once more, despite everything, an irresistible empathy came forward to grind away the sharp edges of his resentment.

"I've no idea," he said, with a pale smile. "Showers of them, no doubt. Showers of Radhas and showers of Sedgwicks, but I only know one of each. Someone helped you once, right? Without worrying how many others there were. I think I know who that was now. I can't fix everything, I know that, but I can't help trying to fix what's in front of me."

A spasm of pure, unguarded emotion passed over the face of his former boss. Sedgwick dropped his head away, rubbing a hand over his mouth. After a moment, he cleared his throat. Lifting his head, he held out a hand. "Good luck. In case I don't see you again, I should confess that what they said about you in Gosport turned out to be true; but as usual, they didn't know the half of it."

With a slight grin, Conor shook the outstretched hand. "Thanks. They left out the best bits about you, too."

He had gone just a short distance across the cricket pitch when he heard a single word echoing behind him. He turned and looked back at Sedgwick with a curious frown.

"What was that?"

"Paregoric," Sedgwick repeated. "More technically known as camphorated tincture of opium. It's the secret ingredient she puts in the cough medicine, so you're smart to be careful with it. It works on stomach bugs, too, and in controlled doses, it moderates the effects of withdrawal." His face lit up with one of the rare, natural smiles that Conor wished he had seen more often over the past several months. "Tell her I'm doing okay, *yaar*, and ... give her my love."

When Conor turned to continue walking, the night surrounding him was reaching its deepest, blackest peak. In the distance, he knew there was a footpath that bisected the field, serving as an informal boundary between the property of the Gymkhana and the even larger grounds of the public Azad Maiden that lay beyond it. He couldn't see it. In fact, he couldn't see more than twenty feet in front of him, but he knew he could get there. With every twenty feet he paced off and left behind, he would be able to see twenty more ahead of him, and that was how he would find his way to it. It was a painstaking way to complete a journey, but it was all anyone could expect when walking through darkness.

17

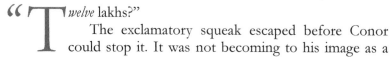

"*Twelve* lakhs?"

The exclamatory squeak escaped before Conor could stop it. It was not becoming to his image as a stone-cold gun for hire, but the figure so astonished him that he was thrown off balance and out of character. A lakh was equivalent to one hundred thousand rupees, which meant Mehta was demanding over a million of them.

A week earlier, the bar owner had made it known he would soon be entertaining bids for Radha's *sar dhakna*, literally the "veiling of the head." The term referred to a traditional ritual within the Hindu marriage ceremony, but it also served as a euphemism for the purchase of a dance-bar girl's virginity. Conor thought it unlikely that a bidding war among patrons would have gone as high as six lakhs. He had been quoted double that price for the privilege of preempting the game and jumping to the head of the line.

Pulling the mask of indifference back over his features, he angled his head to regard the face dominating the wall behind Mehta while he recovered from his shock. The iconic namesake of the Marilyn Monroe Bar gazed back at him. Her hooded eyes, highlighted in dragon fruit-pink, retained their seductive allure despite Warhol's garish handiwork.

"It is a very large sum," Mehta acknowledged, with a small

smile. "More than you expected and maybe more than you can afford?"

Conor remained silent, privately debating whether he had the stomach to argue about it. He looked at the bar owner with calm speculation, wondering why he felt such an intense loathing for the man.

There was nothing special about Rohit Mehta to distinguish him as any more venal than the other pimps and drug dealers he'd run across in Mumbai's hotspots. If anything, Mehta appeared to take pains to present a kindlier face to the world than many others he'd met. He had a large, round face encircled by a tuft of white hair and fitted with enormous glasses that gave him a slightly goggle-eyed appearance. He spoke in tones of muted modesty and wore a perpetually cherubic expression that could be taken for soft-headedness or the onset of senility.

Conor didn't believe it was either. Rohit Mehta was not that old and hadn't become one of the richest men in the district by being dimwitted. He was quite positive the portrayal of a genial, soup-stained baba was as much an act as the one he was putting on himself. He thought it might be the shameless hypocrisy of the performance that prompted his unusually strong antipathy.

"You must understand," Mehta said, breaking the silence, "the price is very high because I would be so much happier not to lose her. Radha is like a daughter. It is my joy to have her close to me. In my old age, she is like the jewel—"

"Oh, give over." Conor cut him off with a flash of irritation. "It's a peculiar sort of father that condemns his daughter to drug addiction."

"Condemns? I condemn?" Mehta regarded him with a wide, saucer-eyed stare. "How could I? It is the guests who brought gifts, and my Radha accepted. She is very strong-willed, and now she will have what she wants. How can I refuse her?"

"Rubbish. Even if you didn't start her on it, you've perpetuated it. You could have ... oh, Christ, never mind." He stopped, pinching the bridge of his nose to moderate the eruption of temper. "You want twelve lakhs, you'll get it. I'll be back in about three hours. Make sure she's still here."

He rose and headed for the door and in a parting glance saw Rohit Mehta's disguise slip. His lips opened in a wide, salacious grin, exposing a line of stubby teeth stained a lurid shade of red from years of chewing betel nut. It was the face of a predatory animal, lifting its head from its bloody pursuits with leering satisfaction. In the background, Marilyn's fulsome, fluorescent lips provided a bizarre, echoing accent to complete the scene.

He returned to the main bar and saw Raj had retreated to a corner and folded himself into one of the small white couches against the wall. Conor skirted the edge of the dance floor and approached with a casual salute.

"*Thik hai*, Raj. *Chalo*. Let's get out of here."

Even though Raj had watched his advance from across the room, the skeletal young man jumped at the direct address. Conor resisted the urge to swear with impatience. "Sorry, *yaar*," he said, limiting his tone to mild sarcasm. "Didn't mean to sneak up on you. I'm ready when you are."

"Radha." Raj accompanied the illogical reply with a timorous head toggle.

"Ehm, right." Conor turned with slow reluctance to look at the figures revolving around the dance floor.

He had not looked for Radha earlier, not wanting to draw her attention before reaching an understanding with Mehta. Now that he had, he was conscious of even more reasons for nervousness. He thought it likely she would be eager to leave with him, and it was equally likely she would have the wrong impression of what leaving with him signified. He wasn't looking forward to the explanations that might be required and wasn't about to go into them with her now.

He walked to the edge of the dance floor, and she saw him immediately, peeling away from the nucleus of women at center stage. She twirled forward with a step that was more graceful than most, but also unsteady—a sign that she was probably floating in the after-effects of a heroin-induced haze.

The string of bells around her ankles jingled as she planted her bare feet on the floor and stood before him with her arms crossed. An impish smirk lit her face, but her large, hazel eyes were shining with affection. Except that she had the sharp wit and impudence of a teenager, Conor could easily have believed her to be closer to nine or ten rather than thirteen. The top of her head reached no higher than his waist.

"How long have you been here tonight?" he asked.

"What time is it now, please?" Radha demanded with exacting formality. He glanced at his watch. "It's after midnight. Twenty five minutes after, to be precise."

"Then it is two hours, twenty five minutes since I am dancing. To be precise."

"What did you have to eat today?"

"Oh, I have eaten too much today, so many rotis and dal. And rice. Rice I had also."

"Hmm, I don't think I believe that." Conor held out his hands, and without protest, Radha put out her own. Like the questions about her diet, this also had become a routine she submitted to with amused patience.

He turned the palms of her hands up, ran his eyes over the inside of her arms, and breathed a sigh of tentative relief. As far as he could tell, she was still only snorting the heroin, or "brown sugar," as she called it. If she had graduated to injecting, there were no visible signs of it. Her arms were smooth and unblemished. He knew she could fool him by injecting the drug elsewhere but doubted she would bother to hide it.

"Okay now, Mommy?" Radha inquired sweetly, returning her hands to her hips with an impertinent wriggle. "All this nonsense about eating, *bhaiyya*. I see you, and what am I to think? Always you are coming and talking, and always you are skinnier, each time."

"We're not talking about me. We're talking about you."

"But I am talking now." Radha smiled brightly. "This subject is too interesting. Tell me, what did you have to eat today?"

"Many rotis, and dal. And rice."

"Oof!"

Her comical exclamation, coupled with the impatient stamp of her foot, gave Conor the first good laugh he'd had in a while. "You'd better get back to dancing," he said, taking a few steps back from the dance floor. "I have to go, but I'm hoping to be back a little later."

At this, Radha's smile faded, and her small, heart-shaped face crumpled. "Always you are coming back, and always going away again, but without Radha. Radha stays where she is. Dancing."

"I know. I'm sorry."

Conor swallowed hard. He didn't dare tell her of the conversation with Rohit Mehta and of the terms they had reached. There was still the small matter of gathering up 1.2 million rupees during the next three hours. He wasn't entirely confident he would manage it and wouldn't risk raising her hopes.

She wasn't letting him off easily, however. Pressing her palms together and holding them in front of her face, she appealed to him with quiet supplication.

"Con-ji, will you do this thing for me? Will you take me from this place?"

"Radha, please don't ... " He took her hands again and gently pulled them apart.

"It is because I am taking the brown sugar?" Her eyes were now shining with tears. "You don't like it. I know this. It is why you don't want me?"

"God, no," Conor groaned, miserably. "It's true, I don't like it. I want you to stop taking it but that's got nothing to do with—

ah jayz, please don't cry. Listen, I promise I'll be back later, in about three hours' time. We'll talk more about it then, right? We'll think of something, together."

Radha's tears continued to fall, but her face brightened slightly as she looked up at him. "In three hours?" she asked, dubiously.

"In three hours," he said and meant it. Unless he was lying somewhere either unconscious or dead, he would be coming back for her, tonight. With or without the money, he would be taking her from Rohit Mehta tonight.

She nodded, and he saw she didn't entirely believe him. With two small fingers, she wiped her eyes—careful to avoid smudging her makeup—and composed herself with a few deep breaths. When she spoke again, the exhausted sadness in her voice troubled him more than the tears.

"I am tired from this, *bhaiyya*. There is nothing good here for me."

"*Síocáin*," Conor whispered, brushing his hands down over her hair with a light, soothing touch. "*Síocáin, mo chara.*"

He watched the melancholy heaviness in her face give way to confused wonder, and realized for the second time that night he had unconsciously slipped into the language he had learned to speak before any other.

It confused him as well, and for a few seconds, Conor felt the atmosphere inside the bar change. It was as if a barometric shift had swallowed up every breath and noise, leaving room for just a single, echoing sound—a voice repeating the Irish words in a soft, comforting drone, directing them at him, not Radha.

Síocáin, mo chara. Peace, my friend.

The moment passed but left behind the sharp aura of premonition, a ghostly tap on the shoulder that sent a tremor of dread along the length of his back.

Not much longer. Something was coming.

18

Standing in the nearly deserted lane outside the Monroe, Conor squinted at a platoon of rats streaming purposefully along the opposite wall and tried to restrain a mounting frustration.

There were many undesirable consequences to be catalogued from the practice of having a semiautomatic handgun strapped to one's chest. In particular, there were two he found problematic. The first was that the shape and weight of the pistol against his side had become so habitual that its absence now felt unnatural. Whenever he was not wearing it, the abnormal lightness prompted jolts of neurotic panic, as though he had lost or forgotten something important.

The second, more worrisome side effect was the temptation generated by ready accessibility. During moments of high aggravation, the urge to yank it out and blast away at something— just to slake the desire for deafening explosion—lurked provocatively beneath the surface.

He had returned to the Jyoti flat to retrieve the Walther before heading for Kamathipura, but although it was again strapped under his arm, he was not seriously considering a murderous assault on the rats. He couldn't deny, however, that the present dispute with Raj was making his fingers itch to take hold of something or someone.

The debate—all the more infuriating for being unexpected—

had been going on in Hindi for the past several minutes, and he was nearing the end of his limited patience. He had to get going, primarily because the available minutes were inexorably ticking away, but also because of the god-awful burning stench wafting from an alley a few feet away from them. The noxious, unidentifiable odor was scratching at his lungs, threatening to revive the tickle that had remained blessedly dormant for the past several hours. He took in a careful breath and renewed the argument with a tone of authority he hoped would settle the matter.

"We are not going to stand here discussing this endlessly, Raj. I have said that we need to work in Juhu tonight and time is growing short. So let's go. Quickly, now."

The young man flinched as Conor completed the command by cracking the back of his hand sharply against his left palm, but Raj's obtuse expression did not waver.

"It is the night for collections in Kamathipura, Con-ji," he protested in a frightened, wheedling voice. "The collections in Bandra-Juhu are for tomorrow night."

"Which you have said ten times now," Conor fired back in exasperation. "So, for the eleventh and final time, I'm telling you the plan has changed."

"I know nothing of this changing plan."

"Well, I'm sorry you didn't get the memo," Conor sighed, lapsing into English. "Jaysus, even the Indian mafia feeds on red tape. Suddenly he's a bureaucrat waiting for paperwork."

"*Kyaa, saab?*" Raj's head dipped to one side in nervous curiosity.

"I said it is useless to consider what you know or don't know," Conor resumed in Hindi. "What I am telling you is the only important thing."

"But why, *saab*? Why Juhu tonight?"

Because that's where all the money is, and I only have three hours to get it.

This was not the response Conor intended to give to an admittedly reasonable question, but it was the naked, mercenary truth. When he had returned to the Jyoti earlier that evening, he had retrieved more than just the Walther. In his knapsack, he was hauling a cargo of pristine five-hundred-rupee notes that he'd been hiding in the flat. They were banded together in sixteen bundles of one hundred notes each. That represented eight lakhs, and it wasn't enough.

The money came from his account at a Colaba district bank, which had been created for him in London presumably by the same busy administrators who had assembled his briefing books, passport, and other operational ornamentations. It was intended to support basic living expenses and items of necessity, but he'd liquidated it a week ago, when the scheme for extracting Radha from her predicament had first occurred to him.

Conor had worried that the abrupt withdrawal of the entire amount would set warning bells ringing in the halls of British intelligence. After two weeks, it seemed clear that no inquiries were forthcoming. Either the disappearance of eight hundred thousand rupees was a matter of routine for the MI6 accountants or no one was paying attention to him at all. Neither prospect was comforting.

He had naively assumed eight lakhs would be more than enough for his purpose, but in fact he was four lakhs short. He needed to find the difference somewhere, and at this late hour the only plausible strategy for getting it was to hoover up whatever was owed to Ahmed Khalil from the swishy nightclubs and upmarket bars of Juhu.

With its long, narrow beach and luxury hotels, the northern suburb was ideally suited for his purpose. It was by far the most productive source on their route, not only because it was a wealthy enclave where appetites were satisfied without regard for expense, but also because it was the neighborhood where Ahmed Khalil had the greatest number of "clients" in the smallest geographical area. He and Raj could complete their collection activities in half the time it took to visit the same number of clubs in central Mumbai.

The weakest link in the strategy appeared to be the sudden intransigence of his jittery associate, whose devotion to routine was the one thing stronger than the fear of his bodyguard. It was an imbalance Conor could tolerate no longer. Raj's question still hung in the air between them, and before answering it, he gathered up his entire reserve of cold-blooded menace.

"Juhu is tonight because I am saying it is, Raj, and that is enough. Now, I don't know what the fuck they are burning in that alley, and I don't want to; but if you don't shut up and start walking, I will throw you down into it."

It was not so much the words as the icily quiet, deadly tone of his voice that achieved the desired effect. He set off at a brisk pace toward the end of the lane, and without further protest, Raj meekly followed.

"Aren't you going to put the bag on the floor?"

"Why?"

"Why?" Conor bit the inside of his cheek, fighting the irrational urge to laugh out loud. There was apparently no limit to the slapstick delight God gained from placing him in ludicrous situations. The flicker of hilarity died quickly. He leaned forward in the low, uncomfortable chair with his hands on his knees and dropped his head with a sigh of fatigue.

"Because that's what you always do, Raj. We come into the foyer, you sit there, and I sit here. You drop the bag by the table, and we wait. The old guy comes and takes it away. We drink the chai. I eat the chocolate biscuit, and you eat the plain one. We divide the payment and leave. We've been here a few dozen times, and that's how it always goes. I would have thought you'd be anxious to get some order back in tonight's agenda."

"Tonight, I will hold the bag."

Conor lifted his head at the sharpness of the reply. He looked at Raj, who stared back at him with a gleam of fearful suspicion in his eyes.

He was glad to have not forced the issue while they were standing on the beach in Juhu. It looked as though this might be the most difficult step in the whole reckless enterprise, and if it wasn't going to go smoothly, it was as well to have it sorted in the privacy of the drop house foyer.

As a means for assembling a large amount of cash in a short amount of time, his strategy had succeeded admirably. He needed four lakhs to add to the eight he was carrying, and by his estimate, the Juhu excursion had netted a little over six. The only step he had not accounted for was the delicate business of getting the duffel bag of money away from Khalil's loyal bagman, but since Raj appeared to have an inkling of his intention, there seemed no point in further delay. As he rose to his feet, the young man shrank down into his chair, clutching the bag even more tightly.

"Give me the bag, Raj," Conor began softly, in Hindi. "You don't have to be afraid. I'm not going to hurt you, but I need you to give me the bag. Just put it—"

"No, *saab*. I will not."

The young man's face was clenched with dread, but the reply came in a strong, definitive voice. Conor's hands had been raised in the placating gesture he might use to calm a horse about to rear in foaming panic. At the unexpected response, they fell to his sides in surprise.

"You ... what? Look, I don't have time for this. Put the bag down on the floor."

"If you take the money, then I must inform on you," Raj insisted again. "They will kill you, *saab*. They will kill you instantly."

"The thought has occurred to me," he said, drily. "It's no

concern of yours, though. I'm the one with the gun, remember? That's been my unique contribution to this show from the beginning. They'll know you had no choice."

"I will keep this bag. I do have a choice."

"No, you don't."

To reinforce the point, Conor lifted his jacket and indicated the holstered Walther, but Raj shook his head.

"If I give you this bag, they will kill you, *saab*," he repeated, stubbornly.

It was too much, really. An accumulation of sorrows, frustrations, and resentments boiled together inside Conor in a cocktail of emotions, and he felt unequal to the task of mastering them. The "talent for repose" finally deserted him. He snatched the gun from its holster, aimed it at the long, narrow face, and snarled in a voice he did not recognize.

"And I'll kill you if you don't, you goddamned moron."

Raj wrapped his arms around the duffel and closed his eyes, trembling violently. "I have a choice," he whispered.

Conor stared at him for several seconds. With a quizzical huff of disbelief, he lowered the Walther and addressed Raj in English. "Holy mother of Christ, are you joking me? Now you're brave? You've been jumping at the sight of your own bleedin' shadow from the day I met you, and now suddenly, you're a ... "

He stopped. Dropping his eyes, he looked bleakly at the gun in his hand. "I don't know what you are. I don't know what I am, either." He snapped the gun back into its holster and offered a wan smile as Raj's eyes fluttered open. "I'm sorry, Raja-ji," he said, reverting once more to Hindi. "I'm not going to shoot you."

"What *will* you do, *saab*?" Raj asked, clearly not convinced.

"Something you won't like much better, I'm afraid," Conor muttered.

He lunged forward and seized Raj by the back of his shirt, pulling him from the chair and dragging him onto the floor.

The weight pulled Conor down as well, and he soon discovered that although slightly built, his colleague was no ninety-pound weakling. Raj thrashed and kicked with a wild, wiry strength that caught him by surprise, and all the while, he continued to hug the duffel bag against his chest in an unshakeable grip.

For several minutes, Conor had a bigger fight on his hands than he'd anticipated, one he briefly worried he might even lose. He was not as strong as he'd been a month ago, and his breathing grew ragged as he struggled to contain the spinning dynamo beneath him. He finally succeeded in flipping Raj onto his stomach so that his face was pushed against the ceramic tile. He pinned him there by planting one knee on top of his back and one hand on the back of his neck.

"Bloody hell," he panted, sucking in air with urgent, wheezing gasps. He reached a hand down to pull at the bag that was still entangled in Raj's arms and now also trapped under his stomach. "You'll be the death of me long before Khalil's goondas, you silly plonker. Now, will you ever just let go that bag and—"

The door at the end of the foyer opened abruptly. He had been half-expecting that complication, and as the familiar figure appeared with the usual tray of snacks, he again pulled out the semiautomatic and trained it on the elderly man, motioning him to close the door.

"Sure, I didn't think we had enough going on yet. Come on out here, baba-ji." He waved the gun at the chair Raj had involuntarily vacated. "Sit down for a minute, and we'll be right with you."

The man raised one eyebrow in mild interest. He closed the door, moved into the foyer with methodical dignity, and placed the tray on the table. Looking at them both without a hint of fear, he gave a disdainful sniff and sat down. Conor pressed his hand more firmly against the back of Raj's neck and bent down to whisper in his ear.

"If I let you up, will you let go the bag so we can get this over with, now?"

"No, *saab*," Raj whispered.

"Well, that's honest, anyway." He straightened and rubbed Raj's head gently. "I'm sorry, *chotta bhai*. I don't know what else to do. I wish I could be smarter, for both of us."

He moved Raj's head to one side, and with a prayer that he had sufficiently practiced the technique when it was taught to him, delivered a hard blow to the slender, exposed neck with the butt of the gun. Immediately, the body beneath him went limp as Raj collapsed into unconsciousness.

Moving quickly, Conor rolled him onto his back and unwrapped his arms from the duffel bag. He transferred the four lakhs to his knapsack and without a glance tossed the bag with its remaining money over onto the floor next to the old man. Turning his attention back to Raj, he made sure he was breathing easily and pulled a cushion from the foyer's second chair to prop under his head.

Sitting back on his heels, he regarded the slack, sleeping face with its sparse collection of baby-soft whiskers. It looked even younger now. He watched for another minute, reluctant to move or take his eyes away, reflecting on the surprising, desperate display of courage he had witnessed. When a small sniff reached his ears he remembered the third person in the room and lifted his head to look at him.

"Are you alone in the house tonight, ji?" he asked, quietly. The older man's head moved sideways in a single twitch of affirmation. Conor acknowledged this with his own head wag and indicated Raj.

"I think he'll only be out for ten minutes or so. Will you stay with him?"

The head moved a second time, and the man's face remained unreadable. Conor rested a hand on Raj's shoulder. "Here is the best kept secret in Mumbai. The mafia boy with a noble heart. He was more concerned about what they would do to me than what I might do to him. He deserves a better life than this."

"Fine words, my boy, but what are the actions?"

Startled by the sound of the dry, gravelly voice addressing him in English, he turned again to the older man, who was on his feet, fastidiously smoothing the wrinkles from his immaculate white kurta. Despite the comment, his face contained no trace of judgment or disapproval, but there was a note of challenge in his voice as he gazed at Conor.

"We can run fast and very far away," he continued in the same dispassionate tone. "But we cannot escape our actions."

Conor stiffly rose to his feet with a sad smile. Picking up his knapsack, he gave a final nod to the brown, wrinkled face before turning away. "I know we can't escape them, ji, and thank God for that. If we could, think what monsters we would all be."

He stepped out into the early morning darkness and stopped on the doorstep, absorbing the old man's warning and feeling the words take the shape of prophecy as they sank in to his soul. He leaned back against the closed door and felt the momentum of the past few hours floundering in a sea of lightheaded weariness. Methodically, he rubbed his fingers against his eyelids until the dizziness receded, and then, still feeling breathless, Conor began moving forward again.

There was a damp, soot-smelling thickness in the air, a miasma made visible in the halos of mud-yellow haze surrounding the streetlights along the road. The temperature was mild, but he felt chilled to the bone. He also noted the shaky, internal trembling that had begun after bringing the handle of his gun down onto Raj's neck was not going away.

Looking down the road, he saw the taxi that had ferried them to Goregaon East still parked where he'd instructed the driver to wait. It looked empty, but when he came up beside it, he saw the driver and his "assistant" were indeed still inside but curled up in the back seat, fast asleep. He was not especially gentle in rousing them. The two boys—each undoubtedly too young to have a driver's license—sprang awake with beaming smiles of reassurance.

"*Jaldi chalo.*"

He accompanied the command with another finger-snapping, hand-cracking performance, and the boys responded immediately. The shorter of the two scrambled into the driver's seat, and although his eyes barely crested the top of the steering wheel he applied himself fearlessly to the urgent request to "go, quickly."

As the car roared and bounced its way back toward central Mumbai, Conor pulled out his phone and punched in the number he'd known all night he would eventually have to dial. It took five rings before the call was answered. After a few seconds of rustling movement, a voice responded in a sleepy voice tinged with fear. With an exhalation of remorse, he plunged ahead.

"Meera, is that you? Yes, it's Con. No, no, there's nothing wrong. Listen, I'm sorry to be calling you so late."

"It is not 'so late' that you are calling, Con," Bishan's wife responded. Her voice now contained a note of relieved amusement. "It is 'so early.' What manner of nonsense are you getting up to, before sunrise itself?"

"It's a little too complicated to explain right now, but I'm afraid I need to ask a favor of Bishan Singh. Can I—"

Before he could finish the request Bishan was already on the line, filled with concern and firing questions. Conor came quickly to the point.

"Bishan, I need a ride. And I need a driver who won't tell anyone later where he took me. Can you help me?"

"Why do you ask this question?" Bishan scolded. "I am coming. Where are you?"

"I'm not there yet, but I'm headed to the Marilyn Monroe

Bar. Can you wait for me at the end of the lane? I'll meet you there in about an hour."

"The Marilyn Monroe Bar, you say?"

He heard Bishan's tongue pull loudly against the back of his front teeth.

"Yes, the Monroe Bar," he replied in a neutral voice.

"The Marilyn Monroe Bar in Kamathipura?"

"That's the one."

"Okay, Okay, in one hour," Bishan said with forced vigor.

"Look, Bishan, I know what you're probably thinking, and it's—"

"No need, no need, my friend." Obviously mortified, the Sikh's deep voice rose to a higher pitch. "I am coming in one hour, absolutely. No problems. I will be seeing you soon. Bye for now."

Conor snapped the phone shut and threw it onto the seat next to him with a groan.

"Jaysus, will this night never end?"

19

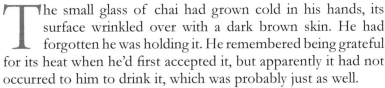

The small glass of chai had grown cold in his hands, its surface wrinkled over with a dark brown skin. He had forgotten he was holding it. He remembered being grateful for its heat when he'd first accepted it, but apparently it had not occurred to him to drink it, which was probably just as well.

He had been neglecting more than the tea. Behind his desk, Rohit Mehta was rocking back in his chair and regarding him with droll interest, while next to him one of the floor managers meticulously counted the stacks of rupees piled in front of them. Conor realized he had been sitting in a semiconscious stupor. He had an imperfect recollection of arriving at the Monroe and making his way to the back office. He also realized that at some point during this indefinite period, he had developed a blistering fever.

The sight of the coagulating tea set off an alarming turmoil in his stomach. He quickly put the glass on the desk and moved it to one side, out of his line of sight. By the time he had conquered the urge to be sick, a cold sweat had puddled in the area around his lower back.

"Are you feeling quite well, *yaar*?" Mehta inquired, solicitously. "You are looking somewhat gray about the face, I am thinking."

"I'm all right," Conor replied, hoping to convince himself if no one else. "Is he almost done?"

Rohit Mehta directed a look of mild inquiry at the floor

manager, who looked up from his labors with obsequious reassurance.

"Yes, Mehta-bhai. It is nine lakhs, thirty-three thousand till now, and these many piles still to count."

When he at last placed the final note on the last pile of rupees, the floor manager gave a sigh of satisfaction, and Conor climbed wearily to his feet.

"Where's Radha?"

Rohit Mehta looked surprised. "She is just there, next room over, sleeping. You passed by her coming in, yes? You did not see?"

He didn't remember seeing, but he found her on a couch in the sitting area outside Mehta's office and thought he hardly could have missed her. It took some time to wake her, and a little more time before she was able to respond to him with any sort of lucidity.

"Is it three hours, already?" she asked, sleepily.

"It's a bit more than that." He smiled down at her. "Are you ready to go?"

Radha shot upright as though released by a spring and stared at him, instantly wide-awake.

"I am going with you, *bhaiyya*? You are taking me?"

The bright, anxious hope in her eyes was almost more than he could stand. He'd never given the matter a moment of serious thought, and it was an odd time to start, but here now, in a dance bar in the heart of India's reddest red-light district, with fever tingling along his nerve endings, he looked at the young face of an incipient heroin addict ... and thought about fatherhood.

"Yes, you're coming with me," he said. "If you want to, that is."

"You have paid for it? It is for *sar dhakna*?"

"No. It bloody well is not for *sar dhakna*." Conor's exclamation echoed in the empty room, making her jump in startled fear.

"Sorry. I didn't mean to yell." He sat down next to her on

the couch. "Listen to me now, Radha, because it's important for you to understand this. I'm not here to take you away so that I can ... ehm, that is ... you're still very young. I know you're not a child, exactly. But ... well, to me you are. So we could never, I mean—ah, for the love of God, tell me you understand what I'm saying to you here."

Radha was regarding him with a look of patient understanding. "Yes, I understand, Con-ji. I am like sister for you. I know this about you since long time. I was not thinking you would take my virginity or make me wife to you."

"Oh." Conor was momentarily stumped for further comment.

"But what I am asking is did you pay Rohit Mehta for *sar dhakna*? It is the only way for me to leave."

"Let's just say we reached an understanding."

"There is no understanding with Rohit Mehta without rupees." She leaned forward, eyes gleaming with curiosity. "How much did you pay for me, *bhaiyya*?"

"Radha," Conor pleaded, getting slowly to his feet again. "Could we please talk about this another time?"

"Yes, except for this question," she insisted. "How much did you pay for me?"

Conor rubbed a hand over his eyes in exasperation. "Twelve lakhs."

"Twelve lakhs?!"

He thought her squeal somewhat reminiscent of his own when he'd first heard the figure.

"Did you not think the price was too high?" Radha asked in amazement.

"I thought it was surprising," he admitted, "but I didn't think it was either too low or too high. He could have said anything, and he would have been wrong. You are not a sari or a piece of jewelry, Radha. You're a young lady, and you are without price. Our first rule, if you are going to come with me, is that you will never speak to me or anyone else as though you thought you had been purchased. Is that agreed?"

"It is agreed."

He smiled at the look of dignity on her face and held out his hand. "Then, what are we waiting for? *Chalo*."

They stepped out into the predawn darkness, and when they emerged at the end of the lane, Conor thought the look on Bishan's face was worth twelve lakhs on its own. If he had been feeling better, he might have appreciated the moment's comic potential: the shameless, thirty-two year-old *gora* trotting along, leading a thirteen-year-old bar girl by the hand. He settled Radha into the back seat of the powder-blue Ambassador and then rested his elbows against the hood of the car next to Bishan.

"I know what this looks like, *yaar*," he said to his friend, "but it's not what it looks like."

"Please, Con, there is no need," Bishan began before Conor interrupted him with an angry obscenity in Hindi.

"Stop blushing at me like my bleedin' grandma," he snapped. "She's thirteen years old, for Christ's sake. Do you think that little of me? Think I've come to India to whore around, de-flowering children? Is that what you think?"

Bishan's eyes immediately filled with tears of wounded remorse. "I am sorry, my friend. It is very early morning, and I am confused. I was not thinking of anything, but only trying to understand why you are here in Kamathipura at five a.m., and why there is a young girl falling asleep in the back of my car. I meant no offense. Forgive me."

Conor turned and put his back against the car. He shook his head with a grimace of self-disgust. "No, forgive me. You're one of the kindest men I've ever met, Bishan Singh. You've come out to this shite neighborhood at the crack of dawn to help me and what do you get in return? I'm sorry, Bishan. I'm really, really sorry."

Sliding down the side of the car until he was almost sitting in the dirt, Conor put his face in his hands. He thought it felt rather comfortable. He was shivering again, and it seemed a bit warmer here, close to the ground. He thought it might be nice to sit like this for a while, maybe catch a few winks.

He felt the powerful arms of his friend lifting him up, steadying him for a moment, and then gently guiding him into the passenger seat of the car. Once the door was shut, he collapsed against it, murmuring thanks in an assortment of languages. Bishan climbed into the driver's seat and regarded him with a look of profound worry.

"You are very ill. There is a hospital close by. I will bring you."

"No," Conor protested, struggling into a sitting position. "It's just a fever, and it'll be gone soon. It comes and goes like that."

"A fever that is coming and going is not a good thing, Con."

"Yes, right. I know. I'll get it checked, but not now. We need to go to the Jyoti, please, Bishan. After that we need to go to Mahim."

By the time they reached the apartment complex, he had recovered enough to insist that Bishan remain with Radha while he retrieved the packed luggage he'd left there earlier. After the previous evening's revelations, and even before hatching the plan to defraud Ahmed Khalil, he had known it would be madness to remain in the flat. Too many people knew where he'd been living. It would be the first place they'd come looking for him.

After retrieving his bags, he returned to the Ambassador bathed in sweat and trembling with exhaustion. Bishan took the bags from him with a small sigh.

"You are finished here?" he asked, quietly. Conor nodded.

"Yeah, finished."

When they rolled to a stop under the covered parking lot of Kavita's building in Mahim, Radha was still sleeping in the back seat. Conor pulled the door open and crouched next to her, but then hesitated.

"I hate to wake her up," he said, looking up at Bishan. "I can carry her upstairs if you get the bags."

At this, Bishan's attitude of reluctant compliance evaporated. Taking Conor by the elbow he pulled him up with a ferocious hiss. "*Bas*! Enough! Idiot. You are shivering head to toe and barely standing on two feet. If you carry your own self upstairs, this will be an astonishing thing. I will bring the child, and I will return for all the baggages. If by this time you have not yet reached, I will carry you as well."

Conor could not help laughing at his friend's indignant rant, but the deep rumble it produced in his chest quickly sobered him. "*Accha*. I get the message. You're probably right."

It belatedly occurred to him that it would have been courteous to phone ahead before turning up so early in the morning, but he reasoned that although their timing might be unexpected, his appearance with Radha would not come as a complete surprise. Unable to think of a way to help the young girl, he had sought Kavita's advice, and her response had been characteristically succinct and generous.

"Bring her to me."

Coming from anyone else it might have sounded like a casual suggestion, but from her, it had the force of a gentle command. He'd been grateful for its unambiguous clarity. It was a directive he could embrace without confusion, an assignment that made sense. As a result of what he'd recently learned, it made even more sense now. Kavita apparently had some experience with the kind of intervention that was going to be needed.

He was able to make it up the stairs under his own steam, but only just. As they reached the third floor landing, he stopped to catch his breath and noted that Kavita's uncanny internal radar had provided an early warning of his arrival after all. The door was once again ajar, and the aroma of fried eggs wafting into the hallway signaled she was expecting him.

The collapse of Conor's mythic appetite had been a source of dismay in the Kotwal household over the past few weeks. Kavita's daughter, Parvati, had tried coaxing it back to life with a variety of recipes, but it was only when she surprised him one day with a traditional Irish breakfast—complete with grilled tomato and brown bread—that her efforts met with any success. It had become one of the few meals he could be persuaded to eat, so it was presented to him regularly.

Leaning against the stairway wall, he looked at Radha, still sleeping in Bishan's arms, and felt the tension melting from his tight, stiffened muscles. He was tired—dangerously exhausted, in fact—and there seemed little promise of rest or safety ahead of him. He sensed the approach of calamity as surely as he could sense the trickle of perspiration sliding down his face; and topping everything else was the unavoidable fact that he was going to need a doctor and some serious drugs to tackle whatever had fastened onto his lungs.

He pushed it all to the back of his mind, because for the moment he was savoring a quiet sense of victory, and because for the moment he knew he was safe. Kavita Kotwal was safety itself. Rest and refuge at the edge of chaos.

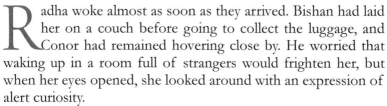

20

Radha woke almost as soon as they arrived. Bishan had laid her on a couch before going to collect the luggage, and Conor had remained hovering close by. He worried that waking up in a room full of strangers would frighten her, but when her eyes opened, she looked around with an expression of alert curiosity.

"You belong to this place, Con? These are your families?"

"In a manner of speaking," he said, marveling at her self-possession. "They are my very good friends, and we're going to stay with them for a bit. We could both do with some rest and recuperation."

"What does it mean, 'recuperation?'" she asked, raising herself from the couch.

"Well ... " he hesitated. He knew what the word meant for him, and that it would mean something rather different for her, but it wasn't the time to discuss it. In fact, confronting Radha with the news that her heroin supply had dried up was a task he hoped to avoid altogether. He was counting on Kavita to venture into that hornet's nest and was happy to plead cowardice as an exemption.

"It's a fancy word that means our friends are going to look after us," he said. "Which begins with breakfast, and since you are awake and alert—ah, no, don't be pulling the long face, now. It's not optional. Most important meal of the day."

They joined the family and Bishan, who looked happier now with a mug of chai and a plate of hot rotis in front of him. Conor introduced Radha and seated her among Parvati's three daughters. The four girls exchanged greetings and stared at each other with shy fascination.

He slipped into the chair next to Bishan, and as Kavita began circling the table serving the eggs, she regarded Conor with a look that made him squirm. He had been doing his best to hide his weariness, but her penetrating gaze made the futility of that effort obvious. When she tried to slip a second egg onto his plate, he stopped her hand with a gentle squeeze.

"Let's not be overly optimistic. I'm trying to set an example, but I can probably manage just the one."

"This is not managing well enough, *beta*."

Kavita turned his face toward her. The faraway look in her eyes so reminded him of his mother's that his throat ached with the pressure of suppressed grief.

"You have had some fever today also," she said. It was not a question.

"Coming and going," Bishan grumbled in disapproval.

Conor confirmed the observation with a small grin. "Coming and going, just like Bishan Singh's patience. I'll likely get the fever back sooner than his good opinion of me."

"Idiot. God forbid it." Bishan gave his shoulder an affectionate thump and pulled at his beard in embarrassment.

Kavita touched Conor's cheek, and before he could protest, she had smoothly transferred another egg onto his plate. "Set a finer example, even. Eat the two eggs."

He watched Radha closely during the meal, and after Bishan departed, and the table began clearing, he at last saw the change he had been dreading since they'd left Kamathipura. Beneath lowered lids, her eyes began darting around the room, miserably avoiding his gaze as her fingers clutched nervously at a small cloth purse she'd placed on her lap.

Conor silently swore at himself. Why had it not occurred to him that she would bring drugs with her? Didn't he always check for cigarettes before he went anywhere? Even now, when he was trying to quit, the reflexive slap against his pockets was a habit as tenacious as the craving itself, a constant reminder of the persistence of addiction. How could he have imagined she would blithely come away without knowing her next fix was secure? And even the one after that? As a crushing fatigue descended over him, he wondered exactly how much heroin she might be carrying in her little cloth purse.

A little over an hour later, Conor's eyes flew open and his head jerked up from his arms, which had been resting on top of the now-deserted dining room table. A deep, shuddering cough had shocked him awake. It was alarmingly loud and even more alarmingly painful. As he reached groggily across the table for the water pitcher, several more followed. He smothered the noise with a table napkin and snatched his arm back to wrap it around his chest.

"Shit, that hurts." He squeezed his eyes shut.

The dose of medicine taken the previous evening had served him well for almost twelve hours, but its effect had finally evaporated. As he braced against a third wave tearing up through his throat, Kavita materialized at his side. She brought one of the ubiquitous brown bottles down on the table with a decisive thump.

"Next patient," she said.

Conor jumped at her sudden appearance and dropped his head back onto his arm. "Do you buy those bottles by the case? Everyone in Mumbai seems to have one."

"Yes. I do." Her head wiggled a cheerful assent. "And the recipe I mix by the gallon."

"Well, give us a shot of it, woman," he croaked. "I'm after choking to death here."

"Drink water first. Medicine after." She poured out a glass of water and set it in front of him.

"Where's Radha?"

"Radha is sleeping." Kavita nodded at the bottle on the table. "She will sleep for some hours now, but she will feel very unwell later. She is in my room."

"That little cloth purse, I should have noticed it earlier. I'm sorry, *ji.*"

"Nonsense," she chided. "It will be well. She cannot bear to be parted from this small bag, but she will be. By and by, she will be free from all of it."

"I admire your confidence. You make it sound simple." Conor sat up with a sigh that started him coughing again.

"Not simple though." She rested a hand on his back. "For a time, she may hate you for this, *beta*. You must prepare. Because you love her, it will be hard for you."

Lifting the water glass, he discovered he needed two hands to hold it steady. He drank and sat back, breathing delicately and realizing that for the moment, there was little more he could do for Radha. While it felt good to have executed an operation that had actually gone according to plan, he had again reached the end of a road without knowing where the next began.

Having at least partially blown the cover of a sketchy American operation and now having stolen from one of the most dangerous dons in Mumbai, there were not many roads from which to choose. Crying uncle and heading for home was still the most obvious, but even now he wasn't ready to pull the emergency brake.

The prospect of eventual failure was ever more likely, and his zeal for the original objective of bringing a nebulous, money-laundering mastermind to justice was even weaker than when he'd started, but what remained was an idée fixe he could not relinquish. He had signed on to this misadventure to find his brother and try to save him, although whom or what he was trying to save him from was even less clear than when he'd started.

If Curtis Sedgwick was to be believed, the next move was out of his hands, and his impatience at the forced immobility was aggravated by a jittering anxiety, signaling in his brain like a distress code. Its message continued to elude him, and if he couldn't decipher it, he at least needed to do something to keep it from driving him mad. He looked at Kavita with an inquisitive frown.

"Are you working in the *zopadpatti* today, ji? Maybe I could come along and—what's so funny?"

Kavita's low, musical chuckle was like a tonic to his soul. "You are a good man, Conor. Very kind and loving, but many times you are too ridiculous. No *zopadpatti* today. Today, you sleep. Come now."

She provided him a pair of light cotton pajamas and ordered him to shower off the lingering fumes of the Kamathipura streets. When he was finished, she pointed him to the bedroom at the end of the hall that her granddaughter Surabhi had vacated. He stood in its doorway, reluctant to assume occupancy. A large window with lacy, flower-print curtains filled the wall opposite the door. Near the window, a rocking chair piled with stuffed animals sat on one side of the bed. On the other, a school desk and small chair had been placed in the corner, below a bulletin board plastered with the faces of bare-chested movie stars.

Holding his clothes—and his gun—in his hands, he looked blearily around the room and finally walked in and slipped the Walther under the bed's pink, fringed pillow. Kavita returned and insisted on tucking him in, pulling the cool sheets into place while scolding his peevish resistance. As his mother had often complained, Conor was intransigent in illness. He loathed being pampered and fussed over, but he had never won any battles with Brigid McBride, and he didn't win this one either.

His eyelids were already drooping when Kavita presented a dose of her paregoric potion. He squinted at the contents of the small glass with its iridescent sheen of mustard oil floating on top.

"I don't think I need it after all. I'm nearly asleep as it is."

The dangerous flash in Kavita's eyes warned him that like Bishan, her tenderhearted patience was not inexhaustible. He swallowed the shot without further protest. The warm glow began spreading through his chest, reminding him of the previous evening's events and of a request he had not yet fulfilled.

"I forgot to tell you earlier," he said sleepily. "Curtis Sedgwick sends his love. He wants you to know he's doing all right."

"Ah, this is good." Kavita smiled. "I was worried for him. Curtis has not come to see me in many months. I knew he was your friend. Parvati was telling me he came to collect you that first evening but asked that we not speak of him with you."

"I'm not sure 'friend' is exactly … well, anyway, he's fine." Conor regarded her thoughtfully, his esteem growing even stronger as he considered what it must have taken to tame Sedgwick's demons and drag him from the brink of oblivion. "He must have been quite a challenge." His eyes irresistibly dropped shut again. "Sedgwick is hard to manage under the best of circumstances."

"Yes, a challenge. He was very sick and very angry for some long time. And very strong." Kavita gave a soft laugh. "Too strong for a tiny one such as me but not too strong for Tom. Always Curtis was sneaking and peeking, looking for escape, but Tom-ji would not allow. He was more stubborn even, no matter how many bumps and bruises. I think Curtis would not be so fine now, if not for him."

Tom-ji.

Of course. Sedgwick knew Thomas. Kavita knew Sedgwick. Kavita must know Thomas. It was a flawed syllogism but a perfectly reasonable one in his mind. If he'd been able to construct it sooner, he and his brother might have been home by now.

Tom-ji.

Conor had surrendered to exhaustion. He had descended too far into twilight to pull himself back, but an ironic smile played over his face as he repeated the name to himself like a lullaby.

"He always hated being called Tom," he mumbled as sleep reached out, greedily pulling him under its black veil of silence. "Neither of us ever liked nicknames."

"Who the hell are you?"

The question rustled over Conor's vocal cords in a hollow scrape, which startled him almost as much as the large, square face filling his field of vision. Seeing the flower-print curtains rippling against the open window, he knew he was still in Surabhi's bedroom, but the fuzzy gray light was too indistinct to help him judge the time of day. It could be early dawn or approaching dusk. In either case, it seemed to suggest he had been asleep—or maybe more accurately, unconscious—for quite some time.

He had opened his eyes to discover the face looming over him in extreme close-up, close enough to distinguish the individual pores on a very broad, mahogany forehead. Above the forehead was a shock of thick, carefully coiffed black hair. Below it, a pair of chocolate-brown eyes stared at him, their air of detachment accentuated by a surgical mask obscuring the bottom half of the face. The sea-green mask gave the voice behind it a muffled, otherworldly quality.

"Doctor Francis deSa. Breach Candy Hospital."

Like the eyes, the voice was unemotional, with the casual, irreverent tone of a young man, and an accent that sounded more British than Indian.

Conor blinked several times, trying to bring his surroundings into focus. He felt groggy and stupid, as though just waking up from a weekend bender. He cleared his throat before venturing another question.

"You're Kavita's doctor, I suppose?"

At this the eyes narrowed, signaling that the invisible mouth of Dr. deSa had twitched in affection.

"Yes, I am the personal physician of *Shrimati-ji.*"

The doctor had rolled him onto his left side and was running a stethoscope over his back. Beyond his shoulder, Conor could see Kavita moving back and forth in the rocking chair.

"What time is it?" he asked her.

"It is just coming on to five o'clock in the evening," she said, nodding peaceably at him.

"So, I've been asleep for nearly eight hours?"

"*Haan ji,* this is so; eight hours plus three days."

"You're joking me."

"Not joking, *beta.* You reached on Monday morning. It is now Thursday afternoon, so four days total. Not always sleeping, but you were having high fever, and I think you are not remembering being awake."

"I guess not." He gave a weak, nervous laugh. "Christ, four days. Stop the lights."

Dr. Francis deSa stood upright. He removed the stethoscope and then the mask, revealing a rigid jaw and a haughty self-confidence. He turned abruptly from Conor to face Kavita. "He is stable. I believe we were correct to begin treatment immediately, but the test results should be ready in two weeks, and then we will have more useful data."

Conor hiked himself onto one elbow and threw a hard stare

at the stiffly averted profile. "Treatment for what? What test results? I don't remember any tests."

"That is not surprising." Dr. deSa glanced back at him. "You were delirious when I took the samples. We are testing for tuberculosis. On average, the cultures take two weeks to develop."

"Tuberculosis." The syllables rolled from Conor's tongue like the inflections of an occult chant. "You think I have TB?"

"I'm almost certain you do," Dr. deSa said, with smooth confidence. "Possibly complicated by pneumonia, given the high-grade fever onset."

"Gently, Francis," Kavita said. "It is a matter of routine for you, but it is a troubling shock for him."

"It's all right, Kavita," Conor said, his voice flat. "It's actually not that big of a shock."

He felt strangely composed. It was almost a relief to say the word out loud. The suggestion of it had floated through his mind more than once during the past few weeks, but until now he'd not had the nerve to believe he was dealing with something so dangerous.

The next, most obvious question was one he didn't intend to ask. He thought he knew the answer and was content to leave it unspoken to avoid causing pain to someone who didn't deserve it. Unfortunately, the self-important family physician was not finished displaying his intellect.

"It is most likely you were infected by Kavita. The epidemiology makes sense. I saw her immediately after her flight from London, and her disease was highly active at that time, quite infectious. You were in close proximity for the duration of the flight, and I understand that after the flight—"

"Yeah, okay," Conor said, curtly. "We get the picture, Francis. So, what do I do now?"

A flush of annoyance colored Dr. deSa's smooth, self-assured face. "Once the test results are finalized, we may need to correct the therapy. Until then, continue bed rest and reduced activity. Continue the course of antibiotics I have prescribed and continue the palliative treatments *Shrimati-ji* prepares for you."

With these instructions, the house call ended. As Kavita steered Dr. deSa from the room, Conor dropped back onto his side and closed his eyes, still feeling oddly calm. Even without a definitive diagnosis, he was grateful for the unambiguous, if insensitive, analysis of the young doctor and for their clarifying effects. The sharpness of a knife existed only in theory until a finger pressed against it.

He dozed off again. The next time he woke, he was still on his side facing the window, and a far more compassionate pair of brown eyes met his gaze.

"Please God, I haven't been sleeping for another three days?" He smiled at Kavita.

"One hour only."

She had pulled the rocking chair closer to the bed, and her kind, wise face was creased with mournful regret. He lowered his brow in a half-serious scowl.

"Don't be starting up with that, now. You'll destroy me entirely with a look like that. Anyway, it'll be all right, you know. Something you maybe don't know about the Irish is we don't go easily where we don't want to—we're a mulish, balky lot, right enough. If my mother were here, she'd tell you I'm even balkier than most."

"She has been here." Kavita's head toggled a rhythmic reinforcement of this unexpected announcement. "Many times you were talking with her these three days during your fever. I heard this myself."

Conor smiled. "It wouldn't surprise me. What did we talk about?"

Kavita shook her head. "I could not understand. You spoke the language of your region. Strange sounds, but beautiful."

"I seem to be doing that a lot lately. So, how could you tell who I was talking to?"

Kavita lifted her chin and aimed it at a point somewhere behind him. "He knew. He sat and listened and understood each word."

Conor had not realized anyone else was in the room. With a wave of premonition tickling his scalp, he pushed up to a sitting position and turned to face a pair of squinting, ocean-blue eyes. He had forgotten how much they looked like his father's, and until that instant, he had not realized how much he'd missed them.

"Heard you were wanting to see me," his brother said.

Conor absorbed the facetious tone and the gruff, thick country accent like a man taking in the first rays of sunshine after a long confinement. It was almost too bright to look at, but the warmth was delicious. He felt an affectionate, loopy expression stealing over his face but returned volley with the sarcasm he knew was expected.

"Wanting you, Thomas? Divil a bit. What put that into your head, at all?"

21

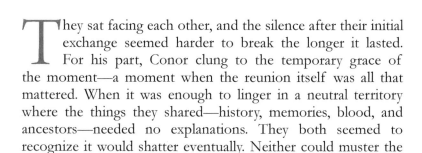

They sat facing each other, and the silence after their initial exchange seemed harder to break the longer it lasted. For his part, Conor clung to the temporary grace of the moment—a moment when the reunion itself was all that mattered. When it was enough to linger in a neutral territory where the things they shared—history, memories, blood, and ancestors—needed no explanations. They both seemed to recognize it would shatter eventually. Neither could muster the courage to produce the first crack.

Predictably, it was Kavita who ended the suspense. She rose from the rocking chair, and as she circled Conor's bed, Thomas's eyes followed her with resigned understanding. She came to a stop next to him and placed a hand on his shoulder.

"One must make a start. You are the eldest."

"Right." His brother's fingers brushed over hers before falling away. "I'm just thinking maybe he needs to rest a bit more. I can come back in the morning."

Conor started up with an alarmed yelp, but before he could form a coherent protest, he was interrupted by Kavita's melodious laugh.

"In this way you will escape? So easily? He has been resting. Soon, he will need to rest again, but for now it is not what he needs. The voice of his brother—this is what he needs."

Without another word, she glided across and out of the room, pulling the door shut behind her. They both watched her leave and stared at each other again until Conor broke the silence.

"You've been here before."

Thomas nodded. "I lived here for a few weeks, mostly right here in this room."

"Helping Sedgwick through withdrawal," Conor said.

"Yeah." His brother surveyed the bedroom with a perfunctory glance. "We'd nearly destroyed the feckin' place by the time we were done. It's the first time I've seen it since then. I hadn't seen Kavita in a while, either. You've been spending a lot of time with her, I gather."

"I met her on the plane from London. Was that an accident, or did she already know who I was?"

He held his breath, not sure he could bear having the question answered, since it meant confronting the possibility that even Kavita Kotwal had been secretly yanking his chain from the beginning. Thomas shook his head.

"Not until I showed up Monday night. I know it seems hard to believe. Bizarre coincidence or fate, whatever you want to call it. Anything's possible where Kavita's concerned." He moved his head in exaggerated imitation of the South Asian head toggle. "You know how she is."

"I do, indeed." Conor released his breath and added hesitantly, "Does she remind you at all of Ma?"

"What do you think? Christ, sometimes I almost believe she is Ma." His brother's smile died abruptly, and he dropped his eyes to stare at the folded hands in his lap. "How is she?"

So, beginning with sorrow, Conor thought. He felt the emotion grip him with a strength he had not permitted in many weeks, wondering if his brother was about to feel the peculiarly nauseating force of it for the first time and thinking it was no more than he deserved. "Thomas, I don't know what anybody has been giving you for news about home. So, I don't know whether you've heard—"

"Of course I've heard, for fuck's sake." Thomas sucked in his breath and released it with a shudder. "Sorry. I have heard. I know about it. I was just wondering—"

"How she's doing now?" Conor fired back acerbically. "I wonder that, too. I haven't seen her myself for a good while. She wasn't very well the last time I did."

Thomas nodded but made no further response. Conor looked at his bowed, motionless head, beginning to register how much the man had changed—or more specifically, aged—in six years.

The brother he remembered was a powerful giant of a man, three or four inches taller than his own six feet. He was broad-shouldered, ramrod straight, and as solidly built as the boulders on a Slieve Mish mountaintop. The man before him now seemed like a clever but not quite believable imitation.

The massive, thickly calloused farmer's hands were the same, but there was something new about the way they rested awkwardly in his lap. Something tentative and helpless. There was likewise something unfamiliar about his posture, a slumped, stooping flatness that made him seem smaller than Conor remembered. His hair was combed flat against his skull in the same closely cropped style, but its color was now more silver streaked with black rather than the reverse, and its neatness contrasted with a patchy gray beard that ranged raggedly over his face and down his neck.

The only thing that seemed unchanged was his face. It had always been lined and weather-beaten, and those remarkable eyes—colored like the horizon where sea meets sky on a cloudy day—had always held a hint of jaded resignation. The difference now was just a matter of degree, and it tugged at something inside Conor.

"Anyway," he said, attempting to lighten the mood, "no matter how she was feeling, if she could see what you look like, she'd be having a run at you with the razor."

Thomas grunted a quiet laugh, but when he raised his head to

Conor, his face was solemn. "And if she could see what you look like, she'd be cutting my throat with it."

Conor dismissed the statement with a sniff, but gave himself a surreptitious self-examination. He didn't look as bad as that, did he?

"And what about the farm, then?" Thomas asked. "The cows and all?"

"All right, I suppose," he replied absently. "I haven't seen them in a while either, you know."

He was looking at several large, fading bruises along his upper arm and wondering what the hell had happened there before remembering Raj had landed a few vigorous kicks in that region ... how many nights ago? He shook his head and gave his brother a sly glance.

"We had to give up on your sheep, though, Thomas. It was too hard keeping track of them."

He thought it a gentle enough jab to open a dicey subject but saw the remark had stung more deeply than he'd intended and again felt his face redden with irritable impatience. What did the fecker expect, after all? That they would go on nattering about the cows, their silage, and what the weather had been doing on the Dingle peninsula? What right did he have to sit looking so wounded and put upon, when he was responsible for everything that had brought them to this point? Now that he'd finally turned up, he could bloody well face it.

Thomas had apparently reached the same conclusion. The small school chair creaked as he shifted and sat up straighter. Placing the palms of his large hands flat against his knees, he nodded an invitation at Conor.

"Go on and tell me about it now."

"Tell you about what?" Conor demanded snappishly.

"About what happened after I left," Thomas replied. "About how you've been getting on for the past six years and about how you managed to get roped into playing Paddy the Secret Agent for a pack of British eejits."

Conor gave him a narrow look of suspicion. "Have Curtis Sedgwick and his crowd really not briefed you on all that? Have they not told you the whole story by now?"

"Sure, they're always telling stories, Conor." His brother's tone was flat. "They're good at that. I'd like to get the tale from your side of it."

"Well, I'd like to hear a new one altogether. Why can't we start with yours?"

"We'll get around to that."

"When?"

"When I say so."

He briefly considered fighting about it. For as long as he could remember—at least since their father had died—this was the pattern in their relationship. Thomas made the rules, and because he presented them with such self-assurance and absolute authority, Conor had never found sufficient cause to question or disobey.

Things had changed since then, however. Now, he had both cause and opportunity, supported by a few new talents his brother would no doubt find surprising. He had his own brand of authority, and if he chose to reveal it, a new capacity for ruthlessness in drawing on it.

He didn't reveal it, though. Thomas didn't yet know how much his little brother had changed, and Conor wanted to keep it that way for as long as he could. He wanted to lie in the long grass and play the naïve younger sibling. It wouldn't be difficult; he'd grown accustomed to pretending, and that was part of the problem. He had been an artist of a different sort once, but now it seemed his only virtuosity was in the art of deception.

He pulled a face at Thomas. "Have it your way. As if that was a change."

In the process of considering how to begin and how much to include, Conor discovered something even more surprising. He had been telling himself that this odyssey was about rescue and redemption, that he was bound by familial duty to an age-old command to seek and retrieve the prodigal son. It was noble and selfless ... and it wasn't true.

The truth was that until Frank had shown up the previous September, he had no idea where his brother was, no means of finding out, and no expectation of ever seeing him again. The truth was that he had started down this road—had learned to shoot, lie, steal, and smother his humanity under layers of "tradecraft"—because it had been the only route offered for getting something he only now realized that he craved: freedom from an internalized bitterness he had never fully acknowledged or expressed.

Someone—someone he loved and trusted—had taken something irreplaceable from him. He had carried the burden of that betrayal within his heart for years and had traveled a long way for the chance to lay both his grievance and his uncomprehending sorrow at the feet of the one responsible.

So he told his story—a memoir of fragmented identity—for the first time to the one person he most wanted to hear it. He spoke without much outward emotion, but the details were powerfully suggestive of the feelings he'd endured: the shame of encountering a neighbor on the stoop as he was led from his Dublin flat in handcuffs; the humiliation of submitting the resignation of his position with the National Symphony to a stone-faced personal assistant when the conductor refused to see him; the emptiness he'd felt in reading Maggie Fallon's formal, carefully worded letter to break off their engagement; the hopeless rage in adjusting to a new daily routine and of trying to remember everything he'd once assumed it had been safe to forget; and then shame again, and guilt, for the death of both a cow and her calf because he had been too proud to ask his snickering neighbors for help with a breached birth.

With these details, he was more honest and expansive, but when he launched into the description of his latest incarnation as an amateur operative, he began to equivocate. He didn't lie, exactly, but he was careful to shape the few details he did provide so as to cast himself in the most humbling light. He made much of the insults suffered at the hands of Lawrence Shelton and of his chaotic arrival in Mumbai. He made very little of what had followed after, doing his best to cement the image of Paddy the Secret Agent in his brother's mind and leaving the darker aspects of his recent history unspoken.

When he finished, Conor felt unexpectedly refreshed, and with a ripple of smug satisfaction, he noted the tale had taken its intended toll.

Thomas was slumped low in the chair again, his face pale, one hand shielding eyes that had disappeared into slits of squinting pain. Conor knew the look. Thomas had always been prone to sudden, blinding headaches that came without warning and disappeared just as quickly. Their mother believed the *chuisle Dé* was exceptionally strong in him and that he resisted it too fiercely. Conor's righteous satisfaction faded as he watched his brother's face grow even whiter.

"Listen," he began, but got no further as Thomas lurched up and stumbled to the door. A few seconds later, he heard the bathroom door slam, followed by sounds of violent sickness. Thomas stepped back into the room some fifteen minutes later and looked at him with a sheepish shrug.

"Jesus, are you all right?" Conor asked, watching him cautiously.

"Yeah. It's gone, now."

"You did say you wanted to hear it."

"I needed to hear it," Thomas corrected. He sank back into the chair with a tired sigh and rubbed the heels of his hands against his eyes. "And you needed to tell it."

"I did," he agreed, and then he added, "sorry."

"Are you?" Thomas's bloodshot eyes regarded him ironically. "Sure, you were always one for pulling on the hair shirt. What have you got to be sorry for, in all this?"

"For wanting it to hurt."

"Ah, well, no crime in that," Thomas said mildly. "You can't say I don't deserve it, but I don't deserve to be treated like a fool, either."

"What's that supposed to mean?"

Thomas's face twisted into a scolding grimace. "It's a load of shite, trying to make me believe you're the worst bogtrotter ever recruited by MI6 and that you've been nothing more than a fool on holiday for the past six months."

"How do you know I haven't been?"

Thomas leaned forward, reached under the bed, and drew out the Walther semiautomatic. Conor stiffened. His eyes shifted involuntarily to the pillow on his bed.

"Yeah, it used to be there," Thomas said with a faint smile. "The doctor found it a few days ago. He was trying to get a tube down into you for his sputum sample, and you were thrashing around in a fever. He pulled this out, much to his surprise, and you latched onto his fucking throat like a trained killer. He'd nearly browned his pants by the time I pulled you off him."

"I don't remember it," Conor said, feebly.

"Clearly. But I don't think I would have believed you, even without this." Thomas tossed the gun to him. "It wouldn't fit the pattern. I've never known you to be a bungler at anything you ever tried."

"Ah, for ... go away outta that, Thomas." He caught the gun cleanly, and after a slight hesitation, he tucked it back under the pillow.

"I won't, though," Thomas insisted. "It's the truth, and

you know it. A lot of things come naturally to you. It's a gift. I don't know—maybe in this case it's a curse. But you can't deny it. You've only to set your mind to be good at something, and before long it's almost second nature. You've mastered it. Take farming for instance." Thomas gave Conor a furtive, half-wistful glance. "You've mastered that as well by now, I'm guessing. It was a great relief to me, you know, when you came and said you'd rather go play the violin in Dublin than stay and work the farm with me. I remember it like yesterday. You were scared—thought I'd be disappointed—but do you know, if you'd stayed, you'd have turned yourself into the best bleedin' farmer in the west of Ireland, and then what the fuck would I do? I actually thought it would be easier without you. That was my first soft-headed mistake but not the biggest."

Conor reflected on this for a moment and then lifted his head with a smile. "Sounds like the beginning of your story, now."

Thomas choked out a mirthless laugh. "I suppose it is."

"Well, don't tell it yet." He eased himself gingerly up from the bed. "I'm tired of sitting around here in my underwear. Push that bag over here. I want to go out for a while."

Thomas frowned anxiously. "I don't think you're supposed to be getting out of bed."

"Yeah, whatever. Fuck it." He pulled a clean shirt and a pair of jeans from his luggage. "I've been in bed for four days, and anyway, fever is episodic in TB. I'll feel like shit again soon enough, but I don't feel too bad right now."

"How do you know so much about it?" Thomas asked.

"There's no shortage of tuberculosis in the slums of Dharavi," Conor remarked, drily. "I've been working with Kavita in the clinics there. The doctor thinks I caught it from her, but I might have picked it up there as well. Doesn't much matter. The real question will be whether the tests show a straightforward infection or an MDR strain."

"And what's that, then? MDR?"

"Multidrug resistant. Much harder to treat. Harder to cure."

Thomas rubbed a hand over his mouth, absorbing the information in silence. "Could do with a stiff drink," he said finally. Conor nodded.

"This was my point."

"Fancy a little Jameson's Limited Reserve?" Thomas asked.

"Hell, yes, but I've whistled for it in every five-star hotel bar in Mumbai. I haven't found it yet."

"You're whistling in the wrong bars," his brother said with a crooked grin. "I know a place."

22

Conor gaped around the room, hardly able to credit the evidence of his eyes. One minute he had been in the cacophonous center of a Bandra shopping district, the street teeming with homeward-bound workers, begging children, and a continuous flow of honking, fuming traffic. The next minute, he had stepped through a door and was transported home.

The interior of Durgan's Irish Pub was so authentic, so uncannily evocative of bars he'd known from Dingle to Dublin, that the overall effect was one of momentary dizziness. It was as if the needle of an internal compass had been twisted to a familiar but unexpected setting.

"It's unbelievable. It even smells like Ireland." He closed his eyes and breathed in an aroma both sweet and acrid.

"That'll be the peat fire." Thomas cocked his head at the massive fieldstone fireplace anchored at one end of the room. "It's mad altogether, really. It'll be thirty-three centigrade and the air-con cranked full blast, but there's always the peat fire going."

"How did you find this?" Conor asked.

His brother's eyes slid from him evasively. He turned away toward the bar—a long, handsome specimen of dark, polished wood featuring an array of long-handled taps advertising Guinness, Smithwick's, and Murphy's. He pointed Conor to an empty area of the room.

"Let's have a drink first. Get yourself a seat in the corner there, and I'll bring it over."

Conor made his way to the table Thomas had indicated, taking time to browse among the photos lining the walls. They were a stock collection of the most famous, most frequently photographed Irish landscapes, but he lingered over them affectionately, as if absorbing images from a family album.

He paused at the fireplace and had to agree the great expanse of fieldstone was a bit overdone, a bit too "Bunratty Folk Park," but the homely little bricks of peat in their various misshapen sizes still produced a twinge of nostalgia. He wondered what logistical hurdles were involved in importing genuine Irish turf into India.

When he reached the corner table, he pulled one of the chairs back, throwing a casual glance at the photo centered over it ... and froze. It was another landscape, a very familiar one, but not famous. It was a particular view of Ventry Harbor off the coast of the Dingle peninsula. He would have known the harbor anyway, but this angle he particularly recognized because it was a vista that could only be seen from the upper pasture of the McBride family farm.

Staring at the photograph, a flash of intuition pulsed through him, and when Thomas arrived carrying a bottle of Jameson's and two whiskey glasses, he spun around with an accusatory glare.

"You're Durgan, aren't you?" He couldn't decide whether the concept was appalling or hilarious. "You own this bloody bar, don't you?"

Thomas set the bottle and glasses down on the table with a heavy sigh. "I'm not Durgan, and if we're to be completely accurate, the European Union owns this bloody bar."

"The European—oh, mother of God, take me now." Conor dropped into the chair. "The grant money? Are you coddin' me, Thomas? Frank Murdoch has sworn to me you're laundering money for terrorists. Are you telling me you scarpered with two hundred and fifty thousand pounds just so you could open a fucking pub in fucking India?"

"Calm down. It's more complicated than that." Thomas took a seat across from him and filled their glasses. "I'm going to tell you, but like I said earlier—let's have a drink first."

He took the glass his brother offered and drank the whiskey off in one gulp. It did calm him down—a little too much.

"I'd better get you something to eat," Thomas mumbled. He disappeared again and returned with a steaming bowl of Irish stew and a plate of brown bread. The novelty of it made Conor forget he had no appetite. He devoured everything with a hint of his former gusto while his brother watched him, eyes crinkled in fond amusement.

"Why do you suppose we never got married, either one of us?" Thomas asked when Conor sat back from the table and regarded him expectantly.

"You're changing the subject," he objected.

"Not really. I'm just easing into it."

"Oh, all right. Fine." Conor rolled his eyes and pushed his plate away. "The question is why we never got married. Who the hell knows?" It didn't seem politic to raise the issue of Maggie Fallon again. He gave a short laugh. "Maybe because we've never been in love."

"Speak for yourself," Thomas said with a sniff.

"Oh, is that right, then?" Conor grinned and leaned forward with an attitude of greater attention, but Thomas made no further comment.

"Laura Mahoney?" he ventured. "Was it her?"

"Never mind," Thomas muttered. "Doesn't matter."

"Her sister, Mary Ann?"

"All right, shut up."

"Right, so." Conor bit the inside of his cheek and sat back to look at the growing crowd gathered round the bar. It appeared to be mostly a collection of sunburned Australians.

"Patricia Boyle? Janey Sylvester? It wasn't that mountainy girl, wore the gansy down over her knees—Moira something or other?"

"It might be someone you don't even know," Thomas said, glowering.

"Well, why'd you bring it up, if you don't want to talk about it?" Conor asked in exasperation.

"Because it's the start of the story, which I'm getting to if you'll give me half a feckin' chance."

"Okay. Brilliant. Get on with it."

"You went off to the Dublin Conservatory," Thomas began. "And that was fine with me. I could run things the way I wanted, be in charge, and not have to worry about you arguing for your own ideas. I thought I knew what I wanted. Turns out I didn't."

Thomas looked thoughtfully into his glass and swirled its contents. "After a while, I hired a couple of men to work for me. I didn't know them and didn't like them much, but they did what I told them to, so I couldn't complain. It went on all right for a few more years, but it just wasn't the same. And then one weekend, I went to a wedding—"

"Whose?"

"Declan Garvey's."

"That aul' eejit," Conor said, dismissively.

"Yeah, that one," Thomas nodded. "I woke up on Monday morning after a three-day hangover, and I realized I was still single and was probably going to stay that way. I saw that I'd likely go on being a bachelor farmer, living on the edge of the Atlantic with my queer old ma who had more to say to the fairies than she did to the neighbors, most of whom were scared shitless of her anyway. It gave me a peculiar feeling. Like I was suffocating. Started to feel a bit desperate, really."

Conor swallowed painfully. The observation struck a nerve and extinguished the last of his pleasant, whiskey-induced buzz.

"I'm acquainted with that particular feeling myself," he said. "I had to become you, remember, once you got tired of it."

"I know, but I never expected—oh, hell." Thomas passed a hand over his eyes. "We'll get to that, later."

"These men you hired, where did they come from, were they local?"

"No, couple of hard cases from Armagh."

"Damn," Conor said, softly.

"Yeah." Thomas gave a melancholy nod of regret. "Anyway, I started drinking too much in my room at night, and when that seemed too pathetic, I started drinking too much with the lads from Armagh. It was them that turned me on to this 'pub-in-a-box' scheme. They're filling me with stories about their buddy Bobby Durgan, who's over in America. He's going to build Irish pubs all over the world. Pretty soon, I'm on the phone with him. Everything you need comes in a kit that arrives by ship in cargo containers, he says—walls, floor, bar, furniture, everything, right down to the bloody knick-knacks and buckets of turf. He's had a plan for India, and he's looking for investors. I'd go there, take delivery on the kit, get the thing built, and then be in charge of running the business. I know, I know," Thomas said, acknowledging Conor's dumbfounded stare. "I don't know what I was thinking. I was off my nut, drunk nearly every night, and the whole thing got away from me."

He paused at the sound of a raucous cheer from the other end of the pub. The Australians—a football team, if size and numbers were any judge—looked ready to settle in for a week. They'd moved to a collection of tables next to the bar and had erupted in song. He waited, a wistful, half-envious tolerance in his eyes and continued when it was over.

"Before I know it, the lads and I are at the bar filling out application forms for an EU business loan—they told me it was a business loan, anyway—to get cash for the investment; all dead simple, low-interest, start making payments as soon as I've got money coming in the door. None of it felt real, to tell you the truth. It all seemed like a bit of *craic*, something that would take a long time and then might never happen anyway, but in the meantime I could pretend I had great expectations."

Thomas emptied his glass with a slow, long sip and pulled a cigarette from his shirt pocket. As he lifted the lighter to it, he looked at Conor and stopped.

"Sorry, I forgot."

"No, go ahead. Wish I could join you." Conor nudged the ashtray forward. "The place is full of smoke anyway. Doesn't seem to be bothering me."

"No sense risking it." Thomas slipped the cigarette back into his pocket. "Better for both of us."

"Thanks."

They regarded each other for a moment without speaking.

"Conor, it's good to see you," Thomas finally said, his voice cracking.

"Same here, mate."

"I'll get back to it, now."

"When you're ready."

Thomas took a deep breath. "Well, it didn't take a long time, and once it got rolling, it all happened fast. I get a phone call from the EU's man in Dublin. Did I not get the award letter for my grant, he asks me, which of course I hadn't. I thought it was a loan, I tell him, and he laughs at me. No, sure it's a grant, free and clear, nothing I'll need to be paying back. So where's the money then, I ask him, and he gurgles away at me again. Must have thought me a right culchie. In the bank, of course, wired to the account on the application. Then he rattles on about metrics and objectives, how excited they are about my innovative ideas, and that he'll be coming over in a few days to look at the sheep; and the light finally dawns that I've been fucked. It wasn't an EU business loan. It was an agricultural grant based on an application full of lies."

He paused again and glanced at the whiskey bottle with an air of troubled speculation. Silently, Conor picked up the bottle and put it down on the floor next to him. A flicker of annoyance passed over his brother's face, but then it melted into a sad smile.

"Good lad," Thomas whispered. He cleared his throat and continued. "So I go off to beat the lard out of my Armagh drinking buddies, the bowsy little wankers, and they're all soft talk and reassurance. They're going to look after me. I'm one of them now, and I'll be taken care of, as long as I go with the program and don't make trouble. I'm to come over here as planned and get the pub running as a front for this money-laundering gig Durgan is putting together for a Mumbai gangster. After a while, they'll let me come home again. I'm part of the brotherhood now, they say, and as long as I'm loyal, they'll be good to me and to my family. Well, Jesus, we all know what that means."

Thomas shook his head. "I didn't have much time to think, and I wasn't in very good shape for thinking, anyway. They had me out of the country by the following day, and I"—he broke off with a frown and then finished weakly—"I ended up here."

This last, prevaricating statement sounded clumsy. Conor picked up on it and shot Thomas a quizzical look.

"I get the idea you just skipped ahead a few chapters. You're leaving out some interesting details, I'm thinking."

"No more than you," Thomas countered, his chin jutting in defiance. "I'd say we've both got details we're not proud of and maybe not ready to talk about yet."

It was harder to detect, but there was something even in this that seemed slippery. He gave his brother a look of cool assessment before ceding the point. "Fair enough. I have to ask though, Thomas. Did it never occur to you that once you'd skipped the country, the EU would look at the other name on the application, and that Interpol and the Garda and every other pillar of justice would be falling down on my head?"

"It didn't." Thomas's voice choked with sudden emotion. "It didn't, because I didn't know your name was on it. I didn't send you those papers, Conor. The last time I saw the bleedin' things, they were spread across the bar in Matty Jack's pub. I didn't know you'd been pulled into it until almost a year after I got here."

Conor could see that this was the absolute truth. Thomas leaned over the table, put his face in his hands, and was silent. He gazed at the large, scarred hands for a long moment, feeling shaky and unmoored. At last, he took a breath—he could never get one deep enough to be satisfying these days—and released it with a slow whistle.

"I've half-hated you for years, thinking you tricked me on purpose and ruined my life."

"I did ruin your life. What's it matter that I didn't mean to?"

"Quite a lot, as a matter of fact," Conor said. His lip twitched ironically but soon he felt a cold mask settling over his features.

"Who are these people?"

Thomas pulled his face from his hands and looked startled by what he saw. "You might say the IRA, three or four times removed." He regarded Conor warily. "Castoffs and dead-enders from the Irish People's Liberation Organization, which was a splinter group from the Irish National Liberation Army, which had splintered from who-the-hell-knows. They're not much to do with Ireland anymore, or republicanism, and they're for damn sure not an army. They're just criminals for the sake of it, to get rich and build a reputation as a player among the mafias of the world."

"That's a start, but it isn't news to anyone. You'll need to be more specific than that, Thomas," Conor said. "British intelligence is looking for names and locations, particularly for the ringleader—Frank's 'wizard.' That's what your immunity depends on, in all this. We can't go back home and get this shut down without—"

"We can't shut it down," Thomas broke in, abruptly. "I can't go home yet, with or without immunity. There's more to it, now. There's a lot of moving parts you don't know about in all this."

Moving parts. With a groan, Conor remembered where he'd heard the same term recently. For a few welcome hours, he had forgotten all about Sedgwick and his gauzy machinations.

"Sedgwick and his friends—we haven't even gotten to that part yet," he said, realizing that after all this, they were only half-finished. "He wouldn't tell me what their angle was."

"And he must have told you I wouldn't either." Thomas looked away with a stubborn frown. "We agreed it's better for you not to know."

"That's nice you both agree, but I don't," Conor said. "You can't seriously expect that I'll—"

Thomas put up a placating hand. "Okay, Conor. Let's not fight about it tonight. It's another long story altogether, and you're already knackered. I think we'd better be getting you back."

"I'm not tired," Conor said, sharply.

It was an unconvincing lie. Thomas smiled, the corners of his eyes crinkling again with affection. He got to his feet and rested a hand on Conor's shoulder. "Well, I am. I'm a lot older than you, little brother. I wear out faster."

23

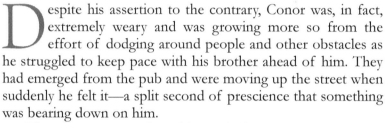

Despite his assertion to the contrary, Conor was, in fact, extremely weary and was growing more so from the effort of dodging around people and other obstacles as he struggled to keep pace with his brother ahead of him. They had emerged from the pub and were moving up the street when suddenly he felt it—a split second of prescience that something was bearing down on him.

His reflexes were at low ebb. He had time only to tense his muscles, crouch, and half-turn before feeling the assailant's blow against his side. He went sailing into a display of clay water jugs that shattered and crashed around him, and then slammed into a wall beyond before crumpling to the ground.

"Shit."

He heard the familiar voice cursing somewhere above him as he scrambled to find his footing.

"You. Follow me and guard the alley. You. Take this and pay that guy for the pots before a riot starts and then go wait in the car."

A pair of hands jerked him to his feet, and before he could recover his bearings, he was being frog-marched down an adjacent dead-end lane. Near the end of it, he could see Sedgwick's white SUV parked at an angle.

"Didn't see that one coming, did you, Danny-boy?" Sedgwick

growled into his ear. "You're not the only one who can pull a fast one."

"Sure," Conor shot back. "But when I take a crack at you, it doesn't come out of my wallet."

"Shut-up, smartass. You just make me want to draw this out a little longer and enjoy it more."

With a sudden twist, Sedgwick turned and threw him against the wall again. There was very little light in the alley, but as he went down, Conor saw Thomas at the top of it, straining to escape from two muscular men. He recognized them as the *taporis* that had administered the savage beating in the Sewri godown two months earlier.

"Sedgwick!" Thomas shouted. "What the hell are you doing? He's sick, for fuck's sake."

"Oh, I know he's sick," Sedgwick snarled. "Believe me, that word is getting around. But he's not half as sick as I'd like him to be."

Conor climbed to his feet again, and with a desperate intake of breath, launched himself at the shadowy, blond figure. He was knocked down again by a precisely aimed shot to the ribs. He fell down onto his back, chest heaving.

"Leave him alone!" Thomas roared.

"I will," Sedgwick purred. "As soon as he stops getting up. Are you finished getting up, McBride?"

He was too winded to speak, but as he saw Sedgwick's hand move in the darkness he rolled away and snatched the Walther from its holster. A second later, he and the American agent had guns trained on each other in a stalemate.

Sedgwick's eyes widened with surprise. He was silent for several seconds, glaring at Conor impatiently.

"Damn, you are such a pain in the ass," he said. Without turning his head, he called up to the *taporis*. "*Arrey*, let him go. Let the *gora* come down here. Stay there and make sure no one else does."

The two men released Thomas and stepped back as he raced toward Conor.

"Nice and easy, Tom," Sedgwick warned, as Thomas, seeing the standoff, pulled up with a startled grunt. "Let's all slow down and stay calm so that we can try not to fuck this up. Could you see from up there that Conor was pointing a gun at me?"

"No, it's too dark," Thomas said, shifting his gaze between the two of them.

"Good," Sedgwick said. "Finally, I get a break. Put the gun down like a good boy, McBride. Tom, tell him to put the goddamn gun down."

Thomas looked at Conor in amazement. "I thought you left it under the pillow. What's going on, here?"

"Oh, quite a lot, really," Sedgwick remarked, sarcastically. "Haven't shared the news of your recent escapades with your big brother, Con? Can't imagine why not."

Conor said nothing. He was still breathing hard and struggling to hold the gun steady. He couldn't yet manage talking as well.

"The crux of it," Sedgwick continued, "is that Ahmed Khalil sent me to kill you, and the *taporis* are here to make sure I do. If I don't, they have instructions to do it themselves and take me out in the process. Now, I've got a number of pretty good reasons to ice you, McBride, but oddly enough, I don't feel inclined to do it. So here's the plan. While the Khalil boys stand guard up there, I'm going to march you down to the car, throw open the rear hatch, fire a few rounds in your general direction, and then pack you into the back and drive you away."

With a snort, Conor managed to find his voice. "You're an awful feckin' eejit, if you think I'm believing that."

Sedgwick gave a low, ironic laugh, shaking his head. "I was afraid of that. This was going to be very straightforward until you pulled the gun out, but now we're stuck role-playing a Fort Monckton case study. You've got to decide if I'm telling the truth, or if I'm going to plug you as soon as you drop your arm.

It's a tough call. I am pretty pissed at you, and you know why. Not a whole lot of trust between the two of us right now."

He glanced at Thomas. "This is how it's been with me and your brother, for the most part. We end in a draw."

"Bullshit," Conor said. "I've kicked your ass more than once."

He could easily believe that Sedgwick was compromised for his indirect responsibility in letting a thief loose—a foreign one, no less—within a prestigious Indian mafia organization. Not only had Ahmed Khalil lost money, he had been made to look like a fool, which was worse. That part of the story was plausible, but he was far from convinced that the ridiculous scenario just outlined represented Sedgwick's true intention.

"Looks like we're going to need your help, Tom," Sedgwick said, grimly. "He isn't going to trust me, but I'm sort of hoping you will. This is the only way it's going to work. I'm trying to save the bastard's life as well as my own."

Thomas had been standing off to the side, watching them in dazed confusion. Now, he rubbed a hand fretfully over his head and turned a questioning look at Sedgwick. "I don't understand any of this. What's Conor got to do with Ahmed Khalil, and why would Khalil want him—"

"There isn't time," Sedgwick said gently but with a note of urgency. "Please, help me out here before it's too late."

Thomas sighed, and to Conor's horror, turned toward him with a look of firm purpose. "Put away the gun, Conor. I've known him a long time, and I believe what he's telling you. If I didn't, would I put you in danger? I don't know what the hell is going on but if he says this is the way we've got to do it—"

"You don't know what's going on, and that's the point," Conor hissed. "You don't know what I've done. It doesn't matter how long you've known him, you don't know what you're getting into with this. He's got good reasons for wanting me dead or at least missing. We don't need to make it easier for him."

"We don't have a choice," Thomas argued. "It's three against two, and I've got no weapon. Those two at the end of the lane would finish off at least one of us."

"Not necessarily," Conor said, and added with some reluctance, "I'm a pretty good shot, Thomas. We might be able to—ah, fuck."

His brother had moved in front of Sedgwick, effectively shielding him. He walked up to Conor and squatted down, hand outstretched. "Trust me, then, if nobody else. I know I've not spent ten weeks in a training camp learning to read faces and pick the liar out of a crowd, but we've got our own special instincts as well, you and me. Give it to me, will you now? I don't want to see you killing anybody."

"Instincts can be wrong, even if they're special," Conor said, but he saw further argument was useless. He lowered the gun, and with practiced efficiency engaged the safety and tucked it back under his shoulder.

Thomas dropped his hand, his brow creasing sadly. "*Deartháirín ó mo chroí.* I can remember when it was the fiddle you had to have with you everywhere. Did you bring it over here with you?"

Conor looked quickly away. The line of Irish was from a sentimental song their father had often played—"little brother of my heart." It had a gentler sound now than in the days when Thomas had teased him with it.

"No," he said, curtly. "I haven't had the fiddle with me for a long while."

"Ah, well." Thomas sighed, and, standing upright, pulled Conor to his feet.

"Progress. This is good," Sedgwick remarked. "Next item. Do you know the Candlelight Bistro on the Causeway down near the Sassoon Docks?"

Sedgwick directed the question to Thomas, who nodded.

"Excellent. I'm going to fire a shot in the air, and you're going to take off up the alley. It'll be fine. They don't even know who you are. I'll pick you up in front of that restaurant in about an hour."

He stepped back and pulled the trigger. "Now, get the hell out of here," he shouted and then called out to Khalil's *taporis*. "Let him go. We don't need him, and Mustafa, I told you to wait in your goddamned car."

As Thomas ran back up the alley, Sedgwick directed a cold, angry stare at Conor. "What the fuck is wrong with you? What were you thinking? Did you have any idea what kind of position you would put me in with your idiotic heroics?"

"I didn't," Conor admitted. "I'm sorry. It seems obvious now, I suppose. It never occurred to me Khalil would hold you responsible. Is Raj all right?"

"Oh, sure, Raj is fine," Sedgwick snapped. "He was robbed at gunpoint and knocked unconscious and had to spend a few hours wondering if he'd be decapitated, but he's great. Raj was smart. He reported you as soon as he woke up. Some of us have been looser with the rules. A little more soft-hearted, if you know what I mean."

"I know what you mean. I'm sorry," Conor repeated.

"Yeah, sorry, sorry," Sedgwick mimicked. He grabbed his arm and yanked him forward, planting the gun at his back. "Let's go."

At the end of the alley, he lifted the hatch of the SUV, revealing a large, bloodstained bundle lying across the back.

"What the hell is that?" Conor looked at the bundle distastefully.

"Your dead body," Sedgwick said, with relish. "Trussed and ready for its disposal next to the Sassoon Dock. This evening, the part will be played by the fresh carcass of a young water buffalo."

"This is really the plan?"

"Yeah, this is the plan. You still thought I was going to kill you, McBride?"

"I've got to be honest, I thought you might try," Conor admitted. "Or at least go on beating the crap out of me."

"It's tempting." Sedgwick smirked in sour amusement. "Now, get against the wall there. Once you're down, I'll heave you into the back. I'll dick around for a while with the door open, looking like I'm wrapping you up. There's a tarp on the floor of the back seat. By the time I shut the back, you need to have scrambled forward and moved under it. Are we clear?"

"Clear." Conor peered into the rear of the SUV and then walked over to the wall. "What do you want me to do?"

"Fall down when I shoot you."

"Yeah, I get that," Conor said patiently. "Any particular direction? Slumped against the wall? On my back, stomach?"

"Oh." Sedgwick chewed his lip. "On your back; easier to pick you up from that angle. I guess. Hell, I don't know. I've never tried this before."

"Hmm. That's a comfort."

Conor watched with an odd, watery feeling in his stomach as the agent chambered a round, took aim, and then hesitated. "I'm going to spray the wall to the right of you. Don't fidget or jerk around, for God's sake."

"I won't."

"Okay." Sedgwick raised the gun again.

"Wait a minute. My right or your right?"

"What difference does it make? Don't fidget in either direction."

"Right."

In the next instant, the area next to his right ear and shoulder exploded in a fusillade of bullets. He closed his eyes as fragments of concrete flew out from the wall, and then, sinking to his knees, flopped onto his back and lay motionless.

"Conor. Jesus, are you all right?"

He opened his eyes to see Sedgwick crouched over him, rigid

with alarm. Conor gave a slow, solemn wink, and the agent's face relaxed.

"That was—damn, that was pretty convincing. You really looked like something hit you."

"Something did. I think a few bits of concrete went into my arm."

Sedgwick leaned in for a closer look. "Yeah, you're right. You'll have to dig those out later."

After being unceremoniously dumped next to the bloody bundle in the rear, Conor fumbled his way forward as instructed until he was arranged awkwardly on the floor of the vehicle, under a tarp. A few minutes later, Sedgwick slid into the driver's seat and started the engine. They rolled up the alley and then came to a stop, and he heard the window slide down. Sedgwick spoke gruffly to Khalil's men. "We're done here. Follow me to the docks."

The car began moving again, and although it would have been safe to talk, they rode to the southern end of the city in a tense, unbroken silence.

The Sassoon Dock was the site of Mumbai's largest fish market. It looked onto a large harbor on the city's bay side, where fishing boats arrived daily to unload a variety of sea creatures that moved from baskets to handcarts to trucks, eventually making their way to plates in every corner of the city. At first light, the market would be busy, and by early morning, jammed. At this time of night, the area would be marginally quieter, with most of the activity centered on the main jetty, where boats would be arriving throughout the night and jostling for mooring space.

The docks were located at the southernmost end of Mumbai, in the Colaba district, and although he could see nothing, Conor could tell by the smell when they had arrived. The SUV shuddered over the rutted roads of the harbor area for what seemed like miles before finally coming to a stop.

"Shouldn't be more than a few minutes," Sedgwick said over his shoulder as he exited. A moment later, the rear hatch was lifted again.

He listened to the grunts of effort as Khalil's men lifted out the stiffening "body" and then heard their swearing fade into background sounds of lapping water and a clamor of fishing vessels. It might have been only a few minutes, but to Conor, perspiring heavily under the suffocating tarp, it felt like hours before he heard an engine revving and then speeding past. Shortly after, Sedgwick jumped back into the car, chortling.

"Stupid bastards—thank God for that. It worked like a charm, at least for now. I got them to stuff it under a pile of fish guts, and they're practically puking from the stench. Not anxious to hang around and chat."

"Glad to hear it," Conor said, shifting uncomfortably. "Can I get up now? I could use a bit of fresh air myself."

24

By the time they arrived to collect Thomas outside the Candlelight Bistro on the Colaba Causeway, he'd had ample opportunity to work up a towering rage. Barely waiting for the car to stop, he threw himself onto the front seat and shut the door with a violent slam.

"What the bloody hell have you been up to?" he demanded, accosting Sedgwick with a vicious scowl.

Conor saw the agent's head pivot sharply toward his brother. At first, he appeared ready to meet the challenge with equal hostility but then took a deep breath and turned his eyes back to the road. Putting the car in gear, he transferred his aggression to the clutch, and the SUV lurched into traffic, heading north.

"I think you'd better be asking Conor instead of me."

"Well I'm asking you," Thomas said. "As I've asked for the past two months without a straight answer. You were going to come up with something simple. 'Safe but scary' you told me. You'd have him begging to go home within a couple of weeks, you said. Whatever happened to that plan?"

"That plan," Sedgwick said irritably, "became obsolete once I learned he was a bloodless SOB who can see around corners and be a shrewd, deadly fucker when he feels like it. I brought him into the Khalil organization because it was easy, and I didn't have time to be creative and then, to be honest, I unexpectedly—and rather foolishly as it turns out—got comfortable working with him."

He shot Thomas a sideways glance, and his anger relaxed into an affectionate grin. "This probably comes as a shock, but your little brother is possibly the most gifted recruit British intelligence has sent into the field in ten years or more. There aren't too many with both the skill and the stones to cheat Ahmed Khalil and then vanish like a puff of smoke."

In the backseat, Conor slouched a little further into the shadows as his brother swiveled around, one eyebrow raised in astute observation.

"It's not as shocking as you might think," Thomas said wearily. He peered at Conor. "Are you all right? You look like you've got a fever again."

"No, it's just ... ordinary, stress-induced sweat. I'm all right." Conor pushed the damp hair from his forehead and tried shifting the conversation to a more practical topic. "Listen, can we discuss our next move, since the dumping of my remains is checked off the program? I can't be flouncing around town, now that I'm dead, and I can't hide at Kavita's flat indefinitely."

"Nothing to discuss." Thomas turned back to face the road with an air of finality. "You'll be going back home."

"I'll be doing no such thing," Conor answered with equal resolve. "At least, not alone."

"Conor, there's no point in arguing."

"I agree, no point at all in arguing, because I've—"

"There's no point in either of you arguing." Sedgwick's voice was pitched to command attention. "It's not up to you. It's Walker's call."

Conor saw his brother's back stiffen.

"You'd better not be suggesting what I think you are."

"I'm not suggesting, or recommending. I'm informing."

Sedgwick paused to concentrate as he steered the SUV through a disordered intersection before continuing. "The decision's made, and it's not up for debate. Walker wants him dealt in on this."

"Walker can go to hell," Thomas said angrily.

"Who's Walker?" Conor sat up and leaned forward.

"Greg Walker," Sedgwick said. "Introduced to you as Grigory Lipvin. He's a counter-narcotics agent with the US Drug Enforcement Agency."

"The DEA?" He sat up even straighter. It was not especially illuminating information, but it did validate one technicality—Sedgwick had told the truth in swearing that he wasn't working for the CIA.

"Yep. Special Operations Division."

He looked at Conor in the rearview mirror, his cool, gray eyes indistinct in the darkness. He seemed prepared to reveal additional details but before he could, Thomas erupted. He sent a fist crashing onto the dashboard and bellowed a sound that seemed halfway between a sob and a roar.

"Goddamn it, shut up! You promised me. You said you would keep him clear of it. I don't care what Walker wants. We agreed a long time ago that he would never hear about any of this."

"He's got to hear about it," Sedgwick retorted. "He's the one that forced the issue, so he's got to hear it now. I have no options; the man is my boss."

"One of your bosses," Conor interjected.

"Yes, fine, one of them," Sedgwick conceded. "Anyway, he's the one calling the plays I have to roll with now, especially after the stunts you pulled this week. You managed to impress him and piss him off at the same time. He realizes now that it's too risky to send you back to London, and we can't leave you in Mumbai. We put on a show tonight for the two dumbest taporis in Mumbai, but it won't hold up for long. Khalil will realize soon enough that he's been tricked again. He's also got an eager accomplice in your old friend Rohit Mehta, who wasn't pleased to hear that he was holding wads of money stolen from his boss. Needless to say, he wasn't allowed to keep it. We can't even set you up to get arrested. With so many people wanting you dead, it's too dangerous now to lock you up—they'd get to you in jail.

There'd be hell to pay if word got around that we let a foreign agent go down when we knew he was compromised, particularly if he got killed by the gang we'd infiltrated ourselves."

"So, I'm not going to London, and I can't stay in Mumbai. Where are you proposing that I go?"

"North," Sedgwick said, with a wary glance at Thomas. "The plan is to give Con the paramilitary monk a new assignment with a new outfit. You're going to be attached to the DEA's operation as the bodyguard for your brother, who is on his way north as well."

"Not a chance." Thomas spat the words ferociously. "Not a bloody, fucking chance. If that's what you've in mind, then stop the car right now. You can count us both out of it. I'm done. I'll take my chances with the feckin' British before going along with any more of this horseshit."

To Conor's surprise, Sedgwick abruptly brought his foot off the accelerator. They were on the MG Road near the main Fort campus of the University of Mumbai and not all that far from the Bombay Gymkhana. Braking to a stop on the side of the road, the agent turned to regard each of them in turn. His face looked tired and strained, but again he addressed Thomas with uncharacteristic restraint.

"We've been together on this for a long time, Tom," he said. "A few phone calls to the right people, and you could sabotage the whole thing, but that's been true from the start. I somehow knew I could trust you, and after a shaky start, I've tried to be someone you could trust, too." He indicated Conor with a nod. "I know what he means to you. I know what I promised, and ... I know what I owe you. I can't believe after coming this far and knowing what's at stake that you'll set this whole operation on fire; but if you want out of it, take him and go. I won't stop you, but I can't protect you, either. Or him."

Thomas stared ahead, and in the windshield's ghostly

reflection, Conor could see his features hardened in sullen indecision. He sat back in his seat and remained quiet. After a few tense minutes, his brother's face crumpled.

"What will you be doing, then?" Thomas asked, his voice grown hollow. "You were supposed to play the bodyguard."

Sedgwick released a long sigh of relief. He put the car back in gear, and they started forward again. "Don't worry, there's still plenty for me to do. Anyway, he's better at it than I am. You'll be safer with him."

Conor cleared his throat tentatively. "I don't suppose anyone wants to explain what this DEA business is all about or what I'm meant to be guarding him from?"

"All in due time," Sedgwick assured him. "We've still got a long night ahead of us."

"He needs to be in bed," Thomas objected. "The doctor says he's got TB."

"I know." Sedgwick again looked in the mirror at Conor. This time, the darkness did not obscure a sarcastic gleam creeping back into his eyes. "Kavita passed along that news earlier this week. She's wracked with guilt for not making you get tested earlier, so she's had me playing community health worker for the past few days, finding everyone who's ever shaken hands with you to make sure they get a skin test. That's made me even more popular with the *goondas*, as you can imagine. I assume you're on antibiotics?"

Conor nodded. "I've been pretty careful around people for the past few weeks. I sort of had a feeling ... " he trailed off with a self-conscious shrug.

"Ah, yes, the McBrides and their famous intuitions," Sedgwick said. "We'll have to take our chances around you now. Where you're going, you should get a couple more weeks of recuperation before your services will be required."

"And it looks like we're going by train?" Conor observed that the SUV was rolling up to the main entrance of the rambling, Gothic pile formerly known as Victoria Terminus, now renamed Chatrapati Shivaji, the main railway station for Mumbai.

"Correct," Sedgwick confirmed. "You'll be riding in style, too. Wait till you see it. You're in for a treat."

"You said north. Care to narrow it down a bit?" Conor asked. "More than half the country is north of here."

"Rishikesh." Thomas's sepulchral, dispirited intonation made the word sound like a feeble expletive. "We're going to Kavita Kotwal's ashram in Rishikesh."

25

"I've never known a cheaper bastard," Thomas sighed.

"He is pretty tight with the *baksheesh*," Conor agreed. "I've noticed that."

"They'll get it out of him eventually, but he always has to make a bleedin' production of it. Probably still has his confirmation money, the mingy little blirt."

"Just part of his winsome charm."

Thomas aimed a skeptical squint at him, and they both chuckled. They were in one of the main halls inside the train station, dwarfed by vaulted ceilings and soaring cathedral-like arches, trying to hold their ground as the only bodies at rest in a swirling tide of motion. They were standing where they'd been told to and had no occupation other than to watch the American agent reveling in his element.

He was arguing with a growing clutch of railway staff and curious onlookers, trying to confirm both a train and a departure platform for their journey. Apparently, they were traveling via the Kotwal family's private carriage, and it was still parked on a siding somewhere, waiting to be hitched to one of the many trains in the station heading north that evening. Sedgwick was bargaining for the best route to Rishikesh.

The city was located in the foothills of the Himalayas in the Indian state of Uttaranchal. Conor remembered Kavita had referred to the state as her "home region," but how she came to have an ashram there and why they were going to it was just another mystery that remained to be explained.

In fact, beyond the immediate prospect of a train ride, Conor had very little grasp of what was going on and thought he probably wouldn't like it once he did. At one time, he would have found such ambiguity insufferable, but India had taught him patience, as had the surprisingly disheveled, bumbling universe of international espionage.

Whatever the Americans were up to, and whatever results his latest mutation to DEA operative might yield, at least he was in no immediate danger of a mob assassination or of being separated from Thomas. Apart from the heaviness in his chest reminding him of his indifferent health, he felt more sanguine about the future than he had for months. Watching Sedgwick approach them, quivering with irascible energy, Conor felt content to let someone else direct the agenda. For now.

"Tom, what are you carrying for rupees? I don't have any small money, and I'm damned if I'm going to give one *paise* more than this is worth."

Thomas pulled a roll of bills from his pocket with exaggerated patience. "How small does it need to be? I doubt I've got anything to suit tight-fisted assholes like—"

"Just hand it over. I'll bring you the change." Sedgwick swiped the money from Thomas's hands and headed back across the hall.

"Sure I'll not be seeing any of that back again," Thomas grumbled, philosophically. "But he'll be quicker about it at least, now he's working with my money."

"Why do you let him call you Tom?" Conor asked. "You never let anyone at home get away with that."

Thomas shrugged. "I tried to get the upper hand on that for a while, but it wasn't any use. It's what he wanted to call me, so I had to give up on it. He usually gets his way."

"I've noticed that as well." Conor lifted his gaze to survey the stained glass windows and elaborate iron railings above them. "I'm sure this will be no exception. He's as tenacious as he is cheap. I wouldn't want to see what he's like on heroin."

"Hopefully, you never will," Thomas said, quietly.

Conor winced, regretting the offhanded tone of his remark. "Sorry. That sounded more flippant than I meant it to. How long has he been clean?"

"About two years. This time. I know he acts the prick a lot," Thomas said, "but it's mostly out of fear. He thinks he needs an edge to keep himself alert."

"You're fond of him, aren't you?"

Conor studied him, intrigued by the idea that a friendship existed between his brother and the American agent. He had occasionally felt sympathy for Sedgwick, and they had shared a fractious camaraderie, but the nature of their association hadn't been conducive for building mutual warmth.

"We've come through a lot of shite, and we've done a few things for each other." Thomas's forehead puckered. "I suppose you could say I'm fond of him, but don't take it the wrong way. We're not sweethearts, for fuck's sake."

Conor laughed but was surprised to also feel a small twinge of something that bore a passing, if not precise, resemblance to jealousy.

As Thomas predicted, the bargaining process moved at a brisker clip with Sedgwick in possession of the "small money" surrendered to the cause. Before long, he was striding back with an air of smug satisfaction.

"Got it for practically nothing," he boasted. "The carriage will be hitched to the Chennai Mail on Platform 6. You leave at forty minutes past midnight."

"Hell of a bargain," Conor observed. "You paid for a train going south when we're supposed to be going north."

Sedgwick waved a dismissive hand. "It disconnects you at Pune, and you get hooked to another one going up to

Ahmedebad, then on to Agra, and so on. So it takes a little extra time. No big deal."

"How much extra time?" Thomas asked suspiciously. "How long will it take?"

Sedgwick shrugged. "I don't know. Five, maybe six days, but most of that is just getting to Agra. It's a fairly straight shot after that."

"Six days! Jaysus, we could be there by supper tomorrow night if we booked the AC chair car on an express, like normal people."

"Yeah, well, normal people in a chair car express aren't undercover and on the run, looking to cover their tracks. On top of that"—Sedgwick stabbed a thumb in Conor's direction—"the chair car folks wouldn't appreciate having his microbes cycling through the AC system."

"Ah. Fair point there." Thomas looked at Conor with renewed concern. "How's the form, by the way? Feeling all right?"

Conor pursed his lips, diffidently considering the question. "Not too bad. Only half-smothered. I'm about ready for a chair of some kind, though."

"Well let's head over to your palace on wheels," Sedgwick said. "No reason they can't roll it to the Chennai Mail with you inside it. It's sitting on Platform 28 right now."

Trailing along at the rear, Conor found it a little ridiculous that a railway station could be so enormous. When he trudged down a flight of stairs onto Platform 28, he felt as though they'd marched halfway back to Bandra. Ahead of him, Thomas and Sedgwick had continued farther up the platform to buy food from a trackside vendor, but he wasn't hungry, and he'd walked far enough.

He stopped in front of the rail car that would be their mode of transport for the next six days and eyed it doubtfully. It didn't look like much, at least from the outside. A 1920s-era Pullman edition, its drab, black-and-olive paint job was chipped and dull, and the washed-out lettering on the side proclaiming it the "Redwood Special" did not evoke visions of luxury.

Although several of the pitted and scratched windows glowed with a sallow light, the curtains had been drawn over most of them, obscuring whatever lay inside. At the end of the car, however, he saw that one window had remained uncovered. Through it, he caught sight of a darkened living room and the dim outline of a plump, overstuffed sofa. It looked particularly inviting.

A door at the end of the room led out onto a rear observation deck, and with a hopeful grunt, Conor walked over to the stairs leading up to it. He took hold of the railing, but before he could pull himself up, the door above flew open and a dark shape emerged. It tumbled down the stairs and collided with his midsection. Just as quickly, it bounced off again and began speeding away from him, a long length of fabric flapping out behind it.

Conor staggered back and then spun to look at the rapidly retreating figure.

"Oh, shit!" He began to run, frantically motioning at Sedgwick and his brother, who were just strolling back, loaded down with greasy-looking bags.

"Grab her!" Conor shouted. Their faces gaped as the small form dodged nimbly around them and continued on without breaking stride. He broke through the two of them, cursing in explosive gusts. "Are you made of stone, for Jesus' sake? Radha, stop! Wait!"

He didn't have a prayer of catching her at this pace, but at the far end of the platform, she became entangled with several children and their mother. The woman—wearing a full-length, black chador—was still gripping Radha by the wrist, scolding her clumsiness, when he stumbled up and dropped onto one knee.

With her back to him and all of her energy focused on escape, Radha did not notice him. She twisted furiously in the large woman's grasp, spitting a stream of obscenities worthy of the crustiest South Asian sailor. She wore a bright yellow *salwar kameez*, and her *dupatta*—a wide ribbon of cloth that matched the rest of the outfit—clung precariously to her shoulder at one end. The other end dragged along the ground near Conor's foot. He picked it up and draped the loose end over her opposite shoulder.

"Rad ... Radha ... " He began, forcing out syllables between breaths.

The reaction was instantaneous. Perceiving a new threat at her back, Radha wrenched her hand free from the burly woman and snatched at the soiled end of her *dupatta*. With a cry like that of a goaded animal, she whirled around and found herself eye-to-eye with her adversary. She stared at Conor and the contorted snarl on her face changed to awe-struck wonder.

"Con-ji! I was not believing it."

Her arms dropped limply to her sides, and Conor allowed his muscles to relax. Rocking back, he rested an arm on top of his knee and regarded her with anxious bewilderment. What the hell was going on? Who, or what, was she running from, and what was she doing here in the first place?

Before he could venture any questions, Radha's face became animated again, and she launched herself at him. Her small hands pounded at his chest and shoulders with a hysterical frenzy, and she began a litany of her own questions, a cross-examination punctuated with outrage and reproach.

"Now you are come, *bhaiyya*? Where have you been keeping until this time, please? Why did you go away? What is making you treat Radha so badly? Why taking her from Rohit Mehta, and leaving her in some too horrible place with bad people?"

He could have easily caught hold of the little, balled up fists, but he let her continue pummeling him in rhythm with each indignant exclamation. He was too surprised to stop her.

"Horrible?" Conor stammered weakly. "What bad people? What are you talking about, Radha?"

"Her!" She pointed wildly over his shoulder. He swiveled on his knee to look behind him, and saw that Thomas and Sedgwick had caught up and were accompanied by Kavita, who stood looking at them placidly.

"It happens I was wrong, *beta*," she said, a corner of her mouth lifting in a wry smile. "She is hating me and not you."

As if in confirmation, Radha burst into tears and threw herself against Conor. Hiding her face against his shoulder, she poured out her story between sobs. "She would not let me leave that room. She locked the door. She is watching me always. She took away ... " Radha faltered but then continued in a rush. "She took away all my things and is making me to take some sticky, burning drink, and I was being so sick, *bhaiyya*!"

"Sounds vaguely familiar."

Conor heard Sedgwick's soft remark behind him but ignored it. He put an arm around Radha, trying to soothe her. "Shhh, sweetheart. It's all right now. Nobody is trying to hurt you. Kavita's been trying to help you and me as well. You and I have both been ill—she's had her hands full with the pair of us."

"Also? You are being ill?" Her voice, muffled against his shoulder dropped down to a low conspiratorial whisper. "She must be a very bad woman, Con-ji. So wicked. She is poisoning us, I think."

Despite her seriousness—or maybe because of it—Conor could not suppress a gasp of laughter. When she lifted her head to look into his face, however, he sobered immediately. Gently but firmly, he pushed her away from him and gave her arms a reassuring squeeze as he got to his feet.

"Sure it only tastes like poison, love. The best medicines always do. *Shrimati-ji* is a legend you know, a very great healer. I can't think she's been unkind to you. You're not trying to make me believe that, are you?"

Reluctantly, Radha shook her head, and from lowered lids, glanced at the small, elderly woman with a new expression of tentative curiosity.

"Of course not." He looked inquiringly at Kavita. "What are you both doing here, *ji*? Why did you bring her?"

"My recommendation," Sedgwick said, before she could reply. "Your business agreement with Mehta is null and void. Khalil took his money back, so the little 'godfather of the dance bar' wants his property back; and since he and Khalil have had their *taporis* on the prowl for you for the past three days, he'll want to pry information out of her about you. He's not likely to be gentle, because he doesn't have much to lose. You can't sell a *sar dhakna* more than once."

"And you will not be here to protect her from this," Kavita added quietly. "Mumbai is not safe for you and now also not safe for Radha."

"Thanks to me." Conor brushed a hand over his eyes and saw Sedgwick regarding him with a half-sympathetic smirk.

"You know what they say, dude. 'No good deed goes unpunished.' I hate to say I told you so."

"Then don't," Thomas said.

Conor bobbed his head gratefully at his brother, for the remark and also for not resuming a demand for explanations that he had some right to expect at this point. After a moment of uncomfortable silence, Kavita gathered up a corner of her shawl and tossed it over her shoulder with an impatient sniff.

"Good deed, bad deed, what deed? This is some rubbish talk. Come. Ashram is there. Clean air and healthful foods are there. Massages and other Ayurvedic treatments also there. A good place, with many good things. Why such tension? It is nonsense making."

Conor turned back to Radha, spreading his hands in appeal. "What do you think, *choti bahan*? You came away with me once already. Do you trust me enough to try it again?"

"I trust you. I will come with you, Con-ji," she said, in a strained voice. She had been listening closely to their conversation, and her face was gray with fear. Repeatedly, her eyes met his and flicked skittishly away, a little guiltily, he thought. "I trust also your friends if you are saying it is good," she added. "But, Rohit Mehta—he is angry with you, and he is angry also with me? I was not knowing this. He did not sound—"

Again, she glanced up and away from him. This time, the look of guilt was unmistakable, and they all saw it.

"Son of a bitch," Sedgwick breathed. "I knew she would be trouble."

Conor made an urgent motion for him to be silent. Keeping his voice low and calm, he encouraged her to continue. "He didn't sound angry when you spoke to him, is that it? When was that, Radha? When did you speak to him?"

"Just now." Her voice was barely audible. "Some little while ago."

"How did you contact him?"

Without looking at him again, Radha reached through a slit in her *salwar kameez* and pulled Conor's mobile phone from her pocket. Kavita hissed a sigh of disappointment.

"All of your things we brought to rail car. This phone she is taking from your room there."

He nodded, keeping his eyes on Radha. "You spoke to him a little while ago, and he told you what to do. What was it?"

"He told me to run," she whispered, "that he was coming and fetching me. I was frightened, *bhaiyya*. I was not wanting to go to a faraway place on a train. The woman—*Shrimati-ji*—she was telling me you also would come, but I was not believing it."

"Where is he meeting you? What did you tell him?"

He had continued speaking in tones of quiet composure, but it seemed to only frighten her more. Her small body quaking with terror and remorse, she raised her eyes to look at the large metal sign hanging from the ceiling above their heads. Platform 28.

26

With an oath of barely contained rage, Sedgwick walked several steps away and slammed the bags of food he had been holding into a trash bin. He stood for several seconds with his hands on his hips, glaring down at the bin, but when he returned, his face was composed and his voice clipped and businesslike.

"Okay, we've got to get out of here, now. And by now, I mean right now. Get back down the platform to the private car. It's got to connect with the next train out of the station, wherever it's going. I'll go figure that out. Tom, do you still have money? There's a station engine attached to the Pullman, and the engineer is in it already, I saw him there earlier. Pay him whatever it takes to get the fucking thing moved out into the yard. We've got to get it away from this platform. Kavita, get Radha out of sight. Lock her in the bathroom, if you have to. Take the phone away from her, obviously. Conor, you need to—Christ, you look like hell. Tom, look after your brother. He's ready to drop."

Sedgwick tossed this final observation over his shoulder while sprinting to the nearest stairs and taking them three at a time. Conor watched him go and turned to find the others staring at him.

There was no use denying that he was in poor shape. Whatever air he was taking in felt like it was being strained through a ball of damp wool lodged in his throat. His brother scrutinized him more closely.

"Are you all right?"

"Not great," he admitted, "but not ready to drop. I will be, though, if I have to hike around this feckin' place anymore. Go on and have yer man get the train started. It's got to come back this way to get out of the station. I'll just wait and crawl on board when it gets here."

Thomas opened his mouth to object but then closed it again and nodded. With one challenge put to rest, Conor turned next to Radha. She was still badly frightened, her face pale and tear-stained.

"*Chuisle*, it'll be all right." He gave her cheek a light pinch and then turned her around to face Thomas. "This is my own *bhaiyya*. His name is Thomas." Conor shot his brother a playful glance. "You can call him Tom, though. He won't mind. Go with him and Kavita-ji. I'm going to wait here and rest a bit, and we'll all leave on the train together."

"Do you promise this, Con-ji?" She searched his face. "You will not go away from me, again?"

"I can't promise anything, Radha," he replied. "All I can say is that I'm not planning to go anywhere."

Surprisingly, his candor seemed to satisfy her. With a solemn nod, she took the hand Thomas offered, and the two of them set off together, following Kavita back to the private car.

He looked around for a place to sit, or more accurately, collapse. There was nothing. He shuffled over to one of the steel girders holding up the roof. First he leaned against it, and then, sinking down to the ground, he slumped against it. The crowds had thinned considerably in this section of the station. The people milling about earlier had disappeared from the platform, and there were few on the adjoining ones. In the distance, he heard voices and the low-throated hum of engines. Against all reasonable expectation, he found himself falling into a doze.

About ten minutes later, his catnap was disrupted by two noises occurring simultaneously: a distant, high-pitched squeal of train wheels and a much closer explosion of gunfire.

He had the Walther out before he was fully awake. He slid up into a low squat, pressing against the column at his back, and peeked around the edge of it.

The shots had sounded from one of the pedestrian bridges suspended over the tracks, and Conor spotted Sedgwick, half-hidden in the shadows on the far side of the bridge. He stood within twenty feet of the staircase, gun gripped in one hand at chest level, but those last twenty feet were completely exposed. He was pinned in a shallow alcove, safely shielded but trapped.

He couldn't tell if the agent had seen him, and he could not identify the enemy. Along the bridge, bystanders skittered like ball bearings dropped on the pavement. Some were running back to the terminal while others threw themselves to the ground. Several huddled together behind a sheet metal structure—a snack stand, he surmised—at the center of the bridge. Everyone seemed to be shouting.

He took in the panoramic mayhem and pulled his head back, letting it rest against the steel column. The surreal tableau resembled nothing so much as a shooting gallery. It seemed eerily similar to the weapons simulation facility at Fort Monckton. Hit the right targets and rack up points, hit the wrong ones and—well, no, on second thought, it wasn't similar at all.

"Shit," Conor sighed.

Briefly closing his eyes, he reviewed his options and made a decision. He repositioned himself to face forward, and bracing an arm against the girder, stepped out from his cover to squeeze off two quick shots.

A deafening crash sounded as the bullets hit the top of the snack stand. The roof lurched up and spun sideways while the rest of the structure skewed to the right with a stuttering screech. It was abrupt and dramatic, just as he'd hoped. He stood perfectly still to watch its aftereffects. The success of the strategy depended on being able to see something he recognized and to see it in time.

People who'd previously been upright dropped to the floor in fresh panic while others already down tried to flatten themselves more completely; and in the space of an instant, he saw a particular sort of movement from a figure crouched near the snack stand. He flexed his wrist an inch to the left and fired. The figure jerked spasmodically, screaming as he was struck, while at the same time a bullet glanced off the steel next to Conor and sent a shower of sparks streaming over his head.

"Target good, ten points for me," he whispered shakily, ducking back behind the girder. More bullets ricocheted off the girder and surrounding pavement before another set of shots signaled that Sedgwick was drawing fire to give him cover. Conor darted out and immediately had the gunman in sight but had no clear shot. He put a few more rounds into the collapsing snack stand and ducked back, swearing. The air around him popped and pinged as the barrage shifted to him again.

The pattern continued until he finally saw an opening. He took the shot while Sedgwick bolted for the stairs, also firing as he ran. The figure on the bridge, seemingly hit from both directions, crumpled without a sound.

Conor's eyes swept along the bridge as the silence continued. He emerged from hiding and was heading toward Sedgwick, who was yelling something as he raced down the stairs. The ground in front of Conor erupted in a series of tiny explosions.

"Second gun, second gun! There were two of them!"

Conor dove, half-rolling and half-crawling back to the relative safety of the steel girder.

"He's too close to this side. I don't have an angle," Sedgwick called from the stairwell when the shooting stopped. "I can't even see him. Cover me, and I'll come over to you."

"Christ, no, don't!" Conor shouted. "There isn't enough here to shield both of us."

"Then I'll go back up and—"

"And be gone for your tea in about ten seconds. He's right by the top of the stairs. You can't do anything, Sedgwick. Just stay where you are, for fuck's sake. He's got no shot at you there."

"Well, what do you want to do, then?"

"Haven't a clue," Conor mumbled. He was close to the end of the little strength he'd had to begin with and what breath he could muster was coming in hoarse gasps. He also needed to reload.

"McBride, did you hear me?" Sedgwick called. "Are you all right over there?"

"Yeah, yeah. Just hang on a minute."

He popped the spent magazine from the Walther, and with shaking fingers, pulled the spare from his shoulder holster. As he snapped it into place, he looked up and saw the station engine come into view. It was chugging slowly up the platform with the Pullman car in tow, gliding onto the scene like the proverbial *deus ex machina*. Conor watched its approach with grim determination.

"Right. We'll have to make this work."

He wiped his palms against his shirt and took a firmer grip on the gun. He waved it at the engineer, motioning for him to keep the train moving, but the wild-eyed man cowering in the cab needed no such encouragement.

"Get ready to run for it," Conor shouted to Sedgwick. "You first. I'll count it off and you'll go on three, right?"

"And who's going to cover you running for it?" Sedgwick countered skeptically.

"If I hit him, I won't need it, and if he was any good, he'd have got me the first time."

"Not a smart plan. It's too dicey."

"Too dicey?" He very nearly laughed. "Get on your mark and

get ready, you horse's ass. One, two ... three!"

Sedgwick sprang from the stairwell as Conor opened fire. He took the first three shots while still protected behind the girder, and the next several he released on the run. Since they were all more or less blind, he aimed them high, unwilling to risk an indiscriminate spray at the bridge. Ahead of him, Sedgwick twisted and began shooting as he continued running. With the additional firepower providing at least the illusion of cover, Conor stopped in the middle of the platform and took more careful aim.

"What the hell are you doing?" Sedgwick yelled. "Keep moving, for God's sake! Get on the train!"

"It's all right," Conor murmured, mostly for his own benefit. "I've got him."

In the next instant the dark shape on the bridge pitched over the side, and after a drop of forty feet, landed facedown on the rails of Track 27. Conor swayed forward a few steps and dropped down to brace his hands on his knees as Sedgwick arrived at his side.

"The other one. Is he dead as well?" Conor asked.

The agent gave him a level look. "What answer would you prefer to hear?"

He hung his head, not responding. Sedgwick put a hand on his shoulder.

"Come on, ace. That station engineer looked like he wasn't stopping until he hits the ocean. We'll never catch him if we don't get going, and we don't want to be around when the police get here."

"A bit weird that they're not already, isn't it? We made enough noise."

"Yeah, I thought that, too." Sedgwick looked up at the shrieking pedestrians on the bridge with a frown. "Those guys didn't strike me as Rohit Mehta's typical lowlife *taporis*. They don't usually carry guns. Something even weirder—they were clearly targeting me. Unless somebody already discovered what really got buried down at the Sassoon Dock, Khalil had no reason to come after me."

"What do you think it means?"

"Damned if I know," Sedgwick said. "Anyway, we don't have time to figure it out now. We need to run for it."

With his head still down, Conor tried to fortify himself with a deeper breath and failed. "I don't think I can do that."

"You can do it," Sedgwick insisted, putting a hand under his arm. "Your brother will have my guts for garters if you don't."

Straightening slowly, Conor began an acerbic remark, but the words caught in his throat. Doubling over again, he struggled for breath around a spasm of gagging coughs while pressure mounted in his lungs like a tightening knot. Sedgwick caught him as he fell and lowered him to the ground. Still coughing, Conor pressed his hands on the pavement, bracing against the unbearable pain in his chest. He felt something give way and finally could breathe again. He opened his eyes and stared at a spot between his arms where the concrete was stained with a dark patch of blood.

"Oh. Fuck." He gazed at the spot in mild, surprised annoyance.

Sedgwick knelt in front of him, white-faced, his anxiety yielding to tentative relief.

"That's it? 'Oh, fuck,' like you just snapped a friggin' shoelace? You've just—literally, it looks like—hacked up a lung and scared me shitless, and that's all you can say?"

"Sorry."

"You should be." Sedgwick sat on his heels and pressed his hands against his eyes. When he looked up again, he brightened. "Here comes Tom. He must have managed to get that bug-eyed engineer to pull over and wait for us."

Thomas was coming at a run, peppering them with questions

as he approached. "Are you all right? What the hell was it about, then? Are they gone? Are they—holy mother of God ... " He broke off as he saw the body lying across the tracks, and registered even greater alarm as he caught sight of the blood. "How bad is it? Where are you hit?"

"No, it isn't ... I didn't get shot," Conor stammered. He drew a hand across his mouth and gave a slight start as he looked at it.

"Here." His brother pulled out a handkerchief and passed it to him, his weathered face twisting in anguish. "Sedgwick, we're mad to be hauling him away to the mountains. Christ, there's nothing up there. We ought to be taking him to a hospital to see a doctor."

"I've seen one already, Thomas," Conor said quietly. He wiped his mouth and wadded the bloodied handkerchief in his hand. "And he's seen all he needs to of me. The drugs will either work, or they won't. It's only been a few days."

He put a hand against his side and took a cautious breath, the deepest one he'd managed all day. "To be honest, I'm feeling a bit better. Maybe I shook something up in there."

"Then get up and start moving," Sedgwick said briskly, looking at his watch. "We've got ten minutes to hook up with our train."

They half-dragged and half-carried him down the tracks and up the stairs into the Pullman. Within twenty minutes—after one of those Indian feats of organization that pulls improbable success from a cauldron of chaos—it was smoothly riding along at the end of the ten o'clock train to Nagpur.

As soon as he stepped on board, a quick glance was all Conor needed to recognize he had seriously underestimated the charms of the "Redwood Special." Unlike the shopworn exterior, its interior was designed to satisfy the creature comforts of the most discerning maharajah, or, in this case, mobster. With plush, royal red carpeting and upholstery; gold-plated fixtures; marble accents; and a dining room complete with crystal chandelier, the car was nothing short of a rolling mansion.

Unfortunately, he got no immediate chance to enjoy its amenities and no immediate answers to the questions that were piling up at an accelerating rate. He had barely eased into the comfort of the long-awaited couch when he was being forcibly dosed with a handful of antibiotics, followed by a paregoric chaser. Fiercely, he fought to hold his ground against the soporific haze stealing over him.

"Sneaky bunch, the lot of you," he croaked, scowling as Kavita put a hand to his forehead, lips pursed in diagnostic concentration. "Like a feckin' ambush. Well, you won't get out of it that way. I'll not be going quietly until I get answers. Let's have the story you promised, Sedgwick, and hurry up about it."

"Afraid it's going to have to wait a little longer," Sedgwick said. "I'm getting off the train at Nasik to head back and see if I can figure out a few things. I'll catch up with you again in Agra. You've got a twelve-hour layover when you get there."

He shifted his gaze to Thomas and found no help there either. "You'll not be getting anything out of me. This was all his idea. Let him tell it."

"Okay, then. Fine." Conor struggled obstinately against the insidious embrace of the sofa cushions and turned back to Sedgwick. "We've got a few hours before Nasik, so start talking. Like you said earlier, we've got a long night ahead of us."

From their respective chairs across the room, Thomas and Sedgwick exchanged an ironic glance. The agent's face quivered, and Thomas responded with a half-suppressed snort. A few seconds later, they were both convulsed with laughter.

"Do you not think it's long enough already, you silly gack?" Thomas gasped. "You're cracksome, little brother, no mistake. I love your spunk, but Jaysus, have a look at yourself. You're covered in dirt, pale as the white bull of Connaught, and have bloodstains all down the front of you. You're looking like something the tide wouldn't take out."

Conor looked down and winced in distaste. Contrary to Sedgwick's presumption, the sight of a moderate amount of his own blood pooling on the pavement—where it had no business being—had produced a substantial shock. As supporting evidence making the diagnosis more certain, he could have done without it. The sight of the rusty stains drying on his shirt was just that last bit of melodrama that proved too much for him. His resistance disintegrated.

"You're right," he whispered and closed his eyes.

27

For a week, the Redwood Special continued its hopscotch journey from one scheduled train to another, attaching and uncoupling from each like a faithless consort. It rolled from Aurangabad to Nagpur to Ahmedabad, clattering across the powder-dry Indian countryside in a zigzag pattern; and apart from brief intervals when he was made to sit up and swallow something, Conor slept through most of it.

After defying it with such persistence, his capitulation to illness was so complete and his exhausted surrender so out of character that Thomas and Kavita became openly anxious for the return of his "cracksome" obstinacy.

They had valid grounds for concern. When he was awake enough to be sensible, Conor was unnerved by the intensity of his symptoms. No matter how still he kept, everything ached, and the awareness of each laborious breath produced such fatigue that he worried he might unconsciously stop trying.

Complicating his condition was the emotional residue from having killed two men in a violent gun battle. Although he slept continuously for several days, hardly conscious for ten minutes at a time, it was never enough. His sleep was restless, filled with noise and jumpy images. Frequently he would wake, sweaty and gasping, wondering if it was possible to sleep twenty hours a day and die of exhaustion.

Fortunately, the antibiotics did find traction and encouraging signs appeared as they gained the upper hand. His lungs began clearing; the quick, shallow snatches of air lengthened; and the painful scrape in his chest subsided. These were all positive developments, but as it turned out, the most important accelerant to his recovery was Radha.

At first, out of an abundance of caution, he had asked that she not be allowed into his room at all, but she misinterpreted that directive and suffered from it more than he realized. Still fragile in her own recovery, Radha was confused and forlorn, feeling somehow to blame for bringing sickness on the rescuer who had twice delivered her from Rohit Mehta.

Because she was kind, Kavita took pity on the young girl's misery, and because she was wise, she found an answer for it. When Radha appeared at Conor's bedside one afternoon, her eyes peeking anxiously above a familiar, sea-green respirator mask, he was completely undone. A happy glow of affection shot through his heart at the sight of her. He couldn't summon the will to even try turning her away.

"What are you doing here, little one?" he asked softly, in Hindi.

"I am becoming nurse," came the muffled reply, in English. "Kavita-ji has asked me. She is doing many, busy things, and she is somewhat old, *bhaiyya*. I am to be helping her."

"*Accha.* I see. What assignment has she given you?"

"Bringing food," Radha replied briskly. "And watching you eat. You must be sitting up now, Con-ji. You cannot eat soup lying down flat like this."

Hiding a smile, he pushed himself up and helped her to lift the tray onto his lap. She slid it into place and took up a position at the foot of his bed, regarding the tray expectantly. He tilted an eyebrow at her.

"Are you really going to watch me eat it?"

"*Haan ji.* Each bite, even. So strict I will be."

Her hazel eyes above the mask twinkled with such devilish

glee that he couldn't help laughing. It didn't hurt as much as he might have expected.

With the addition of Radha's tender, half-comical ministrations, Conor's recovery gathered momentum, and he began venturing from his bedroom to the sitting room couch for extended periods. Relaxing there one evening, his mulish character at last resurfaced when Kavita presented the nightly dose of cough medicine from her trusty brown bottle. When he flatly refused it, complaining he was tired of feeling half drunk all the time, he saw her share a satisfied smile with Thomas. She put the bottle away, and after some experimentation, came up with a narcotic-free alternative that was nearly as effective, and—perversely—tasted twice as bad.

Owing to the haphazard route, the journey to Agra took four days longer than originally planned. When they pulled into the Cantonment Station on a Monday morning, they had been traveling for ten days and were looking forward to the twelve-hour layover. Palatial accommodations notwithstanding, they were all anxious for a break from the Pullman. Even Conor had recovered to the point of becoming stir crazy and insisted he was strong enough for an outing.

They were gathered for breakfast in the crystal-encrusted dining room discussing what to do with their brief hiatus when Thomas paused with the butter knife in his hand and glanced around the table sheepishly. "I've been rambling around this country for nearly six years and would you believe I've never seen the Taj Mahal?"

He was slathering butter over slices of toast and tossing them onto the plate in front of Conor, who was eating them as quickly as they arrived. His appetite had resurfaced with a vengeance, and ever since his brother had been stoking him like a coal-burning furnace.

"Ah, it is very beautiful," Kavita sighed. "The precious stones, the inlay, and marble carvings, the tomb of Mumtaz, and the names of God. A sight that 'creates sorrowing sighs, and the sun and moon shed tears from their eyes.' These are words of emperor Shah Jahan. Yes. You must go, both of you."

She toggled her head at Conor and Thomas with a genial smile. They did not make the mistake of underestimating its mildness.

"Well, I guess that's settled," Conor said drily. "What about you and Radha, though? Do you not want to see it as well?"

Kavita waved a hand breezily toward her young nursing assistant. "Another time. Radha and I will be keeping busy while you are making the tour. Some shopping, some visiting."

He turned to Radha to see how this arrangement sat with her. She beamed at him with eager reassurance and gave a small bounce in her chair. "Yes, this is so. Kavita-ji and I will be keeping very busy while you are seeing these tombs and stones."

He smiled back at her, marveling that such a transformation from bitter enemy to fervent acolyte could be accomplished in the course of ten days. He also breathed a prayer of gratitude that the hard, desperate hunger he had seen in her at the Mumbai train station had also been wiped away. Radha's eyes were now as they were meant to be—not downcast or frightened or fidgeting restlessly in search of a fix, but shining with intelligence and expectation. Her resilient spirit humbled him and reminded him that he bore some responsibility for ensuring the fulfillment of its promise.

They emerged from the Agra train station into a warm, March morning, and the usual assortment of auto-rickshaw drivers collected around them. Conor knew any eye contact led to protracted exchanges that ended in disappointment for everyone. He did his best to politely ignore the drivers and set his gaze on the middle distance, where it came to rest on a gleaming black sedan with tinted windows. It idled smoothly in a parking area across the square, providing a sharp contrast to the battered, colorless vehicles surrounding it. Thomas had noticed it as well.

"Friends of yours, I suppose, *ji*?"

"Yes, Tom." Kavita squinted up at him with a smile. "This car is coming from Agra cathedral complex on Wazirpura Road. You will come join us after your touring."

Conor and Thomas shared a puzzled glance.

"Who do you know at the cathedral?" Conor asked.

"Archbishop." Kavita put a hand on Radha's shoulder, and they set off across the square with the sound of her low, infectious laugh still hanging in the air.

"Well, naturally. The archbishop." Thomas shook his head. "She looks like she's up to something, don't you think?"

"She's always up to something." Conor shrugged. "We'll find out eventually, I imagine. Now, before we get into it with this crowd, do you fancy a cab or an auto-rickshaw?"

"Auto-rickshaw," Thomas replied immediately. "I'm after starving for a bit of adventure."

*S*hould guilty seek asylum here,
Like one pardoned, he becomes free from sin.
Should a sinner make his way to this mansion
All his past sins are to be washed away.

With the guide booklet lying open on his lap, Conor read the words again. It was from the passage Kavita had cited earlier—the Mughal emperor, Shah Jahan, extolling the marvels and near divine powers of the mausoleum he had created as the final setting for his priceless jewel, the beloved Mumtaz.

In front of him sat the thing itself, shimmering like a mirage under the hot afternoon sun. He and Thomas had explored every inch of it, along with its surrounding gardens and outbuildings, and were resting now in the shade of the *Darwaza-i rauza*, the monumental structure that served as the main gateway into the compound. He shut the booklet and returned to a contemplation of the living postcard before him, soaking up the atmosphere and the irony.

Here he was again—the serial penitent—once more casting himself on the doorstep of another religion's iconic shrine seeking absolution. He didn't feel it and wasn't surprised. Despite the medieval emperor's assurance, he didn't expect the Taj Mahal to supply the same measure of peace he'd found in the cool stillness of the Jain mandir. Maybe it was because the Taj technically wasn't a mosque and therefore not actually a house of worship. More probably it was because blowing off a man's kneecap didn't share the same order of magnitude as shooting him to death.

He glanced at Thomas and blinked. "Did you say something?"

"I did, yeah," Thomas replied. "I said you've gone awfully quiet. We walked around a fair bit. Have you overdone it, do you think?"

"No, I'm fine, I was just—I don't know—daydreaming." He faced forward again, focusing now on the watery replica of the monument in the long reflecting pool.

"Want to talk about it?" Thomas asked quietly.

"Not really, no."

"You hadn't any choice, Conor."

"I know that." He wished his brother would stop talking. The familial sixth sense often floated forward when it was least wanted.

"So then, you shouldn't feel as though—"

"Thomas, for the love of Christ."

"Right." Thomas brushed a hand awkwardly across Conor's back and got to his feet. "I'm going for a bottle of water. Do you want one?"

"Sure."

Watching him disappear through the huge, red marble archway, Conor felt a twinge of regret for the rebuke and envious appreciation for the unchangeable nature of his brother. Thomas was older and sadder and encumbered with his own weight of guilt and self-reproach, but fundamentally he was the same person he had always been. Whatever he had been doing, it had not altered the essential man. He was simply himself—stolid, straightforward, and at home in his own skin. He was a model of stability in contrast to the splintering psyche of his younger brother.

When he returned, Conor accepted the water with a nod of thanks and apology. He took a long pull, and with his elbows on his knees, rolled the plastic bottle between his hands, staring at it. "When you're doing whatever it is that you're doing, have you ever needed to ...?"

Again, Thomas intuitively understood what remained unspoken and shook his head. "I've never carried a weapon— that's Sedgwick's department. I wouldn't know what to do with it if I had one."

"I'm glad," Conor said, his voice growing husky. "It generates its own sort of addiction, I've found. You want to get rid of it, but after a while you're afraid to be without it. You start learning things about yourself you didn't want to, and it ... changes you because you can't unlearn them. As much as you might want to, you can't go back to not knowing or to who you thought you were before you did." He looked at his brother with a brief grin. "Sorry. I'm talking shite. That barely made any sense, even to me."

"Conor, please," Thomas whispered. "Please, will you not let me put you on a plane and send you home? Before he got off the train, Sedgwick told me what you've been doing for the past few months. We had a hell of a fight over it. I've seen for myself how good you are with the gun, little brother, and I can see what it's doing to you. You don't belong in this mess."

"No more do you," Conor said, calmly. "You may as well give over, Thomas. You want me to go home, I want you to come with me, and neither of us is going to get what we want. We're stuck on this ride until it winds down or crashes, so we might as well face it. Sedgwick has told you what I've been up to, but I'm still in the dark about you. If he doesn't show up by the time we leave tonight, you're going to have come clean and tell me what's going on. Agreed?"

"Yeah. Agreed."

With a groaning oath, Thomas deflated and seemed to age even more, right there in front of him.

28

In obedience to Kavita's informal command, they set out to locate the cathedral complex in the early afternoon. In the Wazirpura neighborhood of Agra, the Catholic archdiocese had established a sprawling, well-tended enclave that their driver found without difficulty. They coasted through its gates and up a wide avenue lined with bougainvillea, passing signs for various buildings that were just visible beyond thick stands of trees. It seemed the grounds housed a number of schools and convents in addition to the main cathedral.

The auto-rickshaw circled around the church and deposited them in front of the main building, in a wide courtyard that was empty when they arrived, but by the time Conor had finished paying the driver, Kavita had appeared, walking alongside a priest in a long, white cassock. He was a handsome, middle-aged man, tall and slender, with skin the color of rich, burnished copper. He walked with a graceful, dance-like gait, which he was tactfully moderating to match the stride of his companion.

"Your Grace," Kavita said, smiling fondly as they approached, "I am presenting to you now my two good friends, these brothers Conor and Tom. Now boys, you will please shake hands with his Grace the Archbishop, Cecil de Cunha."

Like dutiful schoolchildren, they both stepped forward.

"Very pleased to meet you, Your Grace." Conor deferentially took the warm, brown hand extended to him.

"It's ... Thomas, actually," his brother said with a note of apology, shaking hands in turn.

"Like the saint," Archbishop de Cunha replied. His voice, deep and mellow, held a hint of dry amusement.

"A pretty far whack from that, I'm afraid, Your Grace." Thomas flushed with embarrassment and glared at Conor, who had choked off an involuntary laugh.

"Oh, yes?" The archbishop regarded each of them with a raised eyebrow and then relented with a nod. "Yes, a 'far whack.' All of us."

There was something regal about him, and yet his dark eyes, framed by large, square-rimmed glasses, radiated peaceful, good-humored warmth. He and Kavita seemed well suited and entirely at ease with each other. So well suited, in fact, that Conor narrowed his eyes with a flash of intuition. "The two of you wouldn't happen to be related at all?"

Archbishop de Cunha's face lit up with a broad smile, and Kavita's gurgling laugh rang through the courtyard.

"Very good, *beta*. Very clever. He is my nephew." She reached up to give the taller man an affectionate pat on his chest. "My sister's son. I was bringing Radha here to meet him and to be showing her this place. We have talked of many things together. Now I will be talking to you, and we will see what is to be done."

"Something needs to be done?" Conor asked.

At this, she and her nephew exchanged a nod of understanding. The archbishop inclined his head to each of them and wished them an enjoyable visit. With swift, stately elegance, he returned to the building, leaving the three of them standing in the courtyard, looking at each other.

Conor's question had come out sounding strained and overly casual. He'd seen the sign for St. Patrick's Junior College for Girls when they entered the complex and had immediately understood what Kavita was plotting. Just a few evenings earlier, they had discussed the question of Radha's education, after she'd gone to her room. He hadn't expected things to progress so quickly and was surprised by how conflicted he felt about it.

It was unquestionably the right thing for her. She would be safe, comfortably beyond the reach of Rohit Mehta. She would be given the chance to learn and thrive in a stable environment. If it was not for this that he had committed larceny to bring her out of Kamathipura, then for what? She deserved the opportunity; it was his duty to facilitate it. And yet, it was difficult—more painful than he had ever imagined—to think of leaving Agra without her.

"Do you not think so?" Kavita prodded, gently. "Truly, she is *choti bahan*, 'little sister' to you, and you are very loving, but is it being wise to carry her with you, where you are going? Will you carry her farther even, one day, when you are going home? There is a place for her here. Is it not better for Radha to remain?"

"Yes. Of course it is." He forced the words past the dryness in his throat. "Have you talked with her? Does she want to stay?"

She nodded. "We have talked. I believe she wants it, but so devoted she is to her *bhaiyya*. What you will be wanting—this is very important to her."

"I understand, *ji*. Where is she?"

"She is just there by the church, sitting with Curtis. He reached this morning also." Kavita motioned across the courtyard with a sigh. "This troubling matter, not so easy to fix, I think."

Beyond a large garden of flowering shrubs, the Cathedral of the Immaculate Conception sat at the center of the compound. It was a long, Victorian-style confection, painted in creamy yellow. On the steps in front of the main door, Radha and Sedgwick sat together. Their heads were bowed, almost touching, their attention focused on Sedgwick's right arm, which was turned up and lying across her knees.

Thomas sucked in his breath, and Kavita wagged her head sadly. "Yes. He is struggling also, Tom-ji. He will not speak of it to me. I think maybe he does not understand even, but you see how it is."

Conor could see it well enough also. With his shirtsleeves rolled up to the elbows, Sedgwick's lean, tanned arms were plainly visible, and the trails of angry red marks scored along the underside of each looked raw and painful, even at this distance. Radha appeared to be rubbing them with ointment. He couldn't see Sedgwick's face, but it was clear that he was speaking and that she was listening intently. Every few seconds, she looked up at him, her eyes wide and solemn.

"Oh my God," Conor breathed, feeling a queasiness in his stomach. "Does that mean what I think it does?"

"No, it bloody well doesn't," Thomas said brusquely, but then added in a softer voice, "At least ... I mean, Christ, I hope not."

"No, you are right in this," Kavita reassured him. "He is taking no drugs. He is remaining strong, Tom-ji."

Thomas breathed a sigh of relief. "It's the scars," he explained, seeing Conor's confusion. "In some ways, it's good they never faded. They remind him what he's been through, but he says they sometimes itch like hell. That's how it works on him now, tickling at him when his defenses are low. He's managed to fight it for two years, but every so often he tears his arms apart, usually in his sleep."

They watched Radha carefully roll the sleeve down over Sedgwick's right arm and reach for his left. Thomas grimaced in sympathy. "I haven't seen them this bad in a long while. I'm surprised he's letting her do that for him, though."

"I asked him to," Kavita said, acknowledging with a shrug that it made Sedgwick's submission a foregone conclusion. "It is good for them to know one another better, for her to understand the menace of the thing that reached for her and for him to accept tenderness and help another, as he has been helped."

"I wonder what brought it on," Conor mused. He felt a

reluctant, growing respect for the agent, for his perseverance in what had to be a weary struggle. "Do you suppose he had another run-in with the Khalil gang?"

"I doubt it," Thomas said. "If anything, he's better when he's kept busy."

"You were very angry with him," Kavita suggested. "So much yelling that first night on the train."

"I had good reason to be angry. Ah, go on now, Kavita," Thomas scowled, his face incredulous. "You're not saying he's ripped his arms to pieces because I yelled at him. Sure we've yelled at each other before, fairly often as a matter of fact."

She took his arm, giving it a small shake. "He is afraid that soon he will miss your yelling. Radha has her *bhaiyya* and Curtis also. You too have been big brother to him, and this bond is everything for him. He grew well with you caring for him. This business of yours moved slowly, but now it becomes quick. When it is finished, you also will go away. He sees this already, and it is frightening for him. You had not seen it."

"No. I hadn't thought that far ahead." Thomas looked down at the tiny woman, his surprise changing to distress. "That's a hell of a thing to put on me, you know. A hell of a thing."

He abruptly turned and made a quick circuit around the courtyard's central fountain. Conor saw he was close to the breaking point.

"When do I get some rest from all this?" Thomas hissed desperately. "I promised to see it through with him, but am I meant to stay a fugitive my entire life?"

"Thomas, take it easy," Conor began, but his brother flung an arm in his direction and continued in a strangled voice.

"I ran away. I abandoned obligations and left my family to suffer the consequences. Is it wrong that I might like to go back and clear my name, and—please God—beg my own mother's forgiveness before she dies? Is that what counts as betrayal now?

Is that considered desertion?"

"*Bas.*"

Kavita's voice was not loud, but the word cracked emphatically in the courtyard. Thomas looked as though he'd been punched. He sank onto the edge of the fountain at the center of the courtyard, and she came to stand before him. Conor followed and sat down next to him.

"I'm sorry, *ji*. I didn't mean to be yelling at you," Thomas said, morosely. "I do understand what you're saying. It's no one-way street, after all. God knows Sedgwick has been there for me plenty of times."

He scrubbed his hands over his face and then looked at them both with a weary sigh. "So, what now?"

"No more of this nonsense, talking of 'betrayal' and 'desertion,'" Kavita said. "Be a bit more calm. Matters will arrange themselves without such drama. Only let him know that it is well between you. Help him to know that your strength will find him, even if you are not here."

Thomas rolled his eyes with a faint groan and looked at Conor. "I'm not much good at this."

"Nope, me either," Conor said. "Looks like we both have some work to do, *bhaiyya.*"

Thomas nodded. "It seems unfair. No matter what we do, we're always leaving someone behind."

"In time, we leave everyone behind, *beta*, but something of us remains, always."

Kavita had turned to look at Conor as she spoke, and her eyes filled with a bright, sad sympathy. Again, he felt the return of that portentous, jittery tapping at the back of his brain. It was a whisper of something he couldn't quite hear. He could only feel its feathery breath, freezing his heart.

It wasn't long before Radha led Sedgwick—unshaven and noticeably subdued—over to the courtyard, and the two brothers stoically took up their assignments. Thomas and Sedgwick returned to the train station in preparation for their departure that evening. Conor asked Radha and Kavita to show him some of the places they had seen during their visit to the cathedral. They strolled around the gardens and came to St. Patrick's Junior College, where the archbishop joined them, as if by chance. He guided them through the building, introducing teachers and describing the studies underway in various classrooms they passed. When they had finished, Conor sat with Radha in a small grotto behind the cathedral as twilight descended.

"Do you think it is a good place, Con-ji?" she asked, watching his face anxiously. "Would you be happy for me to be staying here?"

"I think it's a very good place," he assured her. "I'd be happy for you to stay, but more important, I think you will be happy here. Do you think so as well?"

Her face relaxed in relief. "Yes. I think so, and I am glad you think this way, too. *Shrimati-ji* says I will be learning so much, and if I am studying well, then in some time I will go to university. I can become nurse, Con-ji! A good one! Really and truly."

"You're a good one already, love." He put an arm around her. "Really and truly."

They had supper with Archbishop de Cunha, and after the meal, Conor brought Radha out to the courtyard where a cycle rickshaw had arrived to escort the new pupil to her quarters. A smiling nun in a gray habit was waiting, along with a friendly young girl who had clearly been brought along for moral support.

Her small bag of clothes and personal items had been sent over from the train earlier in the afternoon. Conor put it into the rickshaw, and after taking a steadying breath, he turned to face her. The moonless night wasn't dark enough to hide the look of pain on her face.

"Will you be coming back, Con-ji?" she asked in a small voice.

"Will you be visiting me sometime?"

He hesitated, wanting to lie and knowing he couldn't. He took another shaky breath. "I don't know, sweetheart. I know that I want to, and if I can, I will."

She nodded, lips trembling. "You will be going back to your home place."

"Yes. I think so."

In the next instant, her fine, small features had broken into pieces, and Conor was on his knees, pulling her into his arms. Her felt her tears soaking his shirt and tried desperately not to add his own to them. When she had cried herself out and grown quiet, he lifted her up into the rickshaw and gently pulled her arms from around his neck.

He arranged the *dupatta* that was always falling from her shoulder and then, smoothing her hair, kissed the top of her head and stepped back. She caught his arm and gave it one last squeeze. "I am missing you already, *bhaiyya*," she said, bravely meeting his eyes with sad composure. "And you? Also? Are you missing your Radha?"

Conor nodded, fighting to keep his voice level. "I am," he said, softly. "I am already missing my Radha."

29

The archbishop's sedan returned Conor and Kavita to the Cantonment Station with just fifteen minutes to spare before the train's seven o'clock departure. The streets of Agra were even more engorged with traffic than earlier, but the uproar seemed remote as observed from within the hermetically sealed vehicle. A muffled echo was all that penetrated its quiet interior.

Conor spoke little during the ride to the station. He felt bone tired, emotionally whiplashed, and the car's supersonic air conditioning was aggravating his lungs. He hunkered down into the soft leather and dispiritedly watched their progress through the city, trying not to breathe too much.

He rallied when he arrived on board the private car and found Thomas and Sedgwick lazily sprawled across the sitting room furniture, sipping mango *lassis*. Whatever "brotherly" conversation had taken place during the previous hours, it apparently had gone off successfully. Sedgwick still hadn't shaved, but he was again cloaked in his preferred "dramatis persona," caustic wit sharpened and at the ready.

"God almighty, McBride. Are you ever going to get rid of that damned cough?"

"I'll keep you posted." Conor kicked the agent's feet aside so he could more easily access the sofa. "I was fine until I got locked in the archbishop's bloody icebox of a car."

"Have the other *lassi*." Thomas indicated the extra glass on the coffee table. "Maybe it'll help."

"It won't," Conor assured him but reached for the glass as he sat down. "It has to taste like shite, or it isn't any use. Kavita will be here any minute with my evening shot of floor polish, so we'll all get some relief soon. How's everything coming along on this end?"

His eyes shot a question at Thomas over the rim of the glass, and his brother twitched a brief smile in response. "Oh, grand altogether. How about for you?"

"Yeah, fine. Sort of. It'll be fine."

He finished the sweetened yogurt drink, put the glass on the table, and coughed. "Told you." Conor shrugged apologetically as Kavita sailed in with resolute purpose.

"Not a moment too soon, *ji*," Sedgwick remarked. "I was ready to kick him and his moth-eaten lungs out the back door. I guess this means lights out for you, pal."

"Ah, that's where you're wrong, pal," Conor said. He winked at Kavita and shuddered in swallowing the dose. "Brand new recipe, same unparalleled flavor. I can go all night, if that's what it takes."

Taking the empty glass, she smiled in approval and gave Sedgwick a subtle gesture of command as she left the room. Conor settled back on the sofa, regarding him with relaxed expectation. "Will it take all night, do you think? I'm ready when you are, so tell me a story."

The light mockery in Sedgwick's eyes softened a few degrees. "Can't say you haven't earned it. Where do you want to start?"

"How about with that gang who were shooting at us at the train station—what have you got on that?"

"Bupkis. A hinky feeling with nothing to show for it." Sedgwick ran a hand over his face and looked startled at feeling its light stubble. "They were too well trained and well armed to be from Mehta's outfit—or Khalil's for that matter. Plus, when I got back, I confirmed the lid was still on our Sassoon Dock rope-a-dope, so they had no reason to come after me."

"What about the police at the train station?" Thomas asked. Sedgwick shook his head with a worried scowl.

"They weren't saying anything, no matter how many rupees I waved at them. That alone puts up the hair on the back of my neck. Somebody's paid them a bundle not to talk, or they're afraid to. Either way, not good."

In the pause that followed, the Pullman's coupling mechanism suddenly engaged with an echoing, metallic belch. The three of them jumped in unison and then settled back, grinning uneasily. The train lurched forward and began moving slowly out of the station.

"Okay, so if it isn't related to Khalil, it must have something to do with this other game the two of you are—no, sorry." Conor stopped himself. "I know. Not a game. What about it, though? British intelligence thinks this is a money-laundering scheme to arm a Kashmiri terrorist group. Is that what the DEA is up to? Because maybe your customers aren't satisfied with the service; maybe they sent a few representatives to Mumbai to let you know."

"Tom is the launderer for Pawan-bhai. That's nothing the DEA started, although we took advantage of it." Sedgwick pursed his lips and frowned thoughtfully at Conor. "And, the terrorist part ... " The agent looked to Thomas, as if seeking permission. His brother heaved a mighty sigh of resignation and glared at the ceiling.

"There are no terrorists," he growled. "Never have been."

"There have never been any terrorists?" Conor swiveled a glance back and forth between his brother and Sedgwick, uncertain who was going to pick up the thread.

"Technically untrue, in the general sense," Sedgwick said mildly. "Naturally, there have always been terrorists. You find them on every continent, and in every—"

"Oh, leave off, for fuck's sake," Thomas said. He pulled his gaze down from the ceiling. "We're not talking about the general sense. This particular 'story,' I suppose you can call it, has nothing to do with actual terrorists."

"What's it to do with, then?" Conor asked.

"Fake terrorists," Sedgwick replied promptly.

"Uh-huh. So far, I'm not mesmerized by this story. Please tell me it gets better than this."

"Not much," Thomas said. "Just give it to him straight, Sedgwick. The whole thing is bunged together with chewing gum and butcher's string if you ask me, but it will make more sense if you tell it properly."

"Okay, okay." Without preamble, Sedgwick abruptly shifted forward in his chair and gave Conor an unblinking stare. "Have you ever heard of a man called Vasily Dragonov?"

"No. Who is he?"

"You really don't know?"

"I just said so. You think I'm lying?"

Sedgwick regarded him for another few seconds but relaxed as Thomas let out another impatient sigh. "I just wondered whether his name got mentioned in any of your briefing books. Vasily Dragonov is one of the biggest drug and arms traffickers in the world. Although they don't get much support, the DEA—more specifically, Greg Walker—has been trying to nail him for twenty years. MI6 and the CIA give lip service to the idea, but they also use him as an informant for operations they're running from Colombia to Kosovo. Dragonov craps out a few nuggets of information for them every so often, and somehow they forget they're supposed to be capturing him."

"Shocking. I'm absolutely gobsmacked," Conor said tonelessly.

"Disillusioning, isn't it?" Sedgwick grinned. "Anyway, Walker got tired of the bullshit, and he's pretty high up in special ops now. The agencies have reciprocal agreements for information sharing, but he got permission to set up a sting operation and fly it dark and silent. He planned it to look so authentic that any national agents who came sniffing around would peg it as one more Dragonov project they could use as leverage for their next information download."

"How does it work?" Conor asked with a weary sense of déjà vu. He'd been asking the same question—to Frank, Shelton, Sedgwick, and his brother—for months now.

Before Sedgwick could respond, Kavita returned bearing a tray with their evening sweet. It was a fragrant, steaming bowl of *gajar halwa*, a warm carrot pudding made with cardamom and sugar and garnished with roasted cashews.

"Once again, Kavita-ji, your timing is impeccable," Sedgwick observed. "We were just getting around to you."

She placed the tray on the table and sat down next to Conor, whose stomach was burbling in anticipation. Thomas quickly picked up a plate and passed another across to Sedgwick. "Get what you can now. Last night he put away most of it on his own."

"About time. He could use a few pounds." Sedgwick threw a speculative glance at Conor. He spooned a serving onto his plate and continued. "Your brother might think it's chewing gum and butcher's string, but really, it was genius. The challenge is to lure Dragonov to a place where he can be captured, and that's damn near impossible. He's too smart to walk into a trap, but Walker has been studying this guy a long time. He's done psych profiles, analyzed his habits, changing interests—all that shit. He came up with an idea for taking something this guy treasures and turning it against him, and the lynchpin in the strategy is our very own *Shrimati-ji*. Kavita Kotwal."

Incredulous and alarmed, Conor stared at the pint-sized figure sitting next to him. Eyebrows shooting up and eyes widening in what he assumed was a droll imitation of his own expression, she looked back at him.

"Land of surprises, no? So much we did not know of each other, until few days ago only."

"I'm beginning to wonder how much I'll ever know of you, Kavita-ji." Conor sighed. "How in the name of Jesus and Mary do you figure into all of this?"

Instead of responding, she inclined her head toward Sedgwick, and with a wink of affection, he gave her one of his rare, unguarded smiles.

"Years ago, Dragonov got religion. He became fascinated with Hinduism and then got fanatical about the practice of yoga—*asana*, *pranayama*, *dhyana*—the whole shooting match. Completely obsessed with it, on a mission to find his true guru. It just so happens that one of the preeminent teachers of the *ashtanga vinyasa* system of yoga is also the most unorthodox guru in India, known in Rishikesh as Mata Saraswati Devi, but also known as Kavita Kotwal, the Devi of Dharavi and the wife of Mumbai's biggest Hindu crime boss."

Conor had put an arm over the back of the sofa and was watching Kavita in open amazement. "Spiritual guru, humanitarian worker, all-around angel of mercy, and mafia wife—that's a lot to reconcile in one small body."

"*Haan.*" Kavita's head toggled, and she laughed quietly. "Problem is always husband, but what is so different? Where is the married woman in India who has no husband problems?"

Sedgwick regarded her affectionately. "Our smartest move was at the beginning, when Walker decided to approach Kavita first. Once she was on board, Pawan-bhai didn't stand a chance. Walker left the recruitment in her hands, and it was done within a week."

"He is older now." Kavita shrugged. "He begins to have some thought for his place on the wheel of *dharma.*"

"Well, it wasn't completely altruistic." Sedgwick smirked. "The price for his cooperation was to overlook the money-laundering racket and to collect intelligence on his biggest rival, Ahmed Khalil. That's how I got hired. I was brought on to infiltrate Khalil's organization."

Conor nodded as another piece of the mystery slipped into place.

"Pawan Kotwal agreed to act as front man, a paying customer for Dragonov," Sedgwick continued. "He'd pose as a gang boss turned radical, looking to arm a Hindu paramilitary group in Kashmir. We'd run negotiations through Dragonov's middlemen, and with some innocent small talk, start making references to Kavita and her ashram, hoping they would take the information back and plant it on Dragonov like a virus, get him wondering if she might be his true guru. We knew it would take years, planned it that way, in fact. We'd build a steady relationship as a predictable customer, keep dangling this tantalizing bit of tinsel at him, and look for him to make a grab at it. The key was having the right middleman for our side of the relationship, which turned out to be Pawan Kotwal's money-launderer. Your brother."

The revelation was not entirely surprising. Conor absorbed it with a curt nod while Thomas pushed himself up from his chair and pulled out a package of cigarettes. He indicated the door leading to the rear observation deck. "I'm off to the patio for a smoke."

"Now?" Conor looked at him in irritation. "Can't you wait, for fuck's sake? We're just getting around to your part."

Like smoldering brush exploding into flames, Thomas turned on him in a fury. "Yeah, thanks, I'm aware of that, Conor," he barked. "I've been living it, and I bloody well know how it goes, don't I? I don't need to hear the whole feckin' thing all over again. Let him carry on with it. He's on a roll."

The small sitting room shook with the crash of the rear door slamming shut and then settled into numb silence.

30

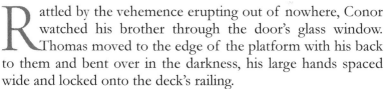

Rattled by the vehemence erupting out of nowhere, Conor watched his brother through the door's glass window. Thomas moved to the edge of the platform with his back to them and bent over in the darkness, his large hands spaced wide and locked onto the deck's railing.

"What the hell was that about?" Conor breathed, weakly. "What's wrong with him?"

Sedgwick was standing and also gazing out at Thomas with an expression that was unfamiliar to Conor. With its polished glaze of cynicism stripped away, his face seemed tender and defenseless, particularly when he turned to Kavita, as though seeking reassurance.

"It is not about you, *beta*," she said gently. "Let him be."

"Isn't it always about me?" His smile was pained and apologetic. "Self-absorption is a signature element in people like me."

For a moment, it appeared he would go after Thomas anyway, but finally he sat down again with a sigh. "It's Robert Durgan, the bastard who tricked him into the money-laundering mess in the first place. He hates him, and he's scared of him, and he can't stand talking about him. I've never met the guy, but I'd cheerfully kill the fucker if I ever got the chance. Walker nearly did. It was a reasonable strategy, but when it blew apart, he almost lost it. He gets so deep into the cobwebs of his obsession that he ... shit. Sorry."

Sedgwick flashed a humorless grin. "I'm in the cobwebs too, I guess. You don't have a clue what I'm talking about, yet."

"No," Conor said. "Listen, if you want to take a break from this ... "

Sedgwick shook his head. "Let's get through it. Otherwise he'll stand out there all night. He's as bullheaded as you are."

"Go on outta that. I'm not as bad as him."

They looked at each other, and suddenly both were smiling. For the first time Conor felt a bond with his one-time boss, surpassing anything they had previously shared. They were like two younger siblings, commiserating over the autocratic disposition of a big brother.

"Where was I?" Sedgwick leaned back in his chair. He put a booted foot on the coffee table, but Kavita quickly shifted it off again with a light slap against his knee.

"Talk more quickly, Curtis," she instructed, gathering the empty plates onto the tray. "I will be bringing chai in a short while."

"You've got to hand it to Pawan-bhai," he continued, when the two of them were alone. "He figured the best assurance of DEA protection for his money-laundering operation was to get Durgan into the game, and Walker agreed to it. Kotwal gets Durgan to come out of his hole and fly to Zurich to meet Walker—who's posing as Pawan-bhai's business manager—about a special project. Now, this guy stood to make a tidy sum out of all this, plus whatever extra business came his way from the intelligence I pulled out of the Khalil gang. Sweet deal. Unfortunately for him, the dickhead overplayed his hand."

He gave a derisive shake of his head, as though still amazed at how events had transpired. "Walker flew over and met him for dinner, and it went bad from the beginning. Durgan acted like a *goonda*—Abdul Hassan with fewer brains. Acted as though Walker should be grateful he was there at all. Instant enmity. He tried to play the big mafia man, talking about his deals in Johannesburg and Sofia, but Walker said he was so far over his head it was laughable. Everything about him felt bogus. He seemed like a guy pretending to be another guy who was pretending to be someone else."

"Not unlike myself, lo these many months," Conor remarked mildly.

"Well, you're a lot better at it," Sedgwick said. "By the end of the meeting, Walker knew he could never trust the guy enough to work with him. He told Durgan next to nothing, said he'd be in touch, and flew back the next morning. It was all sackcloth and ashes for a few days after that, until I made the casual suggestion that we cut the boss out altogether and just go straight to his man on the ground instead. Walker told me to give it a shot. And that's … " He hesitated before finishing. "That's how I met your brother. He came on board, and we got the thing underway and have been working on it ever since."

"Just like that?" Conor threw a jaded look across the room. "You said 'Tom, would you ever like to help Pawan-bhai stock up on rocket launchers for the liberation of Kashmir?' and he said, 'Right so, I'm your man.'"

"It took a few more conversations than that." Sedgwick offered a weak smile. "In the end, I just told him the truth."

Conor's brow arched in ironic surprise. "You were honest with him from the beginning? Why?"

"I'm not sure I know myself," Sedgwick said. "He was in pretty bad shape when I met him, Conor. He'd just found out what Durgan and his boys had done to implicate you in that EU grant fraud, and he was drinking pretty heavily. I thought about taking advantage of that, I'm ashamed to admit. I sat with him a few nights, watching him get drunk and staying sober myself, and then one night he spilled his whole story. The next night I got drunk with him and told him mine. We sort of recognized each other at that point—two fuck-ups looking for a chance to do something right, for a change."

He took a breath and said no more. Silence filled the room, disturbed only by the hypnotic sound of the train's wheels rhythmically thumping against the seams of the tracks. Conor could tell the agent was anticipating his next question and dreading it. The temptation to ask it was strong. He had spent more than a few idle hours wondering about the personal history of his controlling officer, but with a hint of regret, he passed on the opportunity.

"So, now I know how it got started," he said. His voice conveyed a dry sense of wonder. "The next question is how does it end?"

Sedgwick's shoulders slumped, and he regarded Conor with an odd smile of relief and regret. "The details around 'how' are still sketchy but the 'when' is starting to look firm. Tom meets with these guys three or four times a year, always at the ashram. The middlemen have spent time with Kavita, and they've clearly been taking back reports. When we heard you were coming, Walker figured we were getting onto thin ice with MI6 poking around, so he risked a big move. Tom met with them just before you arrived and said he was ready to make a twenty-million-dollar purchase on behalf of Pawan-bhai and that he was hoping to celebrate the next phase of the relationship by hosting Dragonov at the ashram. A month ago, we finally got what we'd been waiting for all these years. He's agreed to come, and we've been getting ready ever since. That week I told you I was in Dubai, I was actually up in Rishikesh with Walker and Costino scoping out a capture strategy."

"Costino." Conor's brow wrinkled in vexed recollection. "Is that your squeaky little intern, Kovalevsky?"

"Oh, right." Sedgwick gave a soft laugh. "Tony Costino. He's older than he looks. He does legal analysis and manages the admin, but he spends more time brown-nosing his boss than doing his work. When I got back to Mumbai ten days ago, the two of them had left for meetings in DC to brief the top brass. My assignment now is to get us all in place at Rishikesh and wait for instructions."

"Uh-huh." Absently biting his thumbnail, Conor drifted into brooding contemplation. His attention wandered from Sedgwick and fixed instead on the window behind him. Its mirror-like reproduction of both the room and its occupants permitted occasional, indistinct glimpses of the darkened landscape rolling past. The scenes were likely no different from those that had scrolled over the glass for the past ten nights, but his inability to pierce the reflective glare triggered a claustrophobic anxiety.

After so many months and so much effort devoted to misdirection, he had hoped the truth, once dragged forward, would reveal something sordid and ignoble and that he could shame his brother into abandoning it. That's what he'd been hired to do, wasn't it? He hadn't expected anything like this.

In many ways, it was a preposterous scheme, but its objective was neither sordid nor ignoble. To sabotage it would be irresponsible and probably just as dangerous as letting it run its course. Fate had fixed its seal on it, and as he acknowledged its victory, the unfixed dread that had plagued him for weeks sank that much further into his bones.

With a reflexive start, he realized Sedgwick had not stopped talking. Swearing silently, he pulled his mind back to focus on the room's interior rather than whatever lurked in the impenetrable darkness.

"There's something else I need to tell you," Sedgwick was saying, "before we try to get your brother back inside for his chai. You're not going to like it."

"Won't I?" Conor asked, somewhat lethargically. "Brilliant."

Sedgwick acknowledged the sarcasm with a shrug. "We thought one of the agencies might get wind of something and turn up; but we didn't expect them to focus on Tom. I'm contracted as

MI6's primary NOC—a nonofficial cover agent—in Mumbai, so luckily they tapped me to babysit the first agent they sent. He was pretty easy to confuse as long as I kept a bottle of vodka in front of him. Walker and I stuck to the original plan. I told the guy I'd heard Tom was doing business with Dragonov for terrorists in Kashmir, figuring that would be enough for MI6 to bury it, but not long after we got rid of him, we found out they'd recruited you."

He glanced out the back door at Thomas, who had taken a seat on the wrought iron bench that was bolted to the floor. Elbows on his knees, with a cigarette dangling from one slack hand, he sat watching the rails race away and disappear into the distance.

"The thing is," Sedgwick went on, "when we first got the word on your MI6 recruitment, it didn't come from the London office or Fort Monckton. We got it from Tom, who got it from Durgan."

Conor followed Sedgwick's gaze, unconsciously mimicking his brother's posture. He estimated that Thomas was on his third cigarette, and the craving to smoke one himself made his fingers twitch. He dropped his head with a resigned sigh—not shocked, just weary.

"And Durgan must have got it from someone inside MI6."

Sedgwick nodded. "You're a quick study, as usual. Tom was so panicked about you that he's never even wondered how Durgan could have known about a covert operative recruitment, which was just as well, but obviously the rest of us were curious. Walker had already decided Durgan was just another middleman in the money-laundering ring, a buffer to keep the real leader behind a curtain. That leader might have a mole inside MI6 who feeds him information, but there's another possibility we have to consider."

"And what's that?" Conor asked dully.

"That the leader is also a high-level informant, protected just like Dragonov is, and that MI6 owed him something."

Apparently, his capacity for shock was not altogether dead. At Conor's gasp, Sedgwick bowed his head. "Yeah, I know. Black ops are black in more ways than one. It might be a red herring, but in some ways it makes sense. Walker tells Durgan there's a new piece of Kotwal's business in the offing, but then nothing happens. Durgan maybe catches on that he screwed up the meeting and confesses to his boss, and they begin speculating that Kotwal has done an end-run around them, taking his extra business straight to Thomas. The boss bides his time, but when MI6 comes knocking, he trades information for a favor: find out if his man in India is two-timing him. They agree, but keep the whole thing at arm's length by sending an expendable agent, and before it even gets underway, they have Durgan leak the information to see if it scares Tom enough to prompt a confession."

Conor had to admit the plot had a certain self-contained elegance. He could see Sedgwick was inclined to believe it but wasn't as certain he did. "It sounds pretty convoluted. What does Thomas think?"

The agent's eyes again took on a look of strained discomfort. "We didn't tell him."

"You didn't tell him? Why the hell not?"

Seeing Conor's indignation, Sedgwick leaned forward. "Listen, from the very beginning of this, he's never much cared what would happen to him, but he's petrified about what anyone might do to you. If the strategy was to scare him by bringing you into it, it worked. Tom almost broke with us once he heard about it. We only kept him on board by promising to look after you. He already has a pathological fear of Durgan. If he thought the agency that recruited you is actually mixed up with him ... well, let's just say it scares me to think what he might do—what kind of bargains he might try to make."

"What scares you?" Conor asked with caustic sarcasm. "Just that he'll somehow banjax this ramshackle shell game you've had him running for five years?"

"No, shithead," Sedgwick spat back angrily. "I'm not worried about the fucking shell game. I'm worried about him, and God knows you make me wonder why, but I'm worried about you, too. Haven't you seen enough of mafia etiquette by now to know how it works? It's the same all over the world. The boys in charge don't let you walk away from them, and they punish traitors. You saw what it looks like in Sewri, and if I hadn't swapped you out for a water buffalo, you'd have gotten a taste yourself. You think the Irish version is any better? That they'll go easier on your brother? Or you?"

"Oh my God." Conor slumped backward until he collided with the back of the sofa. The blood that had rushed to his face in irritation drained away again. "I get it. If you're right, I can't bring Thomas back to report to MI6. They'll debrief us, dish it to Durgan or his boss, and turn us loose for them to find. We're fucked."

"Well, don't give up the ghost so easily." Sedgwick's expression softened. "You do have a few friends in the DEA. We may be ramshackle, but we're better than nothing. Do you at least understand why I don't want to share all this with your brother right now?"

"Yeah, yeah," Conor assured him quickly. "Jesus, we can't tell him. He'd go off his head—try to trade himself in exchange for me, and we'd probably both still end up on the rack. Again, that's if you're right. Anyway, I'll go along with it. We'll do it your way."

"Thank you." Looking exhausted, Sedgwick let his head drop back against his chair. With his eyes closed, he absently rubbed at the scars on his left arm.

At least, it looked like his eyes were closed. A minute later, his head popped up and he scowled wearily at Conor. "Why the fuck are you staring at me like that?"

"Oh, sorry." Conor's eyes snapped back into focus. "I wasn't really—away to the hills for a minute. I was just wondering about Frank and where he stands in all of this. Either way, he must be getting pretty impatient. I've been here a couple months, and he's not learned a bloody thing."

"No doubt." Sedgwick's smile grew wide as he settled back and closed his eyes again. "I've been filing reports on our progress tracking your brother through the Khalil organization. If Frank knows the real connection has always been with Kotwal, my letters home must be driving him batshit crazy."

31

He took the stairs of the ashram's dormitory two at a time, animated by the conviction that he was late for something but not remembering what. Hurrying to the end of the corridor, he'd just breached the doorway of Kavita's apartment when he tripped over her.

"*Arrey!*"

The Hindi exclamation was second nature to him now. It spilled automatically from Conor's mouth, along with a few saltier expressions he had known a good while longer. He stumbled to avoid toppling onto the seated figure beneath him.

"Jayz, Kavita, I'm sorry. I didn't see you there."

"It doesn't matter."

She looked up, glowing and serene. She was sitting in the lotus position, wearing loose-fitting white pants and an embroidered white kurta. Her long hair was plaited into a braid that ran straight down the middle of her back. She looked unusually youthful and perfectly relaxed.

"It might have mattered if I'd landed on top of you." He studied her curiously. "Why are you sitting so close to the door?"

"The place of greatest light. It is right here, in this spot exactly." She closed her eyes, and with palms facing the floor, cupped hands over an invisible bolus of energy.

"*Accha.*" Conor nodded, respectfully. Of the many things that befuddled him about India, this wasn't one of them. The pervasive spirituality of its people and their belief that the border between worlds was a billowy, translucent thing at best was not a foreign idea to him.

In the world of Celtic mysticism, the concept was called *caol áit*, "thin places." His mother knew them and had an enduring hunger to be near them. Throughout his childhood, she had dragged him on innumerable forced marches to holy wells, portal tombs, and monastic ruins. The spell of the numinous was overpowering in the spots she favored, and for a boy who was happier avoiding such experiences that was precisely the problem. It was far less potent than hers was, but his own susceptibility to the vibration of *chuisle Dé* had sometimes rattled him to the marrow of his bones—often enough to engender a wary, arms-length respect for *caol áit* in all its forms, wherever it occurred.

As Kavita caressed the air in front of her, Conor indulged in a bit of reverie, regretting his adolescent obstinacy and wondering what he wouldn't give now to follow his mother across a dolmen-strewn cow pasture to see her perform a ritual that would look a lot like the one he was watching now.

After a moment, he recalled his original purpose and reluctantly shifted his eyes to the rest of the apartment, searching for evidence of a forgotten obligation.

Sedgwick and Thomas were sitting at one end of the dining room table staring glumly at the blank screen of a laptop. Seeing the data cable trailing from the side of it, Conor finally remembered what he was late for—a meeting to dissect the latest e-mail correspondence from Dragonov's underlings. They had been expected to make contact by three o'clock that afternoon with the final details for the arms dealer's visit. Glancing at his watch, he winced. It was almost four o'clock.

"Have they been yelling for me?" he asked Kavita, in a low voice.

"Not as yet," she replied, without opening her eyes. "There are issues."

"Issues? What issues?"

"Power cut." Kavita solemnly pointed a finger at the ceiling. "What to do? No power, no Yahoo."

Lowering her hands onto her knees, she opened her eyes and regarded Conor with a sigh of satisfaction. "You are looking well, *beta*. You have had a good trek, I think, on the paths by Lakshman Jhula? Fresh air and healthful exertions are there in your face. Rishikesh is being good to you, yes?"

He smiled. Kavita's sentence structures routinely wandered beyond accepted rules of English idiom, but he wasn't sure it was accidental. Her poetic phrasing often evoked deeper truths, and this was a case in point.

Rishikesh had indeed been "good to" him. The antibiotics deserved some credit, as did Kavita's prepared concoctions, but the ashram and its surrounding community had a living, purposeful quality that had achieved the effect of a wholesale transfusion. After only a week, every ounce of anything tired and sickly had been siphoned out, replaced with the fortifying mixture of nature and spirit that permeated the atmosphere around him.

That afternoon he had tested his growing stamina with a long walk near Lakshman Jhula, one of two pedestrian bridges that spanned the Ganges, connecting the city center to its east bank where most of the ashrams were concentrated. That his ramble had obscured the day's more serious business was a tribute to the east bank's peaceful, otherworldly ambiance. That Kavita knew about the excursion was an added surprise.

"How did you know where I went?" he asked.

"Prateek was here." The twinkle in her eyes belied her neutral tone. "Complaining that you prefer trekking to his yoga instruction."

"Hmm. Right. Prateek." His nose wrinkled in distaste. He'd had no great desire for such instruction to begin with, and the mandated lessons with Prateek the "uber-yogi" had done nothing to change his mind. He found him an intimidating, overpowering presence, and his demonstrations of pranayama—the ritualized breathing exercises central to yogic practice—left Conor both spellbound and faintly nauseated. During exhalation, the sixty-year-old master could draw his abdomen into such a state of concave extremity that one half-expected an imprint of the man's spine to appear on his stomach.

"I guess I did scarper a bit early on him. He's just too much yogi for me, I think."

"Come, sit." Kavita patted the floor next to her. "We will practice *pranayama* together, you and I."

"Oh ... ehm."

"Yes, come, come. You must learn to breathe properly."

"He can learn how to breathe later, Kavita," Sedgwick's voice called from the dining room. "McBride, get your butt in here."

Caught halfway between sitting and standing, he offered an insincere pout of apology and then spun in his tracks and hurried to the dining room.

"Nice of you to find time for us in your busy schedule," Sedgwick said.

Conor joined them at the table, and now all three of them sat facing the laptop, like petitioners before an oracle. He raised an eyebrow at Thomas. "What have I missed?"

"Exactly nothing," Thomas said. "We're waiting for the bloody power to come back."

"What about the BGAN?" Conor asked. "Couldn't we try that? Nice to get some use from it after hauling it all the way over here."

"Shit, I forgot you had it." Sedgwick's eyes widened hopefully.

"What's a bee-gan?" Thomas asked.

"Broadband Global Area Network," Conor replied. "Fancy yoke that connects a laptop to the Internet via satellite link. I don't even know if it works or not."

"Get it and let's try," Sedgwick said. "We can set it up out in the garden. Bring your laptop, too. The battery is dead in this one."

He retrieved the BGAN from his room, and a few minutes later they were sitting on the ground in Kavita's Ayurvedic medicine garden examining it. The equipment was remarkably compact—a white, rectangular panel slightly larger than the laptop and a single connecting cable. When the rapid beep of the terminal indicated a successful link to the satellite, he switched on the laptop. After a moment, an intricate, horizontal tree diagram appeared on the screen.

"What the hell is that?" Thomas asked, leaning in for a closer look.

"The log-in screen," Conor sighed. "I'd forgotten about it. There's a nine-character password entry for each line of the diagram."

Sedgwick gave an incredulous snort. "There's got to be at least twenty lines. There's no freaking way you remember the password for every one of them."

Without responding, Conor began tapping on the keys, humming to himself and occasionally lifting a hand to let his fingers wiggle above the keyboard. As the lines filled up, Sedgwick's smirk faded.

"It's a musical password." Delighted, Thomas bounced a fist against his knee.

Conor nodded. "It's a good chunk from the staccato jig section of the Korngold concerto. I'm a bit rusty. Let's see if I played it right."

He hit Enter and grimaced as the screen went black. A second later it lit up again, icons popping up as it whirred to life. Another few strokes established the Internet connection, and he handed the laptop over to Thomas.

"All yours," he said. "Go get the mail, and I'll get us a snack."

When he returned with a bowl of fruit a few minutes later, the mood had darkened. Sedgwick was on his feet pacing the garden, while Thomas remained seated on the ground frowning pensively.

"It doesn't make any goddamn sense," Sedgwick fumed. "Look through it again. Does it read like they're afraid of a trap? Why would they be suspicious now?"

"Maybe because it *is* a trap?" Thomas said, *sotto voce*. He pulled the laptop closer and silently read the message again.

"More issues?" Conor asked, lowering himself to the ground.

"You might say that, yeah. Change of venue." Thomas gave him a sidelong glance and looked up at Sedgwick. "I don't know, it looks pretty straightforward. He doesn't want to sully the holiness of the ashram by doing business here."

"Oh, for ... they've been doing business here for the past five years!" Sedgwick squawked.

"Dragonov hasn't," Thomas replied.

"What about Conor?" Sedgwick demanded. "Are you sure they're not nervous about him?"

"Doesn't sound like it. They're congratulating me for expanding business inside the family, looking forward to meeting him, and seeing me. And why wouldn't they?" Thomas added, still staring at the screen. "I've been a good customer all these years. They trust me, poor bastards. They're fine with everything except the location."

He turned back to Conor. "They're saying Dragonov wants us to meet him in Gulmarg a week from today. We'll take care of business, and then he'll fly us all down to the airport in Dehra Dun, and we'll drive over here."

"Where's Gulmarg? Far away?"

"Far enough," Thomas said. "It's in Jammu-Kashmir, about eight hundred kilometers north of here, a little west of Srinagar. It's a ski resort."

"A ski resort, in India? No shit?"

"Yeah, yeah. Up and coming destination. They're trying to make it the Aspen of the East."

"Can we stay focused on the problem here, please?" Sedgwick snarled. "Why Gulmarg? What the fuck is in Gulmarg? He likes to ski?"

"I think he's got some investment property there, actually," Thomas said. "I remember his lads mentioning it a while back. Said they were heading up there after our meeting."

Sedgwick rounded on him with an accusatory glare. "You never mentioned that. Seems like it would have been a good piece of news to share, don't you think?"

Thomas flushed angrily. "We talked all kinds of shite. It didn't matter until now, did it? Why would I care where they feck off to once I was done with them? Why would you?"

"All right. Hang on a minute." Conor put a hand on his brother's arm. "We're not on to a productive line of discussion with this."

"You've got something brilliant to suggest, I suppose?" Sedgwick jeered.

"I do, yeah," he replied drily. "I suggest you stop stomping about, blattering like a six year old, and I suggest we consider the options. Sounds to me like there are two: either we tell them to feck off and call it a day, or we hump it up to Gulmarg. I doubt your man Walker is much interested in the first. So unless there's an alternative I'm not seeing, we might as well talk about the second. Tell me if I'm missing something here, Agent Sedgwick. Do we have a choice?"

Sedgwick continued stalking the garden for another minute before coming to a stop in front of them. Locking his fingers together, he placed both hands on top of his head and released a sigh of defeat.

"You're not missing anything. Too much is invested to pull

back now. It just got a lot more complicated and a lot more dangerous, but we're taking this guy down, so it looks like we'll be humping it up to Gulmarg to do it."

32

During daylight hours, the temperature in Rishikesh rose quickly, achieving a deliciously even, therapeutic warmth by midafternoon, but the air often grew damp and chilly once the sun disappeared, and it had been dark for over an hour.

Without taking his eyes from the scene unfolding in front of him, Conor reached for the jacket he'd left lying on the steps. A gathering breeze—visible as an iridescent wrinkle sweeping across the water under the moonlight—gave the evening an extra bite. It fluttered the orange robes of a priest who was descending the steps of the ghat, accompanied by a young man cradling a bundle in his arms. They were about to perform sanjayama, the ritual immersion of ashes that was part of Hindu funeral rites.

Conor shivered as he pulled on the jacket. He was out of practice with cooler temperatures after several months in the humid soup of Mumbai. Apparently, it was even colder farther north. Reports indicated winter held a firm grip on the region they would be heading for in the morning.

He and Thomas had come to the ghat that evening to escape their pre-departure anxieties, leaving Sedgwick to contend with the manic demands of Walker and Costino. The two DEA agents had arrived earlier in the week. After three exhausting days of role-playing and worst-case scenario spinning, Conor thought the preparations had moved into a counterproductive phase of obsessive-compulsive repetition.

At the first opportunity, he and his brother fled the premises, joining the throngs of pilgrims and tourists flocking to the Ganges for aarti. The ceremony took place each evening on the wide, marble ghat of Parmarth Niketan, one of the oldest and largest ashrams in Rishikesh.

The boisterous, jubilant service of music, song, and fire had ended now, and the crowds had dispersed, but the two of them continued to sit in the darkness, reluctant to return to a world so far removed from the joyful pageantry they'd just witnessed.

"I've often wondered what happens to them," Thomas said.

"You have?" Jerking his gaze from the priest's slow, stylized movements, Conor gave Thomas a glance of surprise. His brother did not often indulge in the contemplation of metaphysical mysteries. "The dead, you mean? What happens to their souls and ... like that?"

"The dead!" Thomas's forehead puckered in consternation, and he gave a hoot of laughter. "I'm not talking about the dead, you eejit. I'm talking about those things."

He pointed down at the river's edge where a boat-like basket of flowers with a small, guttering flame at its center bobbed on the water. It was one of many that worshippers had launched onto the river during the evening ceremony—a prayer of light offered to Mother Ganga, in thanks for her divine, eternal light. The basket had become trapped between two rocks.

"I was just wondering how far they get," Thomas explained. "Do they wash up on the beach farther down? Or maybe there's some special wallah who goes down to catch them, so they can use them again?"

"I wouldn't be surprised. There's a job for everyone in India."

Conor smiled, charmed by the imagery of someone stationed downstream, patiently waiting to catch the prayers of the faithful. Now that he'd seen it, the shipwrecked boat of marigolds troubled him. Impulsively, he jumped up and ran lightly down the stairs. Bracing one hand against a rock, he plucked the basket from the water and put it down again in the free-flowing current. As he climbed back up the stairs, even in the darkness, he could see Thomas grinning at him.

"Laugh if you want." Conor gave a self-conscious shrug. "It's a prayer. It shouldn't get stuck there."

"I wasn't laughing," Thomas assured him, gently. "I was just thinking you're so much like Ma—in a good way. I'm even a bit more like her than I used to be. I've been up here a lot over the years. I've spent hours sitting right here, staring at the river. There's something about it, isn't there? It pulls at you, no matter where you are, even when you can't see it. Gets under your skin, somehow, and you find yourself wanting to get back to it. Know what I mean?"

"I do."

Caol áit.

After a moment Conor added softly, "She'd be proud of you, Thomas. She never stopped believing in you."

"Ah, Jaysus, don't. Please." The protest came out as a thin, strangled whisper.

"All right, I won't, but it's true all the same. She never did. Not once."

They stayed out for as long as they dared, like truant schoolboys, but at last they shuffled back to the ashram. When they slunk back into the conference room Walker had appropriated for their planning sessions, Sedgwick glanced up from a map he'd been studying, looking too tired to be angry with them.

"I was beginning to think you weren't coming back at all." He leaned back with a yawn and pushed a handful of hair from his forehead.

"Sorry to be gone so long." Thomas gave his shoulder a friendly squeeze. "You look like hell, incidentally. Are you ever going to bed, at all?

"Walker wants to do one more run-through," Sedgwick said dispiritedly. "By the time we get to Gulmarg, we'll be so overrehearsed, it will be a miracle if they don't see through it."

"Where is Walker?" Conor asked.

"He's ... " Sedgwick twirled a hand wearily at the door as it opened with a bang. Walker strode in with a brisk, powerful stride. Seeing Conor and Thomas, he stopped and glared at them.

"Where the hell have you been for the past two hours?"

"We needed a bit of a break," Thomas replied. "We took a walk down to the ghat for the aarti."

"The ghat. You walked down to the ghat. For the aarti." Walker jammed his fists onto his hips. The small, dark eyes behind his wire-rimmed glasses flashed even more dangerously.

Standing at attention with his shirtsleeves rolled up to expose a pair of hairy, muscular arms, Walker perfectly embodied a number of caricatures Conor could name—gym teacher, drill sergeant, or some kid's particularly scary-looking dad. He had decided, however, after reflecting on it for three days, that he didn't actively dislike Walker. The senior agent was tense and often irritable, but he was too candidly earnest to be despicable.

"Gentlemen, is there something unclear about the mission we're engaged in, here? Something confusing about the significance of it? This is a deadly serious business. We're not tourists on vacation."

"Japers, are you serious?" Conor gaped with extravagant surprise. "Is this not the luxury package tour? It's been such a fucking laugh-riot so far, you can see how I got confused."

"Very funny. Very glib." Walker scowled and aimed an accusing eye at Sedgwick, who gave a helpless shrug.

"What can I say? He's Irish. They're glib." He bowed his head over the map, lips forcibly suppressing a telltale tremble. "Anyway, we've got the two of them back, so now where's Costino?"

"I sent him to bed," Walker said. "He's got first shift driving tomorrow. He needs to be fresh."

Thomas and Sedgwick shared a glance of withering irony.

"Cute little hoor," Thomas whispered. "Always works the angle to his advantage."

"Okay, men." Walker checked his watch, threw his leg over a chair, and dropped into it. "Let's run through this plan from the top."

The plan, insofar as they could control it, was kept as simple as possible. Having lost the home court advantage, Walker had attempted to regain the initiative by immediately flying to Srinagar with Costino, and from there they had driven to Gulmarg to execute a thorough site and perimeter inspection of the new venue before coming to Rishikesh.

The designated rendezvous was Gulmarg Alpine Cottage. Discreet inquiries confirmed a Russian investment company had indeed purchased the hotel within the past eighteen months, with an eye toward transforming it into a timeshare resort. The new owner was expected to be there with some associates on the following Thursday. He would take up residence in the presidential suite.

Their next stop had been the police headquarters in Srinagar. With no jurisdiction in India to make an arrest, the DEA needed to enlist local authorities for Dragonov's apprehension. Walker had always known they would have to file an international arrest warrant with Interpol. He had just hoped to delay that move for as long as possible.

"Like I said earlier ... " He tossed a copy of the warrant onto the table. "If Dragonov has penetrated Interpol and developed contacts there, we're screwed."

"But your hand was forced," Conor said, parroting back what they had all heard at least three times now. The senior agent seemed to believe repeating the story would have some positive impact on its outcome.

"My hand was forced." Walker's index finger poked the air for emphasis. "We needed authorities in place up there immediately.

So the arrest warrant got filed early."

"And the Criminal Investigation Department in Srinagar has booked a two-person team at the hotel posing as buddies on a skiing vacation," Sedgwick chimed in mechanically. "They're in the room next to the suite."

"Hope they know how to ski," Thomas said, with a small smile.

"Now, we keep this very clean and natural," Walker continued. "Thomas will have the listening device. He's got their trust, and they haven't searched him for years. You both get inside the room, go through all the chitchat. We'll run through the lines again in a minute—"

Conor groaned and slouched down into his chair.

"Which is one of the most important parts of this whole damned operation," Walker enunciated imperiously. "If you don't get him on tape saying what we need him to, the prosecution has no good case, and we're wasting our time. Eventually, you get around to the payment. You log in to our bank account, you transfer the payment to the joint account, and when it's done you give the verbal cue and we—"

"Whoa. Hang on a minute." Conor sat upright. The latest recitation had uncovered a nuance he'd missed earlier.

"You want the cue after the transfer? You want us to actually dump twenty million dollars into an account he can access? Not that it matters to me, but does that sound like a judicious risk with the US taxpayer's money?"

Walker brushed the query aside with an impatient wave. "Legal analysis says it's the only way. Anyway, it's a joint account."

"Yeah, but presumably he shifts it," he persisted.

"He won't have time," Walker said, flatly. "You just give the verbal cue, and CID will come in from next door and make the arrest. Game over. Period."

"But—"

"I believe I said 'period,' McBride."

"Yeah, fine, 'period.'" Conor abandoned further argument with a sigh.

The plan was about as good as it could be. There was nothing to be gained by parsing its components individually but as he tossed around in bed later, Conor mused on Walker's emphatic 'period.' Applied as standard grammatical notation, the period was a reassuring anchor that signaled closure. Used verbally to hammer the lid on question and debate, it had rather the opposite effect.

Lifting his wristwatch from the night table, he angled it against a patch of moonlight, and dropped it back onto the table with a groan. Drowsily, he looked up at the ceiling and began tracing out a dimly visible network of cracks, but at the sound of a long, low creak in the hallway outside his door, he shot out of bed as though catapulted from it.

He paused in the middle of the room before creeping to the door and held his breath to listen. Something brushed softly back and forth against the wood. Taking the knob in his hand, Conor gave it a quick twist and yanked the door open, thrusting the Walther into the opening ahead of him.

Thomas leapt back from the door to the middle of the hall, stumbling and swearing in a guttural whisper.

"I'm getting fairly tired of watching you wave that feckin' thing around, Conor."

Conor lowered the gun with a terse obscenity of his own. "Sure, what do you expect, when you come rubbing up against my door in the middle of the night? What are you doing out here, anyway?"

"Listening. I wasn't going to wake you if you were sleeping."

"Obviously, I'm not."

"Yeah, obviously. Put your goddamned gun in a drawer and come with me. I want your help with something."

He followed Thomas down the hall and into Kavita's apartment. Leaving the lights off, they walked through to the dining room where the laptop snoozed on the table, its revolving screen saver blitzing the room with erratic slivers of color.

"What are you up to?" Conor whispered. His brother pointed him to a chair in front of the computer and sat down next to him, leaning in to speak directly into his ear.

"I hadn't thought about it until you said something," he said. "In a couple of days, you and I are going to be sitting in a room with a Russian arms dealer, and we're going to hoover twenty million dollars out of a US government bank account and put it into his. Then we're going to sit back and pray to God somebody comes to arrest him before he bolts with it. It's a dodgy bit of business, don't you think?"

"I do, of course." Conor frowned and picked at a piece of candle wax on the table. "Wasn't I trying to say so earlier? You might have piped up then about it."

Thomas shook his head impatiently. "Wouldn't have made a difference. Walker wasn't having it. Costino has him dead paranoid about the lawyers. He's afraid they'll somehow take it all away from him if he doesn't do it the way they want. That's fine if it goes according to plan, but what if it goes wrong? What if the DEA can't get its money back? Who's going to take the fall for losing twenty million dollars?"

Abruptly, Conor stopped fidgeting. He rested his hands on the table and sat motionless. "You think Walker would try to pin that on us."

"I don't think he's planning to," Thomas said. "But I can see him making the leap if he has to. We're the ones going into the room and shifting the money, Conor, and who the fuck are we? Two 'joe soaps,' right? A couple of nobodies—except one's on the run for robbing a mafia don and the other's a money launderer wanted for grant fraud. Walker can turn that into whatever he wants, especially if he needs to get himself off the hook."

Conor's initial skepticism died away in a low whistle. "Okay. Fair point, but what can we do about it now, short of bolting ourselves?"

"I've done it already. I thought you could make it better." Thomas reached over and woke the laptop with a sharp tap on its keyboard. Squinting against the eruption of light, Conor saw a login page appear on the screen. There were no identifying characteristics, just plain black text against a stark white background. He stared at it, rubbing a finger over the stubble on his chin.

"What are we logging in to?"

"Vasily Dragonov's new bank account."

"Oh, Christ. Thomas—"

"It's a legitimate joint account," Thomas interrupted. "I set it up by phone with a bank in South America about an hour ago."

"You rang a bank in South America? How the fuck does that work?"

The exclamation was not loud, but it echoed like a shout in the otherwise silent apartment and Thomas flapped a hand in annoyance. "*Whisht*, for the love of God, will you ever keep it down? We'll be having the whole place awake. Yes, I rang up a bank in South America. I've opened and closed bank accounts all over the world for years now, Conor. What about the title 'money launderer' don't you understand, for Jesus' sake?"

"I understand more than I ever wanted to," Conor fired back, acidly. Thomas sighed.

"Well, amen to that, brother. Listen to me now, though. Durgan's got a fellow in South America who opens accounts. I've used him before. It's another joint account, under the name of the same shell company Dragonov used for the other one. I had all the information from when we first opened it. No lawyer in the world could deny this account is identical to the others. The only difference is Dragonov doesn't know about it."

"So he can't get it out, but we can," Conor said. "Come through like heroes in a crisis."

"Exactly."

"Doesn't this seem like the kind of thing the DEA should have thought of on their own?"

"Seems like it," Thomas agreed. His deadpan stare indicated that no deeper comprehension—and certainly no comfort—would be gained from pursuing that line of discussion. He hit the keyboard again to refresh the login screen and Conor bowed to the inevitable.

"Right. You want me to assign a shatterproof password, I suppose."

Thomas smiled. "You're seeing out of all three eyes tonight, mate. Work away with your rare old tune. It'll take up to thirty-six notes of it."

"I should teach it to you as well," Conor argued as he began entering the code. "You ought to know it, just in case something—"

Thomas clapped a hand on his shoulder, pulling him gently around to face him.

"Nothing is going to happen to you, Conor. "Do you understand me, now? Nothing. I'll not let it."

"Yeah. Same for you." He banged a fist lightly against his brother's arm. "Period."

He assigned the password, and when it was done, they stared at the screen until the monitor blinked into sleep again, which coincided closely with the piercing blast of a whistle that made them jump. It came from the garden just outside. All over India, even on the peaceful east bank of Rishikesh, the night watchman was a ubiquitous presence during the early morning hours, traditionally armed with a whistle and a wooden staff. They watched the figure drift past the dining room window like an apparition. When the rhythmic tap along the walkway had faded, Thomas turned to Conor, his face wan and tired.

"I wonder, will it ever end," he sighed. "Even if we get through this, Durgan is still out there somewhere, and that scares me more than all the rest. I've no idea where he is, and I've never understood how he knows so much about you."

"Maybe someone is telling him about me." Conor regarded his brother cautiously. "That's Sedgwick's theory, that someone bigger is calling the shots, someone who can access information about me whenever he wants. He thinks Durgan is just an errand boy. A sort of clown."

"Horse shit," Thomas said without visible emotion. "He's one twisted son of a bitch, the farthest thing from a clown. How would Sedgwick know? He's never met him."

"Walker has. He had that meeting with him in—what?" Conor interrupted his own argument, seeing Thomas shake his head back and forth.

"Walker's never seen him, either. It wasn't Durgan who met him in Geneva."

A sharp intake of air locked itself in Conor's lungs for several seconds before exiting in a gust. "How do you know that?"

"I didn't at first, but then Durgan told me himself, last September, when he called to tell me you'd be coming over here." Thomas stared out the window. "He thought the Geneva meeting was a trap. Walker was going to make a deal on the spot if it had gone well. He'd give one criminal a free pass and a truckload of money in exchange for help catching another one. But Durgan got spooked. He sent Desi to the meeting instead, and Desi made a hames of it."

"Who's Desi?"

Thomas closed the laptop and stared down at it before answering. "Desmond Moore and his pal Ciaran. The two fellows from Armagh I hired, when this whole ball of shite first got rolling. Desi Moore. Poor, stupid bastard."

"Why? What happened to him?" Conor asked.

Thomas rolled his head to look at him with an unblinking gaze. "He's dead. That's the real reason Durgan rang, I'm sure. Wanted to hear the fear in my voice. Said Desi had fucked up. Said he'd suspected for a long time that I had too, that it would be a lot better for me if I came clean with it before you got here. Said if he found out later I'd been cutting him out of something, we'd both be getting the Desi Moore treatment. I haven't had any contact with him since then. Threw the mobile away, shut down the e-mail account, and came up here until Sedgwick called saying I'd better do something with you before Walker had you thrown in jail."

"Why didn't you tell them Durgan suspects something?"

Thomas shrugged. "Too scared. They need me at this point, but they don't need you. What if they tried protecting me by getting him after you instead? Do you understand now, why I wanted you kept out of it? Why I wanted you sent home without knowing what was really going on over here?"

"Yeah." Conor ran a hand over his face before asking the question he didn't want answered. "How can you be certain Durgan killed Desi?"

"Because he sent me a picture, Conor," his brother whispered. "E-mailed it to me. And Desi's face was the only part of him left I could recognize."

Back in bed a half-hour later, Conor's sleepless mind returned again to the symbolic relevance of the 'period,' and to the wistful question Thomas had posed.

Will it ever end?

In a musical composition, a set of chords known as a closed cadence forms the punctuative counterpart to the written word's period. Marking the end of a section within the piece—or more dramatically indicating its conclusion—the closed cadence and its definitive tonic chord signals closure. In doing so, it supplies a fulfillment the pricked ear hardly knew it yearned for: a release of tension, an accession to completion and rest.

He had always reveled in compositions that toyed with that nebulous desire, that withheld gratification until the next measure, and then the next, letting the tension build inexorably as the listener's heart fills, waiting for the instant when the music will crest and resolve.

But then it doesn't come.

Instead of the anticipated closed cadence, the music slides to a "deceptive cadence." It goes up, back, sideways, across—somewhere new. Somewhere unexpected. The musician works the strings, and the process begins again. The ear quivers in exquisite torture, still waiting for release, still aching for a tonic chord.

33

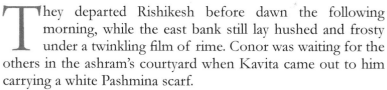

They departed Rishikesh before dawn the following morning, while the east bank still lay hushed and frosty under a twinkling film of rime. Conor was waiting for the others in the ashram's courtyard when Kavita came out to him carrying a white Pashmina scarf.

For the past several days, she'd been supplementing his tropical wardrobe with cold-weather clothes. An endless assortment of long-sleeved woolen kurtas and thick sweaters had been finding their way into his bedroom until he'd felt obliged to stop the madness.

"It's more clothes than I left London with, Kavita," he protested, and she'd responded with unusual severity.

"Again I am telling you, Conor. You are feeling quite well now, but you must take care. Kashmir is very cold just now. It is not good to you. Cold Kashmiri air going down inside your chest is not good to you. It is a very dangerous thing."

Abashed, he'd resisted any further objections and stood patiently motionless as she coiled the scarf around his neck.

He caught a glimpse at her eyes as she finished. They were dark and somber, too much like the eyes he had left thousands of miles behind on a late summer day that felt like a hundred years ago. When her hands moved from the scarf to hover—one on top of the other—over his chest, the gooseflesh surged over his skin in waves.

"You will need all of your strength," she breathed, as though speaking to herself.

"Whatever I've got, *ji*, it's what you've given me." He took her hands and pressed them gently. "We should be back in a few days. I'll see you again soon, please God."

"Yes. You will be seeing me here again, *beta*, but I think it will not be soon."

She tried to smile for him, realizing she had frightened him. Before she could say any more, the others arrived, and Walker was anxious to be going. Conor bent to touch her feet, and she kissed the top of his head. Without another word, they parted.

The furriness of sleep was quickly blown out of them as they crossed the wind-swept Ram Jhula pedestrian bridge to the waiting Range Rover on the opposite bank. The seven-passenger vehicle had been stocked the night before with bottled water and a picnic hamper supplied by the ashram's cooking staff.

Apart from Tony Costino, who was well rested and aggravatingly buoyant, none of them felt inclined for conversation during the first few hours of the ride. The tense quiet inside the SUV gave Conor plenty of time to brood on the troubling emotions Kavita's parting words aroused.

After several hours of useless worry, he put it aside. He couldn't hope to interpret the obstacles Kavita—or, for that matter, his mother—had sensed were ahead of him. Obsessing over it only added to the strain on his overstretched nerves.

Driving helped. They all took a turn in the rotation after Costino's initial stint, and he discovered Indian roads required a level of concentration that erased any inclination to daydream. He volunteered for a second shift when the first was finished. Altogether, he spent a good six hours navigating around various obstacles and marveling at the ever-changing panorama as they rode deeper into Jammu and Kashmir.

Sedgwick was at the wheel now. After fourteen hours on the road, the journey was concluding as it began—in darkness—and the mood inside the Range Rover was one of tedium. Conor stared out the window while his brain whispered nonsense.

Porter cake. Velvet on the tongue. Easy going down. A dense, sweet fantasy, with a perfect blend of nuts, dried peel, and sultanas delivered in every bite.

It was an old television advert from home. Now that the announcer's honey-soaked voice had taken root in his head, complete with the image of a succulent porter cake rotating on a plate, he found it hard to think about anything else. It was an absurd but welcome respite from what had been rubbing against his mind for the rest of the day.

He turned away from the window. The scenery had been spectacular throughout the day, but it was too dark to see anything now, and since they had been steadily corkscrewing up a narrow track against the side of a mountain for the past several minutes, he didn't much mind the obscurity. He twisted around, inadvertently—or perhaps not—kicking the foot of the sleeping Costino, whose puppy-like energy had finally expired a few hours earlier.

"Porter cake," he recited to Thomas, who was in the seat behind him. "Velvet on the tongue."

His brother indicated recognition with a low, animal moan. "Easy going down. Wouldn't I like to tackle a slab or two," Thomas sighed. "That's hitting below the belt. I'd eat the beard of Moses, I'm that hungry."

"Nothing left in the hamper?"

"Raked hollow." Thomas rolled a meaningful glance at the yawning Costino.

"What's porter cake?" their younger colleague asked. He was blinking in confusion at being jarred awake by a shot to the anklebone.

Conor blinked back in light ridicule. "Never had a slice of porter cake in all your sad life? Poor bastard. I could never make you understand what you've missed."

Unlike his verdict regarding Walker, after careful consideration, Conor had determined that he *did* dislike Costino. Heartily. The baby-faced agent he had taken for a recruit fresh from college was actually the same age as he was, which made his pretensions of doe-eyed innocence even more grating.

His pose as an eager-to-please subordinate was a better act than his attempt as a Crimean mobster, but having played a role himself recently, Conor knew how far it needed to settle in for the charade to be convincing. Costino's natural self was not buried deep enough. It needed a sharp eye, but when he paid attention, Conor could detect the shrewd glances and flashes of naked ambition.

Instead of looking annoyed, Costino laughed. "I love listening to you guys, especially in that patois you sometimes use."

"Patois?" Thomas, who did look annoyed, huffed in disgust. Conor merely shrugged.

"It's called *Gaeilge*, and it's actually classified as a standard language, but never mind. Happy to provide the evening's entertainment."

A squeal of brakes sounded as the Range Rover violently swerved to the right.

"Sorry, boys," Sedgwick said from the driver's seat. "Hard to see the turns in the dark."

Walker, riding shotgun and sleeping soundly until that moment, lurched up, instantly wide-awake. "Are we here?" he asked.

"Wherever the hell 'here' is," Sedgwick said. "I'm following your directions. Feels like we're climbing Everest."

"We're through Tangmarg?"

"Five or six kilometers back," Sedgwick confirmed, "and about a thousand feet down."

"Then we're on the Gulmarg access road." Walker put his face to the window, peering into the darkness. "We should be hitting an army checkpoint soon. The safe house is somewhere at the top."

While sounding imminent, the top of the hill proved to be an additional fifteen minutes away, and before they reached it, they encountered the expected checkpoint. The entrance to Gulmarg had closed at sundown, but Walker produced an impressive document festooned with official stamps for the inspecting officers. The gate was raised, and they were given directions for following a restricted military road to their destination.

Hidden among the trees on Gulmarg's western outskirts, the property was owned by the Indian Army, and the Criminal Investigations Division in Srinagar had secured its use for them that night. Walker had called it a safe house, but as Conor climbed from the SUV, weary and stiff, he thought "sheep barn" more accurately described it.

It was perched on the hillside and constructed from rough-hewn pine. A set of stairs and a wide deck had been added—perhaps in an effort to disguise its original purpose. The interior was a single large room divided evenly into areas that emphasized its two main functions: sleeping and eating. Precisely spaced army cots lined the wall on the right-hand side; a dining table and kitchen area dominated on the left.

The CID had also arranged for someone to provide supper. The young man who greeted them at the door with flour-covered hands was clearly taking his duties seriously, but judging from his muscular physique—along with the AK-47 strapped to his back—he was a cook who came with supplemental skills.

The place was rustic but adequate. It was made more inviting by its cozy warmth and by the aroma of Mulligatawny soup simmering on the wood-fired kitchen stove, which also served as the building's main source of heat.

After serving up an enormous amount of food, their cook returned to his barracks, and the rest of the evening yawned before them as a torpid descent into limbo. Having forcefully persuaded Walker to forego another rehearsal, there was little to do except search for innocuous topics of conversation and wait until it was late enough to go to bed. When Walker called lights out at ten o'clock, the announcement met with audible sighs of relief.

After so little sleep the previous night, Conor had no trouble nodding off, but at three in the morning, an acrid odor, combined with a noticeable constriction in his chest, brought him fully awake. The kitchen stove did a fine job of keeping the large room heated but its vents were in less than perfect working order, and it smelled like someone might have banked the fire with something other than wood.

He fumbled in the darkness for his coat and slipped outside. Standing on the front deck he took cautious gulps of the freezing air, mindful of Kavita's warning. The tightness loosened, but he lingered outside, listening to the disembodied night sounds of the forest.

In the surrounding pines, boughs creaked and sporadically shifted to unload parcels of snow, each of them hitting the ground with a noise like a muffled punch. After eavesdropping for a few minutes, he straightened and caught a whiff of cigarette smoke on the breeze. He leaned over the deck railing and saw Sedgwick sitting on a bench in the yard below, looking up at him. Offering a silent wave, Conor descended the steps.

"Stove bothering you?" The agent asked, with a note of apology. "I threw in a few bricks of sheep dung by mistake. I thought I'd cleared out most of the smoke. Did it wake everyone?"

"No, just me," Conor replied, sliding onto the bench. "Lower tolerance, I suppose. How long have you been up?"

"About an hour. Walker's fault. He's invented so many worst-case scenarios I can't sleep wondering which one will happen. It'll be something we never thought of, probably."

"That would make Costino happy," Conor said sourly. "He's panting to see some action."

Sedgwick flicked the cigarette onto the snow with a grumble of agreement. "Costino's lucky he's seeing anything at all. I'd have left him back in Mumbai. He feels like bad luck, exactly the kind of dumbass analyst that field operatives get killed trying to rescue. Makes me nervous."

"In that case, I'm glad he's supposed to stay with the car." Conor grinned, but then added more seriously, "You were supposed to be in the room with Thomas tomorrow if I hadn't come along and nicked your job. Does that make you nervous, too?"

"A little. Not because I don't trust you. It's because I'm a control freak. To be honest though, it would have been riskier with me in the room. I would have—" He stopped. After staring straight ahead for several seconds he gave a slight nod, as if acknowledging an internal dialogue. Without turning, he finished the thought. "I would have needed some kind of disguise. Someone in the room might have recognized me. It's not my first trip to the rodeo with Dragonov and his gang."

Conor stiffened. He hadn't seen that one coming. He almost felt foolish for being surprised by it. "Right. That got my attention. How do you know him? And why didn't you tell me before, for fuck's sake?"

Sedgwick's chin burrowed down into his jacket. "I hoped I wouldn't need to get into it, unless it became relevant."

"Unless it became relevant." Conor languorously exhaled a plume of breath. It was hardly worth the effort of getting angry anymore. "Fine. Whatever. You all think it's better having me drip-fed little squirts of information as it suits you, so who am I to argue?"

"I'll tell you about it."

"Don't put yourself out; I mean if it's not relevant—"

"I *want* to tell you about it." Sedgwick drove a fist into his knee, raised it again, and let it fall onto the bench between them. Conor looked at his averted profile, suspecting he knew what sort of story he was about to hear.

"Ready when you are," he said, quietly.

With his chin still pressed against his chest, Sedgwick slid his hands into the pockets of his jacket. "It was my first field experience with the CIA, in St. Petersburg," he began. "We were cooperating with the DEA, investigating groups that were expanding into arms dealing, using transit corridors they'd established for drug trafficking. The DEA had targeted Dragonov, and the CIA was supposed to gather intelligence on the corridors by infiltrating his drug-running business. He'd delegated most of it to the lower ranks, so that's where they assigned me."

His eyes flicked at Conor and tailed away again. "Like I said, it was my first operation, thirteen years ago. I was twenty-three, and my case officer was a dinosaur from the Cold War era. He'd spent most of his career turning Soviet physicists. He didn't know shit about drug trafficking, but he'd logged thirty distinguished years and nobody at Langley knew what the fuck else to do with him. So he was in charge. He assigned my cover and threw me into it—no backup, no support since he didn't know how—just me on my own, crawling around bars and strip clubs on the St. Petersburg docks, looking for the door to Dragonov's lair."

Sedgwick expelled a bitter laugh. "Well, I found it, and Jesus wasn't I a star. I got hired into a mule gang, taking heroin packets off fruit trucks and bringing them to the docks to get repacked and sent to Helsinki. Within six months I'd learned enough to map the entire transit corridor from Tajikistan to St. Petersburg. The bosses back home were very pleased, and my pals in the mule gang loved me. I ended up in meetings with Dragonov several times. I doubt he'd remember me, but you never know, and I was pretty tight with his men in St. Petersburg. If any of them moved up to the inner circle, and if they ended up traveling with him ... well, it was a risk we were prepared for, but we've got you now, so we can avoid it."

He paused to light another cigarette. Snow had begun falling in fat, cottony flakes, some merging into larger clumps that dropped quickly and broke apart on impact. Conor rubbed them off his jeans as they landed, waiting for the story to continue, but realized the agent was struggling to get it started again.

"What happened?" he asked. "You got caught?"

"Oh, yeah, I got caught. Just not the way you think." Sedgwick's voice turned flat, impersonal. "It isn't all that hard to look like a junkie or even act like one. That's what it was supposed to be. An act. I was supposed to be pretending." He glanced at Conor, a half-flinching squint. "What I was too young and stupid to realize was that once you've nailed it and have everyone convinced, 'looking like' and 'acting like' doesn't cut it. Close isn't good enough once you're inside. I had to be flawless to get trusted, to get good intelligence, and the more I brought out, the more the bosses wanted. They didn't want to notice what I was becoming—just sent me back for more. Of everything. I thought I could handle it and thought I was managing pretty well. Classic argument of a junkie—you're sure you're keeping all the balls in the air, even while you're circling the drain."

He faced Conor squarely and fell silent, offering an opportunity for question or comment. Conor could do nothing with the invitation. The questions he might have asked were not meant for Sedgwick, but for the shameless manipulators who had warped the talent of a twenty-three year old and extinguished his future, without a flicker of conscience.

He had an intimate knowledge of the hazards involved in assuming a false identity, but his exposure to that danger had been a mere flirtation by comparison. He would not have considered until now that he'd gotten off lightly.

He said nothing, and with a wistful smile Sedgwick looked away again. "Well, the short version of all this is that sometime during the second year of the operation, I got picked up in a drug raid. I don't remember it, don't even know where I was. It was four months before my controlling officer tracked me down in prison."

"Oh, Christ, you've got to be kidding."

The agent's breath caught in a choked laugh. "I'm not sure he was looking very hard. It was tricky getting me out without burning the whole operation. I didn't get a lot of sympathy from my superiors. I got a voucher for rehab, then they reassigned me, and then I flamed out, and we started it all over again. And then they got tired of me. That's when I started freelancing. Worked with MI6, did a few jobs for Australia, a few for Canada—fucked up several of them. I was pretty much at the end of the line when Walker dug me up, offering one last chance and the prospect of a little revenge. He's been studying the guy for twenty years, but I'm the only agent who's ever been in a room with him."

"Seems like you made the most of it," Conor ventured. "Last chance was the charm, maybe?"

"No, I was well on the way to wrecking that one, too, before I finally got a grip." A shaky grin skittered over Sedgwick's face. "Some people find Jesus. I found a four-foot tall Indian saint and an Irishman with fists like concrete. Maybe that's what I'd needed all along—the right balance of compassion and violence."

He bent forward, ruffling the top of his head to shake the snow from his hair, and sat up straighter. A trace of sarcasm surfaced as he watched Conor speculatively.

"So, there you have it," he said. "Does it all sound relevant, now that you know?"

"It does, in a way—to me anyway," Conor said, stung by the mild dig and its undeniable justice. "I'm sorry if you felt forced to talk about it."

"I wasn't forced," Sedgwick corrected. "I know the conventional wisdom about me. Most people, I don't give a shit what they think, but I wanted to tell you. It's not a story that covers me in glory, but now at least you know it wasn't a lifestyle choice. I don't know why that matters to me, but it does."

"I never thought it was a lifestyle choice."

"Really?" Sedgwick cocked an ironic eyebrow. "Never?"

"Well—" He was rescued from further embarrassment by the sound of a door opening above them. Costino darted out onto the deck. The glow from the flashlight in his hand bathed his face in moon-colored light, accentuating a look of faint alarm. It gave them both the comic relief they needed.

"Look who it is," Conor chirped up at him. "You've a queer old look in your eyes there, Tony. Which were you thinking, now, that we'd been kidnapped or that we'd deserted?"

34

They were back in the SUV at ten thirty the following morning. The meeting with Dragonov was not until noon, and his hotel was only a few kilometers from the safe house, but Walker's insistence on building in ample travel time met with no resistance. Everyone was anxious to get moving.

Geographically, Gulmarg was known as a mountain shelf. A wide, bowl-shaped meadow sitting twenty six hundred meters above sea level, it had first gained popularity as a hill station retreat for the British during the "Raj" era. Remnant artifacts of their earlier rule still dotted the landscape. A small Anglican church sat isolated in the middle of the meadow, flanked on one side by the world's highest golf course, now buried under several feet of snow.

The Gulmarg Alpine Cottage sat in a high, remote clearing on the opposite side, near the gondola, and Walker's plan for approaching it involved a double-pronged strategy. Midway up a steep, winding road leading to the hotel, a trailhead marked a trekking path to the property. It snaked up through a forested area and ended at the hotel's front entrance. The plan was for Walker and Sedgwick to hike up the path, posing as recreational tourists, while Costino drove Conor and Thomas up to the hotel's small parking area. They would wait for the two agents to emerge from the trail and take up positions outside, and then Conor and

Thomas would make their way to the lobby, leaving Costino to remain with the car.

As Sedgwick predicted, the first crack in this precisely choreographed production was one they hadn't anticipated.

The wet snowfall from the previous evening was now frozen on the road, leaving it slick and treacherous. They reached the trailhead, but as soon as it braked, the Range Rover could progress no further. It lost all traction, wheels spinning uselessly against the ice. The only remedy was to creep back down to a level spot on the road for a new running start. Costino was assigned the task while the rest of them started up the trail.

"Why don't we leave it here?" he protested, turning a pleading gaze from one face to another, seeking an ally. "Won't it look weird for me to drive up alone and sit in the parking lot? Greg? Why don't I come with you? I can be another hiker."

"Because we might need the car, Tony," Walker explained, beginning with ominously exaggerated patience and finishing with a roar. "And if we do, we might not want it to be stuck on the ice, in the middle of the fucking hill. Now, do what I tell you. Get in the goddamned car and figure out a way to get it up there."

"Okay, sorry." Costino backed a few steps away, biting his lip, but then his cold-reddened cheeks dimpled with a reassuring smile. "Good luck, everybody. I'll see you on the other side."

He trotted back to the car and disappeared around the side of it as the four of them started up the trail.

It was a gorgeous route, winding through a hushed landscape of fragrant conifers, but the path was long, rocky and covered in snow, making for a difficult climb. By the time they'd reached the halfway point, Conor's convalescent lungs were protesting. He kept his head down to avoid distraction, concentrating on the effort required, but when he lifted it after a few minutes to check their progress, he saw a shape dart into his field of vision.

A boy? Yes, it was a boy. Hindu.

The population in Jammu & Kashmir was largely Muslim, but judging by his *tilak*—a thick horizontal smear of yellow paste across a narrow forehead—the little boy that materialized in front of him was not only Hindu but also a young devotee of the supreme deity Shiva, creator and destroyer of worlds. He looked to be about ten years old. He was thin, stunted, and dressed raggedly, with a head full of brown hair sticking up in all directions. He had stepped out from the trees onto the path and was smiling up at him with flashing white teeth, holding out a cluster of marigolds, cupped in two small hands.

Where on earth had he found them in this weather?

"Conor. Don't take the flowers, dammit."

"Why not?"

"You know why." About twenty meters ahead of him, Walker glared back in irritation. "They're not free. He wants money for them, and if you give money to one, we'll have a dozen more popping out of the woods, and we don't need that."

Conor stuffed his hands into his pockets, unconvinced. The path ahead and behind them was empty. He didn't believe a dozen small children were hiding among the trees, ready to stream out with fistfuls of marigolds. The boy toggled his head, smiling again, and moved his hands to indicate a small shrine just off the path. It sat atop a broad, whitewashed platform, a cement block with an elaborately carved archway. Within its niche the figure of Shiva—in traditional dance posture—gazed out with cool serenity.

Walker pivoted and strode off up the trail. With a wink, Conor plucked two blossoms from the boy's hands and tucked a grimy wad of rupee notes into the pocket of his threadbare jacket. He put one marigold into the niche and the other into his own pocket and began to turn away, but then he looked again at the child. Warmer temperatures would be on the way soon, but it was an overcast, viciously cold day, and the boy's thin denim jacket was no proper protection against it.

With a furtive glance up the path, he removed the Pashmina scarf wrapped around his neck. It was wide enough to serve as a shawl, and as he quickly wound it around the small body, the child's eyes grew round with wonder. When he was well wrapped, he reached for Conor's wrist and pressed it to his forehead in gratitude. Conor touched his shoulder and stepped away.

"Off you go," he whispered, repeating the words in Hindi and urging the boy in the opposite direction. "Go on home, now. I'll catch hell if he sees you."

He watched the child scamper off down the trail and then started off to catch up to the others. When he reached them a few hundred meters short of the clearing, Walker had called a halt to make final preparations.

The Srinagar Criminal Investigation Division had issued them two police radios for communications. Walker had given one to Costino and kept the second. Checking in now, he learned the two CID officers who had established the listening post in the room next to Dragonov had been joined on the scene by six additional undercover officers—far more than expected. They were stationed at various locations both inside and outside the hotel. He communicated with the officer in charge, confirming that Dragonov and his men were in the suite, and then began a test to ensure Thomas's body wire was transmitting properly.

During the momentary lull, Conor opened his coat to tighten his gun holster. Propped against a tree with his arms crossed, Sedgwick glanced at him and gave a low cry of surprise.

"The Walther? Christ, McBride, who told you to bring it? You can't wear that in there. They might search you."

Conor's eyes stretched in confusion. "I'm supposed to be his bodyguard. What's the use of a bodyguard without a gun?"

"They don't think you're a bodyguard," Sedgwick insisted. "They think you're his brother, and—"

"I am his brother," he retorted.

Walker ripped out his earpiece and marched over to him. "Take it off." His fists were poised at hip-level. "Take it off and hand it over."

Conor shook his head slowly, a steel-tipped dread scissoring into his stomach. He had been on edge from the moment they'd left the safe house that morning but had not felt frightened until now. "No." His refusal was categorical. "I won't bring him in there unarmed."

"Then you won't bring him in there at all," Walker shot back.

"Walker," Sedgwick began in a tone of warning, but Conor waved him to silence.

"If I don't bring him, nobody does. Period."

Walker went rigid with fury, but before he could explode, Thomas put a restraining hand on his shoulder. "I'll wear it," he said. "We already know they're not going to search me."

Looking at Conor, he added, "You'll know where to look if you need it. You're quick as a short-tailed weasel. You'll have it off me about as fast as wearing it yourself."

Conor saw it was the best deal he was going to get. He slipped off his coat. As soon as Thomas had the holster in place, Walker urged them to hurry up the final stretch of trail to the hotel.

He was dragging behind again by the time they reached the clearing. Thomas turned back to give him a hard look. "What's wrong?"

"Nothing's wrong," he panted. "I wasn't prepared to run half-way up the Himalayas this morning, that's all. I'm a little out of shape."

"You're wheezing."

"I'm okay."

"It's a crattling sound. I can hear it from here."

"Yeah, I can hear it too, Thomas, as it's me that's making it. It's the cold air."

Cold Kashmiri air. He wondered if his impulsive surrender

of the scarf had been entirely wise.

The Gulmarg Alpine Cottage was a modern, three-story structure of white pine clapboard, and its empty lobby was like the audience hall of a maharajah. It was long and narrow, lined on either side with low couches. Its ceiling was resplendent, painted with a colorful design of vines and flowers that simulated the traditional pietra dura technique of polished stones embedded in marble.

To register, the prospective guest had to traverse the long space like a supplicant and approach the presence of the front desk manager, who affected the manner of a maharajah himself. Installed behind a half-wall of elaborately carved wood, he observed the approach of Thomas and Conor with regal indifference.

"How are you?" Thomas offered the greeting with a nervous grin. "We've an appointment to see Mr. Vasily Dragonov. Would you ever ring his room, please, to let him know we're here?"

"Sir, sorry, sir." The manager's eyes fluttered shut; his head moved in random directions. "Not possible."

"Not possible?"

"It is power cut. No telephoning, sir. Sorry-sorry."

"Oh, shit," Thomas breathed.

Conor understood the broader meaning of his dismay. Walker had confirmed the hotel was wired for Internet access, but a power cut in Gulmarg had the same effect on its accessibility as it did in Rishikesh.

Fortunately, the complication was one they actually had planned for—he was carrying the BGAN kit in his backpack. They could connect it to make the bank transfer. Thomas's panicky expression was an overreaction, and it worried him. With a quick, surreptitious movement, Conor placed the side of his boot against his brother's, and pressed.

"Maybe you could have someone take us to him," he

suggested. "He's expecting us. I don't think he appreciates being made to wait."

The haughty little manager appeared to conclude the remark was valid. With a peremptory snap of his fingers, he summoned the bellman to bring them to the suite.

"*Tóg go bog é.*" Conor patted his brother on the back as they followed their guide into the stairwell. *Take it easy.*

They continued conversing quietly in Irish as they climbed the stairs, safe in the knowledge that oceans and continents separated them from the nearest living soul who could understand them.

"We're doing all right here," Conor said. "It's going to be fine."

"I know. I guess." Thomas used a glove to sponge a layer of sweat from his forehead. "Foolish of me. It was always meant to come to this, but I didn't think of it until now. It's harder than I would have thought."

"Because they've trusted you."

"They had no reason not to. We bought things. We paid for them. Sure it's rubbish, but I always felt I was playing it straight with them. Until now."

"Play it straight now," Conor urged. "At least pretend you are. They needn't know, not right away. When the hammer drops, and the cops come in, just you look more surprised than anyone."

"*Déanfaidh mé iarracht,*" Thomas mumbled, with a sigh. *I will try.*

35

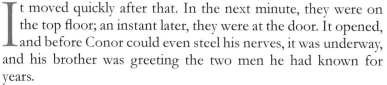

It moved quickly after that. In the next minute, they were on the top floor; an instant later, they were at the door. It opened, and before Conor could even steel his nerves, it was underway, and his brother was greeting the two men he had known for years.

He scanned the room as they stepped into the suite, a large, impersonal space dominated by accents of glass and steel. Like the Jyoti flat in Mumbai, the suite's saving grace was what could be seen from it—a stunning view of forest pines and the snow-covered Gulmarg meadow far below. What was missing from the room was equally noteworthy. Dragonov was nowhere to be seen.

Conor automatically began cycling through options for addressing that development, but then realized it wasn't up to him. The leading part belonged to Thomas. The success or failure of the day rested on his broad shoulders and on his relationship with these men and his ability to tease from them certain words and actions.

He nervously turned to see how his brother would manage under the weight of this and suddenly found it difficult to stay in character. A wave of admiration threatened to undermine his façade of detachment. Thomas had buried his earlier discomfort and stepped into the performance with wholehearted and courageous commitment, displaying an unexpected ease with his role. Releasing a natural-sounding growl of pleasure, he gave warm handshakes to both men, who were Nicholas and Maxim.

In contrast, Conor felt unconstrained by the pressure of conforming to expectations. Their hosts had none where he was concerned. They had no previous experience by which to measure him and showed only mild interest in forming any. They greeted him warmly as the brother of a long-time colleague and client, but for them, his significance ended there. In an indication of how little importance they afforded him, neither showed any interest in frisking him. He floated on the periphery of their attention, a largely ignored spectator free to observe the action without participating in it.

Standing apart, he studied the two of them while pretending not to. Nicholas and Maxim were quite ordinary-looking men. Russian accents certainly, but not overly thick. Middle-aged, average height, paunchy middles, and baggy eyes. Interchangeable.

They led the way into the living room to a set of sofas facing each other next to a window. Rather than sitting with Thomas on the sofa, Conor took a straight-backed chair and drew it back a little to a vantage point that allowed him to keep everyone in view. His disconnection from the scene generated a sensation of vertigo, but also a peculiar feeling of safety, as though he were a disinterested bystander watching strangers through a window.

The meeting began with social pleasantries. There was lighthearted conversation. Laughter. There was vodka. At exactly the right moment—sooner would have looked anxious, any later would seem discourteous—Conor saw Thomas manufacture a bland smile of curiosity. What of their leader? Hopefully, he had not been detained?

No. Vasily was here, of course. He was in the bedroom, resting. He would join them shortly. More vodka. Glasses raised. Salutes. Thomas tossed him a wink and a cheerful smirk. Conor caught the implied message and returned it: the son of a bitch had better show up soon.

Vasily Dragonov finally did appear, abruptly emerging from the bedroom and filling the room with a charged atmosphere. As he advanced toward them, Conor found it impossible to get a fixed read on him and didn't believe it was the vodka impairing his analysis. The man appeared as a slippery physical oddity that defied intense scrutiny, not so much nondescript as indistinct. Precise features were hard to define amidst an abundance of black hair—a thick shock of it on his head, two bushy lines of it across his brow, an all-encompassing growth of it beginning at cheekbone level and descending down over his neck like a silky pelt. He projected a large man's presence, but was under average in height, with a frame that looked solid and dense.

Beneath all the hair, his face shifted like a trick photograph, morphing with every adjustment in angle. Conor noted that his arrival prompted a perceptible change of emphasis in the meeting. The conversation became more formal and sedate; the bottle of vodka was removed to a cupboard.

Thomas talked for a brief period about the ashram and about Kavita. For the most part, Dragonov listened politely, asking few questions. For a man who had traveled upward of eighteen hours from Moscow with the hope of meeting his true guru, Conor thought he displayed a surprising lack of inquisitive interest. Was that suspicious, or merely an indication of a detached, incurious personality?

When the talk turned to business, he felt the prevailing mood change again. The discussion continued with easy cordiality, but everyone suddenly seemed more attentive, Dragonov included. Again, Thomas led the discussion. As he made his way through the agreed script, Conor mentally tracked the reactions it was designed to elicit. Each recorded response from the arms dealer served as a gift-wrapped piece of evidence for the prosecuting attorneys who would be chaperoning the production through its next phase.

Thomas secured Dragonov's verbal understanding that the weapons were being purchased with laundered mafia money, that they would be targeted against Pakistani installations, that the intent was to destabilize the Line of Control and the larger Jammu-Kashmir region, and that the strategy would include targeted attacks on Western tourists, including Americans.

Sprinkled over the accomplishment of this gruesome laundry list were the esoteric details—almost surreal in their banality—of manufacturer end-user certificates, shipping methods, delivery dates, and destinations.

Finally, it remained only to seal the transaction with a bank transfer, which required an Internet connection. Conor watched Dragonov reach toward the lamp next to him and try the switch. Nothing.

At that moment, in what might have been the first spontaneous emotion he'd shown since arriving, Dragonov turned to Maxim and unleashed an intense, furious tirade, entirely in Russian. Clearly, it was meant to be a tongue-lashing, which Maxim immediately took to heart. He surged to his feet and offered a weak, apologetic smile.

"We have been without power since morning. There is no sense of urgency with these people, you know. I must go see if some other means of persuasion might—"

"I think we can help you out," Conor broke in quickly.

It was the first time he had volunteered any comment since the initial exchange of greetings. His voice sounded unfamiliar, even to himself, and every eye in the room swung toward him, as though the chair itself had spoken. Thomas recovered first, covering his momentary lapse with an expansive sigh.

"He's right. I've no head for this shite, but my little brother is determined to teach me a technological thing or two. He's got a battery-powered satellite gizmo in his backpack. We can use that to connect. All we need is a patch of clear sky."

Dragonov exchanged a glance with his two lieutenants. His face was inscrutable, but theirs were not. For a few seconds they hesitated, their eyes shifting indecisively, and for Conor, it was a few seconds too long. His radar went up, and his nerves engaged. They suspected something.

He felt an overpowering intuition building, insisting that they needed to get out of the room. With a herculean effort of self-discipline, he resisted the urge to move closer to Thomas, closer to his gun. Looking at Dragonov, he forced a disinterested shrug.

"Just an option. We can wait for the power to come back if you'd rather."

"Nonsense." Dragonov passed his eyes over him, as if only now deciding he was worthy of closer attention. "Foolish to wait, when you have the means to get it done quickly. Also foolish, however, for all of us to freeze. I assume we may wait here while you search out your patch of clear sky?"

"Of course." Conor nodded and tipped his head casually at his brother. "I'll need you, though. You've got all the account information."

A ripple of irritation slipped almost imperceptibly over the arms dealer's features and then disappeared beneath an answering smile. "Bundle up well," he purred amiably. "Maxim, go along to keep our friends company. Bring the vodka if you like. No harm in a small glass to stay warm."

Moving a few steps ahead of Maxim, Conor and Thomas took the stairs back down to the lobby. As they exited the front door of the hotel, they were met with the spectacle of Sedgwick and Walker, enjoying a picnic lunch.

"Nice for them," Thomas whispered in gruff amusement.

They sat at one of several tables scattered around the snow-dusted clearing, with an array of thermos containers and orange peels spread before them. The officers listening in via Thomas's body wire had presumably radioed Walker to warn of the altered plan. Neither he nor Sedgwick gave any indication of noticing them. A bit farther off, Conor saw an additional hiker enjoying some midday refreshment. It was their "cook" from the previous evening. The young officer had apparently received a new assignment from his superiors.

Conor selected a spot about ten yards away, a table closer to the front door. Dropping onto the bench, he offered a prayer of gratitude for unpredictable power cuts. Because of this one, the denouement in the suite would come with them safely stationed here outside, with only Maxim to subdue and five bodies on the scene to tackle him.

It had little effect on the air temperature, but the sun was now shining brilliantly, setting off a diamond-bright twinkle on the field's blanket of frozen crystals. The brightness made it difficult to see the screen, but at least there was no need to step through MI6's tedious login hierarchy. They were using Sedgwick's laptop this time.

The BGAN set-up worked, but the connection was much slower than in Rishikesh. Maxim loitered near the hotel entrance, looking impatient and unhappy, but there was no hurrying the technology. Anyway, Conor reasoned, if he knew what was coming next, he wouldn't be in such a rush.

It took almost ten minutes to access the DEA's bank account and set up the transfer. As the transaction began processing, a status bar appeared on the screen, tracking its slow, incremental progress toward completion.

"Christ, this is going to take a while." Thomas got to his feet in nervous frustration. He took a walk around the table while Conor monitored the screen.

"Don't pace," he whispered, when his brother paused to peer over his shoulder. "Makes you look nervous."

"At this point, I don't much give a shit."

They both snickered softly as Thomas straightened and began another aimless stroll in the opposite direction. A minute later, the laptop's screen saver appeared, and Conor tapped at the track pad to clear it, but Thomas mistook the movement. He raised his eyebrows in inquiry.

"Transaction completed, then?"

Conor's head snapped up to stare at him, his brain frozen in alarm. His brother immediately registered the unconscious error. His mouth dropped open with a soundless oath. Inadvertently, in the form of a question, he had given the verbal cue signaling the officers at the listening post to move in for target apprehension.

Before either of them could decide what to do or say next, Maxim raised a fist to his mouth, and Conor saw a microphone wire tucked into the sleeve of his jacket. The Russian spoke urgently, first in his own language, and then in English, repeating the announcement.

"Transaction complete. Transaction complete." His voice scraped sharply in the cold, thin air and as his hand went into his jacket, Conor automatically reached under his shoulder, grabbing at the empty space where his holster should be.

"Thomas, Jesus Christ, look out!"

He threw the picnic table onto its side and lunged from the bench, connecting with his brother as he heard the crack of the gunshot. The two of them tumbled to the ground. Frantically, he tore open his brother's coat and ripped out the Walther. More shots erupted around him, shattering the front window of the hotel lobby. In the next instant, he heard the muffled sound of more gunfire, coming from the upper floors somewhere inside the hotel.

Peering over the top of the table, he saw Maxim lying across a shower of broken glass in front of the pulverized window. Looking left, he saw Sedgwick and Walker also braced behind an overturned table, their guns still trained on the lifeless Russian.

"What is it?" he shouted. "What the fuck just happened?"

With a quick check of the front door, Sedgwick ran across the open space, landing on his knees next to him. "It's a trap. Dragonov has more men with him. They ambushed the officers at the listening post next to his suite." His voice was level, but his lips pulled back in an anguished grimace. "The bastards knew it was a set-up. They knew before we got here. Dragonov must have friends at Interpol who saw the warrant and tipped him off. Fucking two-faced traitors. Someone will get a cut, I'm sure. They made sure to wait until the transfer was finished."

The laptop and satellite hook-up had slid from the table to the ground. With the barrel of his gun Conor tipped up the now-static screen and looked at the status bar. In the last few seconds before the connection terminated, the transfer had gone through to the account Thomas had opened two days ago.

More gunshots sounded from inside the hotel, not quite as muffled this time. They ducked behind the table again.

"Who's doing all the shooting? Does everyone in the feckin' hotel have a gun?"

The question, sounding strained and unnatural, came from Thomas. With an icy premonition, Conor spun around to look at him. He was on hands and knees, crouched behind them. As Thomas lifted his head, Conor could see it in his eyes—the expression he'd suggested to cap the performance of a lifetime.

His brother looked more surprised than anyone.

"Thomas. Oh fuck, no. Jesus, Sedgwick, he's hit. He's been shot."

36

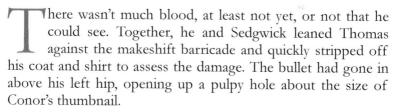

There wasn't much blood, at least not yet, or not that he could see. Together, he and Sedgwick leaned Thomas against the makeshift barricade and quickly stripped off his coat and shirt to assess the damage. The bullet had gone in above his left hip, opening up a pulpy hole about the size of Conor's thumbnail.

"Here's the exit wound." Sedgwick lightly probed an area on Thomas's back. Looks like it came through cleanly, at least." He looked at Thomas. "How much pain?" Thomas shook his head uncertainly.

"None. Just feels peculiar. Cold, like the rest of me. I'd appreciate the shirt and coat back on, if that's all right."

"We should bandage it somehow, in case the bleeding gets worse."

"Here, use these." Conor handed his gloves to Sedgwick. "We'll need tape, string, something. I'll go look."

"McBride, wait! Shit. Be careful."

Eluding Sedgwick's frantic grasp, he sprinted for the front lobby. Sporadic sounds of a gunfight continued somewhere above him. It was impossible to tell what floor, but it sounded closer than before, and from the lingering echo after each shot, he thought the battle might have moved to the stairwell.

The front desk manager had understandably deserted his post. At the desk, and then in the office behind it, he rifled through drawers and cabinets until he found what he needed: a roll of brown packing tape. When he returned with it, the scene had consolidated. Walker and the young CID officer who had been stationed farther across the field had gathered closer. Walker was repeatedly trying to raise Costino on the radio, directing him to bring the Range Rover.

"He's not answering the radio?" he asked, handing over the tape. Sedgwick shook his head grimly.

"Incompetent son of a bitch. He's got it on the wrong setting or else he broke it. No sign of the SUV anywhere, either."

Conor sank down next to Thomas and gave him a close look, trying to disguise a rising panic as Sedgwick improvised a bandage with the gloves and tape. Shivering, his brother managed a wan smile.

"Probably still trying to get it up the hill. Bloody wanker."

Spitting an obscenity, Walker lowered his radio and turned a questioning glare on the young officer. He had been monitoring the second channel and the communications of the CID officers inside. In response to Walker's implied query, he delivered a situation report in a clipped, professional tone.

"Second team has engaged the men who ambushed listening post. They are still on fourth floor. Dragonov is still in suite, number of men with him unknown. The perimeter team has reached, entering through rear door. They are in stairwell between third and fourth floor, Dragonov's men shooting from stairs above. Officer in charge requests reinforcement to opposite side of fourth floor with strategy to flush from top to bottom."

Walker stood with his arms folded, staring out across the clearing. With a deep breath, he turned to Sedgwick.

"How bad is it? Is he stable?"

For the first time, Sedgwick's poker face wavered. He raised his hands helplessly. "I don't ... it doesn't look bad, but it's still a bullet wound, Greg. Who knows what it might have hit going through him. We need to get him out of here. Back to Srinagar."

"But is he stable?" Walker asked again.

"I'm right here, you know," Thomas spoke up sardonically. "Supposing you wanted to ask, I'd tell you I'm feeling fairly stable. Tell us what needs to happen."

Walker pulled the wire-rimmed glasses from his face and rubbed a hand quickly over his eyes. Replacing them, he came to balance on one knee in front of Thomas. Ignoring the others, he put the case to him directly and succinctly.

"I need to take this officer and get inside and see if we can get the initiative back before it's too late. You need to get away from the action. I think the safest and closest option is across the field and down the path. Do you think you can make it?"

"I do." Thomas looked back at him with stony resolve. "Let's get on with it."

With a nod at Sedgwick and Conor, Walker got to his feet. He was already running toward the hotel with the CID officer close behind as he barked out orders. "Go. Get him under cover, and when you find the SUV get him out of here."

Conor and Sedgwick helped Thomas to his feet. Supporting him on either side, they moved as quickly as they dared, wary of aggravating whatever might be bubbling beneath the deceptively small surface wounds.

They intended to place him well down the trail in the area where they'd stopped earlier and then Sedgwick would look for the car. As they neared the spot, Conor stopped, catching sight of Costino a little farther below. He was moving with an indecisive step along the path but hurried forward when he saw them, his mouth falling open at the sight of Thomas. Conor unloaded on him before he could utter a word.

"Where have you been, you useless bastard?" He had a nearly uncontrollable desire to bounce the agent's callow face off the nearest tree trunk. "I see the earpiece, but where's your radio? Where's the car? Where are your fucking brains? I've an itch to crack you open like a walnut, to see if you have any at all."

Costino stopped short. A spasm of nebulous emotion shuddered over his features. "It doesn't work." He lifted the radio and showed it to them, holding it as though it were a foreign object he'd found on the ground. "I tried every channel. I couldn't reach you and couldn't hear anything. The car got stuck on the ice again. It's down there, in about the same spot. What's happened? I heard gunshots. Thomas, are you—"

"Give me the keys," Sedgwick snapped. He snatched them from Costino's fingers. "All you need to know is the shit has hit the fan. Dragonov is up there with a battalion. Are you armed?"

The younger man stared as if hypnotized and nodded slowly. "Yes. I have a gun."

"Well, where is it?" Sedgwick yelled. "Get it out for Christ's sake, and go cover the top of the trail while I help them down to the car."

Costino tugged at his coat and timorously drew a pistol from its inside pocket, looking as dazed as he had earlier in handling the radio.

Conor's eyes met Sedgwick's. He watched the agent's eyebrows arch with fatalistic irony and knew they were sharing the same uncomfortable recollection from their conversation the previous evening.

"Dumbass analyst," Sedgwick said and turned back to Costino with a resigned sigh. "Put it away before you shoot yourself. Wait here for me. Keep your head down, keep out of sight, and stay put. Got it?"

With mute obedience, Costino put the gun back into his pocket. They left him there and continued down the path toward the car. As they rounded a bend, Conor spared one last look up at him. He was standing on the edge of the trail, eyes lowered, shifting from one foot to the other.

Thomas leaned more heavily on them as they descended. Conor caught him wincing as they jostled over a section of uneven ground, and he moved in closer, trying to transfer more of his brother's weight onto his shoulders.

"The pain is worse now, is it?"

"Feeling it a bit more," Thomas admitted. When they reached the small shrine, his stoicism finally weakened. "Let's just sit down there for a few minutes, right? Have a bit of a rest."

Maneuvering across the trail they eased Thomas down onto the platform. Conor was grateful himself for the break, hoping it would diminish a persistent slurp in his chest that he was doing his best to ignore. Facing the shrine, he braced his hands against the stone and dropped his head, peering into the interior. The marigold he had placed there earlier was still snugged up against the foot of Shiva; the god's young disciple was nowhere in sight.

He stared in at the small, lithe deity, unable to form words of prayer in any language. The image dominating his mind was his brother's wound, blood beading up from it like drops of moisture on a pipe about to burst. He turned with his back to the shrine and sat down next to Thomas. In a desperate attempt to contain his fear, he hammered a door shut in his brain, isolating a choir of anxieties shrieking for attention. A static chill moved in to numb his rapidly thumping heart, and a tenuous composure took hold.

It allowed some space to think and reflect on what had gone wrong. Sedgwick thought someone within Interpol had tipped off Dragonov, but something wasn't adding up in that explanation.

He had known it was a trap, yet the arms dealer had come to Gulmarg anyway. Why? For the money? The temptation of a twenty-million-dollar haul was compelling, but was it worth the risk for a man already awash in millions? He recalled the image of Dragonov as a blurry character with shifting expressions, almost camouflaged beneath a bushy abundance of black hair, rolling across the room toward them with a bulky swagger.

Almost camouflaged?

From that tantalizing thought, his mind took a leap and then another one, traveling back several weeks to the scene in the Mumbai train station. Then it returned again to the moment he saw Maxim raise his wrist to speak into the microphone buried in his sleeve. The images came together like puzzle pieces; a picture at last emerged.

"It wasn't anyone at Interpol." Conor's anesthetic fog dissolved in a rush of astonishment. "This sting operation got stung a long time ago."

Sitting on the other side of Thomas, Sedgwick leaned forward and looked at him sharply. "What makes you say that?"

"This is fucking unbelievable." Conor sprang to his feet, nearly shouting now. "Of course they knew what we were up to, that's obvious enough. They loaded up on guns and manpower and tricked us to come here, prepared to turn the tables and blow us away. They knew more than that, though, didn't they? They knew our strategy. That's why they got nervous about the BGAN and going outside. It wasn't part of our plan. It was a contingency, and someone forgot to tell them about it."

"They knew the verbal cue we would use as well," Thomas said. Spots of color displaced the pallor on his cheeks. "You could see Maxim recognized it. He was repeating it just before he shot me."

"And who did he get it from, Thomas?" Conor smacked a fist into his palm. "Apart from the CID officers at the listening post who got it an hour ago, only the five of us knew it, so there's a quisling bastard here, somewhere. I know it's not me, and as you were the first one shot, it's not likely you."

"I see where you're going with this," Sedgwick said quietly. He stiffly rose from the platform and moved to stand in front of Conor, arms crossed. His cool gray eyes regarded him with detachment, but the muscles along his jaw twitched in a rippling spasm. "I'm the one with the back story, which I shared in a moment of weakness, idiotically enough. I never seem to learn my lesson with you, do I, McBride? You think since I've got a history with Dragonov, I must be the one who betrayed the mission, right? What do you figure I'm getting out of it—money or heroin? Or both?"

"Quit actin' the maggot, you stupid fecker." Conor gave the agent an impatient shove against his chest. "Sit down. Would I be standing here yelling all this at you if I thought you'd betrayed the mission?"

Sedgwick took an awkward step backward, startled and uncertain.

"Sit down." Thomas tugged at his arm. "Go on, Conor."

He ran a hand through his hair, trying to order his thoughts for a coherent argument. Then he took a breath and continued. "Dragonov is damned near impossible to lure anywhere. You told me that on the train the night we left Agra. So if he knew this was a trap, what would ever induce him to walk into it? Why would he risk capture by coming here?"

Sedgwick started to respond, but suddenly his mouth clapped shut. Conor saw he had made the first leap already. He nodded at the agent with a grim smile.

"The answer is simple isn't it? He wouldn't. He didn't. I've seen what yoga masters look like, how they move. They're supple, elastic. The guy Thomas and I met today was built like a brick shithouse, and he had less than nothing to say about Kavita or her ashram. I don't know who that hairy little fuck is up there, but I'll bet you twenty million dollars that he's not Vasily Dragonov."

"Holy shit, I think you may be right." Sedgwick's shoulders slumped. "We got baited by our own trap."

"Oh, I'm pretty sure I'm right," Conor said. "Now, while you're taking that on board, here's your next item. You were originally going to be with Thomas in this meeting today, and you're the only one here who would have recognized an imposter on sight. Do you think it's a coincidence that about three weeks ago in the Mumbai train station, a couple of trained assassins came after you, the only DEA agent who's ever been in a room with Dragonov? They targeted you that night but didn't get you. Why do you suppose they didn't try it again?"

"The strategy changed that same night when we brought you in." Sedgwick's face had grown slack. "Coming after me again wasn't worth the risk if I wouldn't see him anyway, at least not before the wire transfer happened."

The three of them looked at each other uncomfortably.

"Yeah, the strategy changed," Conor agreed. "And who, other than us, would have known about that? Walker and Costino. Only the five of us knew the plan. And which one of us didn't follow it?"

"Costino," Sedgwick breathed. "You mentioned his earpiece. I wondered why the moron was still wearing it if the radio didn't work. He's plugged into a different one."

"It figures," Thomas said. "I never could stand the little— ahhh, shit ... " His face twisted, and he pitched forward off the platform, arms clutched at his stomach.

Sedgwick and Conor both jumped to catch him before he could fall to the ground.

"Okay, we've got you." Sedgwick's voice was low, consoling. "No, don't sit on the ground, Tom. Let's get you back up onto the platform. There. Can you put your hands down for a minute? I know it hurts, buddy. I'll be quick, but I need to look."

The soothing hum of his reassurance ended with a stifled intake of breath. Conor also managed not to cry out, but only because his teeth had clamped onto his lower lip with a force that threatened to bite it in half. With the jacket pulled open, they could see his brother's shirt was saturated with blood.

In the continuing silence, Thomas bent forward to have a

look for himself. He stared at the dark, spreading stain for several seconds, muttered a low oath, and closed his eyes. He put his head back against the cement block of the shrine.

"Doesn't look too good, does it?"

"It's a little ... " Sedgwick cleared the catch from his voice and started again. "It's a little messy, no doubt about that. We need to get a real bandage on it. There's a medical kit in the Range Rover. I'll run down and get it."

He stepped back and took Conor by the elbow, drawing him out of earshot. Neither of them could look the other in the eye.

"I didn't think it was as bad as that." Sedgwick stared up at the tops of the trees.

"It's about fifty kilometers to Srinagar?" Conor kept his eyes focused on the ground and kicked at a root with the toe of his boot. "How long will that take?"

"On these roads, about an hour and a half, give or take. We can't waste any more time. There's Celox in the med kit, a coagulating powder. It won't solve the internal bleeding, but it will help, at least for a while. Wait here with him. I won't be long."

Conor watched him go, staring down the path and through the trees to the road in the distance. He walked back over to Thomas and pulled his brother's jacket more tightly around him, raising the zipper up to his chin.

"How's she cuttin'?" He tried to inject some lightness into the question.

"Better," Thomas said, with a quick, unconvincing nod. "It's easing up now."

"Good." Conor smiled at him. He gave his brother a gentle cuff against the side of his head and sat down next to him.

The door inside his head shuddered, but the lock held.

37

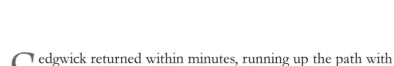

Sedgwick returned within minutes, running up the path with the medical kit and a fresh shirt he'd grabbed from one of the duffel bags. As he began to clear away the blood, Conor took his brother's hand in a wrestling hold, feeling its iron grip as Thomas stifled a gasp and braced against the pain.

Once the wound was packed with the coagulating powder and dressed with a thick, clean bandage, Conor finally broke the silence. "What are you going to do?"

Sedgwick ignored the question. He took a package from the medical kit and ripped it open, removing a square of transparent adhesive.

"This is a morphine patch for the pain," he murmured to Thomas, pressing it on next to the bandage. "There's a big stack of them in the kit, so don't be afraid to yell for more. You should feel it working in a couple of minutes."

Conor waited until he'd again zipped up his brother's jacket before trying again. "Sedgwick—"

"I'm going to help you down to the Range Rover and then go back up the trail and—"

"Bollocks," Thomas hissed through clenched teeth. His face was running with perspiration. "You're coming with us."

"I'm not." Sedgwick closed the kit with a decisive snap. "Walker doesn't know about any of this. I can't leave him stranded, not realizing one of his partners is an enemy."

"What if it's both of them?" Thomas argued. "You'll only get yourself killed."

"Tom, we both know it's not."

With the morphine patch beginning to provide some relief, they got Thomas down the remaining section of trail without stopping again. The Range Rover had not moved an inch. Costino hadn't even tried to make it look like he'd followed Walker's directions.

Conor folded down the rear seats to make a flat surface and scrambled inside, arranging duffel bags to serve as bolsters. He looked through the open hatch in the rear where Thomas sat, gray-faced and trembling, and saw Sedgwick was struggling to conceal his distress.

"I'm afraid it's going to be a bumpy ride, my friend. Don't forget about the pain patches. I'll follow as soon as I can and catch up with you in Srinagar."

With a faint smile, Thomas held out a hand and shook his head. "I don't think I'll be around when you get there. Shake hands now. Don't be mad if I couldn't wait for you."

"Tom, for God's sake," Sedgwick pleaded in a shaky whisper.

"*Síocáin, mo chara,*" Thomas murmured. "It'll be all right."

In the back of the SUV, Conor fell back on his heels, stunned by his brother's tranquil voice and its resemblance to the intuitive echo that had traveled inside him for so long. He felt a hopeless, impotent rage flood over him. Grabbing one of the duffel bags, he slammed it against the back of the driver's seat and struggled for composure, digging his fingers deep into the heavy canvas. After a moment, he exited through one of the rear doors and stood at a distance, watching and listening.

Thomas took Sedgwick's hand in a fierce clasp. "Promise me you'll take care of yourself."

"Don't worry about me. By the time I get back up there, CID probably will have it already solved."

"That's not what I meant." Thomas pressed his thumb against

the agent's wrist and ran it up the inside of his arm. "Promise me you'll take care of yourself, brother."

Sedgwick's face juddered with emotion. "How can I? We both know I'm no good at it. I need the crack of Thomas McBride's fist on my jaw, keeping me honest."

Thomas grinned, raising his hand to form a fist. He faked a quick jab, but then his face grew thoughtful. He repeated the movement slowly until his knuckles gently connected with his friend's chin.

"If you believe it's there, then it will be. Kavita said as much: 'something of us remains, always.' So, now. Promise me."

"Oh, goddammit." Sedgwick's voice disintegrated. He gave Thomas's shoulder a squeeze and turned away. "Yes. I promise. Get in the fucking car. I'll see you in Srinagar."

When Conor had finished settling Thomas, he closed the rear hatch and joined Sedgwick at the trailhead. The agent's washed-out eyes, veiled beneath a tangle of hair, were red with emotion.

"He's nearly out, now," Conor said. "That's the morphine working, I hope?"

"Probably." Sedgwick's brow furrowed. "Are you okay? You look like shit."

"I had the same thought, looking at you."

They shook hands, wordlessly communicating what they couldn't bear to mention.

"We'd better get going," Conor said. "Good luck up there."

"One thing," Sedgwick said. "If I don't show up in Srinagar by tomorrow at the latest, either alone or with, well, somebody—"

"I know. You don't have to say it." Conor nodded. "We're on our own. If ever there were a case for plausible deniability, I'd say this is it. The DEA has never heard of us, there was never an operation to bring in a Russian arms dealer, and none of this ever happened as far as they're concerned. Suits me fine. I've never heard of them either, Walker and Costino. That's my story for Frank. I wish it were true."

"So do I," Sedgwick said. "Oh, son of a bitch, what now?"

A large black sedan had appeared around a bend in the road above them. It successfully navigated the curve but then hit the icy stretch and began skidding. It missed the Range Rover by inches and slid sideways as it passed them before coasting to a stop farther down the hill, against a snow bank.

"Those don't look like CID officers," Sedgwick observed with hollow weariness.

"No, and those are big fucking guns." Conor eyed the two men, armed with AK-47 rifles, as they struggled to exit the car. "Looks like Dragonov sent his entire gang to India. What's the plan?"

Sedgwick bit his lip and gave a quick glance toward the Range Rover. "Lead them away from the SUV. Come on, up the trail. If Tom is still conscious, let's hope he knows enough to stay in the car."

They had a good head start and were able to race well up the trail before their pursuers reached its entrance. At a spot where the terrain rolled in a series of undulating dips, Sedgwick grabbed Conor's arm, forcefully swinging him off the path. Sailing out of control, they stumbled and rolled down an incline before coming to a stop under a thicket of fir trees.

"What the hell." Conor struggled to raise himself, but Sedgwick pushed him back onto his stomach.

"Shut up. We're in dead ground." He threw himself down onto the snow next to him. "The rise in the hill hid us. Lie still and let them go by. If they run far enough up the trail before doubling back, we might shake them, and if we have to shoot it out, it's better if they're not between us and the road."

Conor's legs twitched at the forced immobility. He had moved well beyond any sense of fear where his own life was concerned. The only thing he could concentrate on was the single-minded goal of saving his brother's life. He had no time for this shite.

He also had no choice but to comply, as Sedgwick's hand remained locked against the back of his neck. No doubt the agent sensed his desperation.

The wait wasn't long. Within seconds, they heard the muffled thump of the Russians pounding up the trail, joined soon after by their panting voices, first at a distance and then closer as they came over the rise in the hill. Responding to Sedgwick's urgent pinch, Conor tried to make himself even flatter against the ground. The Russians continued without pause and without glancing either to the right or left. Their retreating footsteps were still faintly audible when Sedgwick released his hold and delivered a succinct command.

"Run."

They clawed their way up the incline to the trail and headed back toward the road, moving as quietly as haste allowed. They raced past the trailside shrine and seconds later heard the sound of voices raised in agitation. The Russians were already doubling back.

"We're not going to make it," Conor gasped. "We'd better take cover. What about the shrine?"

"Too late to go back to it. There." Sedgwick pointed his pistol at a large boulder just ahead of them. "Get ready to fire as soon as we're behind it. We need to pin them far enough back to have a chance against those AK-47s."

Conor's boots slid out from under him as he made the tight turn and fell into position, but Sedgwick was a step slower. The two rapidly approaching figures saw him before he had time to disappear behind the boulder. He took advantage of their momentary surprise to fire a series of random shots and then dove as the answering volley commenced. He landed next to Conor with an explosive gasp of pain.

"Are you hit?" Conor shouted over the sputtering gunfire. Sedgwick's face had gone alarmingly white. He shook his head.

"Shoulder, dislocated."

"Shit. What do you want me to do?"

"I'll get it back in; I've done it before." Sedgwick clenched his jaw. "Just hunker down for a minute. We caught a break. At least one of these guys is a knuckle-dragger. He's going to empty that big banana clip and hit nothing but this fucking boulder."

Conor hunkered down as instructed, and the siege continued. Bullets cracked against the stone and sheared large chunks of wood from the trees around them, filling the air with the pungent scent of pine pitch. Next to him, Sedgwick settled his back against the boulder. With a half-suppressed groan, he torqued his right arm at an angle away from his body, pushing slowly until the joint popped back into place. He slumped forward in relief, but his head came up at a sudden pause in the gunfire and the sound of a metallic snap.

"That's one clip empty," he said. "Take a few shots while they're distracted."

Snaking his arm and one eye around the side of the boulder, Conor began firing. The response was another immediate fusillade, and he pulled back behind the rock.

"They got a little closer, almost as far as the shrine, but I think I just winged one of them. How's the shoulder?"

Sedgwick gingerly flexed the fingers of his right hand. "Fingers are still numb. Should be okay before long. Anyway, the stupid bastards are going to run out of ammunition. Just put out more defensive fire and wait them out."

"We don't have time to wait," Conor fumed.

"Believe me, I wish I had something else to offer."

Conor's fingers drummed against his knee. The Russians kept firing. It was methodical, deafening, and maddening. He wondered if their strategy was perhaps more clever than Sedgwick credited. Every ticking minute brought his brother a step closer to death, and he felt like he was losing his mind. What was happening down on the road? Was Thomas unconscious? Dead already? Or maybe he had heard the gunfight and was even now trying to crawl up the trail, in search of them?

Oh, Jesus.

The compulsion to move, to leap up and out into the open was wildly irrational but impossible to resist.

"Look," he said, turning to Sedgwick. "There's a big tree just there across the path. If you cover me, I'll run across, and at least we'll have a couple of angles—"

"Settle down," Sedgwick ordered. His voice rang with authority, but he regarded Conor with apprehension. "I can't even hold my gun yet. You're going to have to wait."

"There's no time, for fuck's sake! I can't wait! I have to go!"

With that, the secured door in his head gave way, and the darkness that spilled out swept everything before it—all his reason, all his wiser instincts, all his celebrated talent for repose. At the same instant, there was another pause in the shooting. Again, he heard the sound of something hitting the ground with a metallic jingle, followed by a shout of surprise. Without giving himself the chance to think better of it, Conor let a cresting wave of adrenalin carry him forward.

He surged up and away from their hiding place, already firing before he'd cleared the edge of the boulder and before he could even see what he was shooting at. From the corner of his eye, he saw Sedgwick rise with a roar of alarm and awkwardly shift his gun to his left hand to provide covering fire. The shots from the opposite direction began again as the Russians adjusted their aim.

At first, an unnatural clarity flooded through him as he moved, bringing every sight, smell, and sound into sharp focus. An instant later, it was over, and the phenomenon had already reversed itself. A disorienting fog smothered the heightened awareness and dampened even ordinary sensation. He stumbled in confusion, ears ringing. Something was wrong with his eyes. As though trying to see underwater, he crept a few paces forward on the path, peering at the two Russians on the ground in the distance. They'd fallen in a tangle of limbs, mimicking the innocent sleep of lovers. More jarring than this was the thing on the ground in the middle distance. It hadn't been there earlier. It looked like a bundle of red and white cloth.

"McBride, are you all right? Can you hear me? Conor."

Feeling the grip on his arms, he took his eyes from the odd-looking bundle to look at Sedgwick. "It wasn't there before." He feebly gestured up the trail. "What is it? Where did it come from?"

The agent took a deep breath and squeezed his eyes shut. "Wait here." Sedgwick began running up the trail, but after a half-dozen steps stopped and spun around to stare back at him.

It began with a low moan, but as Conor's legs folded, it swelled into toneless keening, a primitive sound exhumed from a lightless place. The protective fog had evaporated. He could see it plainly now, as he had seen it only seconds earlier, a fleeting glimpse of thin limbs sprinting across the trail, of a small carved deity falling to the ground, of a young face turned toward him in astonishment.

It was not a bundle of red-and-white cloth. It was a white Pashmina scarf, soaked in blood.

38

The tables had turned so quickly, in the space of a few minutes. It was Sedgwick now urging him to get up to start moving before more time was lost, but Conor couldn't do it. He couldn't get off his knees. Couldn't even uncurl himself enough to lift his head. He rocked forward, his face inches from the ground, begging for the mercy of a swift, just punishment, knowing it wouldn't come.

It wouldn't come because mercy was what he deserved least. The sacrifice of an eye for an eye was one God apparently had no intention of accepting. Why else was he kneeling there, physically unscathed when he should be riddled with bullets?

Abruptly, Sedgwick heaved him upright and delivered a hard slap against his face. "Goddammit, Conor, snap out of it. Get on your fucking feet and get moving."

Absently touching his cheek, Conor rose and looked at the trail above them. Sedgwick had rearranged the bloodstained scarf to give the child's body the dignity of resembling what it was—a fragile shroud-wrapped scrap of humanity, waiting for its final journey.

"We've got to do something." His voice shook. "We can't leave him here."

"I'll take care of it," Sedgwick said quietly, but Conor continued in a burst of manic chatter. "Listen to me. I'll take him. Put him in the SUV. I'll take him to Srinagar, and—"

"Buddy, you listen to me." Sedgwick took Conor's head in both his hands and held it in a tight grip. "You can't take him anywhere. He belongs here. He probably lives ... lived, nearby. There's a settlement we drove by a few kilometers down, at the bottom of the hill. I'm guessing that must be where his family is."

"Jesus." Conor stiffened his legs to keep them from buckling again.

"I said I'll take care of it," Sedgwick continued. "I promise you, I will. There's nothing you can do for him, but your brother is bleeding to death at the bottom of this hill, and there's something you can still do about that. You have to go. Now."

"Yes. All right," Conor said dully.

As Sedgwick released the viselike grip on his head and stepped back, he looked down to see his fingers still wrapped around the Walther as though glued to it. Holding it by the muzzle, he offered the butt to Sedgwick, who refused it with a shake of his head.

"You can't. Not yet."

Without protest, he tucked the gun behind his back, under his belt.

"It wasn't just you," Sedgwick added. He lifted an arm, gesturing toward the small body, and let it fall to his side again. "You could tell by the ... well, you could just tell. He must have been hiding behind the shrine and just darted across the path before any of us could see. I don't know what he was thinking. Maybe he thought he needed to save the idol. What I'm trying to say is, you're not alone in this. It was me, too. It was all of us."

"Yes, all right," Conor repeated, eyes down.

In their convoluted history together, it was the most generous gesture this troubled, complicated man had ever offered him. He didn't have the heart to tell him how little it mattered. In at least one respect, guilt had something in common with love—it could be endlessly shared without depleting what remained in its owner's soul.

He offered a final salute and hurried down the trail.

Thomas was sleeping when he reached the car but stirred as he opened the rear door to check on him.

"What's been happening?" he asked groggily, eyes still shut.

Conor rested his forehead against the doorjamb and closed his own eyes for a few seconds before straightening with artificial briskness. "How's the pain patch holding up?" He hoped the non sequitur would go unnoticed and that Thomas would not look at him for a while longer. "Will I just give you one for the road? So you don't feel it as much?"

He reached for the medical kit, averting his face as Thomas opened his eyes and smiled at him. "As yer man said, 'bird never flew on one wing.' Lay it on, so."

Almost immediately, he was asleep again, and Conor began easing the SUV down the road toward the meadow. After driving several kilometers, the settlement Sedgwick had mentioned came into view at the bottom of the hill. Several blue-painted cement structures with corrugated roofs were scattered throughout the compound, which had been swept clear of snow down to bare earth. Clearly, the sound of gunfire had not reached this far down the mountain. A group of children were in the open area, kicking around a ball made of plastic bags. On a low wall near the road, a woman in a thick, fawn-colored *salwar kameez* sat stripping the smaller branches from tree limbs, dropping them onto a pile near her feet. She was young, but old enough to be the mother of a ten-year-old.

As the vehicle approached, she looked up. With a toss of her head, she flicked a strand of dark hair from her face and met his eyes with frank curiosity. He looked away, throat closing, and pumped the accelerator to send the SUV shooting down the hill.

As soon as the settlement had disappeared from the rearview mirror, he pulled over and fell out of the car, hanging onto the door as bile rose from his stomach in convulsive heaves. A minute later, he dragged himself back behind the wheel and started forward again. Sweat soaked into his shirt, and he shivered as it cooled and dried there. A skewering pain throbbed between his shoulder blades, and his lungs kept up their low-registered drone. He noted each symptom with apathy. None of it mattered.

There was only one route out of Gulmarg, at least by car. He circled the perimeter of the meadow and navigated the precipitous descent, creeping along the same switchback road they had climbed less than twenty-four hours earlier. It gradually began leveling off, and he allowed his white-knuckled grip to relax. The moment of relief was short-lived.

A disturbance appeared in the distance, coming into focus as he moved closer to it. The road was crowded with vehicles, all of them parked in front of a manmade barrier.

"Fuck." Conor slammed the heel of his hand against the gearshift.

The barrier looked hastily assembled, no more than a collection of large rocks strewn across the road. A group of seven uniformed men were milling in front of it, and as he maneuvered forward, one of them rushed up with a peremptory shout of authority.

"Sir. You must remain here. The way ahead is blocked."

"I have a sick man with me. I need to get to Srinagar and get him to a hospital."

In desperation, he reached into the glove box for the official authorization document Walker had presented at the checkpoint the previous evening. He smoothed out the wrinkled stamps and presented it, along with a solemn pronouncement in Hindi.

"We are on special assignment with the Criminal Investigations Division."

"*Accha?*" The man's eyebrows shot up as he took the document. He examined it with interest but then angled his head, frowning with regret. "Very sorry, sir, but not going down this route. Rock fall is there. The way is closed for next few hours. You must reverse and go to the turning on the left, some three kilometers back. It is trekking route and cart road network connecting to Srinagar via Wadwan. By-and-by, you may reach."

"How long is 'by-and-by'?"

"Perhaps three hours. Perhaps more."

Conor expelled a bark of laughter that came close to spiraling out of control before he managed to swallow it and turn the SUV back in the direction they'd just come. He stared ahead, and with a whisper, surrendered to a power he couldn't compete with or understand.

"Why do you want him so badly?"

He got no answer. And wasn't sure who he was asking.

Although not as bad as he'd feared the trekking route was bad enough. It began with another descent, winding around gullies of snowmelt that drained to a riverbed at the bottom of the valley. Alternately cratered and bulging with half-submerged boulders, the trail was at times a notional thing. Occasionally it disappeared altogether, and he drove in a more or less straight line until he found it again. At other times, a crosshatched pattern of intersections forced a choice among too many options.

As long as daylight held, he felt tentatively confident in his decisions. Although the landscape was dry and featureless, it was occasionally interrupted by small settlements, and his sense of direction remained strong; but if the guard's judgment had been accurate, darkness would overtake them before they reconnected with the main road. He felt far less optimistic about his ability to navigate by the night sky.

Thomas woke at the beginning of the detour. Conor winced at his occasional gasps as the vehicle lurched from one obstacle to the next, but although he begged him to accept further applications of the morphine patch, his brother stubbornly refused. He tolerated the ride for almost two hours, but at a little after six o'clock, as daylight began rapidly seeping away, he summoned the strength to deliver an order that brooked no argument.

"Conor, stop the car now, for Jesus' sake."

Conor hesitated. The SUV continued as if he'd lost the power to control it, but then he lifted his foot from the accelerator and braked to a stop. He pulled up the parking brake and switched off the engine. Silence filled the space around them. He dropped his hands, fingers still tingling from the vibration of the steering wheel, and sighed.

"It sounds like you swallowed a harmonica." His brother's own breath was shallow, his voice reedy.

"Yeah, I suppose it does."

"Did the pills stop working, do you think?"

"I don't know."

"You've been taking them, though?"

"Thomas, will you ever—" He jammed a fist against his mouth, forcing back a swell of hysteria, and continued more calmly. "I've been taking them, yes. Can we stop talking about me, for the love of God?"

"Okay, then." Thomas began to shift his weight but stopped with a sharp groan. "Come back here where I can see you. Let's talk about something else."

He stepped out of the SUV and circled around to the rear door on the passenger side. Lifting the left-hand seat, he moved it back into an upright position and slid inside next to Thomas, who was lying with his head on a duffel bag propped against the back of the driver's seat. Conor looked at him, and suddenly he was ten years old again, fatherless, clinging to his brother's side in a freezing churchyard, believing it was the only anchor that would keep him from blowing away. He turned away and slumped forward, letting the memory shake loose emotions he could no longer contain.

Thomas left him alone for several minutes before reaching over to rest a hand on his shoulder. With a shuddering breath, he lifted his face and tried one last time to bend fate toward his own will.

"The main road can't be too much farther," he said in a thick voice.

"Perhaps." A faint smile played over Thomas's lips. "Never mind about it. I don't want to go on bumping along in the dark, getting shaken to pieces like a—" He broke off, gasping, his face twisting in agony.

"Thomas, please will you let me give you another morphine patch?"

Emphatically, his brother shook his head, eyes squeezed shut.

"Why not, for God's sake?" Conor asked.

"I got to thinking that—ahh," Thomas cried out as his back arched in pain. "I don't want to sleep through it. I don't know why—it sounds mad—but I'm afraid I might miss something. I'm afraid of getting lost."

"Lost?" Conor repeated the word dully, but then stiffened, listening.

He musn't be lost, Conor. You must tell Thomas to come to me.

His mother had issued her final command to him long before he'd had any capacity for understanding it. He heard it again now but not as a tickling, subconscious echo. The directive sounded as clear as the day he'd first heard it, as if she were sitting there next to him, repeating it.

No, it was stronger than that, even. She was there. Everywhere.

Whatever glancing experiences he'd previously had with the

uncanny—the flashes of foresight and irrational anticipation, the uneasy encounters with elemental spirit—all of them crumbled to insignificance in comparison with the staggering sense of presence he felt now. Every nerve in his body was charged with her. The air itself was alive with her.

It lasted less than a minute before it began fading, like the tailing arc of a comet. Even then, it didn't disappear entirely; the essence of her remained. Still shivering, he could feel it hovering around him and knew what she wanted.

Brigid McBride had begun her passage, but she was waiting for her eldest son.

After so many months of angry confusion, Conor at last understood who had really sent him here and what he needed to do. It was time for him to be the anchor now, to deliver his brother safely, and keep him from blowing away. His mother had known it from the beginning. It was the only mission he was meant for in the first place. He smoothed a palm over Thomas's perspiring forehead and tried to clear the sadness from his voice.

"I won't let you get lost. I promised her I wouldn't."

He persuaded Thomas to accept the pain medication in smaller doses by tearing the morphine patches in half. As they experimented with the first application, Thomas clutched at his wrist fretfully.

"We've got to keep talking. Don't let me fall asleep. Not yet."

"I won't."

He looked at Conor, his face haggard with exhaustion and distress. "I'll be out of it, soon enough, but what about you? They'll all be after you now. I wish you could disappear into some new life and leave all this behind, but I don't even know what place is safe. I don't know where to tell you to go."

Where, indeed? Conor pondered the question as he tried to soothe Thomas and settle him down. Perhaps because he was so close to exhaustion himself, he found it morbidly comical to tally up the expanding list of enemies arrayed against him. It began with Ahmed Khalil and Rohit Mehta and continued to include Tony Costino and Vasily Dragonov and almost certainly the elusive Robert Durgan.

And what about Frank Murdoch? His name continued to sit on the list with an asterisk next to it. What was his story? Was he an oblivious pawn in the game of some other dirty MI6 mole? Or was he the lead agent for a blacker operation designed to placate an informant by hanging him and his brother out to dry?

Conor's head swam with uncertainty, but when he looked into Thomas's anxious eyes, his grief sliced through it all. What difference did it make, now?

"Don't worry about me, Thomas," he said, softly. "I've gotten good at disappearing. It's time we talked about other things."

He found a flashlight, hung it from a hook above the door, and turned the car on to provide some heat. Comforted by the warmth and the incandescent glow, they talked—mostly in Irish now—about home, neighbors, and old times, and about their separate and shared experiences with a singularly unusual mother.

Inexorably, Thomas grew weaker, and his temperature soared. The coagulant powder prevented the wound from bleeding through the bandage, but the bruise advancing across his abdomen like a spreading stain indicated that the internal damage was progressing. As the half-doses of morphine became less effective, he began placing the patches on intact, praying the remaining supply would outlast his brother's strength.

As he peeled up one transparent film and prepared to replace it with another, Conor glanced out the window, his eye caught by the gibbous moon appearing over the mountain range. Just two nights earlier, they had watched it rise together, full and luminous, with its light dancing over the Ganges at Rishikesh. Was that where he should go next? Should he take Thomas back to Rishikesh, back to Kavita? He realized he had no capacity yet for considering next steps, but once again, his brother appeared to read his mind.

"Conor, you have to leave me here." Thomas fixed him with a feverish, glassy stare.

"What? Leave you?" He dropped his eyes from the window, appalled. "I'm not going anywhere, Thomas. Not a fucking chance."

"Not now, you eejit," Thomas said. He bit his lip and smiled an apology. "You know I didn't mean now. I can't do it properly without you. I mean when I'm ... when it's done, you need to just go. Go to the airport in Srinagar and fly somewhere, anywhere. Get the hell out of India before anyone can figure out where you went. Can't you understand that?"

"No, I can't understand it," Conor said and knew he was lying again. There was logic in the argument, but the idea of heeding it was unendurable. He slammed a fist against the seat in front of him and then drew his arm back and did it again with greater force.

"All right. It's okay," his brother said, softly.

"I can't talk to you about this, Thomas."

"I see that. I'm sorry I said anything. I won't do it again. I promise."

With a thin sigh, Thomas raised his chin and pointed it at the ceiling of the SUV. Conor watched him continue murmuring as though speaking to someone else. "No, I won't. He'll know. He'll see it on his own."

Not much longer.

Conor pressed the new morphine patch into place and sat back, still watching. His brother sank into its anesthetic fog, his breath now coming in irregular rasps.

A little while later, Thomas looked over at him, lips moving soundlessly while his hand reached for the silver St. Brigid's cross around Conor's neck. Conor snapped the leather strap and planted the cross in the middle of his brother's palm. He closed Thomas's fingers over it to make a fist and wrapped both of his own hands tightly around it.

He bent his head close to Thomas's lips, listening. At first, the barely audible words were unfamiliar, but gradually he recognized them and found himself smiling through his tears.

The Bright Prayer. They had both known it from childhood. It was their mother's favorite. Thomas faltered after the first two stanzas. Conor leaned closer and placed his mouth next to his ear.

"*Cá n-éireoidh tú amárach?*" (Where will you rise tomorrow?)

His brother's smile was broad with relief.

"*Éireoidh le Pádraig.*" (I will rise with Patrick.)

"Right so, good man," Conor whispered. "Keep going. *Cé hiad ar ár n-aghaidh?*" (Who are those before us?)

"*Dhá chéad aingeal.*" (Two hundred angels.)

"*Cé hiad in ár ndiaidh?*" (Who are those behind us?)

"*An oiread seo eile de mhuintir Dé.*" (The rest of God's people.)

"And Ma," Thomas added. He smiled again, with a happiness that left Conor breathless.

"If you can see her, then go to her, Thomas." He was shaking, now—in wonder, in sorrow. "She's waiting for you. Safe home, now. No stops."

"I can see her," Thomas said, his voice suddenly clear. "I can sleep now." The lines of pain fell away from his face and he closed his eyes. "Safe home."

39

"It's not the passage tomb at Newgrange we're making Conor, for all love. It's only a simple cairn—a tiny bit of a one, at that. It's a fine day, and you're a strong lad. It will be finished in no time at all."

"It seems an awful lot of work, Ma. I'm knackered, just from the climb. Why must we do it?"

"It's a lesson for you, isn't it? A lesson I want to teach you."

"Why? What have I done?"

"Ah, Lord, will you give me strength? A lesson, didn't I say? Not a punishment, and I don't know why you'd think—oh, now I see. You're having a laugh at me. If you were searching out some decent stone instead of sporting around, we'd be nearly done already."

"Sorry, Ma. What type of stone is the decent sort?"

"Wide and flat as ever you can find. There, those are lovely ones, now. They're big though; I'll just help you, will I? We'll arrange them so, and then more around here, like this. Good. And that's the outline, done."

"Is it finished, then?"

"You know it isn't. Just you go on with another layer, each stone set a bit in from the edge, do you see? And then you'll go round it again."

"How many times? How many layers does it take?"

"Why, until you can set a stone for a cap, right at the very top."

"You're joking me. As high as that? It'll take forever."

"It won't. You've everything to hand. The builders of Newgrange never had it so easy."

"The builders of Newgrange probably had a horse and cart, anyway."

"God love you, they never had carts—they'd no wheels at all! They weren't invented. They barely had tools and those made of stone as well. Think how it must have been. Stone pounding on stone, prying the boulders up from the ground, chiseling them out of the cliffs. Pulling them up the valley on sleds. Think of the work of it all."

"I've a notion of it."

"You haven't. All those men, pulling at the rocks and going on with it for years, and then carrying sand in baskets up from the sea and mixing it with charred turf to seal everything up and keep it dry. The artists camped around, tracing out their spirals and chevrons, and putting up the standing stones; the priests preparing the chamber and lighting the fires, and the people in the fields, growing the crops and tending cattle, looking at it all and wondering what it meant. Why have you stopped now, *a leanbh*? What's the matter?"

"Nothing. I was just listening to you. It sounded so real, like you were there, watching them build it."

"Ah, wouldn't I have loved it. What a thing to see. Such a place of power. And when it was finished, to be sitting in the chamber on that first solstice dawn, watching the sun strike the passage like a sword made of fire. Watching God reach into every dark crevice, fill it up with light, and gather every soul into himself."

Stone upon stone. Layer upon layer.

Like so, love. Do you see, now? Like so.

He'd been staring at it for a while, ever since waking up, and still couldn't take his eyes from it. He wanted to get closer to it, but the effort of rolling up from the ground to a sitting position had been a skirmish in itself. At the slightest movement, pain blossomed over every inch of his body, and he wondered if the quivering muscles in his legs would even bear his weight.

His hands were especially sore. They were scratched and filthy, like the rest of him, and appeared swollen. They throbbed in sync with the beat of his heart as he stared at the thing in front of him.

The cairn was shaped like an oblong bowl upended and pushed down into the dirt. It stood around four feet tall, with layers of flatter stones starting from the bottom. At about the three-foot mark, the stones became smaller and irregularly shaped, but the structure was solid right up to the top. It had a capstone.

He had built it—his torn, aching hands were proof enough of that—but he had no idea how and no memory of having done it.

The Range Rover had run out of gas; he remembered that much. It had been a little before midnight, and he hadn't been driving very long. He remembered tumbling out into the chilly night and pacing back and forth next to the SUV, screaming. Or maybe sobbing? Maybe both. He didn't remember much else.

Panting, with the disturbing sensation of trying to breathe through a straw, Conor wincingly climbed to his feet. He looked down at the blankets and sweaters scattered around him and had a vague recollection of pulling them out of the car and throwing them on the ground. He had wanted to sleep next to Thomas.

After three circuits around his brother's grave, Conor eased himself down and lay against the cairn, allowing his back to arch and stretch against the stone. He faced the sun, guessing by its path that it was around seven in the morning.

To the left, the terrain with its rocky trail sloped up in a gradual rise, creating a visible horizon over which smoke appeared—thin, dark ribbons rising, expanding, and then disappearing as they bled out over the sky.

There was a village undoubtedly connected to that smoke. Its inhabitants were lighting their fires to cook rotis and boil water for chai, fortifying themselves for the day ahead. There was life going on, just beyond the rise. It fatigued him to think about it, but he knew he would eventually head toward it. Not yet, though. His dead were all he had left. He would stay with them a while longer, where his loneliness was less absolute.

Conor woke again, feeling even more stiff and lightheaded than he had earlier. He lay still, wondering if it was worth the attempt, but finally he pulled himself up and started along the trail. At the top of the rise, the village appeared in the distance. He continued on, stopping frequently to rest. Each time, it took little longer to catch his breath, until at last it escaped him entirely.

The next time he swam up into consciousness, he felt a band like iron tightening around his chest, and then he realized it was a pair of arms, grappling to raise him to his feet.

"Where am I?" He asked the question first in English and then, remembering, repeated it in Hindi.

"Bunagam." The unseen voice behind him was low and musical. "Sir, please lean on me. My cart is just there. American doctors are near the village. I will bring you."

He didn't want to be saved. Mumbling a polite refusal, he tried to settle himself on the dusty ground, but the tenacity and surprising strength of the man's arms defeated him. Conor allowed himself to be brought to his feet, and with painstaking effort, he crawled onto the cart's rough-hewn planks and collapsed. Face down, he remained motionless as his rescuer climbed aboard and urged the oxen forward. The vehicle lurched into motion.

The day had lost most of its warmth, and his fever was climbing. He rolled onto his back, shivering, and slid his hands into the pockets of his coat. His right hand brushed against something small and feathery soft. Conor drew out the marigold with the tips of his fingers, and holding it up between his eyes and the setting sun, recited to himself what his brother had not needed: the last lines of the Bright Prayer.

lig an tsoilse mhór amach. (Let the great light out.)

is an t-anam trua isteach. (Let the wretched soul in.)

Ó a Dhia déan trócaire orainn. (God have mercy upon us.)

A Mhic na hÓighe, go bhfaighe ár n-anam. (Son of the Virgin, receive our souls.)

"And let it be soon," he whispered. "Please God, let it be soon."

40

The nursing aide squinted down at the lunch tray longer than was strictly necessary for the purpose, lips pursed in concentration. Conor imagined she was groping for encouragements that would prove more effective than those she'd already tried. He felt a bit sorry for her as she looked at him with sad reproof.

"You've not touched a bite of it."

She was a stout, rather adorably earnest young woman, with an elaborate cornrow hairstyle that decorated her head like a work of art. The disappointment in her voice pricked his conscience, but not enough to matter.

"Don't take it personally, Jeanie," he said. "Anyway, I drank the tea."

"You always drink the tea," she protested. "But, you can't live on tea."

"No. I suppose not."

An awkward silence followed, but Jeanie was made of stubborn stuff. She had shown that to him a few times already.

"At least you're out of bed, sitting up in a chair. That's more than I hoped for. What about a walk to the solarium? Are you strong enough for it?"

"Probably, but I'm not interested."

"Which is what you say about bloody everything." Jeanie gave him a close look, as though willing him to stand up and walk.

"It's a gorgeous London afternoon, and you can see the park just coming on to bloom. It's lovely."

It was easier to concede the round than continue arguing. With a sigh of acquiescence, Conor followed his nurse from the room.

Kings College Hospital was sprawled across a number of interconnected buildings. They walked down three corridors, crossed an enclosed walkway connecting to a separate wing, and took an elevator to the top floor's solarium. By the time they stopped next to a window overlooking the park, he was completely spent and breathing hard.

"You got me that time," he said, dropping into a wingback chair. "Fair play, but bring the feckin' wheelchair when you come back for me."

"I'll bring it with a supper tray on it." The young woman's pretty brown eyes danced with self-satisfaction. "We'll see how you get on, and maybe I'll let you ride on it yourself. Now, enjoy the sunshine."

Conor settled into the chair, ignoring the view. "They're not paying you enough to deal with the likes of me, Jeanie."

Reflexively, he tried to clear the gravelly scrape from his voice before remembering the effort was pointless. The incision from the tracheotomy had healed, but the hoarseness persisted and appeared likely to do so indefinitely.

Laryngeal nerve damage. In delivering the diagnosis, the Kings College physician could not suppress a sniff of disdain—his editorial comment on what passed for quality workmanship in rural Kashmir.

"I'd like to see you do as much with a jackknife and a hookah pipe," Conor had observed, sarcastically.

He felt a protective appreciation for the ingenuity of the doctors who had saved his life. While the outcome might have been unwelcome from his own viewpoint, he was not so churlish as to resent the effort that achieved it.

Of course, Frank deserved his place on the hero's platform as well. His phone calls to the right people had engineered a medical evacuation the villagers in Bunagam would talk about for years, and the rapid transfer from Delhi to London was an additional testament to his network of influence.

Now that Conor had been more or less delivered to him on a platter, he wondered what further use Frank would make of his privileged connections and to what purpose. He had as yet made no visit to his ailing protégé's bedside, but a few weeks earlier, two men had appeared in Conor's room, flaunting IDs with sinister aplomb and announcing the start of his operational debrief.

Fortunately, they made the mistake of trying to begin when he was still too sick to cooperate. With an abrupt entrance, the angelic Jeanie had sabotaged the interrogation just as it was beginning. Reading the exhausted alarm in his eyes, she had promptly found a doctor to order the two men from his room.

With that miscalculation, the agents forfeited their advantage. Conor had time to form a strategy of his own—namely, to lie—and he exaggerated his weakness until he felt well enough to do it convincingly. When the interviews began again, the agents committed a second tactical error. One of them revealed that Sedgwick was still missing. He preferred not to think too deeply about what that meant. For his immediate purpose, its significance was in knowing that his version of events was the only one on offer. At least for now.

Frank's absence from the proceedings was noteworthy, but Conor felt sure he was reading the transcripts. Although his interrogators had seemed initially satisfied with his answers, two days earlier they'd arrived with a third agent who administered a polygraph test. That seemed a good indication of how his recruiting officer regarded the web of deceit he was spinning.

His head slipped sideways, resting against the wing of the chair. He got little therapeutic effect from sleep these days.

The guttural cries that inevitably shocked him awake were as disturbing as the dreams prompting them. The nursing staff responded to his night terrors with unflagging compassion, but the embarrassment of having to be comforted like a child afraid of the dark only added to the torment. Because he worked so hard to avoid sleep, he was perpetually on the verge of it. He fought to resist its pull now, but the chair was soft and the sun, warm. His eyes closed; his mouth dropped open.

The nightmare hadn't started yet, but a quality of dread was building in his slumbering mind when he felt a light touch on his shoulder. He exploded into consciousness with a yell, coughing in ragged whoops. The face in front of him recoiled in surprise.

"Jesus and Mary," Conor gasped. "You're after giving me a cardiac."

"That wasn't the intent, I assure you." Frank Murdoch lifted a precisely sculpted eyebrow. "Good Lord, you sound ghastly. I'll fetch some water, shall I?"

By the time Frank returned, Conor had recovered on his own, but he accepted the glass and tried to meet his visitor's scrutiny with disinterest.

"What are you doing here?"

Frank smiled. "Hardly an enthusiastic greeting. You're not pleased to see me? How wounding, particularly when I've come with such happy news. Although from your appearance I question their judgment, Kings College Hospital is quite happy to release you at the end of this week. They will be escorting you to the street at eleven o'clock on Friday morning."

"Into whose waiting arms?" Conor asked.

"I leave that entirely to you, dear boy. The captains of British intelligence view your contract as fulfilled. You are free to revel in whomsoever's arms you please."

Careful to hide his surprise, Conor put the glass down on the table beside him with a slight frown. "You're letting me leave?"

"Well, what more could we ask of you?" Frank reached into a calfskin briefcase sitting next to his feet. "You've provided a debrief simply saturated in colorful detail, and your polygraph examination merely confirmed what I already knew ... " As he straightened, holding a thick manila folder in his hands, the playful humor vanished from Frank's face. "That we trained up an agent with talents for fabrication and evasion that have far exceeded our modest expectations."

With lips pressed together in fury, Frank tossed the folder at him. Conor ducked and fumbled to catch the papers as they bounced off the chair and spilled into his lap.

"What am I supposed to do with this?"

"My question as well, Conor," Frank jeered. "What am I to do with this steaming packet of shite? It is hardly more use to me than it is to you."

He rose to his feet and went to the window. Conor glanced at a few of the pages before dropping the pile onto the floor and addressing Frank's slender back. "So, I passed the polygraph test. I would have thought that counted as proof of sincerity."

Frank didn't respond. He didn't move a millimeter. It was a side of the man Conor had not previously seen. He wondered if the tantrum was genuine or another piece of manufactured stagecraft.

"Look, I'm sorry if the story isn't as exciting as you'd like."

"I don't require it to be exciting," Frank said, still facing the window. "I do require it to be true."

"And what makes you think it isn't?" He immediately wished he hadn't spoken. Frank had goaded him into engagement. There was no quick end in sight now. Slowly, with his head tilted to one side, the agent turned from the window.

"What happened at the beginning of February?" he asked.

"At the beginning of February, I was sick as a dog with tuberculosis." Conor gave the pile of papers a kick. "If you don't believe the transcript, you can talk to the doctors here."

"How did you contract it?"

"I don't know." Conor sighed. "I got breathed on. It's India, Frank."

"Where was Curtis Sedgwick?" The questions were coming quickly now.

"In Dubai, I suppose."

"Why?"

"I assumed it was to do with Ahmed Khalil's business, but really, I've no idea. He didn't say."

"He stopped filing reports at the beginning of February. Why?"

Conor summoned up a scowl of incredulity. "Jesus Christ, do you need a picture drawn? He fecked off. Ditched me. He said he had a tip that Thomas was going to meet his gunrunners in a Kashmiri village near Srinagar. I figured we'd go there together but then he dumped me at the train station, said he had to go to Dubai, and I never saw the bastard again."

"Why didn't you report it?" Frank demanded.

Pulling an insolent pout, Conor shrugged. "Not my job. Besides, I was in a hurry to get to Kashmir."

"Where you achieved nothing."

"I ... " Conor faltered. The bald truth of the accusation knocked him off stride. "Where I achieved nothing," he finally confirmed.

"Never saw your brother," Frank persisted. "Or any of his associates."

"No. The car I hired broke down somewhere around Bunagam. I guess I was still walking toward it when I keeled over. Somebody dragged me into the village, called in the Americans, and they found your card in my pocket. And there you have it."

"Bullshit." Frank's tight-lipped fury had subsided. The blunt observation came with a puzzled shake of his head. "It's admirably consistent. Pitch-perfect in its delivery—almost flawless. And it is an audacious raft of bullshit from beginning to end."

"Whatever you say." Conor rested his head against the chair and closed his eyes. It was the third time he'd run through this part of the story. He wondered if it would be as tiring if he were telling the truth. Frank sat down again, crossing his legs and studying him.

"I see two possible explanations for lying," Frank said after several minutes of silence. "One is guilt, the other fear. Let's take the last one first, shall we? What is it you fear, Conor? Are you afraid of me, for instance?"

He opened his eyes and looked at Frank. "Should I be?"

"I should think not. I should think you'd realize that I of all people am in a position to protect you."

"Protect me?" Conor snorted. "How's that been working so far, do you think?"

Frank uncrossed his legs and bent forward, pitching his voice to an icy, even tone. "Let me make this plain for you. MI6 is releasing you. I have no authority to detain you further. If you feel strong enough to drag yourself to the airport, you can even leave tonight and go where you like. Be advised, however, that despite your lack of cooperation, this work will go on. I will ensure that it does. I will eventually learn the truth, and I will get what I want."

"You make it sound quite personal, Frank." Conor held his gaze without flinching. "Why does this interest you so much, I wonder."

"My interests, personal or otherwise, don't concern you," Frank said. "But if I discover that your lies have been a ruse to mask complicity in the betrayal of this mission, there is no hole on earth that can hide you from me, and I will—"

"What? Torture me? Kill me? Or let someone else do it?" Conor fired the questions with intentional force, hoping to surprise a spontaneous reaction in the coldly controlled face. It worked, but not in the way he anticipated. Frank's mouth dropped open in amazement—dumbfounded, guileless, and utterly innocent.

"For the love of God, why would you think that?" he said in a strained voice, as though the question was painful to ask.

Feeling the tension ebb away from him, Conor dropped forward to brace an elbow on his knee, shaking his head. He didn't think it. If Sedgwick was wrong and MI6 wasn't mixed up with Durgan, it was still almost certain he had a friend inside it, but his instincts told him Frank didn't know a thing about it. For whatever reason—and it did seem oddly personal—the agent was clearly still committed and invested in the mission of tracking down the elusive "wizard" he had been talking about from the beginning.

Instincts can be wrong. He'd pointed that out once to Thomas. The thought occurred again now, but even though his brother wasn't there to convince him, he decided to trust his gut. It was time to tell the truth. When he lifted his head, Frank was still watching him.

"I won't believe that you and I are enemies, Conor."

"We're not." Conor sat up with a sigh. "But I have them, Frank. A fair number, actually, and I think you and I share at least one in common. There's a few would like to get at me for what I did to them and a few who think I've got something they want, even though I don't."

Conor thought about the compromised mission in Gulmarg. Sedgwick was missing. Was he still alive? Was Walker? And what about Costino? If he had escaped, he and Vasily Dragonov were no doubt concerned about a certain twenty million dollars that had disappeared. It had been lifted from the DEA's account, and surely by now they'd noticed it wasn't in Dragonov's. Conor had the password for the South American account, but what was the likelihood of the arms dealer believing he had no idea which country—let alone, bank—Thomas had chosen for the deposit?

"And there's one man who thinks he's been betrayed and lied to for years, and he's right about that." Conor paused a few seconds before crossing the point of no return. "Your wizard's name is Robert Durgan—at least, that's one of his names—but I don't know who or where he is or how to find him."

"What happened at the beginning of February?" Frank asked again, gently this time.

"At the beginning of February, I found Thomas, and by the end of it ... I'd lost him again."

41

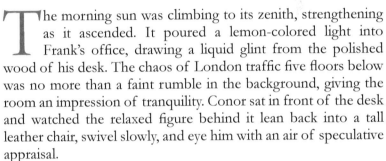

The morning sun was climbing to its zenith, strengthening as it ascended. It poured a lemon-colored light into Frank's office, drawing a liquid glint from the polished wood of his desk. The chaos of London traffic five floors below was no more than a faint rumble in the background, giving the room an impression of tranquility. Conor sat in front of the desk and watched the relaxed figure behind it lean back into a tall leather chair, swivel slowly, and eye him with an air of speculative appraisal.

"I don't think I care for your looks," Frank said, flatly.

"That's surprising," Conor replied. "I was pretty sure you did."

A slight flush colored Frank's aristocratic cheekbones. He flicked his eyes over Conor and looked away with a sniff of impatience. "I refer to your present appearance. Wraith-like. You've gained no weight during recovery, and I think the physicians have exaggerated the state of it. Did they even look at you before chucking you into a taxi this morning?"

"Well—"

"Your skin has quite a sallow look about it."

"Sallow?" Conor held out a hand and looked at it, curiously.

"And your voice still sounds as though you've come off a debauched night of whiskey and cigarettes. Is it painful?"

"No."

"Well, it sounds dreadful."

Conor rolled his eyes. "Jaysus, Frank, you're very hard to please. Did you ask me here just to dissect me? I was under the impression you would have something for me."

With a smooth motion, the leather chair glided back. Frank opened the middle drawer of the desk and removed an envelope. He slid it across to Conor with a rueful smile. "It may surprise you to learn that of the two petitions you put before us, this was by far the hardest. Several markers got called in to secure it."

Conor opened the envelope and shook out the items inside: a US permanent residence visa, an Irish passport, and a piece of folded stationery.

"You know the drill for passports," Frank said. "Don't get caught traveling with more than one. The letter gives details for your alias, should you choose to use it—one F. James Doyle—and it has the refreshing stink of truth to it. Just try not to mention you've been dead for fourteen years."

Conor studied the letter in silence and then tucked the documents into the inside pocket of his jacket. "And the second petition?" he asked, getting to his feet. "Is that secured as well?"

"Nearly there. I'll overnight the final documents to Dingle. You'll be there at least a few days before moving on?"

He nodded, and Frank folded his hands on the desk, regarding him with pensive concern. "Are you quite certain of this? Such a permanent, self-imposed exile? The service has an obligation to provide protection for you. We have a section for that."

"What progress have you made in tracking down Durgan?" Conor asked. "Have you discovered anything yet?"

"Very little," Frank admitted. "But let me again assure you that Agent Sedgwick's poor opinion of MI6 is unwarranted—at least in this instance. No reciprocal relationship exists between the service and Robert Durgan. I've been perfectly honest with you. I've no idea who he is. We're pursuing it. I'd hoped the Mumbai pub might lead to something, but everything was in your brother's name. We've frozen the accounts so Durgan can no longer access them."

Conor smiled, grimly. "I'll bet that's made him happy. Maybe the service itself isn't involved, but you agree his knowledge of my recruitment suggests MI6 must have a mole in here somewhere?"

"It's hard to draw any other conclusion. There's a section for that as well, but I've started my own inquiries."

"And Dragonov?"

"There, we don't come off as honorably." Frank dropped his head to stare at his hands. "I can't touch him as long as MI6 wants to continue using him as an informant."

"God, almighty." Conor exhaled a humorless laugh. "How did I get mixed up with you lot? Britain's best and brightest. So, are you seriously asking me to accept your so-called protection, go back to the farm, milk my cows, and wait for an assassin to crawl out of the woodwork? No. I didn't think so."

A wave of dizziness disturbed his train of thought. He tried to disguise it, putting a hand on the back of the chair, but the ploy was no match for a trained eye. Frank stood up and indicated the chair with a commanding snap of his fingers.

"Sit down. Have you eaten at all today you bloody fool? You're prepared to fly to the earth's four corners to escape men we're not even sure are pursuing you, but it strikes me you're rather cavalier about surviving this illness."

Conor dropped back into the chair, pressing a thumb and forefinger against his eyes. "Survival is a tedious business, it turns out. I'm not sure it's to my taste, but I wasn't given a choice. On the whole, though, I'd rather slip away in a sallow, wraith-like sleep than be tortured to death."

"Christ, what a macabre piece of idiocy." Frank reached for the phone. "Gavin, a tray of sandwiches and a pot of tea, if you please. And have them bring round my car in an hour. I'll be dropping our guest at Heathrow for his afternoon flight home."

As could have been expected, Frank's car was one smooth, comfortable ride, and as he slipped into the passenger seat, Conor couldn't resist a mild dig.

"Of course, it has to be a Bentley. You never go against type do you?"

"I have an image to maintain." Frank's eyes gleamed with self-deprecation. "It can be hell, but I persevere. It's pre-owned and not actually mine. Perhaps that makes me slightly less absurd?"

"Ah, you're all right. I'm sorry." Conor realized he was beginning to dislike himself in this mood of jaded cynicism. "Who wouldn't drive a Bentley, if they could?" After a short pause, he added, "I do appreciate this, Frank."

"It's really no trouble," Frank said. "I live just the other side of Heathrow in Windsor."

"I don't mean the ride. I appreciate that as well, but I meant everything else. It's a lot of money, after all."

Frank's warm, hazel eyes swept over him before returning to the road. "It's a lot of money, but good God, Conor, it's only money, and the service has it. It hardly makes up for what we lack in other areas, and as I already mentioned, purchasing eighty-nine acres of farmland wasn't as dicey as acquiring a green card. I only hope you don't come to regret it."

He already regretted it. He would never stop regretting it.

He had never wanted the farm. There was a time when he couldn't wait to leave it, but when he had returned to it, the land unexpectedly captured him. He grew accustomed to feeling bits of it under his fingernails, holding clumps of it in his hands, and feeling the give of it beneath his boots. At first, it was something he just got used to; he wasn't sure when it turned into something he loved. There was a certain peace in lying down at night, knowing the land was there beneath the floors of the house. That it belonged to him, and he to it.

Selling it now was like tearing out whatever remained of his soul, but Conor didn't know what else to do. He couldn't remain there like a sitting duck, and he couldn't let others go on tending it indefinitely. He also wouldn't have a job once he left home, and wasn't sure where he would find one. He needed the money, and Frank had wanted to do something. This worked for both of them, but it troubled his mind wondering what British intelligence would do with eighty-nine acres of land on the Dingle peninsula.

"They'll resell it, won't they?" he asked. "I mean, they won't go turning it into something clandestine?"

"They won't even know they've bought it," Frank said. "Not for a good long time. Proverbially speaking, I will be keeping it on a shelf for a while. In case you change your mind."

They arrived at Heathrow, and Frank brought the Bentley to a stop at the curb in front of the terminal. He cupped his fingers over his chin, regarding Conor doubtfully. "You *will* keep up with the treatments? A relapse could be particularly dangerous."

"I've got a sack full of drugs. Haven't missed a day yet."

"You'll need to be seen regularly, to be tested."

Conor smiled. "Don't worry. I'll be okay."

"Yes, I believe you will be, in time. I won't embarrass you by asking whether you intend to stay in touch, but as I can't phone you, and as I believe you've mislaid the one I gave you earlier ... " With a typical flourish, Frank produced a card from his vest pocket and passed it to Conor. "A new number. You know what to say."

"Thanks." He accepted the card, and, removing his wallet, gave Frank an amused, sidelong glance as he tucked it into his billfold. "I wonder if there's really any getting away from you, Frank. Like you said, 'no hole on earth.' I have a hunch we haven't seen the last of each other."

Frank laughed. "And your hunches are usually correct."

Conor's answering laugh was brief and wistful. "I am the son of Brigid McBride. My hunches are usually correct."

They shook hands, but as he stepped from the car, Conor looked up at the terminal and was struck with a sudden memory. He bent to look back in at Frank.

"That parting gift you gave me last time, the silver cross—Thomas has it now. I left it with him."

"Ah. Thank you for telling me." Frank's face brightened. "*Slán abhaile*, Conor, wherever it may be."

"You as well, Frank. *Slán abhaile*."

Safe home.

42

Daylight was fading to a gauzy film of dusk when he reached the cemetery. He took a shortcut when it came within view, leaving the road to walk out over a field that gradually sloped up hill to the main gate.

The grass grew long on the hill. Wet from the day's drizzle, it soaked his jeans and caught at the toes of his boots as he climbed. Around him, the fields spread out in their characteristic patchwork pattern, displaying varying qualities of green.

The walk took longer than he'd planned, but the lengthening shadows didn't bother him. This was Ireland, a place where darkness came slowly. It descended with lazy reluctance, stretching itself over hours of deepening twilight.

He gained the crown of the hill and paused to rest, looking down at the landscape. Tidy houses dotted the countryside, and here and there, a plume of smoke rose from a chimney and instantly mated with the mist rushing down to meet it. He closed his eyes and relished the luxury of inhaling deeply.

A gust of wind lashed the hillside while he fumbled with the gate latch, and once inside, Conor paused again, leaning against it. His stamina was improving, but even today's undemanding walk emphasized its limits. After a moment, he straightened and continued into the cemetery. The McBride family plot was marked by a decoratively carved high cross, and when it came within view, he felt a comforting twinge of familiarity. Dismissing fatigue, he walked forward to stand before it.

The monument's original lettering had been smoothed by more than twenty years of weather, making the more recent name in the stone appear harsh by comparison. As he reached out to trace the fresh cut, his fingers trembled. He took a step backward and dropped his hands.

"I wanted to go with you." The new, splintered quality of his voice still sounded strange to him. "I couldn't get there. I don't know what that means. Too strong to die or too weak?"

He pictured his mother's face again as he had seen it last, fading away from him, while his heartbeat stumbled back to its regular rhythm. Her face had been full of love and forgiveness, but he wondered if she could have known what she was forgiving. How much could spirit understand once the body was left behind? Could it look into the mind of a loved one and see the crimes accumulated there? He sank down next to the cross, resting his head and hands against the cool stone.

"God forgive me," he groaned. "I couldn't bring him home, Ma. I couldn't even bury him properly. All I could do was leave him there and run."

Huddled against the cross, he wondered if she could know it was not only his brother he was remembering and that it was not his brother who haunted his dreams.

"Conor? God in heaven, is that yourself there?"

Looking in the direction of the urgent whisper, Conor smiled faintly. "No other. How are you, Phillip?"

"Jaysus, I can't believe it." Phillip Ryan approached through the darkness, his broad face illuminated by a penlight attached to a key ring. "How did you get here?"

Conor squinted as the circle of light landed on his face. "I got a cab from the airport as far as Graham's store and walked from there."

"I just came from Eileen Graham," Phillip said. "She saw you heading this way and swore she was seeing your ghost, and I see why. You look half-destroyed. Are you sick?"

"Not really. I mean, not anymore."

"How long have you been sitting here?"

"What's the time?" Conor asked.

"It's about half-nine."

"So, an hour and a half, then."

"I can't believe it," Phillip repeated. "You look—"

"Half-destroyed. So you said." He put up a hand and Phillip pulled him to his feet with little effort.

"It needs saying again," Phillip said, shaking his head. "Christ, you've dropped two stone at least, and what's wrong with your voice?"

"Dose of pneumonia," Conor said lightly, hoping to modulate the drama. "They had to open up a hole in my neck to get some air in, and I guess they hit a few things they shouldn't have."

"Holy mother of God," Phillip breathed. He aimed the penlight at Conor's throat, examining the scar. "Must hurt like hell, then?"

"It doesn't actually," Conor assured him. "Just sounds like it does. Would you mind running me home, Pip? Now I come to think of it, I'm fairly knackered."

During the ride to the house, he kept the conversation steered away from himself, posing a steady stream of questions and focusing on the last months of his mother's life. She had remained characteristically serene and brave right up to and through her last days, Phillip confirmed. When she knew she was failing, she'd called her sister-in-law to come down from Galway. Honora had moved in and organized the hospice care, and was there at the end with her two daughters, Fiona and Grace.

"I ought to warn you," Phillip said. "You're as popular as a month of rain with those three women just now. Come to that, you're not a great hero around town either." He brought the car to a jolting stop in front of the house and turned from the wheel in sudden anger. "Conor, where in the hell have you been all this time, for fuck's sake? You leave for London on a Thursday to meet with some dodgy Brit about your long-lost brother, and then you don't come home for months? Did you not realize—"

"Of course I did," Conor said sharply. "And so did she."

He looked at the agitated face next to him and felt his resolve weaken. He owed his friend a great deal and couldn't stand the thought of lying to him. Although there was little of his story that was safe for sharing, the urge to confess was unbearable. It would only get harder to resist the longer he stayed. With a resigned sigh, Conor threw open the door of the car. "Come on into the house. I need to talk to you about something."

It wasn't the story he knew Phillip wanted, but he did have news, and realized he needed to tell it now, before nostalgia took a firmer grip, tempting him to say more than was prudent.

An hour later, they sat in the living room with a bottle of whiskey on the table between them. Conor fidgeted uneasily in his chair, staring at the fire. The hissing blaze was too understated to provide much light, but its strawberry hue bounced from the rippled glass of the casement windows, giving their faces an artificial flush. When he could no longer endure the silence, he pushed the bottle forward, and cocked a questioning eyebrow.

"Say something, Pip."

Phillip poured the width of two fingers of whiskey into his glass, stared at it, and then picked it up and took a slow sip before speaking. "Okay. I'm surprised all right. This place is your family's legacy, and if you say the hunt for your brother was a wild goose chase, then I suppose he's not likely to show up again to claim his share of it. It's yours, free and clear. I never expected you'd make the choice to sell it."

"Choice?" The word no longer triggered the withering bitterness in Conor it once had. It just made him feel tired.

"When was the last time I did anything because I chose it?"

"How should I know? Why don't you tell me?"

Conor cringed at the tension in his friend's voice and met the hurt reproach in his eyes with difficulty. "Phillip—"

"You're dragging around an awful heavy load, Conor. Why do you want to be carrying it all by yourself?"

"Because it's mine to carry," Conor said, softly.

"Rubbish." Phillip pushed aside the whiskey bottle and sat forward. "You say you hunted all over India for Thomas because the British fellow said he was there. You say you never found him. Well, what did you find, for Christ's sake? You were gone long enough. What happened over there that's made you want to sell your farm and run off to America?"

When Conor made no reply, Phillip fell back against his chair and stared at him, angry and confused. "Have you got a buyer?"

"I do."

"Who is it?" Phillip waited, and as Conor's eyes fell to the floor, he slammed his glass down onto the table. "Are you joking me? I don't even deserve to know that much for the love of God?"

The chair toppled onto its side as he erupted from it. Conor flinched, half-expecting a fist to come flying across the table at him, but after he jumped up, Phillip's rage appeared to dissolve. He froze, looking uncertain, and stepped over to the fireplace. He squatted down and began jabbing a poker into the heart of the guttering flames.

"When did you decide you couldn't trust me?" Phillip asked quietly, thrusting the poker forward with rhythmic repetition.

"It's nothing to do with trust, Phillip." Conor could read his friend's sense of betrayal in the stiffened muscles of his back and hated himself for it. "Believe me when I tell you, you don't want to get mixed up with any of this. I've already said more than what's good for either of us. I shouldn't have come here at all, but I had to."

"When will you leave?" Phillip asked, after a short pause.

"In a few days."

"Where will you ... oh no, never mind." Phillip's ordinarily gentle voice held a jarring note of mockery he had never heard before. "I suppose that's a great secret as well. Not for me to question or to know."

"Actually," Conor said, carefully, "There's something I was hoping to have your help with, if you're willing. You've been to America, but I haven't. I don't know a soul and haven't a clue where to go. You told me once about that cousin you visited over there, the one that died. Doesn't his widow do B&B now? With a farm attached that she can barely keep going?"

"It's not B&B. It's an inn with a working farm. In Vermont." Without turning, Phillip put the poker down on the floor next to him. He wrapped his arms around his knee and continued staring into the fire.

"Yeah, all right, an inn," Conor agreed, stupidly nodding at his friend's back. "I just thought, you know—me needing a place to go, her needing some farming help. Is it dairy?"

"Dairy, yeah," Phillip said at last, breaking another interminable pause.

"Right."

Conor bit down hard on the inside of his cheek and forced himself to stop talking. After several minutes of absolute, unbroken silence, Phillip twisted on his heel and turned to him. With his back to the fire, his face remained shadowed, but a glimmer of the firelight reflected back on him from the windows, and for an instant Conor saw a glint of something in his eyes he almost would have sworn was laughter. It sent an apprehensive tingle over his scalp, but when Phillip spoke, his voice sounded only stoic and sad.

"At least I'd know where you are. You wouldn't disappear on me again entirely. I'll e-mail Kate and ask her. She'd be happy for a bit of help, I'm sure. She'll be lucky to have you."

He rose stiffly, put the poker back in its stand, and went to lean against the doorway to the kitchen. "It's late, and you need to get some sleep. I'll see myself out through the back."

Conor rose as well but held himself in check, knowing instinctively that he couldn't go to his friend. The evening had introduced something new between them—an awkward reserve had chilled the easy relationship they had long known.

"I'll help with the morning milking," he offered, desperate to begin rebuilding what he'd lost. "Regular time?"

"Yeah, sure, regular time." Phillip shot him a look of cool disdain. "Why wouldn't it be?"

When he was gone, Conor left the lights off and walked aimlessly through each room of the house, his hands resting on tabletops, doorframes, bedposts, and windowsills. A studiously preserved lacuna occupied most of the space in his head, protecting him from memories that tried to assault him with every surface his fingers touched. He ended up back in the tiny kitchen and unlocked the top portion of the half door that led out to the flagstone patio. It swung open, and dampness floated in like the vaporous trail of a night-walking spirit, caressing his face and passing through him with a faint hint of the ocean's echo against his ear.

He stood looking out, considering the idea of a walk to the barn. There were few opportunities left to indulge in the satisfaction of treading through it in the darkness, listening to the peaceful, snuffling sleep of his herd. He lifted the latch on the bottom half of the door, but then he heard a sound like a sharp slap coming from the front of the house. Returning to the living room and switching on a light, he saw a CD case lying on the floor. He recognized it immediately: a recording of Bach's violin concerti.

I can remember when it was the fiddle you had to have with you everywhere.

The memory of his brother's words whispered in his mind, obliterating in an instant its carefully maintained zone of blankness. A tremor ran down his arms to the tingling tips of his fingers. He'd relied for too long on the molded grip of a handgun as his only tactile means of reassurance, and the weight of it—physical and spiritual—incorporated all the compacted mass of a black hole. Now he had an overwhelming desire to feel something else in his hands: the familiar, almost weightless heft of a violin. All at once, he felt like a wayward, thoughtless lover, too long away and with love's object too long from his thoughts. He actually looked at his watch, calculating how many hours he would need to be camped on the Bank of Ireland's steps until it opened, and he could retrieve his Pressenda.

He finally set the feverish preoccupation aside and walked to the stereo system on the bookshelf. He watched with unusual attention as the disc slid silently into the player, and after a pause, Bach's Violin Concerto in E Major erupted from the speakers. A small tickle fluttered in Conor's gut as the three introductory chords sang out to him like a jovial, personal salute.

He let the disc play through to the end. Twice. As the concerti moved through their varied tempos and moods—Allegro, Adagio, Presto, Largo—he lay stretched on the sofa, his left hand roaming over a phantom fingerboard. When the music fell silent for the second time, he stayed motionless, listening to the comfortable groans and creaks of the house and to the satisfying sound of his breath—deep, clear, and almost noiseless.

He woke slowly about six hours later from a heavy, dreamless sleep, the most restful he'd had in months. A tuneful assembly of birds had gathered in the hawthorn bush outside the front door, and the monochromatic light of an overcast dawn was brightening the windows.

Conor sat up, wondering if there was anything in the house to eat. He stepped over to the stereo to shut it off, but as the

CD tray glided out beneath his waiting hand, he froze. A smile of understanding crept over his face. He removed the disc and pivoted to look again at the spot where he'd found it—slapped down in the middle of the floor.

He left the disc on the bookshelf and headed for the kitchen with a lighter step. He was soon to be homeless, but he wasn't alone after all, and he realized now that he never would be. For however long and however far he went, he would carry them with him—his familial *basso continuo*—and the whisper of their mysterious music would soothe and sustain him until the final, closing cadence brought him home.

ACKNOWLEDGMENTS

I want to thank my family and friends—too numerous to name—who have supported me in so many ways as this project inched its way forward. To write and publish a book is an adventure. To do it with the warm encouragement and companionship that I have experienced is a treasure.

In particular, I want to thank those who agreed to serve as Patrons for this publishing project. I am so grateful to each of you, and I dearly hope the result honors your support. In other words, I hope you like it!

Jonathan Barth & Stan Dudek
Margaret Candelori
Peggy & Jim Bouffard
William Bouffard
Patty Carbee
Hon. Nils Daulaire
Reenal Doshi
Holly Gathright & Jim Brown
Claire Guare
Dick & Meghan Guare
Eleanor & Tom Guare
Lynn & Paul Guare

Sadhana & Rick Hall
The Iantosca Family
The Krol Family
The MacArthur Family
Brenda McDermott
Joanne Needham & Andy Johnson
Michael & Cindy Puleo
Ann Louise Santos
Ralf & Mari Schaarschmidt
Jim Wiggins
Susan Z. Ritz

Meet the Author

Thank you so much for letting me share the beginning of Conor McBride's adventures with you. I hope that by now you are as hooked on him as I am! Let's see what kind of trouble we can cook up for him next in Book 2, The Secret Chord (available now, wherever books are sold!)

Many of the settings described in Deceptive Cadence are from my own experiences traveling in both Ireland and India, two countries that captured my heart and are always beckoning me to return. I am a Vermont-based writer who has traveled extensively, but I always return to the small town where I grew up. I have a passion for music (from Classical to Pop and everything in between) and all things Irish, and I love exploring ethnic foods and diverse cultures. I also love connecting with readers to share experiences and new discoveries. I hope you'll connect with me to share yours as well. The themes on my website are: Taste, Watch, Explore, Read, Listen and Learn. Come on over and join in!

www.kathrynguare.com

Connect with me on Facebook:
www.facebook.com/KathrynGuare
Connect with me on Twitter: www.twitter.com/KGuare

39679586R00224

Made in the USA
Middletown, DE
21 March 2019